MURDER
ROUND
THE
CLOCK

ALSO BY HUGH PENTECOST

*Pierre Chambrun Mystery Novels:*

Remember to Kill Me
Murder in High Places
With Intent to Kill
Murder in Luxury
Beware Young Lovers
Random Killer
Death after Breakfast
The Fourteen Dilemma
Time of Terror
Bargain with Death
Walking Dead Man
Birthday, Deathday
The Deadly Joke
Girl Watcher's Funeral
The Gilded Nightmare
The Golden Trap
The Evil Men Do
The Shape of Fear
The Cannibal Who Overate

# MURDER ROUND THE CLOCK

Pierre Chambrun's Crime File

by Hugh Pentecost

DODD, MEAD & COMPANY New York

All of the stories included in this volume originally appeared in *Ellery Queen's Mystery Magazine.*


Published by Dodd, Mead & Company, Inc.
79 Madison Avenue, New York, N.Y. 10016
Distributed in Canada by
McClelland and Stewart Limited, Toronto
Manufactured in the United States of America
Designed by Stanley S. Drate
First Edition

Library of Congress Cataloging in Publication Data

Pentecost, Hugh, 1903–
Murder round the clock.

I. Title.
PS3531.H442M86 1985 813′.52 84-18784
ISBN 0-396-08553-9

# Contents

# Preface

*The Cannibal Who Overate,* the first novel about Pierre Chambrun and his special world, the Hotel Beaumont, appeared in 1962. Since then there have been eighteen more novels about that legendary gentleman and a score of shorter pieces. This book is a collection of some of those shorter pieces.

The late Fred Dannay, who in an incomparable collaboration with Manfred Lee became known around the reading world as Ellery Queen, wrote an introduction to the first of these shorter pieces, "Murder Deluxe," which appeared in the October 1963 issue of *Ellery Queen's Mystery Magazine.*

> In this new detective short novel Hugh Pentecost takes you on the scene, and behind the scene, of a deluxe New York City hotel, with all its bustle, swank, intrigue, suspicion, mystery, scandal, wheeling-dealing-and-doubledealing; with all the excitement, gaiety—and menace; with all the tinsel and gold, the falsities and verities of the human comedy (and tragedy). . . . Is there a locale, a background, more susceptible to crimes and skulduggeries than the self-contained little city of a luxury hotel?
>
> And in this particular beehive of honey-and-moneymaking you will meet Pierre Chambrun, resident manager, whose skill and suavity as "mine host" is internationally famous—a man with tact and perception whose dark eyes could be those of a

> Good Samaritan or of a hanging judge—a man who can be charmingly European or bruskly American—a man who will not tolerate the slightest deviation from superb service or established routine, whether it is a minor complaint from a transient guest or—murder.

There have been two major changes in the setup at the Beaumont since that first novel and the first short piece. A faceless Miss Proctor has been replaced as Chambrun's secretary by the marvelously efficient Betsy Ruysdale, secretary supreme, referred to by Chambrun as "my right arm" and rumored to be a great deal more than that to him in their private lives. I cannot report on the truth of that rumor because what I may know about it has been told to me in confidence.

The second important change involved Alison Barnwell, public relations director, who married her young man, and they both left the hotel to open their own country inn somewhere in New England. Mark Haskell took over as PR man for the hotel, and it is through him that all the subsequent novels and short pieces were recorded.

I am asked if the Beaumont is based on the Plaza, the Pierre, the Ritz? I knew all of those hotels years ago, but none of them is as real to me now as the Beaumont. I know every bar, restaurant, nightclub, private dining room, ballroom, the hospital space, health club, linen closet, storeroom, the kitchen, the wine cellar, the machinery that operates elevators, air conditioning, and every other detail of the life there. It is just as real to me as my own home after more than twenty years. I hope you will come to know it as well as I do and feel as at home there as I do.

HUGH PENTECOST

MURDER
ROUND
THE
CLOCK

# Murder Deluxe

Between the hours of four-thirty and seven A.M. the lobby of the Hotel Beaumont, New York's top luxury hotel, presents a picture that would be unfamiliar to the thousands of rich people who swarm in and out during the other twenty-one and a half hours of the day. It is a little like catching a Hollywood glamour girl preparing for an appearance, in the hands of a masseuse, face smeared with creams, hair done up in pin curls. It is unpardonable to catch her—or the Hotel Beaumont—in such private disarray.

During those secret hours the Beaumont is torn apart and put together again. An army of cleaners, both men and women, bear down on the lobby, the bars, the restaurants, the ballroom, with vacuum cleaners, brass and glass polishing equipment, electrically driven trash wagons, dusters on long poles for cleaning the magnificent chandeliers, old-fashioned buckets and mops. The lights are dimmed, as on a stage after a performance.

The windows of the swank shops off the lobby, displaying jewels, furs, extravagant women's clothing, and a costly nonsense of toys and small gifts, are dark. The mink-draped mannikins in the store windows stare out blankly at the wall-to-wall green carpeting in the entrance halls and lobby, now being curried like a million-dollar race horse. The whole process is carried out with grim precision, beginning precisely at four-thirty in the morning and ending on the dot of seven, with the Beaumont finally stepping out into public view like the Hollywood star stepping before the cameras—shining, glittering, spotless, and smelling rich.

The young woman who arrived at the Beaumont's Fifth Avenue entrance at four-forty-five that morning should have known better. The doorman's attitude said as much, as he unloaded five suitcases of varying sizes, all new airplane-type luggage, from the girl's taxi. The girl was slim, red-haired, immaculately dressed in a dark-green woolen suit. Her handbag and shoes were dark-brown alligator. Though it was gray-dark outside, the girl wore large, black-lensed sunglasses.

She had paid off the taxi before she got out. She swept by the doorman, and carrying one of her suitcases she walked briskly down the long corridor toward the lobby, past the endless mirrors that multiplied her dozens of times, past the glowering cleaning women who resented her intrusion, and up to the reservation desk, where Mr. Carl Nevers, night reservation clerk, gave her his pleasant, professional smile with one eyebrow raised in mild question.

"Do you have a bedroom-living room suite?" the girl asked.

"You have a reservation, miss?" Nevers asked. His quick eye had caught the naked ring finger on her left hand.

Scarlet lips gave him a hard smile. "Do I need one?" And before Mr. Nevers could protest, she had spun the registration folder around and signed the top card in a bold hand:

Laura Thomas
Hollywood, California

The Beaumont was "home away from home" for most Hollywood celebrities, as well as for foreign diplomats, the remnants of the world's royalty, and the special worldwide society of the richer-than-rich.

Carl Nevers knew every regular customer of the Beaumont for the last ten years, by name if not by sight. He had never heard of Laura Thomas, either in his job or in the gossip columns he read daily to keep abreast of stage, screen, and society—or what now passes for society, which is really a sort of "celebrity register." He glanced at the rest of the luggage the doorman had put down in the center of the lobby; he looked at Miss Thomas appraisingly but not discourteously. He had to make the right decision—or Pierre Chambrun, the resident manager, would have him by the ears the next day.

"I think we can take care of you, Miss Thomas," Nevers said suavely. "Suite 14B."

An invisible signal passed between him and the night bell captain, who appeared at Miss Thomas's elbow. The bell captain took the brass key Nevers put down on the shining mahogany surface.

"Will you be staying with us long, Miss Thomas?" Nevers asked offhandedly.

"Three or four days," she said crisply. "I'm not exactly certain."

Johnny Thacker, the night bell captain, slim and wiry, managed four of the five suitcases like a juggler—the girl insisted on carrying one herself. The two disappeared into an elevator.

The Beaumont's face-lifting went on. Carl Nevers stared at the bold signature on the registration card. "Laura Thomas." There were so many new young starlets on the coast that it wasn't too odd he hadn't heard of this one. But lone women were a problem at this hour—five o'clock in the morning. Often they didn't belong here and shouldn't be admitted. In these days it was hard to tell a call girl from a duchess. If you turned down a duchess, Chambrun would flay you alive; if you admitted a call girl preparing for an assignation with somebody's husband, Chambrun might easily fire you. The public relations office would know who Laura Thomas of Hollywood was, so Nevers made a note to find out as soon as Miss Barnwell, the public relations director, arrived at nine-thirty.

A few minutes later the elevator door slid noiselessly open, and Johnny Thacker reappeared. He came over to the desk.

"Who's the babe?" he asked.

"Laura Thomas," Nevers said casually, watching Johnny from beneath lowered lids.

"Who's Laura Thomas?"

"You don't know?" Nevers asked, hiding a sudden qualm.

"Don't know and don't care. Five-buck tip. Hollywood?"

"Of course," Nevers said, feeling suddenly more confident. Call girls are far too practical to give five-dollar tips.

"Something funny," Johnny said.

"Funny?" Nevers's qualms returned.

"She got something live in one of those suitcases—the one she was carrying herself."

"Live!"

"I could hear it whining," Johnny said.

"In a closed suitcase?"

"Yeah. I mean you don't carry a dog or a cat in a closed suitcase. But she's got something in there—something that whines."

"I'll make a note to have the housekeeper check," Nevers said nervously.

The Beaumont didn't bar dogs or cats—the rich often insist on having their pets with them. There had been more than one monkey, many myna birds, and the current movie Tarzan had appeared with a baby leopard on a chain.

But something live in a closed suitcase? Yes, it would definitely have to be checked.

At seven o'clock one of the operators in the telephone office on the third floor plugged in Room 1208 and rang steadily. There was no answer. She jiggled the button on and off. She glanced at the slip in front of her. It was a list of morning calls—calls to wake people. "7:00 A.M. Fisher, 1208." She put her finger on the button and held it there.

Mr. Fisher didn't answer.

Obviously Mr. Fisher had wakened under his own power and was already gone from his room. But the Hotel Beaumont never left anything to chance. The operator called the housekeeper on the twelfth floor and asked her to knock on Mr.

Fisher's door. The housekeeper checked back a few minutes later. Mr. Fisher had hung out his DO NOT DISTURB sign.

"You'd think he'd cancel his call," the operator said.

She had other seven-o'clock calls to make, so she forgot about Mr. Fisher.

At eight o'clock Miss Laura Thomas, wearing a beige wool suit, a mink stole, and her large black sunglasses, and looking as if she'd had a good eight hours' sleep, emerged from an elevator into the Beaumont lobby and walked out onto the street. A block away she entered a drugstore and went to a phone booth in the rear. She dialed a number from memory.

"Hotel Beaumont," a voice said. "Good morning."

"Room 803, please," Miss Thomas said.

"One moment, please."

Miss Thomas could hear the phone ring, and then a man's voice answered—a cold, hard voice.

"Webber here."

"George? Laura."

"You're not calling from the hotel?"

"Of course not. Corner drugstore, as per instructions."

"Everything go smoothly?"

"Like a Swiss watch. The Hollywood plane was on time. I waited for it at the airport and then came in on the bus with the regular passengers. How does it look?"

The man's voice was cold and angry. "Our Mr. Cook is stubborn," he said. "We give him today, and if he still holds out, we put an armlock on him. Call me around four o'clock—from outside—and I'll have some answers for you."

"Don't I see you before then, George?" It was a kind of pouting, flirtatious question.

"You don't," the man said without emotion. "Not until this thing is played out. Now go back to the hotel and make like a movie star."

At eight-thirty that morning the Beaumont's room service provided breakfast for three in Suite 7H. The room service waiter was tolerantly aware that Mr. and Mrs. Clifford Cook and their eight-year-old daughter, called Bobbie by her father, were not accustomed to the luxuries and niceties of the Beaumont's service. Coffee was served in an automatic electric percolator, which kept it piping hot and never overbrewed. A small toaster came with the service. Mr. Chambrun, the resident manager, who was a noted gourmet, had been known to say that he would listen to explanations if someone was accused of stealing a five-dollar bill from a guest's bureau, but he would fire anyone who served the blotting-paper-type toast familiar to hotel breakfasters.

The child, Bobbie, had selected a different breakfast each morning of the three they'd been in 7H. The first morning it had been cereal with a sliced banana, a boiled egg, toast, and milk—probably the same kind of breakfast she had at home. The second day she'd experimented with a chicken liver omelette. Today it was creamed chipped beef.

Mrs. Cook stayed with juice, toast, and coffee. Mr. Cook had started with juice, ham and eggs, toast, marmalade, and coffee. The second day he'd gone to a lamb chop. Today it was kidney stew.

The tips were modest, written in on the checks, but this was made up for in part by a cheerful, friendly approach to the waiter. Nothing high-hat or phony about the Cooks. Small-town New England was the waiter's expert diagnosis.

On the third morning Mr. Cook didn't seem quite as cordial to the waiter as he had been on the other days. He seemed distracted, hardly aware of the waiter's presence. He looked as though he hadn't slept too well. He was a tall, angular man in his middle or late thirties. Sort of a young Abe Lincoln, the waiter thought. Mrs. Cook, a pretty blonde, seemed worried about her husband and was overgrateful to the waiter. Bobbie ran around the table, lifting the silver covers, giving a shrill cry of dismay when she saw what her father had ordered.

"Daddy! Kidney stew for breakfast!"

The waiter gave the little girl a solemn wink and retired.

Bobbie Cook laughed delightedly and sat down hurriedly at her place. "May I begin, Mum?"

"Of course, darling," Anne Cook said. She was watching her husband, who was standing by the windows looking down over Central Park. She finally moved over to stand beside him and put her hand on his arm.

"Cliff?"

He seemed to pull himself back from some distant place and looked down at her with a small, sad smile. He said, "Today is it, you know."

"I know."

"Would you like to be able to live in a place like this for the rest of your life, Anne?"

"Of course I wouldn't, Cliff."

"Or a house just about anywhere in the whole United States?"

"Cliff, I want you happy."

"The best schools for Bobbie? Fancy clothes? Luxuries?"

"I want you happy," Anne said doggedly. She frowned. "I don't really understand, you know. We're doing fine as things are. If you say 'no' how will that be changed?"

A deep frown creased the man's forehead. "I'm not sure," he said. "Hobbs and his man Webber aren't used to having anyone say 'no.' They play it two ways—Hobbs all charm, Webber all menace. Maybe it's just a game designed to frighten me; maybe they really would bite back. My credit made sticky, distribution made next to impossible. There are ways—plenty of ways."

"If they can make millions out of the patents, Cliff, why can't you? That's what I don't see."

"Capital," Cook said. "They have it, and I don't. No matter where I raise it, I'll have to cut someone else in. So why not Martin Hobbs?"

"Why not?"

"It's childish, Anne, but I just don't like him. I just don't want to be in business with him. I don't trust him."

"Then say 'no,'" she said.

"You're willing to risk it?"

"Of course."

He bent down and kissed her gently on the cheek. "Thanks, baby," he said.

"Stop smooching, you two," their eight-year-old daughter called to them. "Your breakfast is getting cold."

Mr. Pierre Chambrun, resident manager of the Hotel Beaumont, was a small, dark man, stocky in build, with heavy pouches under dark eyes that could turn hard as a hanging judge's or unexpectedly twinkle with humor. Chambrun had been in the hotel business for thirty years and had risen to the top of the field. Mr. George Battle, owner of the Beaumont, lived on the French Riviera all year round, presumably counting his money, which never came to an end.

Pierre Chambrun ran the Beaumont without interference or even consultation with the owner. He *was* the Beaumont. French by birth, he had come to this country as a small boy, and now he thought like an American. His training in the hotel business had taken him back to Europe; he spoke several languages fluently; he could adopt a Continental manner to suit an occasion, but the Beaumont was an American institution, and Chambrun kept its atmosphere strictly American.

Chambrun never ate lunch. As resident manager his services were called on most frequently between the hours of eleven and three—people with complaints, people with special problems, members of the staff confronted by one difficulty or another, outside interests using the hotel for parties, fashion shows, special conferences. The arrivals and departures of celebrities, notables, and the just plain rich required his personal attention. Though there were special departments and department heads for handling the intricacies of travel arrangements, publicity tie-ins, and general bowings and scrapings, Chambrun was always close at hand for the emergencies.

He had a gift for delegating authority, but he was always ready to take the full responsibility for "touchy" decisions. He could make such decisions on the instant, and after thirty years in the business, he could tell himself without vanity that he'd never made a delicate decision he later felt to have been an error. A few of them had proved wrong or unworkable, but faced with the same facts again he would make the same judgment.

At precisely nine o'clock each morning he ate a hearty breakfast in his office on the second floor. The office looked more like a gracious living room than a place of business. Chambrun's breakfast consisted of juice or fresh fruit in season, lamb chops or a small steak or sometimes brook trout or a Dover sole, toast in large quantity with sweet butter and strawberry preserve. And coffee—coffee that he went on drinking all day: American coffee for breakfast followed by Turkish coffee, sipped in a demitasse until bedtime. At seven in the evening he ate an elaborate dinner especially prepared to meet the requirements of a gourmet's palate.

Chambrun never looked at the mail and memoranda on his desk until he came to his second cup of coffee and his first Egyptian cigarette of the day.

The memoranda from the night staff usually involved familiar problems requiring tact as well as iron discipline. Despite its reputation as the top luxury hotel in America, the Beaumont was confronted with many of the same problems as lesser establishments. There were always the drunks, the deadbeats, the call girls—the most expensive in New York, but nonetheless call girls—the endless cantankerous guests, the suicides, the heart attacks suffered by elderly gentlemen in the rooms of young ladies not their wives, the whims of elderly dowagers with far more money than they could count, the oddities like the Moslem gentlemen who had insisted on having the bed removed from his suite so that he wouldn't be tempted to sleep anywhere else but on the hard parquet floor.

On this particular morning, his breakfast finished, Chambrun sipped his second cup of coffee and inhaled deeply on his cigarette. He glanced at the list of late arrivals. His eyes stopped at the name of Laura Thomas, Hollywood, California. It rang no bells with him.

The note attached to the Thomas card made him smile wryly. His staff was well-trained. They reported any deviations, no matter how absurd. Carl Nevers, the night reservation clerk, had followed routine. "Johnny Thacker reports the lady was carrying something alive in one of her suitcases. He could hear it whining."

Chambrun reached for the phone on his desk and asked to be connected with Mrs. Kniffen, the head housekeeper.

"Yes, Mr. Chambrun?"

Poor Mrs. Kniffen. She always sounded panic-stricken when she got a call from him, Chambrun thought. "Beautiful day, Mrs. Kniffen," he said.

"Yes, sir."

"I trust your family is all well?"

"Very well, thank you."

"Suite 14B, Mrs. Kniffen. It was occupied last night by a young lady named Thomas. Possibly from the world of the motion picture. The night bell captain reports she was carrying something alive in one of her suitcases. Obviously not an ordinary pet like a dog or a cat. I'm curious, Mrs. Kniffen."

"Yes, sir." Mrs. Kniffen's voice was unsteady. Chambrun could read her like a book. She was remembering the time a box of trained snakes had got loose on the twelfth floor.

"Just an unobtrusive check, Mrs. Kniffen."

"Yes, sir."

"Thank you, Mrs. Kniffen."

As he put down the phone, a small green light blinked on his desk. He picked up the phone again to answer his secretary.

"Mr. Martin Hobbs to see you, Mr. Chambrun."

"Thank you, Miss Proctor. Have my breakfast things removed, and then show him in."

Chambrun's mind was like a well-organized index card file. In his job he had to know everything he was supposed to know—and a great deal more that he was not supposed to know. He knew the obvious, like which men were cheating on their wives and which wives were cheating on their husbands; he knew which guests were spending more than they could afford; he knew all the gossip about everyone. His staff was, in effect, a highly skilled intelligence service. The mental file card dealing with Martin Hobbs was ready for use on a split second's notice.

Martin Hobbs, aged thirty-eight, handsome, great charm, if a little too labored at times. Ten years ago he had been known as "the boy wonder," a young financial wizard from the West Coast, San Francisco's most notable fixture after the Golden Gate Bridge. He'd made a mammoth coup in the stock market that had lifted him to the climate of the fabulously rich. He was ostensibly a promoter and organizer of businesses and business mergers. He was said to hold government contracts in the field of rocketry that would run into billions over a period of years. This meant, obviously, important contacts in government as well as business. To be treated with extra courtesy and special attention at all times.

But, at the bottom of his mental file card, Pierre Chambrun had appended a cliche: What goes up must come down.

A silent waiter wheeled out the remains of Chambrun's breakfast. Chambrun walked over to the sideboard to set his pot of Turkish coffee brewing, took a fresh cigarette from his silver case, and had just lighted it when Miss Proctor ushered in Martin Hobbs.

"Good morning, Mr. Hobbs," Chambrun said, smiling blandly. "Won't you sit down? How can I serve you?"

The blond Viking in a Madison Avenue charcoal-gray suit, a custom-made shirt, and a tie in regimental stripes, flashed Chambrun a bright smile. The word "mask" appeared suddenly on Chambrun's cranial radar screen.

"I've been so deeply involved in this business merger we're

putting through," Hobbs said, "that I've neglected to tell you how perfect the service in your hotel has been and to comment on the extraordinary efficiency of your staff."

"That's always nice to hear," Chambrun said, his hooded eyes studying this famous young man. Something odd here, he thought, something like panic behind that white smile.

"I'd like to impose on you for a rather delicate extra service," Hobbs said.

"We rarely find ourselves unequipped to provide extras, Mr. Hobbs."

"You must deal with the transfer of large sums of cash from your bank to the hotel as a matter of daily routine," Hobbs said.

"We do."

Hobbs reached into his pocket, took out his wallet, and produced a folded check. "I need to have fifty thousand dollars in cash at our meeting today," he said. "Can the people who handle your cash deposits and withdrawals take care of it for me?"

Chambrun made his slight hesitation seem like no hesitation at all. A slow smile began as he glanced at the check. The smile must obviously be completed before he could speak. The check was on a San Francisco bank. It would normally take four or five days to clear. Of course, a quick phone call—

"I can have it for you at eleven-thirty," Chambrun said, "if that is in time."

Hobbs's eyes lowered for an instant to his hands. "You will of course vouch for the fact that it is my check and that the money is being delivered to me. If there's any question, a phone call to my bank—"

Way ahead of you, son, Chambrun thought. "Don't think any more about it, Mr. Hobbs. Do you want the money delivered to your suite or to the conference room?"

"The conference room," Hobbs said. "But I want to be called outside to receive it. Just say there is a message for me. No mention of the money, please."

"I'll take care of it personally, Mr. Hobbs."

Hobbs turned on his brilliant smile. "I'm most grateful, Mr. Chambrun."

"A pleasure to be of service to you, Mr. Hobbs."

Chambrun watched him go, tapping the check gently against the palm of his hand. Then he went to his phone and picked it up. Miss Proctor responded promptly.

"Call Mr. Frederick Tweddell of the San Francisco Trust at his home, Miss Proctor—person-to-person."

"It's only a quarter past seven in San Francisco, Mr. Chambrun."

"Thank you for reminding me, Miss Proctor."

"You—you still want me to make the call?"

"Please," Chambrun said patiently.

At twenty minutes past ten, New York time, Clifford Cook approached the desk in the Beaumont lobby. Mr. Atterbury, head clerk during the day, greeted him pleasantly.

"It turns out that Mrs. Cook and my daughter and I will be leaving for home tomorrow—after breakfast," Cook said.

"We'll be sorry to see you go, Mr. Cook," Atterbury said automatically. "Can we help in any way with your travel arrangements?"

"We drove here," Cook said. "If you'll notify the garage to have our car delivered at ten o'clock, gassed up and ready for the road?"

"Of course."

"I thought of taking Mrs. Cook to the theater tonight—"

"Our theater ticket bureau is just across the lobby there, sir, next to the newsstand."

Cook turned and headed across the glittering lobby toward the newsstand. Before he reached it he came face-to-face with an attractive-looking young man. Except for the fact that he was dark, he could have been a younger version of Martin Hobbs—charcoal-gray suit, custom-tailored shirt, tie in regimental stripes.

"Morning, Mr. Cook."

Cook pulled himself out of his preoccupation. "Oh—good morning, Stanton."

Young Donald Stanton was the most pleasant of Martin Hobbs's entourage. Cook knew that being pleasant was part of a public relations man's job, but with young Stanton it seemed both natural and genuine. He had spent an hour with Cook two days before, asking him courteously about his background, his education, his politics, his business history. Cook, a little puzzled, had been told that "When, as, and if this merger comes off, sir, it'll be my job to include you in our version of the corporate image." Well, Cook thought grimly, it had been a wasted hour.

"Have you ever been to the zoo in Central Park, sir?" Stanton asked.

"No, but I believe Mrs. Cook took Bobbie there yesterday."

"I have a girl who's mad about it," Stanton said.

"Oh?" Cook said.

Stanton laughed disarmingly. "We are going there this afternoon—if!"

"Oh."

"If the big story isn't going to break today, sir. Off the record, sir—and for God's sake don't tell Mr. Hobbs I asked you—is there likely to be a final decision today? Because if there is—no zoo!"

"I hate to interfere with your excursion, Stanton, but I think a decision today is almost certain."

Stanton looked sincerely enthusiastic. "Welcome to the family, sir," he said. "I know how pleased Mr. Hobbs will be."

Cook nodded. But Mr. Hobbs wasn't going to be pleased.

Mr. Frederick Tweddell of the San Francisco Trust didn't enjoy being wakened at seven-fifteen. But when he heard Chambrun's voice, he relaxed. Chambrun was a rare person and a very special friend, as he had been since the two men had first known each other during the war years in France and Germany. He had also been Colonel Tweddell's favorite drinking companion.

"Pierre, you old son-of-a-bottle!" Mr. Frederick Tweddell said.

"Son-of-a-bottle yourself," Chambrun said. "And I have a special one reserved for you on your next trip to New York. But at present a small emergency is at hand."

"You never have emergencies, Pierre—I know you, you're always way ahead of trouble."

"That's what I'm trying to do now—stay ahead," Chambrun said. "I have a check on my desk in the amount of fifty thousand smackers. It's signed by a customer of yours. He wants folding money for it."

"Fifty thousand in cash!"

"By eleven-thirty, our time. Martin Hobbs. Do I cash it?"

Mr. Tweddell's whistle in San Francisco was quite clear in Chambrun's office. "Funny thing," he said, "Hobbs's account here is a personal checking account, not his business account. It just happens I had his folder out yesterday. This is off the record, Pierre."

"I just don't want to be stuck for fifty thousand bucks," Chambrun said. "Off the record, if you say."

"There was a guy in my office yesterday—investigator for one of these Senate subcommittees. He was interested in Hobbs. I couldn't tell him anything or show him anything unless he had a subpoena for our records. But I was curious, so I looked at Hobbs's account after this investigator left. Hobbs has exactly fifty thousand, one hundred and four dollars and seven cents in his account. If there are no other checks out, yours will just make it!"

"And if this account is overdrawn?"

"Before yesterday I'd have said the sky's the limit."

"And today?"

"Not the sky, anyway."

"If I refuse him," Chambrun said, "I'll be in receipt of a telephone call from some political bigwig in the next ten minutes, threatening to chop off my head for being discourteous to the boy wizard. The next day all of the gossip columns will be laughing at me for not trusting one of America's richest men. It would be like turning down a Rockefeller."

"Why does he want fifty thousand in cash?" Tweddell asked.

Chambrun inhaled deeply on his Egyptian cigarette and then crunched it out in the china ashtray on his desk. "I think he may have to go somewhere in a hurry," he said.

"What makes you think that?"

"My gut aches," Chambrun said.

Tweddell laughed. "That gut ache of yours saved my life about six times, Pierre. Trust it. But seriously, this man has some of the biggest defense contracts in the country. Fifty thousand dollars is chicken feed in terms of his general credit."

"But you say the sky's no longer the limit?"

"Look, Pierre, you and I aren't always cautious and careful. We play hunches."

"Hunches based on experience and facts," Chambrun said, his voice hard.

Tweddell chuckled. "So get our your ouija board, chum."

At half past ten that morning Clifford Cook walked into the small conference room on the mezzanine floor of the Beaumont where for the last three days he had been involved with the Martin Hobbs Enterprises. Present when he arrived, after having bought theater tickets for that evening, were Hobbs, young Donald Stanton, Miss Garth, who was Hobbs's pretty secretary and who always left the room when they got down to brass tacks, and, of course, George Webber.

Cook, gawky and angular, his dark hair always in a state of disarray, looked strangely out of place in this gathering. Hobbs beamed at him as he came in and continued to give some instructions to his secretary, who also beamed at Cook as she took down Hobbs's orders on her steno pad. It was apparent to Cook that young Stanton had passed on the word that this was to be D-day, and at least he and Hobbs and the secretary assumed that things were going the way they expected them to.

George Webber was something else again. He was as tall as Cliff Cook but weighed at least fifty pounds more, and not an ounce of it was fat. His eyes were gray and glacial. His jaw was square under a tight slit of a mouth. His voice was a quiet baritone with a cutting edge like a sharp skate on ice. He, too, wore the Madison Avenue uniform, but on him it looked a little out of place. Cook was reminded of an old-time motion picture gangster. The illusion was furthered by a seldom-lit cigar clamped hard betwen Webber's strong teeth.

George Webber was not a man to meet alone in a dark alley. His position in the Martin Hobbs Enterprises was not entirely clear. An official troubleshooter, Cook had decided, brought into action only when the "corporate image" created by Don Stanton and played to the hilt by Martin Hobbs—cordial, courteous, sympathetic, the best of all good fellows—was not producing the desired results. This, Cook imagined, didn't happen often, but he knew he was about to find out just how tough George Webber could be.

"If you'll make those calls and get out those letters, Miss Garth," Hobbs said to his secretary. "Check with me at lunch-time."

"Of course, Mr. Hobbs." Miss Garth beamed at Cook again and left the room.

Hobbs, all smiles, waved to a chair next to his at the head of the conference table. Don Stanton, notebook at the alert, sat across from Cook. Webber stood over by the windows, cigar bristling, looking down at the side-street traffic.

"Well, Cliff, I have the feeling you've arrived at a decision," Hobbs said.

Cook moved awkwardly in his chair, big fingers tugging at an ear lobe. "Yes, I have come to a decision, Mr. Hobbs," he said. "I'm sorry to have been so long arriving at it."

"My dear fellow, you don't make a million-dollar deal in thirty seconds. I wanted you to look into every facet of it carefully."

"I have, and in many respects it would seem foolish to turn it down," Cook said. "But I'm sorry to say that's my decision,

Mr. Hobbs. Thanks for your offer—but the answer is no."

There was a sharp exclamation from Don Stanton—a little like that of a puppy that has had its foot stepped on unexpectedly. Hobbs's smile remained, but it was now frozen in place. Webber turned from the window. The corner of his mouth not occupied by the cigar was drawn down in a sardonic grimace. It was an "I told you so" look, plus a curious kind of relief—as if he were about to be taken off the leash.

Hobbs took a cigarette case from his pocket. His hands weren't quite steady as he extracted a cigarette and put it in his mouth. Stanton leaned forward with a lighter.

"I find it hard to accept that as final," Hobbs said.

"I'm afraid it is," Cook said. He felt a little as though he'd struck a defenseless child. "You may find my reasons a little quixotic, Mr. Hobbs. I've always worked for myself. I've had a modest success with some electrical inventions, including the motor you're interested in. But whatever I've turned out has been mine, and I controlled it. If I sell you the patents, even at the generous figure you've suggested, I—I lose all contact with my own product."

"At a guaranteed salary of fifty thousand a year for the rest of your life," Hobbs said sharply, "you'd have no worries again for as long as you live."

"But I'd be doing nothing. Vice-president in charge of—of emptying ashtrays. My blood is in those patents, Mr. Hobbs. It—it would be like selling my child for cash. Now I'm sure, if you were to draw up a contract with me, I could enlarge my facilities and supply you with a certain number of motors per year."

"You want to be in charge of production at our plants?" Webber asked in his harsh, cold voice.

"No, sir. I want to be in charge of production at *my* plant," Cook said.

"Suppose somebody invents something better next week?" Webber said. "You'd be down the drain."

Cook gave him an ingenuous smile. "But down *my* drain, Mr. Webber."

"It's hard to conceive of a man turning down a lifetime of security simply for the pleasure of running small risks in a small business," Hobbs said. The room was air-conditioned, but tiny beads of sweat glistened on the one-time boy wizard's forehead.

"Or running the risk of having no business at all," Webber said flatly. He took the cigar out of his mouth and waved it impatiently at Hobbs. "It's time we took off the kid gloves, isn't it, Martin?"

Cook felt a small pulse of anger beat in his temple. "Threats aren't likely to change my decision, Mr. Webber," he said.

"My dear fellow, nobody's threatening you," Hobbs said.

"It just seems to be time to acquaint you with the facts of business life," Webber said.

There was a knock at the door of the conference room. Stanton, still looking pale around the gills, went quickly to the door and spoke inaudibly to someone outside. Then he came back and bent down to say something to Hobbs, who promptly stood up.

"Excuse me for a moment, gentlemen," Hobbs said, and went out into the corridor, closing the door behind him.

Webber watched him go, a glint of impatience in his cold eyes.

Out in the hall Pierre Chambrun handed Hobbs a thick manila envelope. "Thousands, five hundreds, and hundreds," he said. "Would you like to count it here, Mr. Hobbs?"

"No," Hobbs said, wiping his forehead with a handkerchief. "I'm sure you don't make mistakes, Mr. Chambrun."

"Thank you," Chambrun said. "But, as a matter of routine, may I ask you to sign this receipt?"

"Of course." Hobbs scribbled his name on the slip of paper Chambrun handed him. "I'm most grateful to you for your prompt and efficient service."

"No trouble at all," Chambrun said. "If there's anything else I can do, be sure to let me know."

Hobbs nodded distractedly, tucked the manila envelope under his arm, and went back into the conference room. He sat down at the head of the table again, placing the envelope on the chair beside him.

"Where were we?" he said.

"We were about to supply our innocent friend with some of the facts of life," Webber said.

Hobbs's shoulders rose in a shrug of assent.

Webber sounded reasonable at first. "The world of big business, of which you seem to have no knowledge, Cook, is a dog-eat-dog affair. The small country grocer has been swallowed up by a supermarket chain. The old-fashioned individual automobile designer has been absorbed by Ford, General Motors, Chrysler, and the like. The wildcat oil speculator sells out to a big oil company. The little man can't handle the enormous problem of mass-quantity distribution. He hasn't the money to make deals on a grand scale.

"No one wants to chop off the little man's head. That small-town grocer is now a supermarket manager, with none of the worries of month-to-month profits. The automobile designer has his drawing board in a Detroit plant. The oil speculator lives high off the hog on his royalties without worrying about pipelines or tankers or oil trucks. The public benefits. Big business can sell its product at a lower price than the small operator. That's the way it is today, Cook. Some of your radicals and so-called liberals may squawk about it—but it's practical, sound business. The loner like you has had his day, Cook. It was a good day, an exciting day, a time of pioneering. But, in exchange for that, he can now have security. You've been offered a damned big hunk of security, Cook."

"I know," Cook said, tugging at his ear again. "If I refuse, I'll be gambling with the future. I may never make anything like the same amount of money. But as I said, Webber—I'll be my own man."

"There is no such thing today," Webber grated.

"I think there is, and I intend to be it," Cook said. "I'm sorry, gentlemen, but I've given this a lot of thought, and I—"

"Have you indeed?" Webber said ominously. "Let me be

frank with you, Cook. We need your patents. We need your motor. It's the best in the market. A contract with you to buy X number of motors won't do. We're dealing in billion-dollar contracts. We must control every detail involved in the manufacture of our product, or the government may decide there's too great an element of risk in awarding their contracts to us. We own the Cook motor, and there's no doubt of our being able to fill the contracts; we don't own it, and there may be some doubts. We can't afford to lose those contracts, Cook. We're in far too deep already. So, like it or not, you and Hobbs Enterprises have to make a deal."

Hobbs instantly took the menacing edge off Webber's words. "So you see, you have us over a barrel, Cliff. So we tear up the agreement we've discussed. If you want more money, obviously you can demand it. Mind you, we're running risks. We offer you fifty thousand a year for life, win, lose, or draw. As Webber has suggested, someone may invent a better motor tomorrow, or six months from now. We don't ask you to be involved in that risk. You're safe, no matter what new invention may come along. But if you want to name a larger figure—?" The smile was cordial, inviting.

"It's not a matter of money, Mr. Hobbs," Cook said patiently, as if to a child. "It's my own independence, my own freedom of action, that I want."

"There's a hell of a lot of freedom of action in a guaranteed fifty thousand a year," Webber said. "Or seventy-five thousand a year."

Cook moistened his lips. "No, gentlemen. No, I'm sorry. I've thought about it and thought about it and the answer is—no."

Webber's face looked curiously like a stone hatchet. He leaned close to Cook's shoulder to put his dead cigar in an ashtray on the table. There was a faint barber-shop smell to him.

"You're not independently wealthy, Cook," he said. "We know that. You depend for your three squares a day on the income from your business. Your wife's comforts come from the same source. Your child's future education ditto. What would become of you if that income disappeared? I'll tell you. You'd have to look for a job with someone else. There are jobs for electrical engineers in many places, you say. Of course you wouldn't be your own man, but you'd get work, you say. But suppose you found yourself blacklisted?"

Webber was standing behind Cook now, and his voice shook slightly, with a kind of cold fury. "Don't you think Hobbs Enterprises could make sure you'd never get a decent job? Don't you think we could put an economic squeeze on you that would ruin your one-man operation in a matter of months, maybe weeks?"

"Are you saying that you will?" Cook asked steadily.

"I'm saying that you're a babe in the woods if you think your personal whims will be allowed to stand in the way of a billion-dollar contract. I'm saying that you're a babe in the woods if you think you can stubbornly hold out beyond our deadline and then expect us to shrug it off as bad luck. I don't know about Martin, but I promise you that, long after you've wrecked our deal, I'll keep twisting your arm until it comes off at the socket."

"Of course it won't come to that," Hobbs said, his charming smile pasted on his face.

Cook stood up. "I think I've had about enough of this," he said. "I don't like being pushed around, gentlemen. If there was any small doubt remaining in my mind, Mr. Webber has settled it."

"Damn it, little man, I'm only talking realities!" Webber exploded. "You can't be a grain of sand in the machinery. No one will let you be that in any walk of life. I've at least paid you the compliment of facing you with the truth."

"Okay, George, you've said enough," Hobbs said. "Listen to me, Cliff. George's bitterness is understandable. We have a great deal at stake. I'd like you to do me a favor. We've spent three days going over this deal. Pretend the annual figure to you is blank in the contract. Know that you can fill it with any amount you think is fair. Go away now, talk it over with your wife, sleep on it, and meet with us once more tomorrow morning. I know that right now you're sure nothing will change your mind. But think about it for twenty-four hours. Is that asking too much?"

Cook hesitated. The red anger he felt at Webber wasn't the best companion to good judgment.

"I hadn't planned to drive home till tomorrow morning," he said. "I'm positive there won't be any change in my point of view, but I'm quite willing to see you in the morning and tell you so again."

Webber had taken a fresh cigar out of his breast pocket and stuck it between his teeth. His cold eyes moved up and down Cook's bony frame as though assessing every ounce of muscle and flesh on it. How much could it take? How much pressure would he have to put in his threatened arm lock?

"Fine," Hobbs said, holding out his hand in a frank, friendly manner to Cook. "Talk it over with Mrs. Cook. After all, her future is involved too."

"We've already talked it out," Cook said. "I know it's hard for you to understand, Mr. Hobbs, but my personal working happiness is what's involved here."

George Webber took the cigar out of his mouth and laughed, never taking his eyes off Cook. "I suggest you repeat my part of the conversation to her, Cook. Sometimes women have an instinct for the truth when they hear it. Which is more than can be said for you, my friend."

Cook turned and walked out of the room, shutting the door firmly behind him.

There was a moment of silence, and then Hobbs whirled on young Don Stanton. "I thought you told us he was coming in on our side!"

Stanton shook his head like a groggy fighter. "He told me he'd decided, Mr. Hobbs. It never occurred to me he'd decide against us."

Hobbs leaned back wearily in his chair, his right hand closing over the manila envelope. "I want you to get something straight, Don. This is a far more critical situation than I think you realize. The government has been led to believe that we already have the Cook motor for use in rockets. Our proposed contracts with them are based on that assumption. The minute that backwoods long drink of water walks out of here and tells some smart government agent or Washington reporter that he hasn't made the deal, Hobbs Enterprises goes up in smoke. Every cent of capital we have has been invested in a new plant and new tooling to meet these new contracts. If the rug is pulled out from under us because we don't control the Cook motor, we're ten times bankrupt."

"I didn't realize how tight it was, sir."

"Well, now you do. For the next twenty-four hours Hobbs Enterprises have got to burst with optimism. I want you to release the notes to the press—the notes we made on expansion plans. Say that I'm setting up an appointment for the day after tomorrow with the banking group—announce that as if there isn't the slightest possible doubt of the outcome."

"Yes, sir."

"Reserve a table for me tonight in the Blue Lagoon Room. That's where your girl sings, isn't it? Arrange for a party of attractive people, and see to it that some of the nightlife boys ask me some questions."

"Yes, sir."

"Okay, get on your horse."

Don Stanton hurried out of the room. When he was gone, the boy wizard leaned back in his chair and closed his eyes. Suddenly he no longer looked like a boy. After a moment he spoke without opening his eyes.

"We don't have any choice, do we, George?"

"None whatever," Webber said. "Not a smidgen of a choice."

Hobbs shook his head from side to side. "It's hard to grasp the fact that a great business empire like this stands to rise or fall on the whim of one stubborn man."

"Maybe you need a few facts-of-life lectures yourself,"

Webber said. "Yours is a paper empire, Martin, built on paper profits. You've reached a crisis where you have to deal with realities. These new government contracts are for real, but you made one mistake. You said you owned the Cook motor, because you were sure you would own it. When you come to sign the contracts and you haven't got the motor, you're through. In come the accountants and the Internal Revenue boys and the Senate committees, and you've had it—and all the rest of us have had it."

"Cook must have a price," Hobbs said. "Every man has a price."

"It would appear our friend Cook is an exception," Webber said. His thin mouth tightened. "Because his price isn't money. But there is a way to buy him, and we have to risk it. It doesn't much matter, Martin, what we go to jail for. Jail is jail. Covering one crime with another is our only choice."

Hobbs sighed. "You think it will work?"

"It'll work," Webber said with grim satisfaction.

Hotel maids don't like to see a DO NOT DISTURB sign hung outside the door of a room. It usually means a disruption of routine. They have to work around that room until the occupant finally comes out.

The maid whose job it was to take care of Room 1208 had been grumbling most of the morning and early afternoon because of the sign outside its door. By three o'clock it was the only room on the floor not done. Mattie Ryan, the maid, called Mrs. Kniffen, the housekeeper, to report.

Mrs. Kniffen remembered there'd been a query from the phone office early that morning—a call for the occupant, Mr. Fisher, for a seven o'clock, which he hadn't answered.

"He must be sleepin' off a giant hangover," Mattie said to Mrs. Kniffen. "The TV's been playing ever since I came on this morning."

"You're sure about that, Mattie?"

"You can hear it plain enough outside the door," Mattie said.

Mrs. Kniffen knew the rules. The slightest thing offbeat, and you didn't wait, unless you wanted Mr. Chambrun down on your back, Mrs. Kniffen called Jerry Dodd, the house security officer. "House dick" or "house detective" were not phrases used at the Hotel Beaumont.

Jerry Dodd, a thin, sharp-eyed man in his middle forties who knew his job as only a man trained by Pierre Chambrun could know it, met Mrs. Kniffen on the twelfth floor five minutes later. They stood outside the door of Room 1208, listening. You could hear the TV set clearly.

Jerry knocked sharply on the door. There was no reply. He took Mrs. Kniffen's passkey and opened the door.

Mr. Fisher was in residence. His room was small but elegant. He sat in the big armchair facing the television set. He was staring at the screen where a midafternoon soap opera was winding its lugubrious course. Fisher's eyes were bulging, but they weren't seeing TV. To Jerry's practiced eye, he was obviously dead—violently dead.

"Heart attack, I guess," he said casually over his shoulder to Mrs. Kniffen, who couldn't see the dead man from the hall.

In a hotel like the Beaumont, which is larger in population than many small towns, sudden death is not an unusual occurrence. Mrs. Kniffen had encountered it many times over the years. Jerry Dodd was an old hand at it.

"I'll call Dr. Partridge," Mrs. Kniffen said, and scurried off down the hall to her own phone.

Jerry Dodd closed the door of Room 1208, remaining inside the room. Mr. Fisher was young to die so abruptly—in his middle thirties, no older. He hadn't gone to bed the night before. He had apparently died while watching his TV set.

There was a bottle of bourbon, three quarters empty, on the table beside Mr. Fisher's chair. There were two glasses, one with a small portion of a drink still left in it. Mr. Fisher had had company before he left this world.

And Mr. Fisher had not left the world peacefully. Every muscle of his body was extended and rigid. He was bent backward, as though his spinal cord had suddenly contracted. Jerry Dodd was no toxicologist, but he had seen the action of strychnine once before—the lightning-fast action, the muscular convulsions, the final moment of agony.

It was obviously a case of murder in New York's most luxurious hotel—murder deluxe.

Like Pierre Chambrun, Jerry Dodd had developed his own sensitive antenna. He moved cautiously to the table, and without touching either glass he bent down and sniffed. He was frowning when he straightened up. He looked at Mr. Fisher's face and his frown deepened. Then he took out his handkerchief, dropped it over the telephone receiver, and picked up the phone.

"Jerry Dodd here," he said to the operator. "Get me Mr. Chambrun, and then call the precinct house and see if you can get Lieutenant Hardy. We got a dead one up here."

"At once, Mr. Dodd," said the operator's emotionless voice.

Seconds later Chambrun answered. "What is it, Jerry?"

"Dead one in 1208, Mr. Chambrun. Fellow named Fisher. Left a wake-me for seven this morning but didn't answer it. D.N.D. outside his door. But the maid could hear the TV playing. Mrs. Kniffen called me, and I just came in. Suicide—maybe."

"Maybe?" Chambrun asked, cool and undisturbed.

"Poison. I'd guess strychnine. But two glasses. Most of a quart of bourbon gone. So he had a visitor. Maybe Fisher hung the D.N.D. outside his door, maybe his visitor did. Doc Partridge is on his way, and I've phoned the cops."

"Okay, Jerry," Chambrun said cheerfully. "Hold the fort. I'll be right up."

In his office Chambrun sipped the last of a cup of Turkish coffee, glanced inside his silver case to make sure he had cigarettes, and picked up his phone.

"Mr. Atterbury at the front desk, please," he said.

"Yes, Mr. Chambrun?" Atterbury said in a moment.

"Who was Mr. Fisher in 1208?" Chambrun asked.

"'Was,' sir?"

"'Was,' Mr. Atterbury."

"One moment, sir." And in one moment: "Mr. Paul Fisher was a private detective, sir."

Chambrun's mouth hardened. "How did we happen to let him register, Atterbury?"

"Letter of introduction from Senator Farrand, sir," Atterbury said promptly. Only such an introduction would satisfy allowing a private detective to register in the hotel possibly to spy on one of its guests.

"Why wasn't I made aware of this, Atterbury?"

Atterbury's brief silence sounded flustered. He was obviously studying the registration card. "I'm sorry, sir. He registered the night Carl Nevers was off for his brother's wedding. I suppose the relief man expected Nevers would make the report, sir, and Nevers—"

"—thought the relief man would make it," Chambrun said impatiently. "We don't run a successful hotel on thoughts of that kind, Atterbury. Not your fault, but make a point of it with Nevers. Senator or no senator, I won't have private investigators making the Beaumont their headquarters."

Chambrun held his finger on the disconnect button on his phone for a moment, then got the operator back. "Get me Senator Claude Farrand in his offices in the Senate Building in Washington. I'll hold on."

There was some delay in reaching the senator. Chambrun, puffing on one of his Egyptian cigarettes, drummed his fingers on the desk. He suddenly broke in on a conversation between the Beaumont's switchboard operator and the senator's secretary.

"Tell the senator," he said, clipping off the words, "it's about an employee of his named Fisher. If the senator doesn't choose to talk to me, tell him I shall release to the press the fact that Fisher was his employee. I say 'was' because Fisher is dead."

The senator was instantly on the wire, booming, oily. "What's all this about Fisher, Mr. Chambrun?"

"He's dead, Senator. He may have committed suicide. He may have been put out of the way by someone. I need facts for the police, and I need them in a hurry."

The senator's breathing sounded as though he'd been running hard. "He wasn't an employee, Mr. Chambrun. Just a casual acquaintance. I gave him a letter to the hotel because he wanted a few days of fancy vacation."

"That won't do, Senator," Chambrun said coldly.

"Look here, Chambrun, can't you tell the police exactly what you know? The man registered at the hotel with a letter of introduction from me. I'll take the next scheduled flight from here to New York. Then they can question me, and you won't be involved."

"As long as you're on the scene, it's your baby, Senator," Chambrun said. "But don't miss that next flight."

He put down the receiver. His hooded eyes moved toward the blotting pad on his desk. Tucked under one of its leather corners was the receipt for fifty thousand dollars in cash signed that morning by Martin Hobbs.

Chambrun was aware that several days ago Senator Claude Farrand had made a speech on the Senate floor attacking the Secretary of Defense in connection with certain proposed contracts being negotiated with the Martin Hobbs Enterprises.

Miss Alison Barnwell—Mrs. John Wills in private life—had been handling the Beaumont's public relations for more than a year. She was extremely good at the job. She managed to look expensive without earning the salary to be expensive. She had a brisk, pleasant manner and a high, proud way of carrying her lovely red head.

Recently married, she was a very handsome woman who had blossomed into something really breathtaking. Every moment of her life was a joy to her now, even the minor exasperations of her job. The Beaumont was an important part of her life, not just a job, since her husband was being groomed by Pierre Chambrun for a top executive position. A close association with Chambrun had developed in Alison something of his possessive and protective feeling for the Beaumont.

It was this feeling that took Alison Barnwell to the Trapeze Bar about five o'clock that afternoon. She was in no hurry to get home from her work since Johnny, her husband, was at a hotelmen's convention in Palm Springs.

There had been a note on Alison's desk that morning from Carl Nevers, the night reservation clerk. "Dear Miss Barnwell: Thought you might like to know that Laura Thomas of Hollywood registered early this morning."

Alison had giggled over the note. Mr. Nevers was as transparent as a windowpane. Ordinarily the list of newly registered celebrities was typed out by her secretary and placed on her desk. Alison's secretary was a walking social and celebrity register. Miss Thomas's name had been ignored by the secretary. Mr. Nevers, therefore, was feeling uneasy. He wanted to know if he'd been guilty of admitting an impostor.

Alison's secretary had brushed away the first inquiry. There was no such person as Laura Thomas—that is, no person by that name of even minor importance. Alison herself had never heard the name. But the signature on the registration card was intriguing. No street address. Just Hollywood—as though that was obviously enough for any postal clerk in the movie capital.

If the lady in question was a fake, the unadorned address was a bold touch, Alison thought. She wanted a look at Miss Thomas. Just before five o'clock, the day bell captain, having been alerted, reported to Alison that Miss Laura Thomas was sipping a martini in the Trapeze Bar.

The Trapeze Bar at the Beaumont is suspended in space, like a birdcage, over the foyer of the Grand Ballroom. The foyer, painted a pale chartreuse with rich cherrywood paneling, is a meeting place for guests when the ballroom itself is not in use. The Trapeze Bar, its walls made entirely of elaborate Florentine grillwork, is popular mainly because it is different. An artist of the Calder school had decorated it with mobiles of circus performers working on trapezes. They sway slightly in the draft from a concealed air-conditioning system. To be seen at the Trapeze meant that you were important, or that you didn't know what you'd gotten yourself into and would find out with a jolt when an obsequious waiter handed you the check.

Mike Maggio escorted Alison from the lobby to the Trapeze Bar and pointed out Laura Thomas sitting alone at a corner table, a chilled martini glass on the table in front of her.

Expensively smart, Alison thought as she crossed the room. There was nothing fake about the mink stole. The black sunglasses added the proper Hollywood touch. Unaware of scrutiny, Miss Thomas tightened her mouth into a hard thin line, which went with the tensions of being famous. It could also go with the tensions of playing a phony role.

Alison stopped by the table. "Miss Thomas?" she said brightly.

The dark glasses turned sharply in Alison's direction. For a fraction of a moment Alison was certain they hid panic.

"Yes?" The girl's voice was cool and completely under control, however.

"I'm Alison Barnwell, public relations director for the Beaumont. May I join you for a moment?"

Miss Thomas hesitated. Obviously she didn't want to be joined. "I'm just finishing my drink," she said, "and I have an engagement."

"Oh, please let me buy you another," Alison said. "I've been looking forward all day to talking with you."

The dark glasses turned toward the martini glass. Clearly another drink was a temptation. Alison sat down at the table without waiting to be asked and beckoned to the captain.

"Two very dry martinis, Mr. Del Greco," she said.

The elegant Mr. Del Greco bowed and retired to the bar with the order. Miss Thomas fished in her dark alligator handbag for a cigarette.

Alison held her small gold lighter for Miss Thomas. "Are

you in the east to make personal appearances, Miss Thomas?" she asked.

"I'm really not interested in publicity, Miss Barnwell," the girl said. There was a false boredom in her voice. "This is the first vacation I've had in a long time, and I'd like to stay out of the limelight."

"That's quite understandable," Alison said, wondering if she sounded as phony as Miss Thomas. She felt it. She laughed pleasantly. "One of the touchy parts of my job is to guess when a celebrity wants publicity and when she wants privacy. Her feelings can be hurt if you make a mistake either way."

"You can be quite certain I want no red-carpet treatment," Miss Thomas said.

"Then we'll just call this an official welcome to the Beaumont," Alison said, as Mr. Del Greco brought the martinis. "To the success of your latest picture." Alison raised her glass.

Miss Thomas's black glasses stared at Alison. "You saw it?" she asked.

"Well, frankly no," Alison said. "I don't get much opportunity to see films in my job, and I was married several months ago, which takes up most of my spare time."

"Lucky you," Miss Thomas said dryly. She sipped her drink.

There was an awkward pause that Alison knew she had to bridge. "Are you perhaps interested in doing something on Broadway, Miss Thomas?"

Miss Thomas seemed to be considering the question, but when she spoke, she figuratively threw a right hook to Alison's jaw. "You really haven't the faintest idea who I am or what I've done, have you, Miss Barnwell?"

Alison blushed. "I'm afraid you've found me out, Miss Thomas. In my job we don't like to admit to ignorance, both out of vanity and an unwillingness to hurt the feelings of a guest."

"My feelings aren't hurt," Miss Thomas said. "All I really

want, Miss Barnwell, is to be left alone." It was pointed and final.

Alison stood up, leaving her almost untouched drink. "I'm sorry to have intruded, Miss Thomas. But it *is* my job."

"Better luck next time," Miss Thomas said, giving Alison a small Cheshire-Cat smile.

Alison walked out of the Trapeze, nodding to one or two people she knew. "That, my girl," she told herself, "was a first-class shellacking."

The fact was, if Miss Thomas was a phony, she played her cards expertly and very, very close to the vest. She had made only one mistake. She had challenged Alison's curiosity so sharply that Alison was determined to find out all there was to know about Miss Thomas—who, what, and why.

The Clifford Cooks had a small domestic problem. Cook had bought theater tickets for himself and Anne. Comedy seemed the best medicine for his state of mind, and the ticket agent had highly recommended the latest musical comedy. Anne had got in touch with the front office to apply for a sitter to stay with Bobbie.

Bobbie was resentful. She wanted dinner in their suite by herself, served by room service. She wanted to watch her favorite TV programs without some nosy sitter to spoil her private fun. She would be entertaining certain imaginary friends who were very much a part of her daily life. Wouldn't there be a housekeeper on the floor? Wasn't the telephone right there?

"If you insist, Mum, I can call the operator every hour—but please, *please* let me have my private party."

Anne was anxious about Cliff. He seemed detached and worried since the morning meeting he'd described in some detail. It was all very well to refuse to submit to threats, but how real were the threats? Cliff seemed to be willing to give in to Bobbie's whim.

"If the sitter service checks with her periodically during the evening, why not?" he said. He had a feeling they wouldn't be staying in places with the rarefied atmosphere of the Beaumont very often in the future. Why not let the child have dinner served in solitary elegance by the room service waiter, in the company of her imaginary friends? "Suppose we have the sitter call you every half hour, chicken? You answer and let her know how you are. If you don't, then the sitter will come up and stay with you."

"Oh, Daddy, you're a doll," Bobbie said.

So Cliff called the sitter service, engaged a sitter for the evening, but explained that Bobbie was to be allowed her solitary grandeur unless she failed to answer the phone. Promptly at eleven, the sitter would present herself, put Bobbie to bed, and stay on in the suite until the Cooks returned. Since they were having a night on the town they might as well hit one of the nightclubs after the theater.

Bobbie was ecstatic. Anne was mildly concerned, but not quite certain whether it was for Bobbie or Cliff. And once the arrangement had been made, Cliff seemed to retreat into the private world of his business problems.

Mr. Paul Fisher's dead body was removed from Room 1208 about five-twenty in the afternoon and taken to the morgue. Lieutenant Hardy, a big, athletic-looking young man who looked more like a good-natured, if slightly puzzled, college fullback than a homicide detective, was not happy. Dr. Partridge, the house physician, and the assistant medical examiner agreed that Mr. Fisher's heart had been sound until he'd swallowed a substantial dose of strychnine, which had knocked him off in a matter of seconds. Laboratory tests to confirm this still had to be made, but Hardy had no doubts of this confirmation.

There was no sign in Room 1208 of any strychnine or of anything that might have contained it.

The nearly empty liquor glass was the one that had contained the strychnine. It was covered with the late Mr. Fisher's fingerprints. The second glass, which had contained a drink without the special flavoring of strychnine, had no fingerprints on it at all. Wiped absolutely clean. There were no other fingerprints in the room, except Fisher's and the floor maid's.

Identification in Fisher's wallet was ample. It contained his driver's license, his license to operate as a private detective in the state of New York, some business cards, two credit cards, and half a dozen blank checks. The address on the credit cards and on the licenses was Fisher's office on lower Broadway. No home address. A phone call to his office was fruitless. No answer.

And apparently Mr. Fisher either kept his working notes in his head or else all notes and papers had been removed by his drinking companion of last evening.

Pierre Chambrun, whom Hardy knew from other occasions, suggested that Senator Farrand might have answers as to the case Fisher was working on. The senator was on his way. Hardy checked on that. Jerry Dodd, the house security officer, had noticed nothing odd about Fisher's behavior—nothing to indicate who Fisher was interested in at the Beaumont.

Chambrun had kept his suspicions to himself. The senator had a right to reveal his own business in his own fashion. But in *his* own way Chambrun was not waiting. His gut still ached.

Returning to his second floor office about six o'clock, Chambrun was pleasantly surprised to find Alison Barnwell waiting for him. Chambrun was fond of his public relations director. He had been indirectly involved in a crisis in her life and found out what a really fine human being she was. She pleased him in other ways. It was a theory of his that women had the responsibility to look attractive on all and any occasions. Alison never failed to meet this requirement.

"One of the things I like about you most, Alison," Chambrun said as he saw her, "is that you're psychic. I was just going to call you at home."

"I wish I thought it was for a date," Alison said. "The evenings are hell with Johnny away. I managed for a long time without him, but now I can't remember how I did it."

"If you haven't anything planned, dine with me here," Chambrun said. "The pot's boiling, and I've got to stay here and sit on the lid. You might be useful."

"Miss Proctor just told me about the heart attack on twelve," Alison said. "I'd be glad to stay if I can be helpful."

"Sun's over the yardarm," Chambrun said. "Care for a drink? I know how you feel about my Turkish coffee."

"May I fix myself a Dubonnet on the rocks?"

Chambrun gestured toward the well-stocked sideboard and sat down at his desk. "It wasn't a heart attack on twelve," he said. "Probably a homicide."

"Mr. Chambrun!"

"And a very sticky one. This is strictly between us, Alison." And Chambrun gave her the details, plus the reasons for his concern about Martin Hobbs Enterprises.

"You think there's a connection?"

He ticked off the points on his fingers. "Hobbs draws fifty thousand in cash, which—in my suspicious mind—spells sudden getaway. Fisher, a private eye, was introduced into the hotel by Senator Farrand. The senator has made loud noises in the Senate about government contracts going to Hobbs. The senator is vastly disturbed over the news of Fisher's death and is on his way here by plane. You don't have to be a clairvoyant to see a relationship among those facts. Which brings me to my reason for having intended to call you, Alison. Hobbs has been here a week. He's never made a move without a blast of trumpets preceding him. I've noticed his PR man hanging around you with a kind of puppy love in his eyes."

Alison laughed. "Young Don Stanton has automatic mouth-watering reflexes at the sight of any pretty girl," she said. "But I'm running a bad second to Toni Blanton, our young singer in the Blue Lagoon Room. He takes her often to the zoo. What I'm missing!"

Chambrun's smile was faint, distracted. "Do you need your records to know how the Hobbs entourage spent last evening?"

"No," Alison said. "He entertained the officers of the Junior Chamber of Commerce at a private dinner. Later on they closed the Blue Lagoon."

"They were in the hotel then all evening?"

"The party was. I can't vouch for any one person, Mr. Chambrun. I wasn't there. Mr. Cardoza, the captain, might be able to help."

Chambrun glanced at his watch. "He's not on for twenty minutes."

"Incidentally, Hobbs has reserved a table in the Blue Lagoon for tonight for ten," Alison said. "Don Stanton wanted to make sure some of the important columnists would be present and cooperative."

Chambrun frowned at his cigarette end. "Either his getaway isn't planned for tonight or this party plan is designed to keep someone's guard lowered. And, Alison, check with Cardoza for me. The Hobbs party consists of Hobbs himself, George Webber, young Stanton, and a girl secretary."

"Miss Garth."

"See if Cardoza remembers any long absences from last night's wingding. The medical examiner guesses our friend Fisher swallowed his hemlock about midnight. I'd say eleven-thirty to twelve-thirty is the critical time. We'll dine at seven. Will you leave the ordering to me?"

"I'd be a fool not to," Alison said, starting for the door. "Cardoza often comes in early to go over any special banquet orders with Mr. Kraus."

Just as Alison reached the door, Chambrun called to her. "My dear child, you came here to see me about something. I haven't given you a chance. What was it?"

Alison laughed ruefully. "Nothing important."

"If it wasn't important, you wouldn't have been waiting for me. Let's have it."

"I just had my knuckles rather soundly rapped by one of the guests," Alison said. "A Miss Laura Thomas."

"The one with the live animal in her suitcase?" Chambrun asked.

"The *what*?"

"Johnny Thacker swears she had a whining animal in one of her suitcases when he checked her into her room," Chambrun chuckled. "Mrs. Kniffen investigated for me." He picked up a slip of paper on his desk. "Five suitcases. Only one of them unpacked. The others locked. No sign of animal life. In what other way is she interesting, Alison?"

"Carl Nevers was worried about having let her register," Alison said. "He asked me, in his oblique fashion, to check on her. She may be Hollywood, but she's no Hollywood celebrity. Personally, I think she's a fake and a very clever one. The question I came to ask you is—do you care?"

Chambrun's narrowed eyes twinkled at her through cigarette smoke. His voice was paternal—but gently and affectionately reproving. "I've told you many times, my dear, that I cannot run this hotel efficiently without knowing everything that goes on in it. But *everything*. Yes, I care to know about Miss Thomas. But at the moment, a moment of crisis, I care more about Hobbs and his possible connection with the murder of Mr. Fisher."

The green light blinked on his desk. He picked up the phone and said, "Yes?" Then: "At once, Miss Proctor." He put down the phone. "Give Senator Farrand your most devastating smile on the way out," he said.

Senator Claude Farrand was a regular guest of the Hotel Beaumont on his visits to New York and had lived there for one long stretch during his service at the United Nations. He had come to know and respect Chambrun over a period of years. On one occasion he had been saved from a dangerously embarrassing moment by Chambrun's quick wit. A little too much old Kentucky bourbon at a dinner one night, plus the alluring and very bare-shouldered wife of a Texas oil man who was a power in the opposition party, had resulted in an indiscreet invitation to the lady to have a nightcap in the senator's suite. The lady had been willing, and she had not been unreceptive to further suggestions. At a critical moment in the senator's romantic campaign, the door of the suite had been opened by a passkey, and Chambrun, smiling blandly, had come in.

The senator had breathlessly retired to do something about his disheveled condition and to put his black tie in order. The wind of his departure still stirred in the room when there was a sharp knock at the door.

Chambrun, cool and unruffled, opened the door to the press. The press, having been tipped off to a possible scandal, was thrown completely off base by the presence of the hotel manager.

"You wish to see the senator?" Chambrun had asked.

They wished to see the senator.

"He's been courteous enough to allow me to show his suite to Mrs. Cardwell. She and Mr. Cardwell are planning a lengthy stay with us, and I wanted her to see what accommodations I could give them." He had turned suavely to the lady. "I trust these quarters will be satisfactory, Mrs. Cardwell?"

The lady, who had lost all zest for the chase, assured him that they would. Chambrun bowed her toward the door.

"In that case, shall we leave the senator to his press conference?"

At which point the senator, cued by Chambrun, appeared from the next room neat as a pin. "Well, boys," he said jovially, "what can I do for you?"

No, the senator would never forget Pierre Chambrun. And now he needed him again.

Senator Farrand was a big man, expensively sloppy in his appearance. He had the deep, booming voice of an orator. But as he came into Chambrun's office he was sweating like an ordinary mortal.

"I came as quickly as I could," he said. "I take it from the way your man Dodd slipped me up here in a private elevator that the police are waiting for me."

"They are," Chambrun said. He wasn't the deferential hotel manager at this moment. He held trump cards in any game with the senator, and he didn't choose to be maneuvered into the image of a fawning servant.

The senator sat down in the green leather chair by Chambrun's desk and wiped his florid face with a handkerchief. "How much do they know?"

"They know that Fisher was a friend of yours. That he registered here with a letter of introduction from you—which, by the way, was naughty of you, Senator. You know damn well I'd have chucked him out on his ear if I'd known he was a private detective. A slipup in routine here is all that permitted him in. The police hope you may be able to tell them what case Fisher was working on."

"Oh, God," the senator said. "Fisher had made no notes? There were no papers or documents to answer that question for them?"

"None."

The senator cheered up noticeably. "Well, then," he said, "things aren't too bad. Fisher was a friend of mine—had done some work for me in the past. In the *past,* Chambrun. He wanted a vacation in a luxury spot, and I wrote him a letter of introduction. I have no reason to think he was working at anything connected with me."

"The police may buy that, but I don't, Senator," Chambrun said coldly. "For certain reasons I won't go into, I can't help you in any such evasion."

"Now, see here, Chambrun, I—"

"You see here, Senator. A few days ago you gave a speech in the Senate condemning some defense contracts about to be awarded by the federal government to Martin Hobbs Enterprises. Martin Hobbs is a guest here at the hotel. There are half a dozen smart Washington reporters who'll make the connection without half trying. I tell you this not to try to advise you on how to handle your problems, but because I will have to point all this out to the police—if you don't. I've waited for you to get here so that you could affirm or deny the connection. You'll have to do one or the other. You can't ignore it."

The senator nodded slowly. He took a leather cigar case from an inside pocket. He busied himself for a moment, clipping off the end of the cigar and getting it burning.

"It's damned awkward, Chambrun," he said.

"I'm sorry to hear it," Chambrun said. "It's damned awkward for me to have a murder in my hotel, particularly since Fisher should never have been registered here in the first place."

"I never dreamed—"

"I know, Senator. In my business I have to dream all the time—or be left in the starting gate."

"Politics," the senator said. "Complex game, you know." He sounded as though he was about to deliver a lecture, and Chambrun's hooded eyes became hostile. "You smell trouble. You get a whiff of conspiracy, and you let go with both barrels, even if they're loaded with blanks. Usually everyone knows it's just politics. You call each other names in public, and then you have dinner together at night. Politics. Sometimes—rarely—you're asked to put up or shut up. This is what happened to me."

"Over the proposed Hobbs contracts?"

The senator nodded. "Hobbs. Young whizbang. Big reputation. But something about that kind of spectacular success, about that kind of easy money—well, it always has a fishy smell to me. I thought it was safe enough for me to take a belt at him. Part of my job—keep jabbing at the administration. But my timing was off and my information incomplete. As it developed, the contracts with Hobbs haven't actually been signed. They will be if everything is according to Hoyle, but they haven't been signed yet. The result is, I'm in the position of having either to support my charges or be too obviously guilty of rank politicking. So I hired Fisher, a competent man, to see what he could find out for me. There could have been better ways to go about it."

"Through the proper committee investigators?"

"Except that I'm not a member of any committee that can properly deal with this contract business. So I hired me a private boy. My political hide will be scorched, Chambrun, if it is revealed that I've personally hired a detective to investigate the administration's business dealings—scorched or nailed to the barn door."

"Unless there is some fire where you thought you saw smoke," Chambrun said.

The senator suddenly looked like an eager puppy dog. "There is some fire you know of?"

Chambrun hesitated. "This much, Senator. It's something to chew on. Perhaps you started something. A proper committee is investigating. I know that directly from Hobbs's bank in San Francisco. The reason I know is that Hobbs asked me to get him fifty thousand dollars in cash on a check drawn against his account there. I wanted to make sure the check wouldn't bounce."

The senator whistled.

"You can add that up with Fisher's murder as well as I can," Chambrun said. "You know better than I do whether your position is a little better than you thought. So tell it your own way, Senator—but tell it. May I call Lieutenant Hardy, the detective in charge, and tell him you're here?"

The senator stood up, blowing air like a whale. He felt a little better. "You may tell him, sir," he said. "You may also tell yourself, Chambrun, that for the second time I am deeply in your debt. Anything—anytime—you want something, ask for it."

Chambrun's smile was thin. "Whatever I have done for you, Senator, has only been incidental to my job of protecting the Beaumont."

* * *

Miss Margaret Hillhouse, who made herself available to the Beaumont for baby-sitting services every night except on Sundays, was having an unusually pleasant evening. At six-thirty she had reported to 7H, the Cooks' suite, where she'd been introduced to Bobbie Cook. Bobbie was a charming little girl, squirming with excitement.

Anne Cook explained patiently what was expected of Miss Hillhouse. Bobbie was to have her private party, her supper to be brought by room service. Miss Hillhouse was to check with Bobbie by phone every half hour. Anne gave Miss Hillhouse an extra key.

"If she doesn't answer you are to come here at once and let yourself in, Miss Hillhouse, and the party will be over. Straight to bed."

"I'll answer, Mum!" Bobbie said.

"At eleven—no later, mind!—you'll come in and put Bobbie to bed," Anne went on. "You'll stay here until we get back. We thought of taking in a nightclub after the theater."

"I'll stay as late as you like, Mrs. Cook. Just enjoy yourselves," Margaret Hillhouse said.

So Miss Hillhouse also had her supper, paid for by the Cooks, served by room service in a small sitting room on the mezzanine. She could hear the dinner music from the Blue Lagoon Room. She was halfway through the newest best-seller and looked forward to a pleasant evening of reading.

At seven o'clock Alison Barnwell sat down at an exquisitely set table in Chambrun's office, a little pop-eyed by what was placed before her. There were cold canapes of stuffed eggs and creamed anchovies; there were hot hors d'oeuvres of crab meat Remick, sprinkled with chopped parsley; these were followed by a deliciously flavored chicken consommé, accompanied by a delicate Rhine wine; then a few mouthfuls of pheasant under glass, with a 1953 Volnay; followed by a few bites of roast veal and artichoke bottoms swimming in a puree of chestnuts, with a 1952 Chambolle; followed by a plain green salad and thin slices of toast and Port Salud cheese and an ice-cold glass of champagne; and finally a fabulous rum cake, Turkish coffee, and a warming Kummel as a liqueur. Pierre Chambrun did himself well.

Alison leaned back in her chair, feeling like an overstuffed Thanksgiving turkey. Chambrun, who apparently dined in this fashion every night, seemed to be delighted by her obvious pleasure. He sipped his coffee, smoked his cigarette, and looked at her like a man who remembers his lost youth with a profound nostalgia.

"I've been so impressed by this that I've forgotten to report back on Mr. Cardoza," Alison said.

Chambrun smiled like a sleepy cat. "I would have asked you," he said, "except that Cardoza leaves nothing to chance. He called me himself. No noticeable absences from the Hobbs party during last evening."

"There were comings and goings," Alison said. "And Miss Garth, the secretary, was not present at all."

"It's a 'could-be,'" Chambrun said. "Any one of them could have visited and murdered Fisher—but there isn't the slightest proof that any one of them did. I've checked with the night staff. No one recalls anything significant. More Kummel, Alison?"

In the Blue Lagoon, Martin Hobbs, George Webber, Don Stanton, and seven assorted guests were beginning a gay evening. On this occasion they were carefully watched by Mr. Cardoza, the captain. Hobbs and Webber each made trips to the men's room during the evening, but went nowhere else. Don Stanton left once, but only to circle around to the dressing room of Toni Blanton, the Blue Lagoon's attractive chanteuse. He returned directly to the table from there.

At the theater Cliff Cook laughed for the first time in days. The musical comedy lived up to the ticket agent's recommendation. Anne Cook called Miss Hillhouse during the first intermission and was reassured—Bobbie was having a ball and had dutifully answered the phone at every half hour. The Cooks decided to go to a nightclub after the theater.

Senator Claude Farrand was on his way back to Washington, having cleared his conscience with the police.

At a few minutes before eleven Miss Margaret Hillhouse made her way up from the mezzanine to 7H. Bobbie had been a little brisk at being interrupted at ten-thirty at the beginning of a TV program. Now, standing outside the door of 7H, Miss Hillhouse could hear the closing theme as the TV show ended. Then she inserted the key Anne had given her into the door and went in. Bobbie Cook was nowhere in the suite.

At ten minutes past eleven Chambrun and Jerry Dodd arrived at 7H, where a frightened and tearful Miss Hillhouse awaited them. Miss Hillhouse, on discovering Bobbie's absence, had called Mrs. Carmichael, who managed the night-sitter service and who had promptly notified Mr. Chambrun.

Chambrun's "gut ache" was acute. Everything that had gone wrong on this day seemed to have a connection with Martin Hobbs. Clifford Cook was in the process of negotiating some kind of business deal with Hobbs, and now Cook's eight-year-old daughter was missing.

Miss Hillhouse, fighting her tears, explained disjointedly how the evening had been arranged. She'd never encountered anything quite like it before, but it had seemed reasonable enough at the time. Everything had gone smoothly. The little girl had dutifully answered the phone every half hour, including the last one at ten-thirty.

Jerry Dodd was on the phone while Miss Hillhouse explained. The kid might be wandering around the hotel somewhere. The staff was alerted. He looked up at Miss Hillhouse while waiting for another connection.

"Eleven o'clock was bedtime," he said cheerfully. "She probably didn't want the evening to end. We'll find her down in the lobby or sneaking a look at the goings-on in the Blue Lagoon. A kid like that can make a federal case out of going to bed."

Then Johnny Thacker came on the phone, and Dodd gave orders for a careful search.

"When do you expect the Cooks back?" Chambrun asked. He didn't feel as cheerfully optimistic as Jerry Dodd. As a matter of fact, he was deeply disturbed. He couldn't somehow swallow all the coincidences of the day.

"They went to the theater," Miss Hillhouse said.

"What theater?"

"I heard them mention a musical comedy, but I can't remember the name of the show."

Chambrun glanced at his wrist watch. Eleven-twenty. The show would be over. "Coming straight home?"

"No, sir. They were going to a nightclub."

"Which one?"

"They didn't say, sir. Mrs. Cook may phone in. She did call during the first theater intermission."

"She may not," Chambrun said. "She'll assume the child's now safe in bed and asleep. Another call would disturb her."

Jerry Dodd came over from the phone. "If she left this floor, she'd probably go by elevator, wouldn't she? Anyone would notice an eight-year-old girl all by herself. They'll pick her up in a few minutes."

Miss Hillhouse began to weep. "Oh, I hope so!"

"Get hold of yourself," Chambrun said sharply. "You have nothing to blame yourself for. You followed your instructions to the letter."

He went over to the phone and asked to be connected with the Blue Lagoon. Mr. Cardoza, the captain, answered in his low suave voice. "Chambrun here, Cardoza. About the Hobbs party. Still there?"

"Yes, Mr. Chambrun. Still going strong."

"Comings and goings?"

"None, sir. Oh, the men's room, the powder room. But no one in the party has gone out into the hotel proper."

"You're positive?"

Cardoza sounded injured. "You told me to watch, Mr. Chambrun."

"Sorry to be edgy," Chambrun said. "If the party breaks up, or if anyone does leave it, call me in my office or in 7H."

"Depend on me, Mr. Chambrun."

"I do."

Chambrun put down the phone. "Jerry, I want someone stationed outside the entrance to the Blue Lagoon. If anyone in Hobbs's party leaves, I want to know where they go and what they do."

Jerry nodded, but looked puzzled. "But what has that got to do with the price of eggs?"

"I wish I knew," Chambrun said. Frowning, he picked up the phone again. "Get me Miss Barnwell at her apartment," he said.

"Johnny?" Alison's drowsy voice said.

"Sorry to disappoint you. Chambrun here."

The sharpness of his voice evidently brought Alison wide-awake. "I'd just dozed off, Mr. Chambrun. I thought it was Johnny calling from Palm Springs."

"We've got new troubles here, Alison. An eight-year-old girl has disappeared. No time to give you the details, but we'd like to locate her parents. They went to see a musical comedy, then planned to go to a nightclub. If you were an out-of-towner, where would you go?"

"El Morocco, Stork Club, Latin Quarter," Alison said promptly.

"Thanks."

"Can I do anything?"

"I'd like it if you were here. If this gets out, the press will be hammering at us—at our sitter system, at our inefficiency."

"Did someone slip up?"

"I don't think so. It may be a false alarm. Jerry thinks the kid just didn't want to go to bed and took off on her own. I hope he's right. I have an uncomfortable feeling he's wrong."

"I'll be there in fifteen minutes," Alison said.

Chambrun held down the phone button for a moment and was then reconnected with the switchboard. "Jane? I want you to call three nightclubs—El Morocco, Stork Club, and Latin Quarter. I want Mr. and Mrs. Clifford Cook paged in all three places. I'll be here unless I tell you otherwise."

Miss Hillhouse seemed to have got control of herself when Chambrun crossed over from the phone.

"Did Mr. and Mrs. Cook have friends in the hotel?" she asked Chambrun.

"Acquaintances," Chambrun said.

"Perhaps one of them got in touch with Bobbie, and she went with them," Miss Hillhouse suggested.

"I've been checking on that," Chambrun said, not explaining how. But perhaps he hadn't done as much in that direction as he should, he thought.

He went back to the phone and talked to the operator again. Had there been any calls to Suite 7H during the evening other than the ones from Miss Hillhouse on the mezzanine? At night there were two operators to handle incoming calls and two to handle outgoing calls. The "out" operators would have handled room-to-room calls in the hotel.

It was asking a lot of them to remember, yet they might. No one was ever put directly through to a room. A name was asked for, the room was called, the guest was asked if he wished to receive the call. Maybe they'd remember talking to a little girl.

But they didn't.

The repeated calls from Miss Hillhouse were all they remembered. The "in" operators could not remember any calls to 7H except one from Anne Cook about ten o'clock.

Jerry Dodd, still hoping the child had wandered off on her own, went out to check in person. But with each passing minute, Jerry's optimism decreased.

At twenty-five minutes to midnight Alison appeared. Chambrun brought her quickly up to date on the evening's events, the arrangements made by the Cooks with Miss Hillhouse, the now almost vanished hope that Bobbie was "making a federal case" out of going to bed. There was a twist of pity at the corners of Alison's mouth as she listened. She could imagine Anne Cook, pushed into this rather unusual arrangement by the child, never forgiving herself if anything serious had happened to Bobbie.

At a quarter to twelve the phone rang, and Chambrun, who answered, heard Anne Cook's frightened voice on the other end. She'd been located at the Latin Quarter. He explained who he was and what had happened.

"Try not to be too alarmed, Mrs. Cook," he said. "It's quite possible she skipped out so she wouldn't have to go to bed. My entire staff is looking for her, and we may have her safely back in your rooms by the time you and Mr. Cook get here."

"Oh, my God," was all that Anne Cook said.

After-theater traffic in New York was heavy, and it wasn't until ten minutes past twelve that Anne and Cliff Cook arrived in 7H. By then even Jerry Dodd's hopes were almost nonexistent. Not a single elevator man, bellboy, or doorman had seen Bobbie Cook. There were, of course, unpatrolled fire stairs. It was not impossible for the child to have gone—or been taken—from floor to floor without being seen. You could actually leave the hotel by way of the fire stairs. The fire-stairway doors at street level could be easily opened from inside, though no one could come in from the street.

Bobbie, accompanied by her imaginary friends, could have gotten out onto the street without being seen. It seemed to Jerry it would be a wise thing to alert the police, who could start looking for her in the neighborhood. He made this suggestion to Cliff Cook and Chambrun. Anne, accompanied by Alison, was hearing the story over again from Miss Hillhouse.

Cook seemed dazed, but he was instantly adamant on this point. "Not the police. Not yet," he said.

Jerry raised a questioning eyebrow at Chambrun.

The final knot was tied in Chambrun's gut. Almost any father in Cook's place would have jumped at help from the police, insisted on it—unless he had reason to suspect a kidnapping, a word that so far hadn't even been mentioned by anyone in 7H.

"Once, when I was a small boy," Chambrun said in a detached voice, "I turned up missing in a hotel my father was managing at the time." It was a complete invention. "I was missing for hours. They finally found me asleep in a broom closet. I take it that eleven o'clock was well past Bobbie's normal bedtime, Mr. Cook?"

Cliff Cook hadn't heard a word he said. But Anne Cook had—she was hearing everything.

"Once in a while she was allowed to stay up to see a special TV show, Mr. Chambrun. Normally she goes to bed about nine. You think she may—?"

"There are a thousand places a child might get into in this hotel, Mrs. Cook—places interesting to a child. I mentioned broom closets. There are hundreds of them. There are special banquet rooms and conference rooms. There are offices. Bobbie could have got into any one of these places, sat down to look at something, and just popped off to sleep." He turned to Dodd. "Jerry, we'll just have to begin systematically and go from bottom to top. Start the wheels."

"Right," Dodd said, and hurried out.

Chambrun turned to Alison. "I'd appreciate it if you'd go down to the telephone office, Alison, and explain the situation to Mrs. Kiley, the chief night operator. I want her to call every occupied room in the hotel. The child may have wandered in somewhere and told some imaginative story. People told that her parents were at a nightclub may have been amused by her and kept her with them, talking. There'll be squawks—but start the phoning, Alison."

Alison went off without a word.

"Miss Hillhouse," Chambrun said, "I don't think there's anything more you can do here. I suggest you go home and get some rest. Take a sleeping pill if you've got one. As soon as Bobbie turns up, we'll let you know. I'll call you myself."

"No!" Cliff Cook said in a harsh voice. He turned on Chambrun and his face was gray as a death mask. "You're not going to find her in any broom closet or banquet room."

"Cliff!" Anne said in a frightened voice.

There was murder in Cook's sunken eyes. "You had a key to this suite, Miss Hillhouse," he said. "What happened? Did you call a confederate or your employer and turn the key over to him?"

The woman stared at him, swaying like an axed tree.

"How much were you paid?" Cook shouted at her. "Did you ever really call her during the evening? We only have your word for it."

"Just a minute," Chambrun said sharply. "She called Bobbie every half hour, and Bobbie answered the phone. My telephone staff can vouch for that. Until ten-thirty Bobbie was in this room."

Cook waved a long arm. "So she wasn't taken till after ten-thirty. You did that to cover yourself, didn't you, Miss Hillhouse? So help me God, if Bobbie is harmed I will personally—"

Miss Hillhouse screamed.

"I want you to go, Miss Hillhouse!" Chambrun said. Cook was a head taller than Chambrun but something in Chambrun's suddenly-hard eyes kept him from interfering. Miss Hillhouse literally ran out of the room.

"Now, Mr. Cook, let's make some sense. Forget about Miss Hillhouse. She followed what I must say were rather unusual instructions from you. You're wasting energy and time considering her a part of any kidnapping plot. Because you think it is a kidnapping, don't you?"

Cook, his legs suddenly buckling under him, sank down in an upholstered armchair, his body slumped forward. Anne was instantly on her knees beside him, holding his face in her hands, whispering his name. "Don't blame yourself, darling," Chambrun heard her say. "How could you dream—?" Her words were suddenly cut off by a deep, choking sob from the man.

"I'll call them, Anne. I'll have her back in no time. You'll see," Cook said. He raised his head as though it weighed a ton. "Thank you for everything, Mr. Chambrun, but we'd appreciate being left alone."

Chambrun didn't move. His eyes were almost hidden by his heavy, hooded lids. He was tapping an Egyptian cigarette on the back of his hand.

"You suspect that Hobbs Enterprises are behind this, Mr. Cook?" he asked quietly.

Cook stared at him, his mouth sagging open.

"It occurred to me somewhat earlier," Chambrun said, as if he were discussing the weather. "Is there something in your business relationship with Hobbs that would make him want to put great pressure on you?"

Cook rose very slowly from his chair, his arm around his wife as if he needed her support. "What do you know about this, Mr. Chambrun?"

"I can only tell you that a series of events today led me to wonder if Hobbs might desperately want you to do something you had refused to do. I use the word 'desperate' because kidnapping is a desperate business, Mr. Cook."

Cook shook his head, trying to clear it. "I've refused to sell them certain patents they need," he said. "If that's the price for Bobbie, then of course I'll sell them." He turned to his wife. "I promise you I will, darling."

"I'd like to tell you two things, Mr. Cook," Chambrun said. "For reasons not connected with Bobbie, I've had Hobbs under surveillance all evening—he and Webber and young Stanton. I know where they are now, and I know exactly where they've been since eight o'clock. None of those three has had anything personally to do with removing Bobbie from this suite. That, of course, doesn't mean that they're not responsible for hiring someone to do the job. But it's almost as though they'd deliberately set up an alibi for themselves for the entire evening."

"So tell me where they are, and I'll go and make the deal with them right now," Cook said.

"They're giving a party in the Blue Lagoon. But before you go to them, Mr. Cook, please keep listening. You're never going to pin this thing on Hobbs or on any of his associates. Maybe Bobbie will reappear after you sign away your patents, and maybe she won't. But if what happened to her will in any way point to Hobbs, I tell you she *won't* appear."

"Oh, my God!" Anne said.

"Our best chance, Mrs. Cook, is to find her and find her quickly," Chambrun went on. "If they haven't got her out of the hotel, we have a good chance of finding her alive."

"You don't believe that," Anne said.

Chambrun glanced at his watch. "She's been gone just under two hours. But we started looking for her only an hour and twenty minutes ago. Unless they got her out of the hotel in the first half hour, she's still here somewhere. What I'm getting at, my friends, is that you can't go to Hobbs and say, 'Return Bobbie and I'll sell you my patents.' If you say it publicly, he'll sue you for defamation; if you say it to him privately, he'll treat you as if you were out of your mind, comfort you, offer to help."

"I can't risk *not* going to him," Cook said. "Suppose I go now to the Blue Lagoon. I won't mention what's happened. I'll tell him I'm ready to sign and want to do it tonight, so that I can—can start home early in the morning."

"Then what?" Chambrun asked.

"They'll send her back!" Cook cried.

"If they can afford to," Chambrun said. "When were you scheduled to see Hobbs again?"

"Tomorrow morning. He asked me to think about it overnight—damn him, I told him another day wouldn't change things. All the time they had this frightful thing up their sleeves to use against me."

"Give me time," Chambrun said.

"I can't," Cook said. "The only thing that matters now is getting Bobbie back, don't you understand? So I'll do what they want me to do."

Chambrun glanced at his watch. "The Blue Lagoon closes at three, Mr. Cook—a little more than two hours from now. Unless I miss my guess, Hobbs's party will ride it out there till closing time. Give me until three. We'll have covered every inch of space in the hotel by then. As soon as our search is complete, I won't ask you to hold back. There's still an outside chance she wandered off and fell asleep somewhere."

"No!" Cook said. "I knew what had happened the minute you called us at the Latin Quarter."

"I find it hard to understand how," Chambrun said, his voice hard, "if you suspected trouble from Hobbs, you went off and left your daughter here under these odd circumstances."

"I anticipated trouble from Hobbs," Cook said, his body twisting with pain, "but *not* this kind of trouble. A business war, yes—that's what I expected, and I was ready to try to fight him. It never occurred to me for a moment they'd attack this way. A war on my credit, yes! A war on my sources of supply, yes. But a war on my child? It never even crossed my mind."

"I'm willing to give Mr. Chambrun his chance, Cliff," Anne said in a low voice.

"They still don't know which way you're going to jump, so they don't know which way they should jump," Chambrun said. "They probably don't know that you're back from your evening on the town. They don't know that you realize anything has happened. They think the baby-sitter has reported the child missing and that we're looking for her. But they have no reason to think we suspect a kidnapping. Let them stew a little while we hunt."

"I don't know," Cook said, shaking his head from side to side.

"I can guess what will happen tomorrow," Chambrun said. "Just before you go to your meeting with Hobbs, you'll get a ransom note. It will demand a sum in cash you can't possibly raise. You'll be expected to sign away your patents in return for a cash advance—" A sour smile moved Chambrun's lips. "Say, fifty thousand dollars."

"I'll go along with you for a while—if Anne agrees," Cook said.

"Of course I agree, darling," Anne said.

Pierre Chambrun walked determinedly to the telephone. His dark eyes were flashing. In less than one minute the full force of the Beaumont's organization, under Chambrun's steel grip and velvet-gloved direction, would be unleashed. . . .

Certain areas of the search for Bobbie Cook were covered quickly and efficiently; other areas were maddeningly slow to take their place in the jigsaw puzzle. Half of the living space in the Hotel Beaumont was made up of cooperative apartments, owned by the tenants. It wasn't possible to walk in and out of these apartments by a passkey. Only some kind of emergency, such as fire, a plumbing leak, some service failure, would justify entry by a member of the hotel staff.

On the transient floors things could be handled more rapidly. The night maid could simply tap on the door with her key, and if no one answered she could let herself in, provided the door wasn't chain locked on the inside. There was always the excuse of fresh towels, or making certain that beds had been turned down. But all of this was tragically slow.

The night engineer, Mr. McNab, and one of the bellboys dressed in coveralls began covering the co-ops from the fifteenth floor up, telling each tenant they found at home that there was a bad water leak on the floor below and entering those apartments where they got no answer and could effect entry. But, at best, it was a long and tedious business.

From the first floor, which was actually above the mezzanine, to the fourteenth, every public room, broom closet, and linen storage cupboard was covered quickly by the night maids on each floor.

No results.

The subbasements, engine rooms, kitchens, pantries, refrigeration rooms, public dining rooms, bars, offices, conference rooms, locker rooms for the staff, powder rooms, men's rooms, smart shops in the lobby—all these were covered.

No results.

In the telephone offices on the third floor, Alison stood beside the bony, grim-faced Mrs. Kiley, who was the night chief, watching the switchboard operators trying to handle the regular service and, in between, methodically calling room after room and apartment after apartment to inquire if anyone had seen Bobbie Cook.

Alison felt angry and a little sick to her stomach as she listened. An unpleasantly large percentage of the people questioned by the operators were annoyed at the interruption and angry at being asked the question. If a stray child was there, wouldn't they have reported it? Mr. Chambrun would hear about this in the morning!

There was a running fire of comment from the operators that would have amused Alison under different circumstances.

"Come on, Mrs. P. Get that bandage off your jowls and answer!"

"Now for old poop face!"

"Here goes a year's tips from that old fanny pincher in 906."

Alison had heard Mr. Chambrun quote figures on one occasion. Eighty percent of the male residents were cheating on their wives. Fifty percent of the wives were indulging themselves with outside lovers. In the telephone office there was a cynical and acid awareness of the ins and outs of hundreds of private lives. Far too many of the guests considered these telephone inquiries an outrageous intrusion, and these guests voiced their resentment and objections without a drop of pity for the missing child. Alison could hardly believe what she saw and heard.

And out of it all came only one discouraging fact: no one had seen Bobbie Cook.

At least, no one would admit having seen her.

Chambrun had established himself in his own office. The Cooks were with him. He had persuaded them there was nothing they could do to help the search. The presence of anyone but a member of the hotel staff in a guest's room would be questioned. The instant there was any news, Chambrun would have it here in his office.

Jerry Dodd, who knew his job, produced a moment's interest. He had routed out the room service waiter who had served Bobbie's dinner. The man, who lived in the Bronx, had gone home at eleven. It had taken him some time to get back to the hotel.

"Edward Hutchins, who served the kid's dinner," Jerry told Chambrun.

Hutchins was trembling with anxiety. Like most innocent people, he saw himself walking up the steps to the gallows to be hanged on a false charge of kidnapping.

Chambrun gave him a reassuring smile, telling him they simply wanted information about the service he'd performed.

A flood of words poured out of the perspiring waiter.

"Please. Take it easy," Chambrun said. "The little girl's parents are anxious to understand."

Hutchins had kids of his own. "She's a fine little girl," he said. "She'll be all right. You'll see."

"Tell 'em what you told me, Hutchins," Jerry said.

"I got the check in the service kitchen," he said. "Service for two."

"Two?" Chambrun said.

Hutchins nodded. "Two. Double order of everything. Two shrimp cocktails. Two filet mignon—both rare. Two baked potatoes. Two green salads. Two ice creams. One milk and one coffee."

Chambrun glanced at Anne Cook and raised an eyebrow. Anne's eyes were filled with tears.

"Her imaginary friend," she said. "It's a boy named Hilary.

She and Hilary—" Anne's voice broke—"she and Hilary are going to be married. He owns a large estate in England, and she's going there to live."

Chambrun nodded slowly. "So you served for two, Hutchins?"

The waiter nodded. "But only the little girl was there."

"She was all right?" Anne asked eagerly.

"She was fine," Hutchins said. "I looked around for maybe a sitter or nursemaid or some member of the family, but there was no one. I asked the little girl if I could come back for the table in an hour. She said fine. Just knock on the door, she told me."

"And you came back in an hour?"

"Sure. They finished okay."

"They?"

Hutchins shrugged. "Both dinners were finished. Both people were hungry. They cleaned up everything on the plates."

"Both dinners were completely eaten?"

"Yes. But I still didn't see any other person."

"If she ate two dinners," Chambrun said to Anne, "our hope that she may be asleep somewhere looks even better. Two filet mignons! Two baked potatoes!"

"Go on, Hutchins," Jerry said. The Beaumont's house officer still had something up his sleeve.

"You don't blame me for being curious, Mr. Chambrun?" the waiter asked hesitantly.

"I approve of it," Chambrun said drily.

"I was interested in the person I didn't see," Hutchins said. "And I found out one thing. It was a grownup."

"How did you figure that out?"

"Ashtray?" Hutchins said, beaming at Chambrun.

"What about the ashtray?"

"On my table. Five, six butts."

"Smoked cigarette stubs?"

"Yes, butts, and smoked right down to the end."

"Of course you didn't save them?"

"Why?" Hutchins spread his hands.

Chambrun turned to look at Anne. "Does Hilary smoke?" His voice was tinged with humor.

"I don't know," Anne said.

"Plain or filter tip, Hutchins?" Chambrun asked.

"Filter. Smoked right down. Brown filter—like Winstons."

Chambrun looked at the Cooks again. They appeared oddly disturbed. "What brands do you smoke?" he asked.

Anne moistened her lips. "Neither of us smokes cigarettes," she said. "Cliff smokes a pipe occasionally."

"Did you have any guests in the suite who might have left a pack around?" Chambrun asked.

"No. There's been no one in our rooms at all, Mr. Chambrun—except the maids, the room service waiters, and a bellboy once or twice."

"Could Bobbie have bought the cigarettes for—for Hilary?"

"An eight-year-old child!" Cook said.

"You're wondering if we'd sell them to her downstairs? I think so. The girl at the counter would assume she was buying them for her parents. Besides, there are cigarette machines all over the place."

"You think an eight-year-old child smoked six cigarettes right down to the filter?" Jerry asked. "And ate two man-sized dinners?"

Chambrun didn't answer, but he was frowning. "When did you serve the dinner, Hutchins?"

"Maybe a quarter to eight. The slip will show," the waiter said. "I picked up the table just after nine. I know because the little girl opened the door for me and then ran back to the TV set. I recognized the show that was on."

"And you never saw a sign of anyone but the child?"

"Sign? Two dinners were gone. Wasn't that a sign? Cigarettes were smoked. Wasn't that a sign?"

"But nothing else? No hat? No coat? No handbag?"

"I didn't look," Hutchins said. "I didn't know anything was wrong then."

Chambrun was silent for a moment. "Thank you, Hutchins. Stop at the cashier's window tomorrow. There'll be a bonus for you for your trouble."

The waiter bowed his pleasure and started out.

"Please," Anne said. "She looked all right? She looked happy that second time?"

"She looked fine, lady. She didn't pay much attention to me because of the TV, but she was fine then."

Chambrun broke a short silence after the waiter had gone. "Do you think she was experimenting with cigarettes, Mrs. Cook?"

"I've never known her to," Anne said.

"But this was a special evening—and a special party for her—and Hilary."

"She's always pretending, always pretending to be someone else. It's possible."

"How much has she been around the hotel by herself?" Chambrun asked.

"Around the hotel?"

"Has she been down in the lobby by herself to buy you a newspaper? To the drugstore for a soda? To the toy store for a present?"

"She's been down a few times on errands for me," Anne said. "Mostly I invented the errands, because she liked to ride the elevator and watch people in the lobby and look at things in the shop windows."

"The point I'm trying to make," Chambrun said, "is that she could have met somebody in the lobby. Would she speak to a stranger freely?"

"She'd talk to anyone who'd even smile at her," Cook said.

"Then it's possible she made a new friend and asked him—or her—up to 7H without mentioning it to you. Part of her big evening."

"It's not like her," Anne said. "It's not like her to keep that kind of secret from me. But I suppose it's possible. Why, though, would the person hide from the waiter?"

The answer to that, Chambrun thought, was unpleasantly obvious.

"If the person made friends with Bobbie for the eventual purpose of taking her away, he'd hide from the waiter," Chambrun said. "And he'd learn from Bobbie the whole scheme of the evening. He'd stay in 7H until Miss Hillhouse made her last call at ten-thirty. He then had half an hour in which to persuade Bobbie to go somewhere with him—or to force her to go."

"You buy that?" Jerry Dodd asked. "Because I do."

Chambrun said grimly, "So where does it get you, chum? Any idea who we're looking for?"

Jerry's jaw jutted out stubbornly. "No, but if she was chit-chatting with someone in the lobby it may have been noticed."

"By the day staff," Chambrun said. "What chance do we have of digging that out before morning?"

After Jerry went off to phone some of the day staff at their homes, Chambrun decided to take a personal hand in one part of the search. He left the protesting Cooks in his office and went to the eighth floor when a phone report indicated that floor was about to be covered.

Number 8B, a three-room suite, was occupied by Martin Hobbs. George Webber was in 803, Don Stanton in 805, Miss Garth in 807.

A phone call to the Blue Lagoon from the housekeeper's cubbyhole on eight reassured Chambrun that Hobbs, Webber, Stanton, and Miss Garth were still whooping it up at their table there.

Accompanied by the frightened night maid and Johnny Thacker, the night bell captain, Chambrun entered Martin Hobbs's suite with a passkey.

Hobbs's suite was neat as a pin. A reasonably elaborate

wardrobe of suits and evening clothes hung in the closet. Expensive luggage was stacked on the upper shelves. Apparently no business papers of any sort were kept here. The bathroom had the usual equipment of razor, shaving cream, tooth brush and paste, hair tonic, comb, and brushes.

Chambrun idly opened the lid of the disposal unit. The Beaumont provided a miniature trash drop in every bathroom for old razor blades, used tissues, empty medicine bottles, and the like. The disposal unit was empty in Hobbs's bathroom.

There was absolutely nothing in the room to indicate that Bobbie Cook had ever been there in her life.

Miss Garth's room was not so neat. She had dressed hurriedly for the evening. But there were no signs of the missing child. Chambrun puzzled the maid and Johnny Thacker by spending some time examining and sniffing at half a dozen jars and bottles of creams and lotions on Miss Garth's dressing table. Eventually he went over to the phone and called Carl Nevers on the lobby desk.

"Do the Hobbs party keep anything in the safe down there, Carl?" he asked.

"Several attaché cases of business papers," Nevers said. "The secretary leaves them here at the end of the day and picks them up in the morning."

That explained the absence of any notes or papers.

Don Stanton's room was negative.

Webber's room was negative—or almost negative. In the disposal unit in his bathroom Chambrun found a small, black screw top from some sort of bottle that had stuck in the unit.

Chambrun took it out, sniffed it, tossed it up in the air, and caught it. He started to drop it back in the chute, then changed his mind and dropped it in his coat pocket.

Chambrun hadn't really expected to find anything incriminating in these rooms—he just wanted to make certain.

* * *

A man's cracking point in a crisis is unpredictable. He may carry through until it's all over and then break apart. It may happen anywhere along the way. Cliff Cook's smashup came about fifteen minutes after Chambrun had left him and Anne in the manager's office, suffering together in a tortured silence.

"They're not going to find her," Cook said suddenly to his wife. "Hobbs got her out of the hotel somehow."

Anne, doubled over as if she were suffering from cramps, shook her head. "We've got to keep hoping, Cliff—until we know for sure."

"I know for sure," Cook said. "Our one chance to get Bobbie back is for me to act before it's too late for them to be able to return her. I'll make the deal they want. I'll make any deal."

"Cliff!"

He'd already started for the office door. "Chambrun's doing his best," he said, "but it isn't going to be enough to find Bobbie. They're too clever for that. They have the money to bribe the whole hotel staff, if necessary."

"I'm coming with you," Anne said.

"No. You stay here, Anne, just in case there is any word. Take it casy, darling. They want what I have to give just as badly as we want Bobbie."

A man under less pressure, with the capacity to think coolly about his problem, would not have followed Cliff Cook's course. But Cook was thinking in a red haze of rage and terror. He would make his deal; he would get Bobbie back; and he would sell his patents to Hobbs. But then, by God, he would spend the rest of his life making sure they were punished. He wasn't thinking of any kind of delicate approach. They would make the deal on the top of the table—no double-talk, no pretenses. A cold, open-and-shut deal.

Mr. Cardoza, the captain of the Blue Lagoon Room, saw Cook approaching the red velvet rope stretched across the entrance to the Beaumont's nightclub. Mr. Cardoza didn't know who Cook was, but he knew trouble when he saw it. Mr. Cardoza could feel the small hairs rising on the back of his neck.

Handling belligerent drunks was an old story to Cardoza—but the look of cold, sober fury on Cook's face was something else again. Cardoza stepped outside the velvet rope and stood there, blocking Cook's way, his suave, professional smile nicely in place.

"I'm sorry, sir," Cardoza said, "but there are no vacancies tonight."

"I don't want a table," Cook said, looking past Cardoza into the supper room. He saw the large circular table where Hobbs, Webber, Stanton, Miss Garth, and a half a dozen others were apparently enjoying themselves. Every last ounce of color left Cook's face.

Cardoza, smiling and smiling, made a half-hidden gesture to one of his assistants inside the velvet rope.

"I want to talk to Mr. Hobbs," Cook said.

"I'll ask him if he cares to come out to talk to you," Cardoza said smoothly.

"I'm going in," Cook said.

Cardoza snapped his fingers, and suddenly there were four white-tied waiters standing behind him. "I'll ask Mr. Hobbs if he cares to come out, sir. May I have your name?"

"Clifford Cook. Oh, he knows me."

Cardoza stepped inside the velvet rope and threaded his way through the crowded tables to the one occupied by Martin Hobbs. He bent down and whispered in the promoter's ear. "There's a gentleman at the entrance, Mr. Hobbs. He wants to see you. His name is Clifford Cook."

"Cook!" Hobbs's voice was sharp, his face slightly flushed from drinking. Webber, sitting two or three places away, was motionlessly attentive.

"It's none of my affair, sir," Cardoza said softly, "but he seems in a highly disturbed state."

Hobbs looked down the table at Webber, whose head moved in an almost imperceptible nod.

"Tell Mr. Cook we'll be happy to have him join us, captain."

"Whatever you say, Mr. Hobbs."

Cardoza moved back toward the entrance. Halfway there he made a gesture to his corps of waiters, and they made way for Cook, who came striding down the room, his eyes fixed on Hobbs.

The young financier rose from his chair as Cook reached the table. He held out his hand in a cordial gesture of greeting. "This is a pleasant surprise, Cliff. Here, take my chair. I'll get another one."

"I'm not sitting down," Cook said. His voice was shaking. Hobbs's smiling face was almost too much for him. "I've come to tell you that if my daughter is safely returned to me—*at once*—I'll sign whatever contract you want me to." The words were clear and loud. Everyone at the table heard them.

"My dear fellow!" Hobbs said.

Webber had risen quickly and was coming around the table to them. "What's this about your daughter?"

"There's no reason to go into details," Cook said, fighting for shreds of control. "You know them as well as I do. Return Bobbie, and I'll do whatever you want me to."

A dozen faces in the area of the three standing men were turned their way. Webber put his hand on Cook's arm. Cook shook it off with a kind of frightening violence.

"You're not yourself, Cook. We'd better talk about this somewhere else," Webber said. "This way."

He turned his back on Cook and headed toward the men's room in the far corner of the Blue Lagoon. It threw Cook off balance, and after a moment's hesitation he followed. Hobbs turned to his guests and gave them a broad wink.

"Stoned to the gills," he said. "Excuse us for a moment." He moved quickly off in Cook's wake.

Webber went straight into the men's room without looking back. The attendant, an elderly Sicilian, smiled and began to run hot water into one of the wash basins. Webber took a money clip from his pocket and extracted a ten-dollar bill from it. He handed it to the old man.

"Just go outside the door and don't let anyone in for a few minutes," Webber said.

"I not supposed to leave—"

"I'm making it nice, dad," Webber said. "If you don't want it nice—"

For ten dollars the old man went out, brushing against Cliff Cook, who was coming in. For ten dollars the old man watched Martin Hobbs follow Cook in. Then the old man went rapidly in search of Mr. Cardoza. For ten dollars! Not for ten dollars or a million dollars would Tony Gardella leave his post. But Webber was much too tough a customer for old Tony to handle alone.

Webber was washing his hands in the basin, bent forward, but his eyes were on the mirror, which reflected the images of a chalk-white Cliff Cook and a visibly alarmed Martin Hobbs.

"What's all this about your kid?" Webber asked, sampling the powdered soap.

"So it's private here," Cook said, almost strangling on the words. "You know what I'm talking about, both of you. Bobbie's gone. She was taken out of our suite while we were at the theater. You took her—or you had her taken."

"My dear Cliff!" Hobbs protested.

"You're accusing us of kidnapping," Webber said, reaching for one of the small handtowels on the glass shelf in front of him. "You accused us of it in front of a dozen people out there." His tone was conversational.

"Just bring Bobbie back, and I'll sign your contract," Cook said.

Webber turned, discarding the towel in a wicker basket to the left of the basin. He was smiling. The white-tiled room glittered with a kind of hospital brightness.

"Maybe it's better we didn't do any business with you," Webber said. "You're an irresponsible hysteric. Do you think people in our position would run that kind of crazy risk just to get your stinking motor?"

"I don't want to talk. I just want action!" Cook said.

"Oh?" A slow, unpleasant smile moved Webber's mouth. "You just want action, is that it?"

Then his foot shot out to give Cook an agonizing kick in the shin. As Cook doubled forward with a cry of pain, Webber ripped a right to the jaw that sent Cook rolling and sliding away on the tile floor.

"George!" Hobbs cried.

"Shut up, Martin," Webber said. "He made a public accusation against us. It's time he was taught a lesson."

Cook was struggling up, a trickle of blood running from the corner of his mouth. His eyes looked glazed. Webber took a step forward and yanked Cook to his feet, his left hand closed on the front of Cook's jacket. Then he punched—pile-driving blows to the stomach and again to the jaw. Cook, flailing futilely with his arms, somehow wrenched away from Webber but fell again, hard, on the glistening tile floor. There were spots of bright scarlet on the white tiles now.

Webber, who had moved with a kind of machinelike precision up to now, seemed suddenly to explode. He sprang on the fallen Cook, pulled him to his knees, kicked him, and then with Cook's face at belt-buckle level he smashed at Cook's nose and mouth, savagely, brutally. The nose flattened out to one side. The mouth was a bloody pulp.

"George!" Hobbs cried. "For God's sake!"

The door to the washroom burst open, and Mr. Cardoza, followed by old Tony Gardella and three waiters, came in. Webber, his fist drawn back for another blow, turned his head quite calmly to look at Cardoza. Then he struck once more into the middle of that drooling mass of agony. He let go of Cook's jacket, and the limp Cook fell to the floor like a sack of grain.

Cardoza spat out a single word.

Webber turned quietly to the wash basin again. He frowned at himself in the mirror. There were several bright red spots on his white shirt front. He moistened the end of a towel and calmly began to work on the spots.

"Get Dr. Partridge," Cardoza said sharply.

One of the waiters ran out.

"Before you call the police," Webber said in that cold, conversational tone, "you'd better ask Mr. Cook if he wants to prefer charges. He accused us publicly of kidnapping his child. I thought this would be more fun than suing him for every cent he has in the world. The stupid son of a—" Then he looked at Hobbs and laughed. "Shall we join the ladies, Martin?"

Half an hour later an ambulance took Clifford Cook to the hospital.

Dr. Partridge had diagnosed a broken jaw, broken nose, a severe concussion, if not a possible skull fracture. Anne Cook, on the horns of two horrors, had ridden to the hospital with Cook on a promise from Chambrun that he and the police would continue the search for Bobbie and that the sympathetic Alison would stay in constant touch with Anne at the hospital.

Chambrun and Alison walked back into the lobby from the side entrance when the ambulance left. Alison was shocked by what had happened. Chambrun was in the grip of an icy anger. Cardoza had reported George Webber's words to them.

"Could they sue Mr. Cook for making a public accusation?" Alison asked.

"They could try. They'd have to prove that somebody believed it and that they were damaged by it."

"You believe it, don't you?"

"I believe it," Chambrun said. They had paused in front of one of the darkened store windows in the lobby. "The problem is that the child's life is still in the balance, Alison. I tried to keep Cook out of just such a situation because now he's made it harder, if not impossible, for them to return her."

"You think they got Bobbie out of the hotel between Miss Hillhouse's last call at ten-thirty and eleven, when she arrived at 7H?"

Chambrun didn't answer. He was looking thoughtfully in the store window. It was a gift and toy shop. There was a display of animals, including all the characters from *Winnie the Pooh.* There was a beautiful French doll, lying in a satin-lined box, her eyes closed. There were circus clowns and cowboys and large stuffed tigers.

"Mr. Chambrun?"

He turned to Alison, and his usually hooded eyes were wide open with an excited brightness Alison had never seen in them.

"Wait here, Alison," he said. He walked across to one of the lobby phones, spoke for a minute, and then rejoined her. "Come with me," he said.

He led the way to the bank of elevators. "Fourteen," he told the operator, and they were whisked upward.

"What's on fourteen?" Alison asked.

"A missing child, I hope," Chambrun said.

"Mr. Chambrun!"

They got out at the fourteenth floor.

"I phoned Jerry Dodd to meet us here," Chambrun said. "He was still calling members of the day staff from the telephone office." As he spoke, another elevator door opened, and Jerry Dodd joined them.

"What's cooking, chief?"

Chambrun didn't answer. He walked down the corridor to the door of Fourteen B with Alison and Jerry at his heels. He knocked briskly on the door.

There was a long wait, and then a muffled woman's voice spoke from the other side of the door. "What is it?"

"I'm the resident manager, Miss Thomas," Chambrun said. "I've come to get Bobbie Cook."

"Holy cow!" Jerry Dodd whispered.

Alison's cold fingers closed on Chambrun's wrist. He stood perfectly still. She wondered if he was breathing. Then, very slowly, the door opened, and Miss Laura Thomas faced them, her glasses black circles in a dead-white face with a scarlet gash for a mouth.

"Her parents have come home?" Miss Thomas asked in a perfectly casual voice.

"Her parents have come home," Chambrun said. "Where is the child?"

"In the bedroom," Miss Thomas said, standing aside.

Chambrun walked quickly through the living room to the bedroom door. Stretched out on the bed, covered by a soft blanket, was Bobbie Cook, surrounded by a collection of dolls and toys. She was sleeping peacefully.

A nerve twitched in Chambrun's cheek, and he let out his breath in a long sigh. He turned back into the living room, and there was a noticeable dampness on his forehead.

"If they'd called me, I'd have brought her down," Miss Thomas said blandly.

"How could they call you?"

"Why, the note!" Miss Thomas said. "The note Bobbie left for them."

Chambrun's silver cigarette case snapped open. He took out one of his Egyptian cigarettes and slowly lit it. "There was no note, Miss Thomas."

"But she left it there—on the table by the door!"

"There was no note, Miss Thomas."

"It must have fallen on the floor—under a chair, or blown away or something," Miss Thomas said. "Oh, dear, I hope they weren't too worried."

"They were worried, Miss Thomas," Chambrun said coldly. "Suppose you tell us exactly what happened tonight."

"Why, I met Bobbie in the drugstore this afternoon," Miss Thomas said. "She was having an ice cream soda. I'm very fond of children. We struck up a conversation. She told me she was going to have a private party for—for imaginary friends tonight while her parents were at the theater. She asked me to come. I—well, it seemed like a charming idea."

"So you went, without discussing it with Mr. and Mrs. Cook?"

"She wanted to keep it a secret," Miss Thomas said. "You

know how children are. And besides, Mr. Chambrun, I'm doing my level best to avoid publicity, as Miss Barnwell knows."

Alison, still in something of a daze, thought that if Miss Thomas *wasn't* an actress she was wasting her talents.

"So each time room service came to 7H, you hid," Chambrun said.

"Of course I didn't hide!" Miss Thomas said, sounding genuinely indignant. "By the purest coincidence I happened to be in the bathroom each time, freshening up."

"Ah, yes, by the purest coincidence. And then, after ten-thirty, you brought Bobbie up here—by way of the fire stairs. Why? Why not the public elevator, Miss Thomas?"

It came out smooth as oil. "You may think it curious, Mr. Chambrun, but at my age I still like to play with dolls. I have a rather unusual collection, and I always carry some of them with me when I travel. I thought it would amuse Bobbie to see them."

"And the fire stairs—seven flights of them?"

"She thought it would be fun."

"And it didn't occur to you to notify the baby-sitter that you were bringing Bobbie up here?"

Miss Thomas looked at Chambrun as though he wasn't quite bright.

"There was the note," she said.

"Ah, yes, the note. The note now mysteriously missing. So, after Bobbie had seen the dolls, you just kept her here?"

"Naturally I thought Mrs. Cook would call when she got in. We didn't expect them till three or later. The child wanted company, but she was tired and fell asleep. So I've just been waiting."

Chambrun nodded slowly. "Let's wake her and see how things check," he said.

He turned abruptly and went back into the bedroom. He put his hand gently on Bobbie's shoulder. "All right, baby," he said.

She stirred, opened her eyes, looked up at him, was puzzled for a moment, and then she gave him a sleepy smile.

"Hello, Mr. Chambrun." She looked past him to the door where Miss Thomas, Alison, and Jerry Dodd were watching. "Gee whiz, Laura, I must have gone to sleep."

"You did, darling," Miss Thomas said. "Something happened to the note we left, and your mother's been worried about you."

"Gee, Mum will kill me!" Bobbie said. "I thought maybe we should have called Miss Hillhouse."

"You had fun tonight?" Chambrun asked.

"It was cool!" Bobbie said. She sat up. "Oh, dear, I hate to leave you, Mignonette." She picked up a small doll from the pillow. "Isn't she terrif, Mr. Chambrun?" She tilted the doll forward, and it made a small wailing noise and real tears came out of its eyes.

"You can have Mignonette if you like, Bobbie," Miss Thomas said.

"Oh, gee, Laura, really, truly?"

Chambrun gave Miss Thomas a look of frank admiration. "You know, Miss Thomas, it may actually stick," he said.

"Stick?" Miss Thomas asked coolly.

"Your story," Chambrun said. "It's a beaut!"

"I'm sure I don't know what you mean. I've told you exactly what happened. Bobbie will tell you the same."

"I'm sure she will," Chambrun said. "Magnificent—nothing short of magnificent."

"There's one thing I don't quite understand, Mr. Chambrun," Miss Thomas said. "If you didn't find the note, how did you happen to come here looking for Bobbie?"

Chambrun chuckled. "I know. That must be puzzling you no end, Miss Thomas. It shows how the best laid plans of mice—and all that. You see, we'd already spotted you for a phony, Miss Thomas. Please don't look outraged. It doesn't become you, and you haven't overdone a single thing so far. As I say, we spotted you, and we were interested. The bellboy who brought you up here yesterday reported you had something live in one of your suitcases. We've tried very hard to find out what it was, without breaking and entering.

"Then, a few minutes ago, I happened to be looking in a toy store window downstairs. I was reminded that, when certain toys, especially dolls, are tilted one way or another, they make wailing or whining noises. That made me think of you, Miss Thomas. It might explain what the bellboy heard. But what would a grown movie star be doing with dolls? It suddenly occurred to me that dolls might be used to entertain a little girl who was not where she was supposed to be.

"Now don't protest, Miss Thomas. I've already told you I think your story may stick. You're just unlucky, and I'm lucky. I played a hunch, and it turned out to be a bull's-eye." He turned to the child. "All right, Bobbie. Thank Miss Thomas for your lovely evening, and then we have somewhere to go."

He walked through into the living room, beckoning to Alison. "Will you phone the hospital, Alison, and put Mrs. Cook out of her misery?"

"Of course."

"Then take Bobbie over there. Explain to her on the way what's happened to her father."

"Yes, Mr. Chambrun—but I still don't get it. Do you think she was really working for Hobbs?"

"Up to her ears," Chambrun said drily. "Cook was supposed to do just what he did to get Bobbie back—offer to sign the contract. Then it would turn out that Bobbie was all right—nothing wrong except that the 'note' got lost—the note that Miss Thomas palmed after Bobbie had written it. But Cook wasn't supposed to accuse them publicly of kidnapping. After that they couldn't go through with it as planned, and Webber took out his anger and frustration on poor Cook."

"So they get away with the whole thing!" Alison said, indignant.

"Maybe not," Chambrun said. "Not if my luck holds."

At a quarter past three in the morning, Chambrun, Jerry

Dodd, and Lieutenant Hardy of Homicide knocked on the door of Room 803. It was opened promptly by George Webber. He had clearly expected someone else. He had taken off his dinner jacket, but he was still wearing the trousers and dress shirt, with a plaid cummerbund and a matching tie.

"Oh, it's you, Chambrun," he said. He glanced curiously at Lieutenant Hardy.

"May we come in?" Chambrun asked.

"Sure," Webber said.

"You know Jerry Dodd, our house security officer? And this is Lieutenant Hardy of the New York police." Chambrun didn't mention Homicide.

"I know you want to talk about that row downstairs," Webber said. His smile was cold. "I lost my head, I guess. That damn fool Cook walked up to our table in the Blue Lagoon and in front of a dozen people accused us of kidnapping his child. I blew my top. But it surprises me that Cook would make it a police matter. He knows I can wipe him out with a defamation suit."

"Mr. Cook hasn't made an issue of it," Chambrun said. He had taken a small black bottle top from his pocket, and now he tossed it up and caught it, over and over, as he talked. "*I'm* making the issue, Mr. Webber. We don't like violence in the Hotel Beaumont."

Chambrun continued to toss the black top up and down. "The kidnapping charge by Mr. Cook was unfortunate, Mr. Webber. The little girl has been found and is safely back with her parents."

Webber's eyes suddenly had the dead, cold look of tiny ice cubes, opaque, unreadable. Chambrun tossed the bottle top up and down, up and down.

"You're not interested in knowing where the little girl was found, Mr. Webber?" Chambrun asked.

"I couldn't care less," Webber said. "For Mrs. Cook's sake, I'm glad she's safe. So just what is it you want of me, Mr. Chambrun?"

"I'm losing my touch," Chambrun said with a wry smile. "I wanted you to ask me what I'm playing with." He held up the bottle top.

"All right, Mr. Bones," Webber said, "what is it?"

"It is the cap from a medicine bottle I found in the disposal unit in your bathroom."

"What of it?"

Chambrun held the top to his nose and sniffed gently. "I suggest it is the top from a bottle that contained a solution of strychnine, which was poured into a drink in Room 1208 last night, resulting in the untimely death of Mr. Paul Fisher, a private detective who was investigating the affairs of Martin Hobbs Enterprises."

Lids narrowed over the ice-cube eyes. "You're kidding," Webber said. "I heard about this man's death, but I had no idea it had any connection with us."

Chambrun sniffed the bottle top and continued. "I can visualize you making a deal, agreeing to the blackmail, and then fishy about your contracts with the government. Perhaps that you didn't have certain patents of Mr. Cook's that you had represented yourselves as owning? You can see why Lieutenant Hardy is interested in this cap from a bottle that may have contained strychnine and why it should have found its way into your disposal unit.

"It's bad luck for you, Mr. Webber. Whatever we may have suspected, we couldn't have proved a thing but for the unlucky chance that this cap didn't go down the chute along with the bottle. What happened? Did Fisher get the goods on you and then try to blackmail you? That's about the only thing that fits the picture of his being willing to have a drink with you."

Chambrun sniffed the bottle top and continued. "I can visualize you making a deal, agreeing to the blackmail, and then having a drink on it. You make the drinks. Bottoms up! It would have to be bottoms up, wouldn't it, Mr. Webber, because strychnine has an extraordinarily bitter taste."

Chambrun sniffed the bottle top again.

Webber turned and moved slowly over toward the bureau. Sometimes iron control is more of a giveaway than hysterical protestations. Slowly Webber opened the top bureau drawer and started to reach into it.

"Just leave it where it is, Webber," Hardy said sharply.

Webber jerked around to find himself facing Hardy's drawn police special.

"Get it, Jerry," Hardy said.

Jerry Dodd went over to the bureau, reached in the drawer, and brought out a compact black automatic.

Not a muscle moved in Webber's face, and when he spoke it was in a cold, matter-of-fact voice. "The whole thing has been a big gamble," he said. "We had to take it because the stakes were colossal. I had the pleasure of seeing that damn blackmailer die in agony. Half a million bucks he wanted, and he thought I would fall for it. I only wish I'd had the chance to pour one for Senator Farrand. You're right, the taste is bitter, and it contracts the spinal cord like a steel spring. It's absolute torture for a moment. Yes, I sure wish the senator could have felt it too."

Chambrun sniffed the bottle top again. "You've forgotten one thing about strychnine, Mr. Webber. It's odorless." He tossed the black top into a waste basket by the bureau. "That was from a mouthwash bottle you evidently discarded."

Webber's face was a stone mask as Hardy snapped on the handcuffs.

Chambrun drew a deep breath. "Like you, I gambled—with the bottle top. Gambled with it because the stakes were, as you said, colossal. Human lives. They're not toys, Webber—never forget it."

# Pierre Chambrun and the Black Days

Pierre Chambrun never eats lunch. As resident manager of the Hotel Beaumont, New York City's top luxury hotel, his busiest and most unpredictable hours are from eleven o'clock in the morning until three in the afternoon. He fortifies himself with a hearty breakfast at nine sharp consisting of juice or fruit in season, lamb chops, or a steak, or brook trout, or sometimes a Dover sole, with stacks of gluten toast and sweet butter, topped off with a spot of English marmalade.

And coffee. Coffee, coffee, coffee. He starts with American coffee—precisely three cups—and then switches to Turkish, which his incomparable secretary, Miss Ruysdale, makes and remakes for him on the carved sideboard in the corner of his elegantly furnished office.

I have a tendency to use cliches in describing the operation of the Hotel Beaumont. I have said in print that it runs like "a beautifully engineered Swiss watch." Even those of us on the staff who know all its secrets, who are, in fact, each a small cogwheel in the works, are often unaware of anything out of order. But to Pierre Chambrun, the slightest deviation from the norm sounds like a broken piston in Jack Benny's Maxwell.

My job is public relations director for the Beaumont. The first item on my day's routine is to go to Chambrun's office on the second floor at precisely nine-twenty-two to discuss the problems of the day. Miss Ruysdale will have preceded me at precisely eight-forty-five. At precisely nine Monsieur Fresney, the head chef, will have brought the breakfast.

Fresney prepares the breakfast menu so that the day begins for Chambrun with, hopefully, a pleasant surprise. At precisely nine-twenty-two Chambrun will pour his second cup of American coffee and light his first Egyptian cigarette of the day. As I walk into his office, he will glance my way, his eyes twinkling in their deep pouches, and offer me some wry comment on the day's problems that starts things off on a cheerful level.

On this particular morning there was no witticism, no "Good morning." The great man sat behind his carved Florentine desk, drumming his fingers. His eyes had that baleful look of a hanging judge that appeared only when things had gone very wrong.

I glanced at his tray. The breakfast steak was only half eaten. God help Monsieur Fresney if the beef had not been absolutely perfect. Chambrun was, I saw by the ashtray, on his third cigarette. I glanced at my watch, wondering if in some fashion I had mistimed my arrival. No, it was now nine-twenty-two and a half.

"Something wrong?" I asked him.

"You have an amazing capacity, Mark, for overlooking the obvious," he said. "For the first time in ten years, Ruysdale is late!"

If there is an indispensable member of Chambrun's staff, it is Miss Betsy Ruysdale. She's hard to describe. Chambrun has many requirements in a personal secretary. She must be efficient beyond all conceivable specifications. She must never dream of an eight-hour day or any regular working hours. She must be chic, but not disturbing. Chambrun doesn't want the male members of his staff mooning over some doll in his outer office. She must eternally anticipate his needs without waiting for orders.

By some miracle Miss Ruysdale manages to meet all these requirements. Her clothes are quiet, but smart and expensive. Her manner toward the staff is friendly, touched by a subdued humor, but she draws an invisible line over which no one dares to step. She is clearly all woman, but if she belongs to some man, his identity is a secret that no one has penetrated. We tell ourselves it can't be Chambrun. Or can it? He neuters her by calling her "Ruysdale"—never Miss Ruysdale or Betsy. Her devotion to him is unquestionably total, but questionably romantic.

Her absence, even her tardiness, on this or any other morning is unthinkable. Only a disaster would account for her absence.

"Would you like me to call her apartment?" I asked.

"That was naturally the first thing I did," Chambrun said. "No answer."

Miss Ruysdale's apartment is only four blocks from the hotel. Neither a subway tie-up nor a traffic jam could account for her failure to appear on time.

"Are you sure she didn't mention being late this morning when she went home last night?" I asked.

"My dear idiot!" Chambrun said. He reached for an appointment pad on his desk. "I'd like you to stand by, Mark, in case Ruysdale doesn't appear very soon. At approximately eleven o'clock, a special French delegation to the United Nations is due to arrive from Kennedy Airport. Paul Lourier has asked me to greet them personally. I know some of them from the black days. If Ruysdale has not arrived, you will take my place and apologize for my absence."

"Of course."

"You will explain that Lourier also cannot be on hand, because of an emergency meeting of the Security Council."

"Ruysdale will show up," I reassured him.

He stared at the empty coffee cup in front of him. This was the point at which Ruysdale usually handed him the first cup of Turkish coffee. The coffee maker was not in evidence on the sideboard. I couldn't help out with that.

Chambrun had referred to "the black days." I knew what he meant. He'd been born in France, but had come to this country at a very early age. During World War Two, he'd returned to his homeland to fight in the French Resistance. It had been a grim time in which many of his friends had died at the hands of the Nazis. Among those who had been close to him in those days was Paul Lourier, now on the staff of the French ambassador to the United Nations.

Lourier had an apartment on the twentieth floor of the Beaumont and he and Chambrun spent what little social time they had in each other's company. Lourier was a relaxed, charming, cultivated gentleman with prematurely white hair and expressive black eyebrows. He and Chambrun had a deep fondness for each other. There were evidently others coming in this special delegation at eleven who had been close to Chambrun and Lourier in "the black days." They would be entitled to special courtesies.

"She would phone if she could," Chambrun said, bringing me back to the present. "I've called the local police precinct. No one has been taken ill on the street—no accident between here and Ruysdale's apartment. Jerry Dodd is going over the hotel from basement to penthouses."

Jerry Dodd is what we call the "house officer" at the Beaumont, head of our security setup. The Beaumont has its problems like any other hotel—the deadbeats, the drunks, the expensive call girls, the cantankerous complainers, the professional hotel thieves who never get caught and the amateurs who always get caught, the suicides, the heart attacks suffered by elderly gentlemen in the rooms of young ladies who are not their wives. And on at least three times so far in my time as public relations director—murder. The hotel is like a small city, and what happens in a small city happens in the Beaumont.

"She's *got* to be all right!" Chambrun said.

I was startled. I'd never heard him sound helpless before.

Jerry Dodd discovered certain aspects of Miss Ruysdale's daily routine that none of us had been aware of before. Her efficiency was such that the machinery hadn't been visible to any of us. It seems that each morning at eight-thirty she entered the Beaumont through the basement entrance to the kitchen where she paused to cast a critical eye on Monsieur Fresney's breakfast preparations for the Great Man. Then she proceeded by the service elevator to the lobby and the reception desk. There Mr. Atterbury, chief desk clerk on the day shift, handed her a list of the new registrations and the check-outs that had taken place since his departure the previous afternoon, plus any special mail addressed to Chambrun. These items were carried to the second floor and her desk in the outer office. She then picked up the phone and called Mrs. Veach, chief telephone operator, reported that she was "in business," and asked for any messages left for the Great Man—or by him.

On this particular morning not a single one of these routines had been followed.

Jerry Dodd had issued a general alarm to the hotel staff—doormen, bell captains, housekeepers, restaurant captains, elevator operators, porters, shopkeepers in the lobby arcade. No one had seen her.

At ten-twenty my desk phone rang. It was Chambrun.

"I'm leaving the hotel for a while," he said. It was without precedent. "You will have to greet the French delegation."

"Count on me."

"If there is any news of any kind, call me at Ruysdale's apartment." He hesitated. "There is a spare key in her desk. Something there may give me a clue."

I didn't stop to wonder at the time whether the spare key was really in Miss Ruysdale's desk or on the Great Man's key ring. I was beginning to catch something of his almost feverish anxiety.

I was at the reception desk when the French delegation—five gentlemen with a multitude of travel stickers on their luggage—arrived at a few minutes past eleven.

"I am Mark Haskell," I said, introducing myself to the spokesman for the group, a Monsieur Jardine. "Unfortunately neither Monsieur Lourier nor Mr. Chambrun could be here to greet you. An emergency meeting of the Security Council has engaged Monsieur Lourier, and Mr. Chambrun is confronted with a crisis here in the hotel. I am at your service, gentlemen, till one or both of them is free."

They were all smiles, undisturbed. Jardine inquired warmly of Chambrun. "It is years since I have seen him."

The delegation had been provided with a suite and four adjoining single rooms on the ninth floor. I went with them to make certain everything was in apple-pie order. There was much jabbering in French, with which I'm familiar, but not fluent. I had room service send them a waiter who spoke their language, and then I departed with much bowing and scraping.

Back at the reservation desk I got a copy of their names from Atterbury and took it up to Chambrun's office. He would want to know who the members of the party were. There were probably other old friends in addition to Jardine.

I felt something ominous in the emptiness of the two offices—Ruysdale's and Chambrun's. The receptionist who sat in a cubbyhole just outside Miss Ruysdale's office—a girl named Sally—just shook her head when I came in. She looked pale and a little shaky. Evidently there was no news.

I went through to Chambrun's desk and put the list of names on his blotter. I wondered where Ruysdale kept the Turkish coffee maker and the necessary supplies. I thought it might cheer the boss if he found it ready for him when he came back. I was looking through the lower reaches of the sideboard when I heard someone come into the office behind me. I turned.

Miss Ruysdale stood just inside the door, looking very chic in a black linen suit, white gloves, white toque, white handbag. There was a fine high color in her cheeks and a curious, almost mystical smile on her lips. I had the crazy notion that she was under the influence of some drug.

"Do you know where Mr. Chambrun is?" she asked in her crisp, businesslike voice.

"I think he may be at your apartment," I said. "Where in God's name have you been?"

The mysterious smile widened slightly. "I have been on an extended hansom cab ride in the park," she said.

I just stared at her.

"At gunpoint," she added.

Most men have had the experience of waiting for some precious female to keep a date—a wife, a girl friend, a prospective girl friend. She is late, late, late. You begin to imagine all the terrible things that may have happened to her—mugged, assaulted, run over by a truck. And then she arrives, only mildly apologetic. She had stopped to window-shop, or have a cup of coffee with an old friend, or she had "just lost track of time." Your anxiety turns to blazing anger. How dare she turn up all in one piece, unharmed, undamaged?

Chambrun was in that kind of rage when he returned, having been summoned by Ruysdale's phone call announcing that she was at last in the office and "perfectly all right." He sat at his desk, his black eyes visible only through slits in their deep pouches. He ignored the Turkish coffee now at his elbow. His hand shook slightly as he held a lighter to his cigarette.

"The explanation had better be good," he said to Ruysdale, his voice dangerously cold.

"It isn't," she said. "It isn't even believable."

"I suggest you try it on for size," Chambrun said.

It sounded hallucinatory. She had arrived, Ruysdale told us, at the basement entrance to the Beaumont kitchen at the usual time—eight-thirty. She had been just about to start down the concrete steps to the door when she felt something round and hard pressed into the small of her back.

"Please don't move or cry out, Miss Ruysdale," a pleasant male voice said. "What you feel is a gun."

You read about this sort of thing happening nearly every day in Fun City, Ruysdale told us, but you know it will never happen to you. Here it *was* happening, and in broad daylight.

Ruysdale is strictly not the hysterical type. I've seen her under all kinds of pressure, and I can vouch for that. I can imagine that her very competent cerebral wheels were turning competently and coolly.

"There is about seven dollars in my purse," she said without turning, standing quite still. "I'd appreciate it very much if you didn't take my driver's license and my credit cards."

"Dear Miss Ruysdale," the male voice said, a lilt of humor in it, "this is not a holdup. I'm going to put my hand on your shoulder and turn you very slowly. Then you will walk toward the vehicle at the curb."

The hand on her shoulder was gentle. She turned, and the man with the gun stayed behind her.

"I'd actually seen the hansom cab at the curb when I walked up, but it hadn't registered," Ruysdale said. "There are a few of them still operating from the square in front of the Plaza. Round the park for ten dollars. The driver, wearing a dilapidated silk hat, sat on top, his face turned away. The horse was old, black, sleepy-looking."

"Into the hansom, please, Miss Ruysdale," the man with the gun said.

Ruysdale looked up and down the street, but there was no one close enough to be helpful. You do what you're told, she thought, when there's a gun at your back. The driver opened the folding doors from his position on top. Ruysdale got in, and the gunman followed and sat beside her. The doors folded in front of them, imprisoning them behind the horse. Ruysdale turned to look at her captor.

"Describe him," Chambrun said.

That vague smile moved Ruysdale's fine lips. "I can't," she said.

"Can't?" Chambrun's voice was impatient.

"He was wearing a rubber mask made to look exactly like Boris Karloff," Ruysdale said. "His hands were white, slim, delicate, well cared-for. He held the gun as if he knew how to use it. The horse started away toward the park."

"What did he want?" Chambrun asked.

The vague smiled broadened. "We drove round and round the park for about three hours," Ruysdale said. "In that time I was subjected to the most charming verbal lovemaking I can ever remember."

"Lovemaking?" Chambrun sat forward.

"He had admired me for a long time, he said. He knew I was unapproachable in the normal fashion. He had chosen this rather melodramatic method to get me alone and tell me what was in his heart."

"Oh, come on!" Chambrun said.

"Is it so impossible that someone should find me unusually attractive?" Ruysdale asked, with just the slightest edge to her voice.

"You are unusually attractive," he said, as if he were referring to a new IBM computer. "But at gunpoint! I admit the rather unusual Freudian overtones, but—really!"

"He quoted poetry to me," Ruysdale said. Her pale eyelids lowered.

> "—What am I? What is any man,
> That he dare ask for you? Therefore my heart
> Hides behind phrases. There's a modesty
> In these things too—I come here to pluck down
> Out of the sky the evening star—then smile,
> And stoop to gather little flowers."

Chambrun made an impatient gesture with his cigarette. "That is part of Cyrano de Bergerac's endless speech to Roxane from under the balcony. Sentimental twaddle! And if I remember your dossier, Ruysdale, you played Roxane in a college production of the Rostand play. You remember the words from that and not because your clown in the hansom cab spoke them so passionately."

"They were nicely chosen," Ruysdale said.

"And provided me with three hours of gut-twisting anxiety," Chambrun said. His eyes narrowed. He was looking down at the names of the French delegation I'd left on his blotter. He brought his closed fist down on the desk. His eyes, bright and cold as two newly minted dimes, turned my way. "Get Jerry Dodd here on the double," he said.

I went to the phone on the corner of his desk. He'd turned back to Ruysdale. "How did he leave you?" I heard him ask.

"I was ordered out of the hansom in the middle of the park, and they clattered off. When I got out he said, 'In my most sweet unreasonable dreams, / I have not dreamed of this! Now let me die, / Having lived . . .' "

"We should be looking for an out-of-work actor," Chambrun said. "Did you happen to notice the hack license in the hansom?"

"The little metal frame where it belonged was empty," Ruysdale said.

"Thank God you were able to pay attention to some aspect of reality, even though the result is negative." He lit a fresh cigarette. Ruysdale, a little slowly, I thought, took his demitasse cup to the sideboard and refilled it with Turkish coffee.

"I dislike destroying your romantic notions, Ruysdale," Chambrun said, after he'd sipped the steaming coffee, "but I'm afraid your adventure this morning was not aimed at you, but at me."

"At you?"

"I am not beautiful," Chambrun said drily, "but I can be

dangerous. What did I *not* do because of your absence this morning?"

"You didn't finish your breakfast," I said.

"You didn't go through the morning mail," Ruysdale said.

"I didn't welcome the French delegation," Chambrun said. He looked at me. "Did you locate Jerry?"

"He's on his way," I said.

Four of the five names, including Monsieur Jardine's, on the French delegation were familiar to Chambrun. The fifth, one Alphonse Dufor, was the name of a stranger.

"I haven't quite got on the rails here yet," Jerry Dodd said. The Beaumont's house officer had arrived in Chambrun's office on the run.

Chambrun was staring thoughtfully at the list of French names. "Why should I be maneuvered away from the job of greeting the delegation," he asked, more of himself than of us. "I've known Jardine for nearly twenty-five years. Like my friend Paul Lourier, he was one of the leaders in the Resistance. Three others I know less well, but well enough. Why should anyone want to prevent my meeting these old friends?"

"The name Dufor means nothing to you?" Jerry asked.

"Nothing." Chambrun's eyes narrowed. "But his face? Perhaps I knew him as someone else."

"You'd be bound to see him sooner or later," Jerry said. "They're booked into the hotel for ten days."

Jerry is a thin, wiry little man in his late forties, with a professional smile that does nothing to hide the fact that his pale restless eyes are able to see and read a great deal at a moment's glance. Chambrun trusts him implicitly.

Chambrun looked thoughtfully at Jerry. "Later might be too late." He pushed himself up out of his desk chair. "Just to be sure, let's pay a visit on Monsieur Alphonse Dufor. Where is he located?"

Jerry glanced at his notebook. "Jardine is in Suite 9A. The

others have 901, 903, 905, and 907. Dufor is in 907."

Chambrun, Jerry, and I headed for the ninth floor, leaving Miss Ruysdale to wonder about her Cyrano. There was no answer to our knocks on the door of Room 907. Chambrun gave a little sign to Jerry, who promptly opened the door with one of his magic passkeys.

Dufor was not in his room. He had left it neatly settled—three suits and a dinner jacket on hangers in the closet. Shirts, ties, and underthings in the bureau. Shaving kit and a robe in the bathroom.

"Jardine," Chambrun said at my elbow.

We went down the hall to the door of the suite. This time our knock was answered promptly—by Jardine himself. At the sight of Chambrun he burst into a volley of French, seized Chambrun by the shoulders, kissed him on both cheeks, and literally dragged him into the suite. He was delighted to see me again. He was delighted to meet Jerry. He was delighted.

"I have a problem, Max," Chambrun said, "and no time to go into detail. Who is Alphonse Dufor?"

Something happened to Jardine's delight. There was suddenly pain in his eyes. "You have seen him?" he asked.

"I have not seen him."

"The past is forgotten and forgiven, Pierre," Jardine said.

"Who is he?" Chambrun said, his voice dangerously cold again.

"You knew him," Jardine said unhappily, "as Jacques Midal."

"Mother have mercy!" Chambrun said. "Where is he?"

"In his room, I presume."

"He is not in his room." He turned to me. "Call the French offices at the United Nations and get me Paul Lourier."

"I tell you, it's all over and forgotten," Jardine said.

I put in the call to the UN, trying to listen to Chambrun at the same time.

"Jacques Midal was one of us in the black days," I heard him tell Jerry. "He was unmasked as a Nazi collaborator by my friend Lourier. He was subjected to torture by Lourier and eventual imprisonment. If any man could have undying hatred for another man, Midal has it for Lourier."

"It is over and dead, Pierre," Jardine said, pleading. "All Midal wants is to live in peace and make reparation for his crimes by being a useful citizen of France."

I found myself connected with the French offices at the UN. Lourier had left there half an hour ago, with word that he could be reached at the Beaumont. I reported.

"Check the front door and the lobby," Chambrun ordered. "He must be stopped from going to his apartment."

I got the day bell captain. We were too late. Lourier had gone up to his apartment ten minutes ago.

We went to the twentieth floor, Jardine with us. It seemed fairly clear to me what had happened. Chambrun had been kept from seeing Dufor-Midal on his arrival. All Midal wanted was uninterrupted time to get at Paul Lourier.

"Why did he change his name?" I asked Jardine on the way up in the elevator.

Jardine shrugged wearily. "The name Midal was a household word for treachery at home," he said. "The man had paid for his crime. His remorse, his reformation, were genuine. He was given the legal right to change his name."

At the twentieth floor Chambrun literally ran to the door of Paul Lourier's apartment. He pounded on it with his fist. "Paul!" he shouted. "It is I, Pierre."

The door opened and the silver-haired Paul Lourier faced us. His face was the color of ashes.

"Thank God you've come, Pierre," he said. "I called your office, and Miss Ruysdale told me you were somewhere in the hotel. She is trying to find you. I was happy to know that she was all right. Please come in."

We went in—but only just in.

Lying on the floor in a welter of blood was a man I recognized as one of the French delegation.

"Midal!" I heard Jardine whisper.

It was a grotesque business. A fencing foil had been driven through Midal's throat and literally pinned him to the floor. It must have severed his jugular. I glanced up at Lourier's mantel. Only one of the crossed foils I remembered as decorations was in place. Next to Midal's dead hand was a gun.

"He knocked on my door," Lourier said in a flat voice. "I had left it on the latch because I expected room service to bring me some champagne. I was on the point of inviting Max and his delegates for a small libation. I called out, 'Come in'—and there was Alphonse Dufor. He had that gun in his hand—and murder in his eyes. I knew he was not in a mood to listen to reason. I suppose he had cause to hate me so much."

"But you tried to reason?" Chambrun asked.

"No time," Lourier said. "I was standing there, by the mantel. He came charging across the room, cursing me. My reflex was automatic. I snatched down the foil from over the mantel and thrust. Miraculously I was quick enough."

Jerry Dodd moved forward and knelt by the gun. He used his handkerchief to pick it up. "French make," he said. He glanced at Lourier. "You were lucky. This is a hair-trigger gadget, but he'd forgotten to take off the safety catch."

"I think not," Chambrun said. He turned very slowly to look at Lourier, his friend. "I think it went like this, didn't it, Paul. You telephoned Dufor's room and asked him to join you. It was time to forgive and forget your mutual grievances. Because the grievances *were* mutual, weren't they, Paul? He had suffered at your hands, but the girl you loved had been brutalized and murdered by the Nazis, thanks to Midal's treachery."

"Pierre!"

"So he came to your room, eager to forgive your part in his horror and hoping for your forgiveness. Instead he got a few vengeful words from you—and a rapier in his throat. The gun is yours, isn't it, Paul? You put it beside him to lend authenticity to your story."

"Pierre, you must be out of your mind," Lourier said, in a shaken voice. "He arranged for the kidnapping of Miss Ruysdale so that you wouldn't see him when he arrived. He needed only a little time to reach me."

"It won't do, Paul," Chambrun said. "How could he have known—in France—about Ruysdale or what my reaction would be to her absence? But you knew, Paul. You knew my habits, my loyalties. You knew this morning that I was safely removed from the scene. It was *you* who needed only a little time."

Lourier leaned against the wall.

"As I remember, Paul," Chambrun said, "you were an actor before the war. May I ask, did you ever play the role of Cyrano de Bergerac?"

"Oh, God!" Lourier whispered.

# Pierre Chambrun and the Sad Song

The projected return of Pamela Powers into the public's awareness was a matter of increasing concern to me as the hour and moment grew closer. As public relations director of the Beaumont, New York City's top luxury hotel, it was my job to make certain that the occasion was placed in the proper spotlight, that the important columnists and critics were on hand to pass, we hoped, a kindly judgment on the Powers comeback, and that the Blue Lagoon Room of the hotel was bulging with celebrities to welcome back Pamela as the toast of the town she had once been.

I had never seen Pamela perform. Fifteen years ago I had been at a midwestern university, in my junior year. I'd never seen the inside of a New York City nightclub, or one in Las Vegas or Miami. Pamela had been the queen of all those places. I'd heard her recordings, of course. I had an album of hers with her picture on the cover—a slim dark girl with wide violet eyes that seemed about to brim with tears. There was a sad and plaintive quality to her songs that made the whole world want to protect and love her. I'd been told that hearing her high, true voice on records was only half the magic, that when you saw her in person, standing in a spotlight by the piano, a long chiffon handkerchief twisted between her fingers, she could tear you to pieces. She was, they told me, an original, a "one and only."

Fifteen years ago Pamela had exploded like a tragic Roman candle, falling to earth in a hundred bright pieces that landed, sputtered, and went out, apparently forever. A combination of alcohol and drugs, they said. Now, in the late hours of the night, you could sometimes hear a disc jockey play one of her records and comment nostalgically on what had once been a great and haunting talent.

Pierre Chambrun, resident manager of the Beaumont and my employer, is a small dark man, stockily built, with heavy pouches under bright black eyes that can turn so hard that your blood freezes if you're guilty of a mistake, or, unexpectedly, can twinkle with humor. He has been in the hotel business for all his adult life. French by birth, he came to this country as a small boy, and he now thinks like an American. His training in the hotel business has often taken him back to Europe, and he can adopt a Continental manner to please a queen. He's an excellent linguist. He's the sole operating boss of the Beaumont, handling his job without interference from the absentee owner.

I think Chambrun's genius as an executive lies in his ability to delegate authority while at the same time always being close at hand to take the responsibility for delicate decisions. His instinct for dealing with people on all levels, from the lowest kitchen helper to visiting royalty, is not something you can learn from a course in hotel management at Cornell University.

We live by fairly rigid outlines at the Beaumont. Chambrun breakfasts in his elegant office on the second floor at precisely nine o'clock. It is always a hearty breakfast because he never takes time to eat lunch. At precisely nine-twenty-two I report to get any special orders for the day. Chambrun will be lighting his first Egyptian cigarette of the day and pouring his second cup of American coffee. There will be a third cup, and then he switches to Turkish coffee, which Miss Ruysdale prepares for him on the carved Florentine sideboard. Miss Ruysdale is an incomparable secretary who seems to know in advance what Chambrun's needs will be even before he has thought of them himself.

The first order of business is to look through a collection of cards sent up by the reception desk—the newly registered guests of the night before. I'm always present for this routine, because it's my job to know if any new celebrity has checked in and if there is any reason for a press release or the special "red carpet treatment."

The hotel uses a code system on these registration cards that Chambrun goes over each morning. The code letter A means that the guest is an alcoholic; W on a man's card means that he's a woman chaser, possibly a customer for the expensive call girls who appear from time to time in the Trapeze Bar; M on a woman's card means a manhunter; O arbitrarily stands for "over his head"—meaning that particular guest can't afford the Beaumont's prices and mustn't be allowed to get in too deep; MX on a married man's card means he's double-crossing his wife, and WX means the wife is playing around; and D means diplomat.

On this particular morning Chambrun was fingering the cards, passing them on to me after he read them. That day we had a famous film star, a Texas oil man with political aspirations, a South American diplomat on a visit to the United Nations. The others were meaningless to me, particularly a Mrs. Donald Jepson. Her card was bare, but Chambrun made two notations on it—A and O.

"A long-gone alcoholic and at last report stone broke," he said. There was a curious questioning glitter in his half hidden black eyes as he saw me put the card on top of my pile without much interest. "Mean anything to you?" he asked.

"I never heard of Mrs. Donald Jepson," I said, "drunk or sober."

"She is Pamela Powers," Chambrun said.

"The singer?"

"The onetime singer," he said. He didn't go on with his collection of cards. "Extraordinary girl."

"Woman," I said. "She quit fifteen years ago. She has to be flirting with forty, or past that."

Chambrun picked up the phone on his desk and flipped the switch on the conference box so that Ruysdale and I could hear Mr. Atterbury's dry voice when he answered. Atterbury is the head desk clerk and an old and trusted hand.

"Morning, Atterbury," Chambrun said.

"Yes, sir?"

"Did Mrs. Donald Jepson have a reservation?"

There was the briefest hesitation. "No, sir. House seat."

The management holds out a half dozen rooms in case some VIP appears unexpectedly. We call them house seats. Only Atterbury and Chambrun are permitted to okay their release.

"You had a reason?" Chambrun asked.

"Yes, sir. I had a terrible crush on Pamela Powers twenty years ago. I couldn't say no."

"She's dead broke, from all accounts."

"I know. My responsibility, sir."

"And will you carry her out of the hotel when she gets screaming drunk and starts climbing the walls?"

"I will, sir."

A tiny smile moved the corner of Chambrun's mouth. "I'd have done the same thing, Atterbury. Good man."

"Thank you, sir." Atterbury's phone clicked off. His day was made.

"Sentimental ass," Chambrun said. He still didn't go on to the next card. His hooded eyes swiveled my way. "Let me know, Mark, if Miss Powers appears in any of the public rooms—bars, restaurants. I'd like to see her again, but I want it to seem casual."

I spread the word. At about twelve-forty-five I was in my office on the second floor when my phone rang. It was Eddie, the head bartender in the Trapeze Bar.

"The lady's here," he said.

I called Chambrun.

"I'm tied up for the next fifteen minutes," he said. "Go down to the Trapeze and keep Miss Powers entertained until I show up."

The Trapeze Bar is suspended in space, like a birdcage, over the foyer of the Grand Ballroom. Its walls are elaborate with Florentine grillwork. An artist of the Calder school had decorated them with mobiles of circus performers working on trapezes. They sway slightly in the draft from a concealed air-freshening system, creating the illusion that the whole place is swinging slightly in orbit.

I saw Pamela as I walked into the Trapeze. She was sitting at a corner table alone—so very alone. I felt an unexpected protective pang for her. She was, somehow, ageless. She was turning a champagne glass slowly round and round and round in her slim fingers.

I stopped at the bar to speak to Eddie and said, frowning, "She's started to booze it up already."

Eddie grinned. "Champagne glass, properly chilled," he said, "loaded with four solid ounces of straight ginger ale."

"Ginger ale!"

"I kid you not," Eddie said. "Shall I send over your usual dry martini?"

"I—I think not," I said.

As I walked toward Pamela's table, I saw her suddenly involved in a tense withdrawal. Did she think I was an unwanted autograph hunter—or possibly a detective? You may ask why I thought detective. It was because, when I reached the table, she stared up at me with those wide violet eyes, and I could see terror in them. I thought with a twinge that she must be a little off her psychic rocker. There's nothing frightening, much less terrifying, about my very amiable professional approach.

"Miss Powers?" I said. "I'm Mark Haskell, the Beaumont's public relations director. I just wanted to tell you how delighted we are to have you with us."

Very slowly her panic seemed to ebb.

"Thank you," she said in a small quavering voice.

"May I join you for a moment?"

"Please do."

I sat down opposite her.

"I don't want any particular attention paid to my being a guest of the hotel, Mr. Haskell," she said.

"That may be hard to control," I said, smiling at her. "You'll be recognized by hundreds of people."

Her tiny smile had a bitter twist to it. "I've long since been forgotten," she said.

"I very much doubt that."

She lowered her eyes. "Did you know that I opened the Blue Lagoon Room here? Seventeen years ago. I was the first star to perform here."

I hadn't known that, but I didn't admit it. "You've been missed," I said.

Just then I saw Chambrun coming across the room toward us. He had on his best "mine host" smile as he bent over her hand and kissed it.

"My dear child," he said.

"Dear Mr. Chambrun," she said. But she wasn't looking at him. The violet eyes had widened. There had been terror in them before. Now it was stark and undisguised. She was staring past Chambrun at the bar. I followed the direction of her look.

Seated at the far end of the bar was a man wearing a black overcoat with an ornate fur collar. He had on a black hat, brim tugged downward. You don't keep your hat on in the Trapeze Bar. He was looking straight at Pamela with cold blue eyes. His mouth was a thin slit over a granite jaw. He lifted a shot glass filled with whiskey and swallowed the contents at a gulp. He looked like a mobster right out of an old Warner Brothers movie. But it was not funny.

Pamela lowered her eyes, and her whole body shook as if she had a malarial chill.

It was two afternoons later that I was summoned to Chambrun's office for a special conference. When I arrived, I found only Mr. Cardoza and Miss Ruysdale with him. Cardoza is the maitre d' in the Blue Lagoon, but he is more than a head waiter. He handles the entertainment and makes sure that only the right people have reservations. He is a dark, elegant gent who looks as if he might be the heir to the Spanish throne.

Chambrun sat at his desk, drumming with his short, square fingers. "Jigs Henning is supposed to open in your room on Saturday, Cardoza," he said.

Cardoza nodded happily. Jigs Henning would jam the place for his four-week stay in the Blue Lagoon. He ranked among the top singers in the business, along with Sinatra, Sammy Davis Jr., and Tony Bennett.

"He's been trying to get out of his contract with us," Chambrun said. "He has a movie offer that would take him to the coast at once if he could accept. I have regretfully refused. But an hour ago I decided to let him off the hook."

Cardoza's dark eyebrows rose. "You have someone to replace him?"

"I have," Chambrun said, with a Cheshire-Cat smile.

"May one ask—?"

"One may," Chambrun said. He leaned back in his chair. "Pamela Powers."

Cardoza stared at him and said, "Oh." It was his way of saying that Chambrun was out of his cotton-picking mind.

"She hasn't had a drink for more than a year," Chambrun said, "and she kicked the drug habit a long time ago. She's been working on her voice for the last ten months. I have persuaded Duke Adler, who arranged all her programs in the old days and acted as her accompanist, to play the engagement for her. She opens Saturday."

Cardoza moistened his lips. "Miss Powers has agreed?" I knew what he was thinking. Pamela was a pro. She wouldn't try a comeback unless she believed in it—except that Chambrun could be ultrapersuasive. If he chose, he could make it next to impossible for anyone to say "no" to him.

"She turned me down flat when I first suggested it," Chambrun said. "Childishly frightened. But I persuaded her that all good performers are scared, even the great ones. It's part of what makes them great. I got her to go to Duke Adler. He reported she was a miracle, her old self. She still refused. Then, an hour ago, she phoned me to say that, if I hadn't changed my mind, she'd do it. You'll have to admit, Cardoza, that a comeback engagement by Pamela Powers will be the biggest attraction you've had this year."

"If she doesn't fall on her face in front of the columnists and critics at the opening," Cardoza said.

"If she's any good at all, they'll give her a sendoff for sentimental reasons," I said.

"Precisely," Chambrun said. "And Duke Adler assures me she'll be better than just good. She'll be terrific, he says."

Cardoza drew a deep breath. "It's your hotel," he said.

"Your confidence in my judgment overwhelms me," Chambrun said drily. He turned to me. "Your job is to notify the press, Mark, and to dust off our prime list of celebrities."

There wasn't any problem about getting the ace columnists and nightclub critics there for the opening. All the tables were reserved before we got halfway through our list of famous people. We ran big ads in the entertainment pages of the papers, announcing that the opening night was already sold out.

I didn't see Pamela Powers again until the Thursday night before the opening. Friday morning to be exact—three o'clock. The Blue Lagoon had closed. Then, in the empty room, Pamela and Duke Adler took over, along with our lighting man. It was largely a costume parade under the lights. Duke Adler sat at the piano, with his pale longish hair and tinted glasses hiding his eyes. He would play the tag end of a song, and Pamela, not really trying, would sing a few bars.

The voice was clear and true, with that strange sad quality

that had made her number one. On cue the lighting man would follow his light plot, and Pamela and Duke would go into a bar or two of the next number. It was an ordinary technical rehearsal, but what I saw of it sent me away deciding that Chambrun was really a genius. Pamela was going to knock them in the aisles.

About two o'clock on Friday afternoon I was in Chambrun's office with Cardoza. We were going over the table reservations with the Great Man. He wanted to be sure that just the right people sat in just the right places. While we were at it, Miss Ruysdale announced that Eddie, the bartender in the Trapeze, was in the outer office to see the boss. Eddie should have been on duty at that time.

Eddie is a chubby, brash young man who grew up on the Lower East Side, knows Fun City like the back of his hand, and has collected more gossip about the hotel guests and the hotel staff than even a Walter Winchell could have managed.

"Thought I'd like to talk to you, boss, where there aren't so many listening ears," he said to Chambrun.

"What is it, Eddie?"

"We got a new customer that bothers me," Eddie said. "The Beaumont ain't the usual kind of hangout for the Mafia."

"Get to the point, Eddie."

"The last five days, along about twelve-thirty or a quarter to one, a guy named Max Wentzel comes into the bar. He sits at the far end and drinks three two-ounce hookers of Southern Comfort. This Wentzel is a gun for the Mafia. I know. We grew up in the same part of town."

"Just visiting you?" Chambrun said.

"He doesn't speak to me," Eddie said. "Like he never saw me before. He sits there, just watching. I get the creepy feeling he's waiting for the right guy to come in to be knocked off. He don't give me reason to kick him out of the bar. But I thought you ought to know."

Chambrun's forehead wrinkled in a dark frown. "He's down there now?"

"Been and gone," Eddie said. "He'll be back tomorrow if the pattern holds."

"Pass the word to Jerry," Chambrun said. Jerry Dodd is the Beaumont's security chief. "I'll drop in tomorrow and have a look in person."

"I thought you ought to know," Eddie said.

"You were right."

By Saturday afternoon I was in the middle of a high-speed merry-go-round. My phone was endlessly busy—people calling and demanding reservations for that night, which we couldn't give them. Customers were ready to hang from the rafters. There were flowers to be arranged for, to be delivered to Pamela's dressing room, and a huge bouquet of white roses to be handed to her on stage after her performance.

About four o'clock I got a call from Eddie. I'd had the switchboard cut off my phone, but they put Eddie through.

"Hate to be the bearer of bad news," he said.

"The bar ran out of liquor?"

"The bar just had an order from room service," Eddie said. "A bottle of booze to Room 822."

"So?"

"Room 822 is where the boss's songbird is living."

"Pamela Powers?"

"Yeah," Eddie said. "Looks like she might celebrate in advance."

"Brother!" I said. "Thanks, Eddie."

I got through to Chambrun and heard him explode.

"Meet me on the eighth floor," he said.

Chambrun's peremptory knock on the door of Room 822 brought no immediate result. He tried again, calling out, "Miss Powers!"

A man's voice answered, asking us to wait a moment. It was a long moment, and then the door opened, and Duke Adler faced us. A cigarette dangled from the corner of his mouth.

The hall lights glittered against the dark lenses of his glasses.

"May I come in?" Chambrun asked, and went in like an aggressive fullback wedging his way off tackle.

Pamela, wearing a filmy sort of peignoir almost the color of her violet eyes, was sitting in an armchair beside the center table. Room 822 consists of a small sitting room and a bedroom. Her hands gripped the arms of the chair so tightly that they were corpse-white. Beside her on the table was a half-empty bottle of liquor and one glass. Chambrun looked at the bottle and then at Pam.

"I'm disappointed," he said in a quiet, cold voice.

Pamela opened her mouth, but no sound came out.

Duke Adler, behind us, laughed. "You got it wrong, Dad," he said. "It's me, not Pam. I always operate half crocked. You knew that, didn't you?"

I remember thinking he was a little tight during the lighting rehearsal. But it hadn't seemed to affect his fingers on the keyboard.

Chambrun's cold black eyes remained riveted on Pamela. "Have you been drinking?" he asked.

She shook her head. Then, suddenly, she was on her feet, her hands gripping Chambrun's shoulders. "Please, Mr. Chambrun, I can't go through with it! I can't! I'd rather die than let you down—but I'd rather die than fail."

"Come off it, baby," Duke said. "Opening-night nerves. You'll be great."

She broke into sobs, then lowered her head to Chambrun's shoulder. "Oh, please—God! Don't make me do it."

Duke Adler's long fingers closed over her wrist. He pulled her away from Chambrun, not too gently. The dark glasses looked down into her tear-red eyes. "Knock it off, baby. Just pull yourself together. You can do it. You know you have to do it, don't you?"

She seemed to make a superhuman effort. She nodded slowly. "Yes," she whispered.

"Is everything satisfactory here with your rooms?" Chambrun asked. Quite unexpectedly he walked past her into the bedroom. I thought that Adler suddenly froze.

Chambrun came back in a few moments, and I heard Adler's breath go out of him in a long sigh.

"I understand your nervousness, Pamela," Chambrun said. "Just know that I believe in you one hundred percent."

"Thank you," she said, almost inaudibly.

I couldn't wait to get out into the hall again to call Chambrun's attention to what was a significant coincidence to me.

"Did you notice the bottle of liquor?" I asked Chambrun when we were alone in the corridor.

"Southern Comfort," he said, nodding. "Did you notice the half-smoked cigar in the ashtray? Adler is a chain cigarette smoker. Pamela doesn't smoke at all. He wasn't in the bedroom."

"He?"

"Eddie's man from the Mafia," Chambrun said. "Tell Jerry I want this room watched. If this Max Wentzel shows up, I want him covered every second."

"Right."

"Pamela will go to her dressing room about seven o'clock to prepare for the dinner show," Chambrun said. "I want you there. Let Cardoza take care of the VIPs. I don't want you to let Pamela out of your sight till she goes on stage. I could swear that girl isn't afraid to sing. It's something else."

"What?"

"I wish I knew," Chambrun said.

"Where will you be?"

"Around," Chambrun said.

I checked with Jerry Dodd, the security officer, about quarter to seven. There had been no sign of Max Wentzel. I waited in Pamela's flower-filled room. At three minutes after seven she and Duke Adler arrived. He had changed into a dinner jacket, but he still wore the dark glasses, and the ever-present cigarette drooped from the corner of his mouth. He frowned at me. "The lady has to dress," he said. I gave him what I hoped was a fatuous grin. "I'm the watchdog to keep out eager autograph hunters and old friends with good wishes—till after the first show."

Adler shrugged. "I'll be back. Want to check the exact position of the piano." He went out.

The minute he was gone, Pamela swung around, steadying herself with her hands on my shoulders. I was aware of a subtle, alluring fragrance when she stood so close. "Please, Mr. Haskell, for the love of God, don't make me do it."

"You're going to be just great," I said. "And whatever else is bothering you, Chambrun and I and the whole staff are standing by. Care to tell me what it is?"

"Oh, God," she said, and turned away toward her dressing table.

Whatever we could have dreamed of in the way of a distinguished audience to welcome Pamela back came to the Blue Lagoon that night for the dinner show. Her dressing room was flooded with goodwill telegrams. It should have been a night of nights for her, but something was tearing her to pieces. I thought at last, when the call boy rapped on her door with a "Ten minutes, Miss Powers," that she was going to collapse. Duke Adler returned and literally dragged her to her feet and shook her.

"Damn you, pull yourself together!" he shouted at her. It was like slapping an hysteric.

She got out into the wings off the little stage. The lights dimmed. The buzz of voices subsided. Cardoza's well-trained waiters avoided even the tiniest click of china or silverware. The curtain parted, and Duke Adler walked out to the piano. There was warm but moderate applause.

Adler sat down and began to play a soft and plaintive melody. And then I heard a choked sob beside me. An ice-cold hand touched mine, as if searching for warmth and courage, and then Pamela Powers walked unsteadily out into the spotlight.

I thought they were going to tear the Blue Lagoon apart. They stood and cheered and shouted. Adler had to play the introduction three times. Then they were silent, with a kind of breathless silence. They were all wondering—could she do it?

The clear small voice began:

"A girl I know,
she is partly mad,
Yet beyond that smile
she is partly sad.
She is partly calm,
she is partly wild.
But she is mostly woman—
No,
She is mostly child."

When she came to the end, the first ovation was tremendous. She had it—all the old magic, all her old skill. I felt myself choking up like a sentimental old-timer. At last they subsided, eager for the next number, and Adler began to vamp the introduction. But Pamela stepped out of the spotlight and down toward the front of the stage.

"Ladies and gentlemen—"

Adler's head jerked up. The lighting man was surprised, but quickly readjusted his spotlight so that it beamed on her. Adler struck a jarring chord and played the introduction louder—completely out of mood with the moment.

"Ladies and gentlemen," Pamela said again, holding up her hands for silence. "Your welcome, your applause, is overwhelming. After all these years—"

They let go again with clapping and cheering, but she begged for silence with her hands. Once more Adler tried the introductory music, but she paid no attention.

"A comeback is a dangerous thing," Pamela said, "but not nearly so dangerous as my real reason for being here. I am here to betray myself, and to betray all the things decent people believe in. I am here to—"

There was the clear sharp crack of a gunshot. I stood rooted in the wings. I saw that Pamela still stood there, apparently unhurt, on the apron of the stage. Pandemonium had broken loose in the Blue Lagoon. At that moment Adler sprang up from the piano bench and started to race toward where I was standing in the wings.

Did I ever mention that I played football on the defensive team at my midwestern college? Instinctively I threw a block into Adler that knocked him flat on his back. Then I was on him. From that somewhat awkward position, I saw Chambrun climbing up from the audience onto the stage to stand beside Pamela. His arm went round her, and he held her very close. He held up his hand for silence.

"Ladies and gentlemen, any cause for alarm is over."

I jerked Adler to his feet. He was still gasping for breath. I twisted his arm behind him and dragged him out onto the stage. At the back of the room I saw Jerry Dodd and two of his men. Mr. Max Wentzel, held between them, looked as if he'd had something of a going-over.

"I want to tell you a story," Chambrun said to the audience, still holding Pamela close. "I tried to persuade Pamela to stage this miraculous comeback, but she was reluctant. She didn't know how you would receive her. It meant so much. She finally refused. And then she changed her mind. I thought it was courage. I was to discover that it was terror.

"It cannot hurt Pamela now for me to remind you that her brilliant career ended when she began to drink—and became a drug addict. She was caught in the horror of both these sicknesses for many years, and then, by her own courage and will, she freed herself. But behind her lay something—I don't yet know what—a crime of some sort. Drug addicts turn to crime when they desperately need money.

"What happened to Pamela during her stay at the Beaumont is quite a story. After she had refused my offer she was approached by the criminal syndicate that handles the distribution of drugs and was blackmailed into accepting my offer of an engagement here. The purpose?" He turned to Pamela. "I think she was about to tell you when an attempt was made on her life. The syndicate had given orders to silence her. Fortunately my staff and I were waiting for just such a move. Would you care to go on, Pamela? You're quite safe now."

"In my second number of each show," Pamela said, her voice low and trembling, "I was to alter the lyrics in a certain way. This was a code that would tell the pushers of drugs exactly where their receiving point was to be and when. I would have to go through with it—or go to jail. I—I've made my choice."

They gave her another full-throated ovation. Chambrun let them go on, then signaled for silence.

"Unfortunately one of the conspirators in this plot is Pamela's accompanist, so she won't be able to go on with her show as planned. But if she will permit me, I could play some of the old songs that made her famous. Would you like that?"

Would they like it!

Chambrun walked across to the piano and sat down. I just couldn't believe it! His strong, square fingers moved through the opening bars of "Bill," the song that made Helen Morgan famous years ago and that Pamela used to include in her repertoire.

Would you believe that incredible boss of mine was just plain great at the piano?

# The Masked Crusader

It began for me on a brisk fall morning. At that time nobody was dead, except on paper. I was looking over the list of newly registered guests from the night before—part of my job as public relations director at the Hotel Beaumont—when my secretary buzzed me from the outer office.

"An old college friend of yours is out here to see you," she said. "Norman Geller."

"Never heard of him," I said.

"I'll send him in," Shelda said sweetly. I knew she was talking in front of this unwanted visitor. Intuition told me I was about to be clipped for the alumni fund by some eager beaver.

"Thank you, Miss Mason," I said, giving it a sardonic reading.

My old college chum walked into the office. I didn't know him, and yet there was something vaguely familiar about him. He was, at that moment, a sort of rumpled Westchester country-club type—tweed jacket, navy-blue turtleneck shirt, gray flannel slacks, custom-made loafers. But he looked a little as if he'd slept in the entire outfit.

"Mark!" he said, holding out his hand, "what luck to find

you here." His handshake was firm but not meant to impress. He saw that I was puzzled. "You don't have the faintest idea who I am, do you?"

"Something stirs, but bells don't ring," I said.

"Norbert Gellernacht," he said. "Little Norbert Gellernacht."

An image came sharply into focus. Norbert Gellernacht had been an eager sophomore in my senior year. He'd worn thick glasses in those days, and he was trying desperately to gain a measure of popularity by writing an allegedly witty column for the college daily. I had thought of him as a pleasant nothing who was never going to make it because he tried too hard. My philosophy professor might have called that a non sequitur.

"Norbert!" I said, unable to think of anything else to say.

"I saw your name on the hotel card in my room," he said. "Public relations director. Boy, was I glad, because I need a friend in city hall."

"Sit down," I said. It obviously wasn't going to be a pitch for the alumni fund.

He sat down in the armchair by my desk and lit a cigarette. His hands weren't too steady. "I changed my name after I sold my first piece of magazine fiction," he said. "Nobody would ever remember 'Norbert Gellernacht.'"

"So you've become a professional writer," I said. "You always wanted to, didn't you?" I thought he must be doing pretty well if he could afford the Hotel Beaumont's prices.

"I used to think so," he said, "until about three weeks ago. I now know that I am just a high-priced salami slicer."

"Oh?"

"Television," he explained.

"That's where the money is, no?"

"This road, paved with gold, leads straight to the alcohol tank or the loony bin," he said, grinning at me. "That's why I need your help, Mark."

"Oh," I said. I was full of "ohs" that morning.

"I am writing a pilot script for a new TV series to be called 'The Masked Crusader,'" he said. "It will star the great Robert Saville, who is, as I daresay you know, a guest in this mink-lined hostelry of yours."

That was one thing I did know—that Robert Saville was a guest at the Beaumont—a suite on the nineteenth floor with half a dozen surrounding rooms for secretaries, valets, and other minions, including a doll who looked as though she did nothing at all efficient with her clothes on. Robert Saville is the current answer to filling the gap left when Clark Gable shuffled off this mortal coil. The difference between Gable and Saville is, I suspect, that Gable was a very decent guy, and Saville is a prize phony. He had already produced one headache for me. His secretary, a sensible-looking girl named Sally Bevans, had come to my office the day Saville checked in.

"It is to be clearly understood, Mr. Haskell," she said to me, "that Mr. Saville's presence at the Beaumont is to be a deep, dark secret. He's here to work with the producers, director, and writer on a film script. Let the word out that he's here, and he'll be swamped."

"By the common people?" I said.

Her smile was amiable. A wise young owl, I thought. "We are only talking to vice-presidents this week," she said.

The next day it was in all the newspapers—plus a couple of TV interviews—Robert Saville was in town, staying at the Beaumont. Our lobby suddenly looked like Grand Central Station at commuter time. I had to assume that Saville's Hollywood-studio promotion man had blown the story.

I ran into the unruffled and chic-looking Sally Bevans in the center of a swarm of screaming female teenagers in the lobby that afternoon.

"Don't blame me!" I shouted at her over the din.

"Title of a popular song," she said.

"Who did blow it?"

"The Master," she said.

"Saville himself?"

"He couldn't stand the loneliness," she said. "He's surrounded by a mere two dozen vice-presidents, and he couldn't stand the loneliness. . . ."

Norman Geller was grinning at me. "Interesting thing about Saville," he said. "Whenever you mention him, people always go into a kind of trance. If you were a girl, I'd know what you were remembering."

"So I'm not a girl, Norman," I said. "What can I do for you?"

"As I told you, I'm writing 'The Masked Crusader,'" Norman said. "It was my idea. I got paid money for it. I got paid money for what is called a treatment. I was then hired to write the shooting script, which means more money and royalties on the original run and all the reruns. Until about ten days ago I had dollar signs in place of eye pupils. Then things got rough. I am on the nineteenth rewrite now. You know why?"

"Why, Norman?"

"Because about fifty people have to get into the act. There's Saville, who has his own personal image about the Masked Crusader. There's the director, who thinks there should be a 'message.' There's the network vice-president for programming, and the network vice-president for development. There's Rachel Stanton, the leading lady, who has *her* image, and there is Walter Cameron, another writer waiting in the wings. And there is T. James Carson."

I knew that Thomas James Carson was the big wheel at the network. Just the other day the papers had reported he'd exercised a stock option that had netted him a million and a half.

"I get three-quarters of the way through the script," Norman said, "and there is suddenly mass hysteria. Hector Cross, VP for programming, thinks the last scene should come first. Paul Drott, VP for development, says the tease should be incorporated in the body of the script and I should think up a new tease. Karl Richter, the director, just looks at me, fish-eyed, and says, 'Where's the message, Norman? I mean you aren't *saying* anything, cookie.'

"Then Saville takes the version over to T. James Carson and insists on reading it aloud to him. Saville is worth so much money to the network and the movie studio that Carson has to listen. But he hates Saville for making him listen, and so he hates the script. 'Interesting, but it needs work—a lot of work.' 'Yes, sir, T.J. What kind of work?' T.J. will make notes when he has a free moment. Of course he doesn't have a free moment. And we're supposed to start shooting next Monday.

"Well, here's my situation, Mark. It's never going to be finished, see? They won't let me finish it. If I don't finish it, I lose a major portion of my rights in it. But I can't finish it. They hang around me like vultures. They snatch each page as it comes out of the typewriter. They come back with suggestions. 'This version is going to be it?' I ask them. 'Yes, Norman,' they say, 'this is it. You're a great guy, Norman, a wonderful guy, Norman, a genius, Norman. This will be *it.*' But they won't let me finish it."

"Sounds wild."

"I've *got* to finish it—and then they can go fly!" Norman said.

"So finish it."

"I need a hideout," Norman said. "That's why I came to you. I need a room here in the hotel that nobody knows about. I mustn't be registered. No phone calls. I want to stay hidden from five thousand vice-presidents and their five thousand private detectives."

"I think something could be arranged," I said.

"Bless you!" Norman said. "I need two uninterrupted days to finish the script—just two days."

I have an apartment down the hall from my office—living room, bedroom, kitchenette. I spend some time there and some time at a nice little garden apartment three blocks from the hotel occupied by my secretary, Shelda Mason. Shelda and I are "like that." Norman could have my apartment for two days without registering. I explained the setup to him, and he was delighted.

"Can I go there now?" he asked. "You could send someone to my room for my typewriter, the script, my razor, my slippers, and a clean shirt."

"It's a deal. You really don't want anyone to be able to reach you?"

"No one! I've been out on the town all night. There are four million messages for me in my mailbox. If there's anything really important, I'll call back. But no one is to reach me."

"Right. They'll call your room. There'll be no answer. You don't answer the phone in my room because it will be for me."

"Mark, you're a doll!"

I took Norman down the hall to my apartment. I fixed him up with a card table he could put his typewriter on. There was stuff in the kitchenette so that he could make coffee and eggs and a variety of sandwiches, so he wouldn't have to call room service. He was almost psychotic about being seen by anyone—word would get back to Saville and the vice-presidents . . .

I was getting some papers together for my morning session with the big boss when my telephone rang. I heard the calm voice of Sally Bevans, Robert Saville's secretary.

"I have to ask you a favor, Mr. Haskell," she said.

"Any time, any place, lady," I said.

"I know that joke," she said.

"I apologize. Just a figure of speech meant to imply a secret passion for you, Miss Bevans."

"This is serious," she said. "We've lost a writer."

"Well, well."

"His name is Norman Geller, registered in Room 1927. He's not there."

"How do you know?"

"Doesn't answer his phone. Hasn't picked up dozens of messages left at the desk for him. He's supposed to be working—matter of life and death, you might say. We have to have a shooting script by Monday. Mr. Saville became alarmed last night and got the housekeeper to open Room 1927 with a passkey. He wasn't there. The page in the typewriter is the same page he was writing late yesterday."

I'd forgotten to ask Norman how he'd spent his time "on the town."

"So he went out," I said.

"Going out is against the rules," Sally Bevans said, a slightly wry note in her voice. "I'm instructed to ask you to have the hotel security officer search the premises. Mr. Saville thinks Mr. Geller may have had a nervous breakdown. He fears suicide."

"And you?"

"I think he just couldn't take it anymore," Sally said. "The point is, if he doesn't finish the script, he's out more thousands of dollars than I can estimate. He may be dead drunk somewhere in the hotel."

"I'll turn the mice loose," I said. "If they come up with anything, I'll have Jerry Dodd call you. He's our security officer."

"Thank you, Mr. Haskell."

"Thank you, Miss Bevans. Would a very dry vodka martini in the Trapeze Bar about one o'clock interest you at all? Over a progress report?"

"It would interest me," she said, "but I'm afraid I'm chained to the chariot wheels."

I called Jerry Dodd and explained things. Norman was to be left unmolested. If Jerry was called by a vice-president or Miss Bevans or the great Saville or even T. James Carson, he was to say he was still looking.

I then called Johnny Thacker, the bell captain, explained the setup to him, and gave him a list of things Norman wanted from his room, with instructions to get them to my apartment as unobtrusively as possible.

The Masked Crusader could now, I felt certain, crusade for the next two days in peace.

Pierre Chambrun, resident manager of the Beaumont and my boss, is a real "original." As his name suggests, he is

French by birth. He came to this country as a very young man, went into the hotel business, and reached the pinnacle as manager of New York's top luxury hotel. The Beaumont, he often says, is not a hotel but a way of life. It is, in fact, like a small town, self-contained, self-sufficient, with its own shops and restaurants, its own police force, and its own "mayor."

Chambrun, short, dark, with very black eyes buried in deep pouches, has a genius for dealing with people, from the lowliest dishwasher to visiting royalty. His staff gives him an almost fanatical loyalty. He has the sense to delegate authority and the genius to be on hand in a crisis to shoulder the major responsibility. They say he has a special radar that tells him exactly where trouble is at the precise moment it happens. "When I don't know what's going on in my hotel," he has said, "it will be time for me to retire."

He didn't know about Norman Geller when I went into his office, but I told him. Anything out of the ordinary gets told, or else.

He was sitting at his carved Florentine desk in his very plush office, the walls decorated by two Picassos and a Chagall—not reproductions, you understand. He was sipping his inevitable demitasse cup of Turkish coffee. The coffee maker was on a sideboard and kept in constant operation by Miss Ruysdale, his indispensable secretary.

He listened with obvious amusement to my account of Norman's problems.

"Millions of dollars on the line for a piece of comic-strip literature. 'The Masked Crusader!' " He snorted, and then his eyes narrowed. "Saville is creating a problem, Mark. The lobby is a madhouse."

"You could ask him to leave," I said.

He frowned. "The network, the Hollywood crowd—important customers," he said. "If Saville wasn't such a vain ass—"

"The funny thing is he comes and goes at will without those silly girls even knowing it," Miss Ruysdale said. "He puts on a gray hairpiece, black glasses, black hat pulled down over his face, and has someone push him right through the crowd in a wheelchair. Who notices an old cripple? I watched him go out this morning, and no one paid the slightest attention. Down the block off comes the hat, the wig, and the glasses, and the magnificent Robert Saville parades down the Avenue. He's made arrangements at the corner drugstore for them to keep the chair for him. When he's ready, he comes back—in disguise."

"Loving every minute of it," Chambrun muttered. "I take it from your story, Mark, that we're going to have to put up with it until Monday?"

"That's when Norman's supposed to be finished," I said.

The buzzer on Chambrun's desk sounded. Johnny Thacker, the bell captain, was in the outer office. He was summoned into the Presence. He looked a little odd to me, as though he might have eaten something that didn't agree with him.

"You get my friend taken care off?" I asked.

"Yeah, I got the stuff to him," Johnny said. He moistened his lips. "There's something your friend didn't tell you, Mr. Haskell."

"Oh?"

"He didn't tell you there was a dead man in his clothes closet," Johnny said.

Norman's room was a mess: ashtrays overflowing, crumpled pieces of paper tossed around the floor, soiled shirts and underthings lying on the unmade bed. Evidently Norman had told the housekeeper he didn't want the maid in his room. Writer at work—DO NOT DISTURB.

Jerry Dodd, the Beaumont's security officer, was already in Room 1927 when Chambrun and I, with Johnny Thacker trailing, arrived. Johnny had done the proper thing, calling Jerry Dodd before he did anything else. Jerry is a slim, wiry man in his late forties, with dark eyes that are never still. He is another of the indispensables on Chambrun's highly efficient staff. The Beaumont has its problems like any other hotel—

deadbeats, drunks, expensive call girls who appear from time to time in the Trapeze Bar, professional hotel thieves who seldom get caught and amateurs who always get caught, suicides, heart attacks suffered by elderly gentlemen in the rooms of young ladies who are not their wives. There are births and normal deaths. And on at least a half dozen occasions in my time as PR director there have been violent deaths. Murder.

Jerry was standing by the open closet door when he came in. He looked around, his eyes bright and cold.

"Better not touch anything," he said. "I've called Homicide."

"That bad?" Chambrun asked.

"That bad," Jerry said. "Broken neck. Looks like he might have been karate chopped." He stepped away from the door so that we could see into the closet. A man was crumpled there, his body twisted into an unnatural position. There was almost a surprised look on the dead face.

"I know him," I heard myself say. "He lunches here three, four times a week. He's asked a favor or two of me on publicity releases. Talent agent name of Frank Hansbury. Handles actors, writers, directors—show-business people mostly."

"Handle your friend Geller?" Jerry asked.

"No idea. Hansbury's being here suggests—"

"It sure does," Jerry said. He turned to Chambrun. "I have a man stationed outside Mark's apartment, just in case Mr. Geller decides to take off."

"I think we better talk to your friend, Mark," Chambrun said.

"I'll join you when I get a man here to cover this room," Jerry said.

Chambrun and I went down to the second floor. Jerry's man was outside my door.

"All quiet," the man said. "He's in there typing away like mad."

I used my key to let us in. Norman, coatless, a cigarette

dangling from a corner of his mouth, was at the typewriter set up on the card table I'd provided. He looked up, frowning. When he saw Chambrun he groaned.

"Now what?" he said.

"Is Frank Hansbury your agent?" I asked him.

"He is, and a damn good one," Norman said. He glanced at Chambrun. "You're the manager, aren't you? You're not going to tell me there's some reason I can't work in Mark's apartment?"

"Are you on the outs with Hansbury?" Chambrun asked.

"He is my rod and my staff, my comforter," Norman said. "I love Frank. But will you please get this over with, whatever it is, so I can get back to—"

"Hansbury is in your room," Chambrun said.

"Who let him in?" Norman said.

"And he's dead," Chambrun said.

That really got to Norman. He stared at us as though he hadn't heard right. "You have to be kidding," he whispered.

"We think he's been murdered, Norman," I said.

"God Almighty, *how*?" Norman said.

"Our man thinks a karate chop to the back of the head," I said. "Broke his neck."

The ash fell from Norman's cigarette. He didn't notice it dribble down the front of his navy-blue shirt. "Geoffrey Cleghorn is a karate expert. Black belt," Norman said.

"Who is Geoffrey Cleghorn?" Chambrun asked, his voice sharp.

Norman started to laugh. There was an hysterical note to it. He waved at the page in his typewriter. "The Masked Crusader," he said.

There were little beads of sweat on Norman's forehead. "What a terrible thing," he said. "I talked to Frank only last night. He—"

"Where were you last night, Mr. Geller?" Chambrun said. "According to Mark you were 'out on the town.'"

"It doesn't matter where I was," Norman said. "I went to

see a friend—about six o'clock last night. I haven't been in my room since. When I came back this morning, I went straight to Mark's office."

"Who is the friend you went to see?" Chambrun asked.

"That's immaterial," Norman said.

"You're going to need an alibi, Mr. Geller."

"Now wait a minute—"

"You do research on the karate skills of your character, the Masked Crusader?"

"Well, sure. I had to know what I could expect him to be able to do. I took a few simple lessons—just to learn the basic techniques. But—"

"You are certainly going to need an alibi," Chambrun said.

Norman sat very still for a moment. Then he lit a fresh cigarette with hands that shook. "Is this official or am I talking to friends?" he asked.

I glanced at Chambrun.

"The police will be here shortly," Chambrun said. "That will be official. What would Hansbury be doing in your room, Mr. Geller? Did he have a key?"

"Not unless he got it from you," Norman said. He had made the decision to talk. "Frank was a very good friend as well as my agent. He knows all about the hell I've been going through with this pilot. Most of it's money hell. I'm supposed to get paid for each rewrite. I told Mark there have been nineteen. But none of them was actually finished—so the network is claiming this is still the first draft. Frank has been fighting them tooth and nail. He's got the Writers' Guild on his side. We've been trying to bypass all the vice-presidents and Saville and get to Carson himself. He's the big wheel at the network."

"So Hansbury came to your room to tell you he'd failed and you blew your stack and chopped him," Chambrun said.

"Oh, cut it out, will you?" Norman said. "I'm the fiction writer around here, Mr. Chambrun."

"So what did happen?"

"I talked to Frank just before I went out last night—around six. He was still in his office. He told me Saville was trying to keep us away from Carson. Saville owns a piece of this package and was afraid if we got to Carson the network might junk the whole project. Frank said he was still trying to set up an appointment with Carson for today. I told him I was going out—for the night. I needed a breather. I told him where he could reach me if it was absolutely necessary."

"Where?"

Norman leaned forward. "Look, Mr. Chambrun, I spent the night with a girl friend, and I'm not going to bring her into it."

"You may have to."

"Like hell I will!"

"Hansbury knew you were going to be with this girl?"

"Yes, and if it's necessary he can vouch—" Norman stopped, his mouth hanging open. Frank Hansbury wasn't going to vouch for anything.

"You're on your own, Mr. Geller," Chambrun said quietly.

Norman looked at me. "If I killed Frank in my room, why would I send you to get my things, Mark? You'd be bound to find the body. If I killed him—and I didn't—I'd make sure you didn't find the body for a couple of days."

"Why a couple of days?" Chambrun asked.

"So I could finish this damned script and get paid for it!" Norman said.

Chambrun sighed. "Let's be realistic, Norman," he said. "You didn't see or hear from Hansbury after you talked to him about six last night?"

"No."

"He didn't call you at your girl's apartment?"

"Not while I was there."

"Which is where?"

"No!" Norman said.

"In this TV project might Hansbury have come to the hotel to see someone else?"

"Sure, they're all here like vultures," Norman said. "Saville, a hatful of vice-presidents like Hector Cross and Paul Drott, Karl Richter the director. Frank could have come to see any of them about the appointment with Carson or about money. He wouldn't have come to my room, though, because he knew I was out."

"Could he have gone to your room to get the script? To make some point about it?"

"He'd know better. He'd know I'd clobber anyone who touched my script without my permission."

"Or karate chop anyone, Norman?"

"Will you cut that out!" Norman said.

Lieutenant Hardy looks more like a puzzled Notre Dame fullback than a Homicide detective. He's tall, square-jawed, a very tenacious and efficient police officer. We were lucky to have him on the case. He'd been in on a couple of other murders at the Beaumont, and he knew us—Chambrun in particular.

"What's your theory about your friend?" Hardy asked me.

We were in Chambrun's office. Hardy had been on the scene for about an hour, going over Norman's room with his technicians and their little vacuum cleaners, powders, brushes, cameras.

"I think not," I said.

"You, Chambrun?"

"If Geller killed Hansbury," Chambrun said, "he certainly didn't mean us *not* to pin it on him. You could say he actually sent us to his room to find the body. I noticed that bedroom slippers were on the list of things he wanted. That would take us right into the closet."

Hardy scowled at the notebook he was holding open in his big hand. "Preliminary report would indicate that Hansbury has been dead at least fifteen hours. Could be more, but not much less—an educated guesstimate by the medical examiner's man." Hardy looked at his wristwatch. "It's now five minutes to noon. That means Hansbury was probably killed around eight, nine o'clock last night. If he came here to see some of the rest of these people it's time we found out." He put away his notebook. "My wife is going to drive me crazy," he said.

"How so?"

"Robert Saville and Cary Grant are my chief rivals," he said drily.

It was the attractive Miss Bevans who answered our ring at the door of Robert Saville's suite. Her thinly penciled eyebrows rose in an expression of surprise when she saw us.

"You have news of Mr. Geller?" she asked me.

I introduced Chambrun and Hardy.

"Police!" she said. "Then something *has* happened to Norman?"

"I think we'd better come inside," Hardy said.

"I'm sorry, but Mr. Saville is in conference. If it's a matter of raising bail or something—"

"I'm sorry, Miss Bevans," Chambrun said. "A man named Frank Hansbury has been murdered. The lieutenant will have to talk to Mr. Saville, conference or no conference."

"Hansbury!" she said. It was a whisper. "How perfectly awful!"

We went into the suite's small foyer. In the room beyond we could hear excited voices, chief among them Robert Saville's pear-shaped tones projecting to the back row of the second balcony.

"I will *not* have a double for my tricks," Saville was blasting. "I will *not* be subjected to jokes about my not doing my own stunts. Therefore the stunts are going to have to be things I *can* do, Karl, and that's that!"

"You'd better let Norman in on the secret," a drawling voice said. "He's got a climbing sequence on the side of a building in the second scene that you just *can't* do, Bob. It's been agreed to from the very beginning. Maybe we'd better change the whole concept and call it 'Little Lord Fauntleroy Rides Again.' "

"You cheap son-of-a—" Saville shouted.

"Sticks and stones, Bobby," the other voice interrupted.

"Hansbury was here last night," Miss Bevans said at my elbow. "I simply can't believe it."

She opened the door, and we walked on stage.

Whatever kind of a jerk he may be in private life, Robert Saville, in the flesh, was impressive. He was tall, dark, with good character lines in his handsome face. His mouth had a weak, slightly pouting look to it, but all in all he exuded masculinity. In all honesty I think the Little Ford Fauntleroy crack was unwarranted. I knew he was an expert horseman, brilliant with fencing foils, and I'd heard he was beating the brains out of the squash pro each day in the courts on the roof of the hotel. He was tanned a beautiful bronze. Caught off guard, as he was when we walked into the room, he still managed an attitude of graceful elegance.

"Would you be good enough to explain this invasion, Sally," he said, looking at Chambrun, Hardy, and me as though we were three cigar-store Indians.

Sally introduced us. "Something dreadful has happened, Mr. Saville," she said. "They tell me Frank Hansbury has been murdered."

"I always knew that jerk would do us in, some way or other," Saville said.

I saw Chambrun's face go stony. He isn't fond of flippancy—unless he's responsible for it himself.

"You'll have to forgive Bobby for exposing his warm human emotions so openly," the blond man by the windows said. He was, I took it, Karl of the Fauntleroy crack—Karl Richter, the director of Norman's opus. He had a Germanic crewcut, and his thin lips were twisted in a sardonic smile. Not a very nice guy, I thought. He gestured toward his almost total opposite—a young man with black hair, worn rather long, who sat deep in an upholstered armchair, his face a blank. "The robot in the armchair is Paul Drott, gentlemen, a vice-president."

Hardy took charge. "Hansbury was found dead, his neck broken, in a closet in Norman Geller's room," he said. "Do the stunts you can do, Mr. Saville, include karate?"

Saville ignored the question. "Sally, call Walter Cameron, and tell him he's going to have to finish the script. Get Hector Cross here. He'll have to know. And tell him to keep it from Carson as long as he can. We don't want Carson flying off the handle till we know where we're at. And send George in here."

"Right away, Mr. Saville." Sally started for the next room.

"Just a moment," Hardy said. "I'm giving the orders here. I heard you say, Miss Bevans, that Hansbury was here last night."

"Of course he was here," Saville said. "He's Norman's agent. He's been in our hair ever since this project got under way. He was here last night before dinner, bellyaching about something or other." He made a sweeping gesture that took in the others. "I told you Norman was on the verge of a nervous breakdown. I told you we shouldn't keep all our eggs in one basket. Wally Cameron should have been working on this script long ago." He turned to Hardy. "Why did Norman kill him?"

"We don't know that Geller did kill him," Hardy said.

"Where is he? Have you found him?" Saville asked. "The little twerp has been missing since early last night. We have a mountain of notes for him, and he's not around. He deserted—powdered—ran out!"

"I understand you got yourself into his room last night," Hardy said.

"With a housekeeper—and Sally," Saville said. "We thought he might be sick when he didn't answer his phone."

"What time was that?"

Saville looked at Sally.

"About a quarter to ten," she said.

"Did you look in the closet?" Hardy asked.

"Why should we look in the closet?" Saville said. "You don't expect to find a writer in a closet, do you?"

"I ask because at a quarter to ten Hansbury was dead and probably in that closet," Hardy said.

"Oh, God!" Sally said.

"When you find Norman, you'll find the answers," Saville said.

"We know where Geller is," Hardy said. "We'll ask him in good time."

"Well, where is he? I've got to talk to him, Lieutenant. The whole beginning of scene three is wrong. He's probably working on it right now."

"What makes you think he's working?"

"That's what he's being paid for!" Saville said.

"I think," Chambrun said in a saw-toothed voice, "I've had about enough of this black comedy, Mr. Saville. A man has been murdered in my hotel. The lieutenant and I are here to gather facts."

"Where is George?" Saville shouted, completely ignoring Chambrun.

"On stage, professor," a new voice said.

The man who came through the bedroom section of the suite was something you wouldn't believe. He was about two inches over six feet with a body right out of Bernarr McFadden's dream world. Muscles, muscles, muscles. He wore a tight cotton T-shirt that exposed them all. There were also gray slacks and white sneakers. This was a man who could bend iron bars and straighten out horseshoes.

"This is my lawyer, George Brimsek," Saville said. "He'll tell me what I have to do and not do."

Brimsek's hair was a reddish crewcut, and he had the coldest gray-green eyes I've ever seen. His smile was pasted on.

Sally made quick introductions and brought him up to date. As Brimsek listened, his biceps rippled. I discovered in due course that he really was a lawyer, but his only client was Robert Saville, and his chief duty was to keep Saville in top physical condition. It was his job to lose to Saville in any public competition—golf, tennis, squash, boxing, foils. The truth was he could have taken Saville in any sport with his right arm tied behind him.

"I think you better answer the man's questions, Bob," he

said. "They can make you do it somewhere else less pleasant, you know." He turned to Hardy. "Do I understand you know where Geller is?" It hadn't been mentioned in his presence, so I assumed he'd been listening from the next room.

"We know where he is," Hardy said. "I want to know about Hansbury's visit to this suite last night."

"That's reasonable," Brimsek said. "He showed up here about seven o'clock. We were just going down to the Grill Room for dinner. I was here, Bob, Sally, and—and you too, weren't you, Paul?"

The vice-president nodded. He seemed to be still in shock.

"There was a lot of shouting," Brimsek said, his smile tightening. "That's been more or less par for the course in our dealings with Hansbury. He has been claiming that Norman was entitled to certain payments for various drafts of the script he's writing. Since there has never been a single completed draft, we claim he's only entitled to payment for that initial draft. Hansbury called us a bunch of crooks and threatened to go to Carson with the whole story. We said he was a chiseling little rat trying to blackmail us. When all that had been said, we went down to dinner."

"And Hansbury?"

"We left him here. It was the only way to get rid of him since he wouldn't accept our invitation to leave. The last I saw of him he was trying to reach Norman on the phone—I assumed."

"Assumed?"

"He was dialing. He had told us he was going to tell Norman not to write another line. I gather he went to see Norman, they got in an argument, and Hansbury got his neck broken. Norman's very good at karate. I know. I taught him."

"You all went to dinner—you, Miss Bevans, Mr. Saville, and Mr. Drott—leaving Hansbury here?" Hardy looked around and got a collection of affirmative nods.

"Dinner was pretty impossible," Brimsek said. "Bob couldn't swallow a shrimp without having to sign his autograph. We came back up here about eight-thirty."

"Hansbury was gone?"

Brimsek nodded. "Gone, leaving a cigarette burn on the telephone table. We began trying to reach Norman then. Bob and Paul had notes for him. He didn't answer. We kept trying. At about a quarter to ten Bob and Sally got the housekeeper to let them into Norman's room. We thought he might be sick or had done himself some harm. Bob's quite right, he was on the verge of a nervous breakdown. Norman wasn't there, so that was that. We went out to find some action somewhere."

"Action?"

Brimsek shrugged. "Bob likes to play poker," he said.

"You went out through the mob in the lobby?"

Brimsek grinned. "We have a way."

"The wheelchair," Chambrun said.

"Oh, so you spotted that," Brimsek said.

"There are four keys to this suite," Chambrun said. "None of them is at the front desk. Who has them?"

"That's none of your damn business!" Saville exploded.

"Might as well tell him, Bob," Brimsek said. "He'll find out." He was being uncommonly cooperative, I thought. "Bob has one, of course. I have one. Sally has one."

"And the fourth?"

Brimsek shrugged. "Sheri has one," he said.

"Who is Sheri?" Hardy asked.

"Miss Sheri Southworth," Brimsek said. "She's a lady companion of Bob's who stays here with him."

"When you rent a suite you can have anyone stay with you you want," Saville said.

"Miss Southworth lives in his suite?" Hardy said.

"Yes."

"Where is she?"

"She's in bed. She's got a bad cold," Saville said.

"Was she here last night?"

"Of course."

"You didn't mention her going to dinner with you."

"I tell you she's got a virus!" Saville said. "She was sick in bed."

"In this suite?"

"Yes, yes, yes!"

"Then she probably knows when Hansbury left. I'd like to talk to her," Hardy said.

"*She's sick in bed!*" Saville shouted.

"Ask her to join us," Hardy said.

Brimsek nodded to Sally, who left to find Sheri.

"We all have our special tastes in women," Karl Richter said. "Bob is neither a romantic nor an intellectual. He just likes them."

Brimsek looked down at his bulging biceps with an amused grin.

If Miss Sheri Southworth had a cold or virus, it was not noticeable. What she did have was a gorgeous shiner. Her left eye was purple and swollen shut. She looked around at us with an amiable grin and said, "I'd really rather switch than fight."

She was something. The blond hair was out of a bottle; the eyelashes were false; ditto the long tapering fingernails. The only things not false were revealed by her negligee.

"Oooh, look at all the lovely men," she said.

"Shut up, Sheri!" Saville barked.

"There has been a murder, Miss Southworth," Hardy said.

"Oooh, how thrilling!" Sheri said. "Anybody I know?"

"Frank Hansbury. Somebody broke his neck," Saville said.

"I understand you were alone with Hansbury in this suite for a while last night, Miss Southworth," Hardy said.

"That Frank Hansbury!" Sheri said. Her gold-tipped fingers touched her swollen eye. "He was only here a little while. On the phone all the time. He was too busy to be interested in me. I came in here for a cigarette, and he didn't even look at me." She touched her eye again, then looked at Saville with her good one. "I behaved myself, Bobby."

"Will you shut up, Sheri!" Saville yelled.

"Can you tell us what time Hansbury left here?" Hardy asked.

"Ooooh, I'm afraid not, Lieutenant," she said. "I really have no sense about time at all. Bobby and the others were downstairs at dinner."

"Do you have any idea who he was talking to on the phone?"

"I'm afraid I don't. I mean, he wasn't really talking to anyone. He kept dialing numbers, but he didn't get any answers. One number did answer, I guess, and he said, 'Is Norman there yet?' But I guess Norman wasn't, because he hung up. Then I went back to my room, closed the door, and I didn't hear when he left."

Hardy drew a deep breath. "You will all keep yourselves available till I tell you otherwise. Don't leave the hotel till you get the word from me."

"Now look here, copper—" Saville began.

"Cool it, Bob," Brimsek said. "The lieutenant can hold us all as material witnesses if he chooses. He's being real polite."

"What about me?", Karl Richter said. "I wasn't even in the hotel last night."

"You stay too," Hardy said.

"Any reason I shouldn't go downstairs for a drink?" Richter asked. "I have a batch of phone calls to make—private."

"You can use my office," Chambrun said.

I was surprised, but I didn't show it. I noticed, as I was leaving, that Paul Drott was getting up out of his chair. He hadn't spoken a word during our entire visit.

Out in the hall Chambrun turned to Karl Richter. "You wanted to tell us something, Mr. Richter?"

Richter's cold face was a mask. "You're smarter than I thought you were, Mr. Chambrun." We were standing by the elevators. He took a cigarette out of his pocket and lit it. "Our Bobby's private life is rather unusual," he said. "Can you guess how it is with Sheri? She is—shall we say friendly?—to his friends, and for that he beats her up."

"I'm sure that isn't what you really wanted to tell us," Chambrun said coldly.

"I enjoyed telling it to you, anyway," Richter said. "But you're right. I wanted to tell you that people like Bob Saville live in a world you may not understand. This is an ordinary guy from upstate New York—Utica, I think. He came from a middle-class family with no dough. He wanted to be an actor, genuinely. He went to an acting school, worked at anything—dishwashing, waiting on tables, night watchman. He got a few odd jobs off-Broadway. A real dedicated guy. Then he hit it big.

"Do you know what he gets for making a movie? Half a million bucks—plus residuals, plus advertising payoffs, plus a share of profits. This TV series, if it sells, will make him several million dollars. He's so damned rich, you couldn't begin to count it. And he's no longer the dedicated young actor from Utica. He's king! If anybody gets in his way, like a writer or a director or a dame or a shoeshine boy—or a talent agent—our Bobby just rolls over him and leaves the remains for the dustman. To him it's unreasonable to imagine that anyone else has any rights. The world is a special-privilege oyster made only for him; none of its rules or laws apply to him. He's not a bad guy, really, but he's lost contact with reality."

"Are you trying to tell us—" Hardy began.

"I'm trying to tell you that, if a waiter brought Bob a cold poached egg, Bob might easily throw him out of the nineteenth-story window. Then he'd turn to George Brimsek and say, 'I lost my head. I'm sorry. Get me out of it.' Up to now George has always gotten him out of it. Don't let the muscles fool you. There is more between George's ears than mush."

An elevator door opened, and we all stepped in. Chambrun turned to me as the car started down. "There's very little hope this story won't leak," he said. "You're going to be swamped by news people, Mark. As far as you know Hansbury died of a heart attack in Norman's room. The presence of the police is ordinary routine. If there are any statements to be made,

Lieutenant Hardy will make them. Have a simple release mimeoed and just hand it out."

I got off at the second floor.

If somebody broke my neck and stuffed me in a closet, the interested parties would be limited. I have no family. Shelda, my secretary, would cry. Chambrun would feel depressed, I think. The police would be concerned, and so would my insurance company.

Hansbury's death touched many more bases, all of them with red-hot publicity angles. There were huge investments on the line. If Robert Saville was in any way involved, his motion picture company stood to lose about $12,000,000 in as yet unreleased films. The network had a penny-ante investment of $250,000 in this pilot of Norman's, plus residuals on other shows, plus half a dozen old Saville movies bought for the late late shows at about $3,000,000 each. This was all real money, plus many other millions they had reasonably expected to make off Saville in the future.

As I sat in my office writing out the phony news release, I could imagine what was going on in a dozen offices here and on the West Coast. Robert Saville must be kept clean at all costs. To hell with who murdered Frank Hansbury, so long as Saville's public image remained unsullied. I knew the Beaumont would suddenly be swarming with high-priced lawyers, high-priced executives, and in all probability, high-priced private investigators.

Nobody would give a damn about Hansbury—no one except a family or a girl or maybe a dog waiting in an apartment somewhere for his evening walk.

And then I began to think about Norman—once known as "little Norbert Gellernacht." Norman's position was sticky, to put it mildly. Hardy would be down on him presently with some pretty deadly ammunition. The scene of the crime—Norman's room, undoubtedly loaded with Norman's fingerprints. The relationship with Hansbury—possibly friendly, quite probably explosive at the moment. The murder weapon—the edge of a hand, precision-skilled. Norman had that skill. He had admitted it. George Brimsek had modestly claimed the role of teacher.

I had a vision of little Norbert Gellernacht sitting under a bright light, surrounded by the accusing faces of Hardy and high-powered lawyers and vice-presidents and even presidents. Norman was ideal guillotine fodder. Norman might well save the huge investments in Robert Saville. Who cares what happens to a writer? Writers are the "nothings" of the entertainment industry, even though the executives keep wistfully chanting that there would be no films, no television, no theater without them. Everybody knows it's actors and directors and executives and vice-presidents who matter.

I went down the hall to my apartment. Believe it or not, I found Norman pounding away at the typewriter when I let myself in with my key. He gave me a slightly irritated smile and went right on pounding.

"Norman," I said, "you're in trouble."

"Be a good boy, Mark, and leave me alone," Norman said. "At this moment Geoffrey Cleghorn, the Masked Crusader, is crossing Fifth Avenue hand over hand on a rope stretched ten stories above the street."

"That's out," I said. "Saville refuses to have any stunts in the script that he can't do himself."

Norman's fingers halted, poised over the keyboard. "Where did you get that?"

"I just heard him say so."

"That punk! It's been agreed from the start that we'd use a stunt man."

"Norman, have you forgotten that Frank Hansbury has been murdered?"

"I haven't forgotten," he said quite seriously. "But the only thing I know to do is finish this script. It means money for me, and money for Frank's estate. His commission."

"Does Hansbury have a family?"

"Divorced. No kids," Norman said, looking back at Geoffrey Cleghorn suspended over Fifth Avenue.

I made what I thought was a joke, because it was the worst thing I could think of. "I don't suppose the girl you spent the night with was Hansbury's ex-wife."

Norman looked up at me, frowning. "I don't know how you found out, Mark, but if you tell anyone I'll break your neck."

I felt a cold chill running down my back. "Norman," I said, "don't use that phrase again."

"What phrase?"

"'I'll break your neck.' There are people who already think you did that to Hansbury."

"Don't be absurd. Frank was my best friend."

"And you were living with his wife?"

"She isn't his wife, Mark. They're divorced."

"And he didn't care?"

"Of course he didn't care. I told you that I told Frank where I was going last night. He even called me there."

"I thought you said you didn't see or hear from him after six o'clock," I said.

"I didn't! He called Gillian before I got there."

That, I thought, would be the phone call that Sheri had heard Hansbury make. "Norman, unless I'm very wrong, you're going to be set up as a fall guy. You'd better forget about 'The Masked Crusader' and start thinking about yourself."

"Who's going to set me up?"

"Quite a lot of people who think of Robert Saville as the equivalent of the gold deposit in Fort Knox," I said. "You've just wrapped up the package. You're a karate expert. You knew how to break Frank's neck. You told him you were going to spend the night with his wife, and he came up to your room to raise hell about it. You chopped him. Opportunity, motive, weapon."

"You're off your rocker, Mark."

"They all say you were on the verge of a nervous breakdown."

"Oh, come on, Mark! Do I look as if I were on the verge of a nervous breakdown?"

"No. And that in itself is suspicious, Norman. The way things are, you *ought* to look like it." I lit a cigarette and my hands weren't too steady. "If Hansbury didn't come to your room to see you, how did he get in there? Did he have a key?"

"Nobody had a key. I was keeping people out so I could work, not inviting them in. Frank didn't come to my room while I was there."

"Then how did he get in?"

"You've got me, Mark. You've been in the room. Were there any signs of a fight there?"

"Only between you and your typewriter," I said.

"Maybe somebody brought him there and stuffed him in the closet after he was dead," Norman said. He looked at me, his eyes widening. "Maybe somebody *is* trying to frame me!"

"I think you can classify that suggestion with the Gettysburg Address for sheer literary clarity," I said. "Norman, you're up to your neck in trouble."

I left Norman and went down to see Chambrun. What I wanted to tell him and ask him had to wait because Lieutenant Hardy was there.

We have a private card file at the Beaumont that lists special information about our guests—their financial status, marital situation, any personal habits worth knowing like whether the guest is an alcoholic or a patron of call girls or an addicted gambler or troublemaker of a special sort. This information is handled by a simple code—A for alcoholic, D for diplomat, O for over-his-head, meaning the guest can't really afford the Beaumont's prices and mustn't be allowed to get in too deep. MX after a man's name means he's a woman chaser double-crossing his wife. WX after a female guest means she's a man-chaser, double-crossing her husband. N stands for general nuisance, a complainer who has no basis for his complaints.

Hardy was going through a little collection of cards that covered Saville and his entourage. That, I guessed, would include Norman.

Chambrun sat at his desk, his hooded eyes half closed. "You will notice," he said, "that the network is paying the bills for everyone. Saville's company may be sharing the cost, but that's not our concern."

"These people just turn on the money faucet and watch it go down the drain," Hardy said.

"The world of expense accounts," Chambrun commented wryly.

Hardy looked at me. "How close are you to your friend Geller?" he asked.

"Not close at all. I haven't seen him since college, and we were just nodding acquaintances there."

"Then you don't really have any reason to believe in him?"

"Not on a buddy-buddy basis," I said. "But the whole thing so far is just too pat for me to swallow, Lieutenant. I've just been talking to him. I'd swear he was innocent—too damned innocent."

"Meaning?"

"That he's been set up as a prize pigeon. These people would do anything to keep Saville off the hook. You heard Richter. My guess is somebody got in a row with Hansbury—maybe Saville, maybe his muscular lawyer. Both of them play karate games. Maybe Hansbury took a swing at somebody and was chopped down. Not planned, not intentional—but murdered. So what to do? If it was me I'd go to the police, admit I had a row with Hansbury, tell them he took a swing at me and that I clobbered him. Self-defense. The worst that would happen would be a manslaughter charge. I might get away with it.

"But Saville can't risk that. Juries sometimes have a way of being rough on a celebrity. The notoriety could cost a lot of people a lot of money. So Saville and Company take the first out that comes to mind. They know Norman isn't in his room down the hall—they'd been trying to reach him. They drag the dead man down there and stuff him in the closet—and leave Norman to face the music when he gets back."

"So answer me three questions," Hardy said.

"Try me."

"This had to be before eight-thirty in evening."

"Why?"

"That's when Saville and Miss Bevans and Brimsek and Drott came back upstairs from dinner. Are you suggesting all four of them would be covering up a murder?"

"It's not impossible."

"Five of them, to be exact," Hardy said. "The tootsie was in the Saville suite too."

"I still say it's not impossible."

"Busy time of night in the hotel. People coming and going. Have you figured the risk involved in carrying a dead man even a few yards down the corridor?"

"They had to risk it."

"Nobody pays much attention to a couple of men handling a drunken friend," Chambrun said, his eyes closed.

"Okay," Hardy said drily. "So we have five people in on a conspiracy. The body is moved by acting as though he's a drunk. Now, your friend Geller says he spent the night with a girl. He'll produce her if he has to. How do these conspirators know he hasn't got a perfect alibi?"

"They have to risk that too," I said.

"Boy, they sure do!" Hardy said. "If he doesn't have an alibi what would his motive be? Hansbury, he says, was his best friend."

My mouth felt dry. I knew what the motive could seem to be, and I knew Norman might not be able to produce an alibi without simultaneously producing a motive.

"They've been trying to set it up for you," I said. "Nervous breakdown. Unendurable work pressures. They quarreled over Hansbury's failure to get Norman paid for the work he'd done. Another slight case of manslaughter."

"Why don't they let friend Norman in on it, then?" Hardy

asked. "Pay him a nice chunk of dough to take the rap—maybe a year or two in jail. From what I hear, that would be an easier way to make a big hunk of money than writing television pilots."

"And let Norman blackmail them for the rest of their lives?"

Hardy's eyes were cold. "Is your friend the blackmailing type? No, don't answer me, Haskell. You don't know. You'd only be guessing." He stood up and started for the door. "The more I try to involve an army of people in this murder, the better I like my chances of pinning it on one single guy—on your friend Geller. His room, he had the know-how, and we'll find the motive. See you around."

Chambrun sat motionless in the big armchair behind his desk. He didn't lift his heavy eyelids when Hardy had gone. But one corner of his mouth moved in a wry smile.

"You are perhaps the worst actor I have ever seen in my life, Mark," he said. "Only a Hardy could have missed the fact that you're bursting with information that will do your friend Norman's case no good at all."

"You mind if I pour myself a drink?" I said. "I missed my usual midday martini."

"Help yourself."

I went over to the sideboard and poured myself a stiff Scotch on the rocks. Chambrun lit one of his Egyptian cigarettes and looked at me through a haze of smoke, as I swallowed most of my drink at one tilt. I came around to the chair beside his desk and sat down.

"This is how it is," I said.

I told him that Norman had spent the night with Gillian Hansbury, Frank Hansbury's ex-wife. That Hansbury knew he was planning just that. If Mrs. Hansbury came forward to supply Norman with an alibi, she would also supply Hardy with a twenty-four-carat motive.

"Maybe not," Chambrun said slowly. "Your friend Norman told us he took off from his room about six o'clock. We know Hansbury was alive at seven, or a little after. He was in Saville's suite making phone calls. If Norman was already at Mrs. Hansbury's—"

"He wasn't. A call came there from Hansbury before Norman arrived."

Chambrun flicked the ash from his cigarette. "Why do you care what happens to Norman?" he asked.

"I'm the chump of all time when it comes to lost causes and underdogs," I said. "And I hate power plays from modern monsters like Saville and Company."

"You're a nice boy, Mark," Chambrun said. "Why not go have a chat with Mrs. Hansbury?"

"Norman would never forgive me."

"Would you care—if it cleared him?"

Mrs. Gillian Hansbury was listed in the phone book. She lived on the East Side in the Eighties. I debated calling her to ask if I could talk to her, but then it occurred to me she might get in touch with Norman in some fashion and they'd be ready with a prepared story for me. I wanted to talk to this woman without her being too well balanced.

I don't recall now that I had any particular picture of what Gillian Hansbury might be like as I rode uptown in a taxi. The woods are full of youngish divorcees living on generous alimony who take love where they can find it. It takes a while for a suddenly single girl to develop a whole new social circle. I realized I'd forgotten to ask Norman how long the Hansburys had been separated. If it was fairly recent, Hansbury's reaction to Norman's teaming up with Gillian could be quite unpredictable.

I think I expected an attractive, probably chic, somewhat hard-boiled gal to answer my ring at the doorbell.

I was accurate about part of it. Gillian Hansbury was rather special to look at: natural red hair, almost violet eyes, a lush figure. She was wearing a shift that stopped about five inches above her knees. A sophisticated, expensive girl-executive type, possibly a former model or an actress. Frank Hansbury had been a talent agent. They could have met professionally.

Before she spoke, after opening her front door tentatively, I saw that she had been crying.

"Yes?" Her voice was pleasantly husky.

"Mrs. Hansbury?"

"Yes."

"My name is Mark Haskell," I said. "I'm a friend of Norman Geller's."

"You're the man at the hotel," she said. She opened the door a little wider. "Come in if you like, Mr. Haskell."

I stepped into a small attractive living room with a wood-burning fireplace. There were many books and a few undistinguished oil paintings that might, I thought, be her own work. On a low table in front of the orange-covered couch was a stale-looking cup of coffee. A silver ashtray was overflowing with butts. The place smelled nice—like a woman.

"Norman sent you?" she asked. "Please sit down."

"He doesn't know I'm here," I said.

Her bright red mouth tightened slightly.

"I want to help Norman," I said. "He's in grave difficulty, and he won't help himself."

"Poor Norman," she said. She sat down on the couch, and I found it difficult not to look at her lovely legs. "I told him he wouldn't be able to retain his sanity if he kept on writing that television script. I've seen writers go into that Waring Mixer too often."

"His troubles at the moment aren't primarily concerned with the TV script," I said.

She looked rather intently at the ashes in the fireplace. "It's been a rugged day for both of us," she said. "Norman and Frank were very close. And I—" Her voice shook a little. She reached for a cigarette in a lacquered box on the table. I held my lighter for her. Her long lashes were faintly damp. She was fighting tears again.

"Norman's in a kind of a two-way bind," I said. "I take it you could provide him with an alibi for last night. He may need it,

Gillian. On the other hand, if you give it to him, you may provide the police with the one thing they need—motive."

She looked back at me, her eyes widening. "Motive for what?"

"At the moment Homicide looks at Norman as their number-one suspect," I said.

"They think *he* killed Frank?"

"They think he may have. They don't know yet about Norman's relationship with you. That would just about sew it up for them."

"How utterly ridiculous!" she said.

"I hope so."

"As far as the alibi is concerned, of course I'll provide it if he needs it," Gillian said. "He got here a little after eight last night, and he left here after breakfast this morning."

I reached for a cigarette of my own. I felt little needles along my spine. "I understood Norman left the hotel around six o'clock last night," I said.

"I suppose he may have," Gillian said. "He's staying at the Beaumont because the TV people insist on his being available twenty-four hours a day. But he has an apartment of his own just off Gramercy Park. He went there to pick up mail and get some clean clothes before he came here."

"He told you that?"

"Of course. He phoned me that he'd had it up to his ears and was going to take the night off. That was around six o'clock. He told me he'd get here when he caught up with whatever he found at his apartment. It was a little after eight when he got here." She shook her head. "I don't understand why Norman's relationship with me would supply the police with a motive."

"You were Hansbury's wife," I said. "Hansbury may have objected to Norman's being here. He evidently knew Norman was coming here last night. The police will assume they quarreled about it, and Norman, who has been doing research on karate, chopped him down. Hansbury did know Norman was coming here. He tried to phone Norman here, didn't he?"

"Yes. About an hour before Norman got here."

"Was he angry?"

"Frank?" She laughed, and it had a hurt sound to it. "He was angry because he couldn't find Norman, but not because Norman might have been here. He couldn't have cared less."

I took a deep drag on my cigarette. "How long have you and Hansbury been divorced, Gillian?"

"Three years," she said.

"Did he have another girl?"

"Girls," she said, tight-lipped. "Girls—plural."

"That was the difficulty? Other women?"

"Frank's business brings him into constant contact with a long stream of glamour," she said. "He should never have married me or anyone else. I should have known it, but I—"

"You were in love with him?"

"God help me."

"But it was all over."

"For Frank," she said.

"And you, too. I mean, there is Norman—"

"Norman is a very sweet guy," she said. She put out her half-smoked cigarette with rather elaborate punchings into the ashtray. "He became a client of Frank's about six months before we were divorced. Norman sympathized with me. He knew I was the one who was hurt. He used to drop around once a week or so for almost a year—just to see how I was. A good friend. He took me to dinner or the theater once in a while. That was all. Then—"

She drew a deep breath and went on. "Then one night we went to an opening and sat around with friends at Sardi's waiting for the reviews. It was a hit, and we all got a little high. Norman brought me home early in the morning and—well, I was grateful to him, and it was about time I—I started to think about living again. That's when it began. Not a love affair, but a pleasant sort of now-and-then thing. That's all it's ever been, Mark."

She looked around the room. "It's saved me from being mauled and clawed and slobbered over by half the wolves in town. Norman has supplied me with what I needed to stay on some kind of an even keel. And I think I've supplied Norman with something that's made him happy without any chains, rules, or obligations."

"And Hansbury didn't care?"

"He didn't care," she said, her voice unsteady. "I see him—I've seen him from time to time. He invites me to lunch, all very gay, very casual, very civilized. He teased me about Norman. Three or four times—" She stopped.

"Yes?" I said.

"Frank had to keep all the bases touched," she said bitterly. "I think he went back to every woman he'd ever made love to, periodically, just to reassure himself that he was irresistible. Three or four times he came back to me, and God help me, I played his game. I helped to reassure him. I guess I'm the kind of nitwit who can only fall really in love once. I guess I used to dream that I'd be so fantastically wonderful that he'd come back to me and stay."

She looked away. "I must not have been." Then she looked straight at me. "You must have noticed that I'd been crying just before you came in. You see—you see, in spite of everything, I loved that miserable two-timer. Only three nights ago—oh, God, Mark!"

She broke down into uncontrolled weeping. She got up and hurried into what I assumed was the bedroom. I felt a little uncomfortable, as though she'd told me more than she meant to. I found myself thinking of the late Frank Hansbury in just the terms she applied to him—a miserable two-timer. You didn't play put-and-take with a girl like Gillian. How what she'd told me affected Norman's position, I wasn't quite sure. Certainly Hansbury hadn't given a damn what happened to Gillian, except as it satisfied his own ego. If she had to, Gillian could make it quite clear that Hansbury would have had no reason to be jealous of or to quarrel with Norman over her.

She came back from the other room, the ravages of tears skillfully repaired. She held her lovely head high and proud.

"I apologize, Mark," she said. "I told you things I couldn't even tell Norman because I—I had to, somehow. I had to tell someone, just once. But now let's think how we can help Norman. If he needs the alibi, of course I'll provide it. And I think I can convince your policemen that I'm the last thing in the world they'd have quarreled about. You and I know that Norman couldn't possibly kill anybody. He's a gentle, sweet nice guy. But there are other people in the picture who aren't."

"The fantasy world of Robert Saville," I said.

"Which is also the fantasy world of Thomas James Carson and his vice-presidents and George Brimsek and Karl Richter. The other night, when Frank was here—" She hesitated, color coming into her pale cheeks, then went on. "The other night Frank told me a good deal about things. We always used to talk shop in the old days. I know things about the great T. James Carson and his vice-presidents and Bob Saville and Brimsek and all the others that would curl your hair.

"And Frank knew a great deal more than I do, Mark. He once said to me, joking, that if he found himself doing badly as a talent agent, he could turn blackmailer and become a millionaire." She frowned and reached for a cigarette. "Frank was in a real mess with all of them over this job of Norman's. They were blandly trying to cheat Norman out of a lot of money. The first thing I thought, when I heard about Frank, was that in the heat of an argument he'd threatened someone with one of his special little tidbits and there'd been an explosion."

"What kind of things do you know about them?" I asked.

"My things are nothing," she said. "Gossip about affairs, who's queer, who's virile, who's not. What Frank had was real stuff—business deals that won't bear scrutiny, blacklistings that would outrage the public if they became known, tax dodges that wouldn't stand investigation, under-the-table bribes to city officials, stuff in the small print of contracts that quietly crucifies decent people. If Frank aimed one of those guns at someone in an argument—" She shrugged.

The telephone rang, and she reached out to the side table and answered it. She looked at me.

"For you," she said.

Only one person in the world knew where I was. Chambrun's voice sounded cold-angry.

"Any luck?" he asked.

"Maybe."

"You'd better get back here on the double," he said. "Someone tried to throw your friend Norman out the window of your apartment."

"Tried?" I said.

"Norman's pretty badly shaken up, but all right."

"Who was it?"

"Stocking mask over his face," Chambrun said. His tone was bitter. "Maybe it was the Masked Crusader. He got away."

It was about five when Pierre Chambrun phoned me. It seems that about quarter past four, while I'd been sitting talking to Gillian, the red light on the switchboard flickered, indicating that the receiver had been lifted in my rooms. The operator plugged in with the standard, "Yes, please."

No one spoke, but she heard a kind of muffled gasping, then suddenly a man's voice, some distance from the instrument, shouted, "Help!" The switchboard girl signaled Mrs. Veach, the chief operator, who also plugged in, listened, and instantly put in an emergency call to Jerry Dodd. By some miracle she found him on her first ring to his office.

"There's some kind of struggle going on in Room 209," Mrs. Veach told Jerry. "Phone must have been knocked over, and we can hear what sounds like fighting—and a man calling for help. It's Mr. Haskell's apartment—"

Jerry didn't wait to hear what Mrs. Veach thought. His own office was in the lobby. He flagged Johnny Thacker, the bell captain, as he raced from the elevators. It was only three or four minutes from the time the cry for help had come over the wire until Jerry and Johnny burst into my apartment.

The living room was a shambles. The card table with Norman's typewriter on it had been overturned. The big overstuffed armchair lay on its back. The telephone on the end table by the couch was on the floor, the receiver off its cradle. The window overlooking the street was wide open. I think I've said it was a brisk fall day, and by that time in the afternoon the wind through the curtains had a touch of winter's chill in it.

Sprawled in a sitting position under the window, on the floor, was Norman. A little trickle of blood ran out of one corner of his mouth. He looked at Jerry, glassy-eyed as a fighter who has been down for the count. The front of his shirt was ripped and Jerry could see an ugly scratch on his chest, as if he'd been clawed.

Johnny Thacker closed the window, and between them they helped Norman to his feet and over to the armchair, which Jerry had righted.

"What happened, Mr. Geller?" Jerry asked.

Johnny Thacker put the phone back on its cradle, ending Mrs. Veach's participation.

Norman moved his head from side to side gingerly, as if he wasn't sure it was still attached to his neck. "Some lunatic barged in here—kind of stocking mask pulled over his head—just charged at me. I—I wasn't ready for him—He dragged me over to the window—got it open and started to heave me out."

My rooms are on the second floor, but the second floor is four levels above the street. You don't get up and walk from that height.

"I—I know a little about karate," Norman said. "I just did manage to clip him one in the throat, and that sent him back away from me, choking. I tried to make it to the door, but he was on me like a wildcat. I had half a chance now because I was ready, but he was no dummy. He knew the holds too.

You—you can see." He waved around the room. "I threw him once, and that knocked the telephone loose. I figured I wasn't going to make it, so I started yelling for help, hoping the operator would hear me."

"She did. That's how we got here," Jerry said.

"He pulled me over by the window again," Norman said. "I managed to get in a good kick to his kneecap. I could hear him gasp with pain, and he staggered back. I saw the counter-punch coming to my windpipe, and I managed to tuck in my chin. His punch was like the kick of a mule, and I went down—partly out, I guess. The next thing—you were coming through the door."

Jerry did all the right things. He notified Chambrun and sent for Doc Partridge, the house physician. He ordered Johnny to stop handling things in the room. He got a wet towel for Norman to use on his cut mouth and scratched chest.

Chambrun and Hardy arrived together in a few minutes, during which time Norman wasn't able to contribute anything more to Jerry. His description of the man was vague—big, powerfully built, strong hands, reasonably gifted in the techniques of karate. He had no look at all at the stocking-covered face.

Chambrun was solicitous. "You're not badly hurt, Norman?"

"Nothing broken—I think," Norman said. "I'm one solid ache, I don't mind saying."

"How did he get in?" Hardy asked.

"Through the door. I was sitting at my typewriter, and he just barged in."

"Door wasn't locked?"

"Of course it was locked," Norman said. His eyes widened. "Sure it was locked. I was keeping people out of here. That's a joke, son."

"Did you hear someone turning a key in the lock?" Hardy asked.

"No-o," Norman said. "But I was typing pretty steadily—

redoing a page of dialogue. If he was quiet about it, I—I might not have heard. I was concentrating—"

Hardy looked at Jerry Dodd. "Hotel thief?" he asked.

"Not ever," Jerry said. "A guy standing outside the door with a passkey, let's say, would hear the typewriter going. A thief wouldn't come into a room he knew was occupied."

"He was no thief," Norman agreed. "He was out to get me. I was supposed to get heaved out the window."

"Why?" Hardy asked.

"I've been thinking," Norman said. "Boy, have I been thinking!"

"With what results, Norman?" Chambrun asked patiently.

"If I went out the window—and there was a little note in my typewriter saying I killed Frank Hansbury and couldn't face it any longer—well, a lot of people would be off a great big hook, wouldn't they?"

Hardy's face was grim. "Could it have been Robert Saville?" he asked.

Norman shook his head. "Not tall enough. Saville's quick and wiry. This man was square and all power."

"Brimsek, the athlete-lawyer?"

Norman grinned and winced. Smiling hurt his mouth. "Not George," he said. "He taught me all I know about karate. I couldn't begin to handle him."

It didn't take long for Hardy to get up a full head of steam. He and Chambrun went quickly to Saville's suite on the nineteenth floor, leaving Norman to gather the scattered pages of his script.

Saville was definitely not alone. Paul Drott, the network vice-president, was there, and Brimsek, and Sally Bevans, busy at a typewriter, and a young man who was introduced as Walter Cameron. Saville had already got in his new writer, and they were deep in what is called a "story conference."

"I just can't stop to talk to you now, Lieutenant," Saville said. "We're revising the script. It has to be ready by Monday. Unless it's absolutely necessary—"

"It is," Hardy said.

"Does Norman know he's not the writer anymore?" Chambrun asked.

"There's always more than one writer," Saville said. "If Norman comes up with something good, fine. But we can't risk it. Wally, here, is—"

"What about Richter?" Chambrun asked. "Doesn't the director usually sit in on story conferences?"

"Nuts to Karl," Saville said impatiently. "He's always trying to work in Significance! This is a straight adventure series. It doesn't have any message except good is good and evil is evil."

"Someone just tried to murder Norman," Chambrun said, as casually as if he were commenting on what a nice afternoon it had been. It was a neat little bombshell. "Evil is evil," Chambrun added.

"Who did it?" the vice-president asked in a small voice.

"It could have been the Masked Crusader," Chambrun said. "Stocking mask over his head and skilled in karate. He tried to throw Norman out the window."

"Knock it off," Saville said angrily. "I'm not interested in gags, Chambrun."

"It's not a gag," Chambrun said. "It just happened—half an hour ago."

A broad smile lit George Brimsek's face. He glanced at his watch. "It is now thirty-three minutes after five," he said. "We began this conference at about three o'clock. Not one of us has been out of this suite since then—not even out of this room except to go to the john. Will that speed you on your way, gentlemen? We have work to do."

"I have been in this business a long time," Hardy said in a harsh voice. "I don't think I've ever run across such callous attitudes as I've found in this room. Don't you even want to know whether or not your writer is hurt?"

"Of course we want to know," Sally Bevans said quickly.

"He was pretty badly beaten up, but he's all right," Hardy said. He fixed Brimsek with a cold stare. "You're the karate expert around here, Brimsek."

"I've just told you, Lieutenant, none of us has been out of this suite since three o'clock."

"Geller has already told us it wasn't you or Saville. Man was a different build and not so expert as you, Brimsek."

"Well, bully for Norman," Brimsek said.

"Why would anyone want to hurt Norman?" Sally asked.

"The suggestion," Chambrun said, "is that the man who attacked him intended to throw him out the window and leave a suicide note in Norman's typewriter, confessing to the murder of Hansbury. That would have ended the murder investigation, got you all off any sort of hook you may be on, and allow 'The Masked Crusader' to be born, unhampered by unpleasant publicity."

"So it didn't work. But how do you tie us into it, Chambrun? We were here. Our hands are clean."

"There is enough money interest in this room to hire a hundred assassins," Chambrun said.

"Oh, my God!" the vice-president said. "I think I better call T.J."

"You just sit tight, Paul," Saville said. "This whole story sounds as if it just came out of Norman's typewriter."

Hardy gave the actor a disgusted look. "It wasn't his typewriter that slugged him in the jaw and clawed his chest," he said. "I'm sending a police stenographer in here to take individual statements from each of you, stating that you didn't leave this suite between three and five-thirty P.M."

"We don't have to sign statements, do we, George?" Saville asked.

The muscular lawyer shrugged. "Here or at the precinct station house," he said. "Please, let's get it over with as quickly as possible, Lieutenant. We're running out of time on a very important project."

Just about the time I got back from Gillian's apartment, Chambrun, Hardy, and Jerry Dodd had returned to the Great Man's office.

Jerry was reporting. "I've checked out the floor maids, the housekeeper for that area, bellhops, elevator operators. No one saw anyone come to or leave Mark's apartment—no reason anyone should have particularly. Certain the guy took off his mask before he came out of the apartment. Nothing to make him stand out from anyone else."

"Except a limp," Chambrun said. "Norman gave him a flying kick in the kneecap. Norman knows how. The man is lucky his leg wasn't broken."

"I've still got to round up that fellow Richter," Hardy said. He was studying his notebook.

"He's in the Trapeze Bar," Jerry said, "or was about fifteen minutes ago. Been in and out of there most of the afternoon. According to Mr. Del Greco, the maître d' in the Trapeze, he must have taken on quite a snootful by now. Not showing it, though."

Chambrun is Chambrun. He didn't ask me a single question about my visit with Gillian while Hardy was there.

"We'll have to move your friend somewhere, Haskell," Hardy said. "I'd like to turn my boys loose in your living room. Geller's attacker must have left a few fingerprints around."

"He can use Miss Ruysdale's office until your men are finished with Mark's place," Chambrun said.

"I'll get him," Jerry Dodd said. "I'd like to ask him some more questions. He didn't see the man's face on account of the mask, but there are other things he might remember now that the excitement's over. There could have been something distinctive about the hands—a scar, a broken finger, the color of the hair growing on them. There might have been a smell—hair tonic he used. And the suit. What color? What kind of material? Shoes? We might begin to build a picture."

"Go ahead," Hardy said. "I'll have Richter brought up here. He may have some ideas."

"Oh, yes, he'll be full of ideas," Chambrun said. He walked over to the sideboard and filled a demitasse cup from the Turkish coffee machine.

Jerry and Hardy took off.

"Well?" Chambrun said to me.

I gave him a blow-by-blow of my talk with Gillian. He listened, eyes hooded, sunk back down in his desk chair.

"The alibi doesn't quite make it for Norman," he said when I'd finished. "Six until a little past eight."

"He was at his apartment."

"You've asked him?"

"No. I came straight here. How is he?"

"He'll do," Chambrun said. "Gutsy little guy. From the looks of things, he fought like a tiger."

"Somebody is trying to pin the tail on the donkey—Norman," I said.

"It has all the earmarks," Chambrun agreed.

Hardy was suddenly back with a couple of typewritten sheets of paper in his hand.

"How do you like this for apples?" he said. "Something we missed in Geller's room—1927. Camera picked it up. Wheel marks on the carpet in the room."

"Come again," Chambrun said.

"Wheel marks! Narrow, rubber-tired wheel marks. A wheelchair!" Hardy said. "There was a wheelchair in that room carrying weight. Someone riding in it."

We had Norman in there fast. He looked a little pale and disheveled. He kept blotting at the corner of his mouth with a bloodied handkerchief.

"We've come up with something," Hardy told him. "Yesterday afternoon, while you were still in your room, did Saville come to see you?"

Norman shook his head slowly. "They wore out the telephone, but I wasn't letting anyone in. I was trying to finish."

"Saville didn't come to see you in his wheelchair?"

"You mean that gimmick he uses for going out through the crowds? No."

"Some other time that day?"

"No. He wouldn't have to disguise himself to come and talk to me. What's up?"

Hardy showed Norman the Homicide report. "There was a wheelchair in your room since the last time the maid cleaned and vacuumed."

Norman's face was blank. "Certainly not while I was there," he said. Then his eyes widened. "Do you suppose that's the way they brought Frank's body into my room?"

For the first time since Frank Hansbury's body had been found in Norman's closet, we had a break in the case. It came as a result of Hardy's efficient Homicide team, which had detected the wheel marks on the carpet, and Jerry Dodd's dogged legwork. Jerry found a witness on the hotel staff—Mrs. Kniffin, the housekeeper on the nineteenth floor.

Mrs. Kniffin is a motherly type who has worked in the Beaumont as far back as the memory of anyone connected with the hotel. In those years Mrs. Kniffin has encountered all the "unexpecteds." Jerry brought her to Chambrun's office where she had a story for us.

"Mrs. Kniffin saw the wheelchair go into Room 1927," Jerry said.

Mrs. Kniffin's plump face showed wrinkles of distress. "I hope I didn't do wrong not reporting it, Mr. Chambrun," she said. "It—it seemed perfectly all right."

"I'm sure your judgment was perfectly sound, Mrs. Kniffin," Chambrun said. "Just tell us what you saw."

Mrs. Kniffin's arthritic fingers twisted the apron of her housekeeper's gray uniform. "That whole corridor was kind of exciting, Mr. Chambrun. Actors and actresses, writers, big-time advertising executives, all scurrying back and forth between the rooms. And, of course, especially Robert Saville. I mean, things were more interesting than usual."

"Robert Saville is a favorite of yours, Mrs. Kniffin?"

Mrs. Kniffin giggled. "I'm too old to admit it," she said. "Spencer Tracy stayed on my floor once. It was a little bit like that."

"For God's sake get to the wheelchair, woman," Hardy said.

"Let her tell it her own way, Lieutenant," Chambrun suggested, giving Mrs. Kniffin an encouraging smile.

"It was last night," Mrs. Kniffin said, "just before I went off duty."

"Which is when, Mrs. Kniffin?" Chambrun asked, for Hardy's benefit.

"Eight o'clock. I always go off at exactly eight. Mrs. Lawler, who takes over, is never late. I guess it must have been about ten minutes to eight. I was in the hall, and the door of Mr. Saville's suite opened, and they brought him out in that wheel-chair."

"Him?"

"Mr. Saville," Mrs. Kniffin said. "I'd seen him before in the wheelchair. It's wonderful what he can do with makeup. He wears a gray hairpiece and black glasses and his overcoat collar turned up around his chin—black hat. You'd never dream it was him. He gets wheeled right by people, and they don't even look at him. A regular Lon Chaney, if you know what I mean."

"I think I do," Chambrun said. "Naturally, you were fascinated when you saw him being wheeled out of his suite last night."

Mrs. Kniffin lowered her eyes. "I have to admit I pretended being busy about something near the linen closet when I really wasn't."

"Quite natural," Chambrun said. "After all, Mr. Saville is a kind of hero to you. Who, by the way, was pushing the chair, Mrs. Kniffin?"

"Why—why one of his people, I suppose," she said.

"You suppose?"

Mrs. Kniffin looked positively kittenish. "I really didn't notice," she said. "A man wearing a raincoat and a hat, I think. But I really didn't notice, Mr. Chambrun. I—I was so interested in Mr. Saville and how he managed his—his disguise."

"So they came out of Mr. Saville's suite. You're sure of that?"

"Of course, sir. I thought they'd be going past me to the elevators, the way they always do when Mr. Saville wants to get out through the lobby without being noticed. But instead they stopped at the door of Room 1927." She glanced at Norman, who was leaning forward in his chair, handkerchief pressed to his mouth. "Mr. Geller's room, sir."

"And then?"

"They went in," Mrs. Kniffin said. "Then I went into the linen room, and Mrs. Lawler was there waiting to relieve me. I went right home."

"Let's not go home quite so fast, Mrs. Kniffin," Chambrun said, his smile gentle. "You say they went into Room 1927. Did Mr. Saville knock on the door or ring the bell?"

"Oh, no, sir," Mrs. Kniffin said. "I was watching him every second. He never moved a muscle. Have you ever watched him in that wheelchair, Mr. Chambrun? He sits there like a statue. It must take wonderful physical control."

"So the other man—the one you don't remember—either knocked or rang the bell?"

"I suppose so," Mrs. Kniffin said. "I—I don't think I ever took my eyes off Mr. Saville. I mean—"

"I understand, Mrs. Kniffin," Chambrun said. His patience bordered on the miraculous. "So someone opened the door and let them in?"

"The door opened, and they went in," Mrs. Kniffin said.

"Did you see who opened it, Mrs. Kniffin? Was it Mr. Geller?"

She frowned. "I—I didn't actually see who opened it," she said.

"And you didn't actually see the man in the raincoat knock or ring the bell?"

"I have to admit I didn't," Mrs. Kniffin said.

"Could he have opened the door with a key, Mrs. Kniffin?"

Mrs. Kniffin stared at Chambrun. "I—I don't honestly know, sir," she said. "Only later, as you may know, Mrs. Lawler let Mr. Saville and his secretary into Mr. Geller's room. They thought something might have happened to Mr. Geller.

They didn't have a key then, sir. Mrs. Lawler used her pass-key. Mrs. Lawler said she was all goose bumps, standing right next to Mr. Saville, talking to him."

Chambrun picked up the phone on his desk. "Please ask Mr. Cardoza to come to my office at once," he said.

Mr. Cardoza is the captain in the Grill Room, where Robert Saville had, in theory, been having dinner at ten minutes to eight last night. Chambrun put down the phone and leaned back in his chair. He made a little gesture of resignation to Hardy. He, personally, was finished with Mrs. Kniffin.

"Try to think hard, Mrs. Kniffin," Hardy said. "Can't you describe the man who was pushing the wheelchair a little better than just a raincoat and a hat?"

"I know it's romantic and foolish," Mrs. Kniffin said, "but I just couldn't take my eyes off Mr. Saville."

"You're sure it *was* Mr. Saville in the wheelchair?"

Mrs. Kniffin smiled at the lieutenant as though he was a backward child. "That is something I couldn't possibly be mistaken about, Lieutenant," she said.

"Thank you, Mrs. Kniffin," Chambrun said.

The old woman hesitated. "I hope I haven't gotten Mr. Saville into any kind of trouble," she said. "I'd—I'd never forgive myself for that."

"Comfort yourself that you've done your job as a member of the staff and as a good citizen, Mrs. Kniffin," Chambrun reassured her.

Mrs. Kniffin, twisting her apron, retired.

Hardy made a growling noise deep in his throat. "Now we got something to twist that fancy creep's arm with," he said.

"Meaning Saville?" Chambrun said, looking at the lieutenant through a pale cloud of cigarette smoke.

"Who else?" Hardy said.

"That may be the crucial question," Chambrun said. "Before you go too far out on a limb, Hardy, I suggest we hear what Mr. Cardoza has to say." His eyes moved past Hardy to the door.

Mr. Cardoza is dark and very elegant. He looks as if he

might be the pretender to the Spanish throne. He is more than a headwaiter. He presides over the Grill Room and the Blue Lagoon nightclub in the hotel. Real princes and kings speak nicely to him to get reservations. I know he rates with the top half dozen indispensables on Chambrun's staff.

He arrived promptly. At the Beaumont, when you get a summons from the second floor, you hop to it.

"Thank you for coming at once, Cardoza," Chambrun said.

"My pleasure," Cardoza said. He nodded to me and Hardy, whom he knew from other investigations. Chambrun introduced Norman, and Norman got the faint classic bow.

"Last night Robert Saville and some of his entourage had dinner in the Grill Room?" Chambrun asked.

One of Cardoza's eyebrows rose. "Indeed he did."

"Could you estimate the approximate time, Cardoza?"

"It would be exact on my table chart," Cardoza said. "They arrived a few minutes after seven and left about twenty-five minutes to nine."

"Any comings and goings?" Chambrun asked.

"How do you mean, Mr. Chambrun?"

"I won't play games with you, Cardoza. We are trying to account for Robert Saville's whereabouts between, say, half-past seven and a little after eight."

"He was with me—God help me," Cardoza said.

"Why do you need God's help, Cardoza?"

"He is an insatiable demander," Cardoza said. "Nothing is ever quite right. He drives my waiters crazy, and he treats them like cattle."

"So he was with you from a little after seven till twenty-five minutes to nine. But he probably left the room at some point?"

"He did not," Cardoza said.

"Not at any time?"

"Not at any time."

"How many people does your Grill Room seat, Cardoza?" Hardy asked.

"The fire laws limit us to two hundred and twenty-six people."

"Were you filled up last night?"

"We are always 'filled up,' Lieutenant."

"And you're trying to tell me that, with over two hundred people in the room, all of them needing attention, you can say positively that Saville never left the room? Not even to go to the john?"

"I am telling you that," Cardoza said blandly.

"I don't buy it," Hardy said. "I don't buy it, because we have an eyewitness who says he was somewhere else."

"Your eyewitness is mistaken," Cardoza said. He smiled, and it was just slightly patronizing. "If you were having dinner there, Lieutenant, I might not be able to swear that you hadn't left the room at some point. You are a pleasant, undemanding, reasonable guest. You would never produce unwanted publicity for the hotel. You could go to the john, as you call it, without creating a sensation.

"But Robert Saville can't push back his chair to stand up without six foolish women trying to rip the sleeve out of his dinner jacket. We have to protect him as best we can from autograph seekers and drooling ladies. Every moment he's in the room is potentially explosive. So in the case of Mr. Saville I know very definitely whether he leaves the room to go to the john or anywhere else. He is never quite out of the perimeter of my vision. Last night Mr. Saville did not leave from the moment he and his party arrived a little after seven until he and his party left at twenty-five minutes to nine."

"What about the others—the people with him?"

"The girl—Saville's secretary—made several trips to the telephone booths in the foyer. Mr. Drott, whom I know well as a regular customer—the network has an account with us—also made several phone calls. The big man, the lawyer, went to the washroom once. But Robert Saville never left the table."

"Thank you, Cardoza," Chambrun said.

Cardoza bowed. "Any time, Mr. Chambrun," he said, and left.

"He's wrong or Mrs. Kniffin is lying!" Hardy said, his anger boiling.

"I think you can be quite certain that Cardoza is right," Chambrun said. "As for Mrs. Kniffin, she wanted it to be Robert Saville in that wheelchair, and so she saw Robert Saville in that wheelchair. A man wearing a gray wig, black glasses, with his face hidden by a hatbrim and a turned-up coat collar doesn't present a sharp picture. Even I might look like Robert Saville in that getup, slumped in a wheelchair, to someone who wanted me to be Robert Saville."

"So much for eyewitnesses," Hardy muttered.

"I think you can depend on Cardoza as a completely accurate witness," Chambrun said.

"Then exactly who was in the wheelchair? And who was pushing it?"

"Norman's suggestion still interests me," Chambrun said. "It could have been Frank Hansbury on his way to be dumped in Norman's closet. He sat there 'like a statue,' Mrs. Kniffin said. Might that not describe a dead man, Lieutenant?"

"And the man in the raincoat and hat—since you're guessing?" Hardy asked with some bitterness.

"In Mrs. Kniffin's ecstatic state, which makes her totally worthless as a witness, the man in the raincoat and hat could have been a woman."

"What makes you think so?"

"Nothing," Chambrun said, smiling. "I just say it could have been, for all the solid facts we have. But you do have a new starting point, Lieutenant."

"Like what?"

"Like Robert Saville," Chambrun said. "Mrs. Kniffin isn't all that worthless to you, Lieutenant. One thing you can be sure of. She *did* see *someone* in a wheelchair, disguised in Saville's wig and glasses. She *did* see *someone* pushing the chair. She *did* see them go into—or be let into—Norman's room. So now you go to Saville and ask him who used his wheelchair and his makeup kit while he was having dinner. Where are those items now? That's a starting point, my friend."

Hardy straightened his shoulders. "This time Pretty Boy is going to sit down and dish it out for me if it takes all night," he said.

"Remember, Brimsek told us that after they had gone into Norman's room with the housekeeper at a quarter to ten, Saville went out in the wheelchair looking 'for action.' Namely, a poker game. Did he find his wig and glasses where they should have been? Was the wheelchair where it ought to have been?"

"There could still be fingerprints on those items," Hardy said hopefully.

Chambrun shook his head. "Mrs. Kniffin didn't say so, but I'd make a small bet the man in the raincoat wore gloves."

Hardy started for the door.

"Just a minute, Lieutenant," Norman said in a small tired voice. "I was lucky this last time. I might not be lucky if they come looking for me again."

Hardy nodded. "You're right. You'll have to stay here till we've given Mark's place a thorough going-over. I'll send a man in here to stand by with you. Detective named Salinger. He's a hundred percent reliable. You want your typewriter in here?"

Norman's smile was pale. "I think I'm pretty fed up with the Masked Crusader," he said. "He got a little bit too real there in Mark's place."

Hardy took off for his confrontation with Saville. Norman didn't move out of his chair. He lowered his head and covered his face with his hands.

"I—I think things are beginning to catch up with me," Norman said. "Poor Frank. Do you really think he might have been in that wheelchair?"

"It was your idea," Chambrun said.

Norman shuddered. "But I didn't really believe it," he said.

Chambrun lit one of his flat Egyptian cigarettes. "I think we'd better bring you up to date, Norman," he said. "Mark has been to see Mrs. Hansbury."

Norman's head jerked up. "So help me, Mark, if you've dragged her into this—"

"She hasn't been dragged anywhere," Chambrun said. "Mark is very much concerned about you. He's a good friend, Norman. He felt someone is trying to frame you and that you'd almost certainly need the alibi that Mrs. Hansbury could give you. He wanted to make certain she'd come forward if she was needed."

"And of course she said she would," Norman said. "But that would mean—"

"It may not be necessary for her to come forward," Chambrun said. "There's a small hitch, though. Mrs. Hansbury told Mark you got to her place a little after eight. You told us you left here about six. Obviously she can't provide you with an alibi for that stretch of time in between—six to eight. That could be the crucial time, Norman."

"I went to my apartment—near Gramercy Park," Norman said. "I hadn't picked up mail for days, and I needed some fresh clothes."

"Did anyone see you there?"

Norman frowned. "I can't honestly be sure," he said. "It's a self-service building. I—I wasn't trying to set up an alibi, you know."

"Let's hope it isn't too important," Chambrun said. He watched the smoke rise from the end of his cigarette. "We're left a little bit high and dry, Norman. Take a look at what we know. Hansbury was in Saville's suite arguing about your payments when they went down to dinner leaving him there. That was a few minutes past seven. Hansbury was still alive then—Sheri Southworth saw him. He made a phone call to Mrs. Hansbury, trying to find you. Now Saville, Brimsek, Drott, and Miss Bevans are all in the clear for the next hour and a half. At ten minutes to eight Mrs. Kniffin saw a phony Saville go into your room. That *may* have been Frank Hansbury, dead, wheeled into your room by Mr. X. If it was Hansbury, he wasn't killed by Saville or Brimsek or Drott—or Miss Bevans. I'm disinclined to believe that Miss Sheri Southworth is a mankiller—in the literal sense."

Chambrun smiled faintly, then went on. "So that brings me to the key question, Norman. Who else in this entourage could have gotten into an angry argument with Hansbury and chopped him down? Because that seems to me to be what happened. Not a planned killing—an explosive, unplanned moment of violence."

"Only Sheri was in the suite," Norman said.

"We don't know that," Chambrun said. "Hansbury was there, and Sheri was in her room. If someone rang the doorbell, Hansbury could obviously have let that someone in."

Norman nodded, moistening his lips. "Frank was furious with everyone. But the person he hated most in the whole setup was Karl Richter," he said.

"Oh?"

"Richter was the one who was really fouling up the script," Norman said. "Karl and his bloody 'significances.' Just when we'd get Saville and the rest of them to agree about a sequence, Karl would blow it for us. He's a crazy egomaniac. He doesn't care about anyone's ideas but his own. He thinks directors are the only important people in show business. If he happened to turn up while Frank was there in the suite, they could certainly have got in an argument."

"He wasn't in the hotel," I said.

"He *says* he wasn't in the hotel," Chambrun said. He looked at Norman. "Is he a karate expert, Norman?"

"I haven't the faintest idea," Norman said.

"Mark, it might be worth having a casual conversation with Richter," Chambrun said. "If he's still in the Trapeze Bar, and he isn't too stoned, you might be able to find out where he was last night between seven and eight without his thinking he was talking to the police. Use your best diplomatic technique."

The Trapeze Bar is suspended in space over the foyer to the Beaumont's Grand Ballroom. Its walls are a kind of Florentine grillwork, and some artist of the Calder school has decorated them with mobiles of circus performers working on trapezes. They sway slightly in the movement of air from a cooling system, giving the unusual effect that the whole place is swaying slightly. It's an extremely popular rendezvous for the famous and the near-famous before the lunch and dinner hours.

It was nearly six o'clock when I got there, and the room was crowded to the doors. I flagged Mr. Del Greco, the maître d', and he pointed out Richter at a corner table.

"I was about to give him the polite heave-ho," Del Greco said. "He has to be potted to the eyes. He's been here for nearly four hours taking in one after another—Dutch gin on the rocks."

Richter wasn't alone. The attractive Sally Bevans was with him.

"Well, well, well," Richter said when I joined them. "The Beaumont's barker." He was deathly pale, but he seemed in control.

Miss Bevans smiled at me. "I finally got that martini," she said. "On the run."

"Sorry I couldn't have bought it for you," I said.

"Join us, by all means," Richter said as I pulled up a chair. "I have been summoned by the Mafia—my name for Saville and Company. I have been explaining to Sally that I'm not exactly in tiptop condition to involve myself in a story conference."

"They need you, Karl," Sally said. "Wally Cameron has come up with a whole new opening sequence."

"Convey the word that I need a little time for rehabilitation," Richter said. "A lot of hot coffee, a lot of cold shower—shall we say, after they've had dinner?"

"I'll report," Sally said. "But I have the feeling they'll descend on you *en masse* when Lieutenant Hardy is through with them."

"So the Law is still chasing its tail," Richter said. "Running in circles can last a long time—long enough for a lot of cold showers. Convey the word, Sally, my dear. Richter will come when Richter is damned good and ready."

Sally made a little moue and stood up. "I'll report," she said.

"Do so," Richter said. "And then rejoin us, my dear, and I'll persuade you to desert the Mafia and become a Rhine maiden." He watched her go, moistening his thin lips. "A really lovely gal," he said. "How is it they so seldom recognize the genuine male as opposed to the counterfeit?" He looked up at the waiter standing by the table. "Once more, please, and whatever Mr. Haskell's little heart desires."

I saw the waiter was about to deliver an ultimatum from Del Greco and shook my head. One more couldn't do that much damage. I looked at Richter. All that was missing was the Heidelberg scar to make him the perfect Prussian prototype.

"This is a wonderful, a magical bar," he said. "I've sat here all afternoon, and the grapevine entwines itself around my ears, and bit by bit I am completely up on current events. I hear the rumor that someone tried to throw little Norman out the window."

"It's not a rumor," I said. "It was a near thing." I found myself looking at his well-manicured nails and wondered if they could have clawed at Norman's chest.

"The police seem unwilling to accept expert help," Richter said. He looked at me hard, as though he had difficulty focusing. I expect he did. "I told you the Mafia would stop at nothing to keep the finger pointed away from them. Your square policeman seems to have rejected that idea."

"Alibis," I said. "The Mafia, as you call them, left Hansbury alive in Saville's suite when they went to dinner. He was dead, according to the medical examiner, by the time they got back. They were all accounted for the entire time. You weren't in the hotel," I added, slipping it in as casually as I could.

"That's correct," he said. "I was not in the hotel. I was on the other side of town, having dinner with my cameraman and my set designer—at Sardi's." His eyes narrowed. "Were you trying to get me to provide myself with an alibi, Mr. Haskell?"

"Why should I?" I said, trying to look fatuous.

"Well, no matter. I have one. But I very much wonder about the Mafia conspiracy. They say they left Hansbury alive. They *say.*"

"Sheri saw him alive after they left. He made phone calls."

"That pet poodle will say anything she is told to say," Richter said. "She's got the bruises to prove it. Conspiracy, my dear fellow. The Mafia is expert at it."

I wondered how much I should tell him. His theory had little needles pricking my spine. "At ten minutes of eight somebody wheeled a man out of the suite wearing Saville's wig—his invalid disguise—and into Norman's room. We wonder if that was Hansbury's body."

"Now you're getting interesting," Richter said.

"But they were all in the Grill Room," I said. "So who did the wheeling?"

"My dear innocent," Richter said, obviously enjoying himself, "it is perfectly simple. There are presidents and vice-presidents at their beck and call. They phone. 'We have had a little accident,' they say. 'We have killed Frank Hansbury. We need to plant his body in Norman's room. Please send someone around to wheel him in.' 'Yes, sir. Right away, sir.' And so they go to dinner, cool as the cliché cucumber. Help arrives. Miss Sheri admits him. Frank Hansbury is dumped. Kaput."

"Hansbury made a phone call after they were in the Grill Room," I said. "We know that for a fact."

"Do you, Haskell?" His smile was twisted. "The Mafia includes among its cohorts actors, mimics. Is the person who got the phone call absolutely sure the voice wasn't an imitation?"

I almost said, she ought to know—she was his wife. I didn't. What I did say was: "It's an interesting idea."

"But hard for the square policeman to absorb, or prove, I imagine."

I tried the fatuous smile again. "While we're setting up alibis, where were you at four-thirty when someone was trying to toss Norman out my window?"

Richter laughed. He waved toward the bar. "Check with your elegant captain over there. He's been hating me since two o'clock this afternoon." He looked at the drink the waiter had brought him and shuddered. "I think I have overestimated myself," he said.

At that point Sally Bevans returned from the phones in the foyer. "I'm sorry," she said. "The words are 'urgent,' 'immediate,' 'pronto.' "

His pale eyes looked her up and down, as though he could see through the chic beige dress. "What a pity," he said. "You could provide the one sure way to revive me, my dear." He stood up abruptly, and I just managed to stop his chair from toppling over. "Do you think I might avail myself of your steamroom and shower baths up at the squash courts?" he asked me.

"Be my guest."

"Thanks." He laughed. "Remember, the Mafia is all-powerful, Haskell." He walked away, stiff-legged, a little uncertain.

"Can I buy you that martini now?" I asked Sally.

She sat down beside me. "I always feel I'm being manhandled when he just looks at me," she said.

I signaled the waiter. Something told me I ought to stop playing detective, but Richter, drunk as he was, had suggested something not out of the realm of possibility. I wondered if this cool chick beside me could be sitting on the truth about a murder. I wanted to call Gillian to ask her if she was quite sure it was Frank who had talked to her on the phone, but I also thought I might not have another chance to catch Sally Bevans off guard.

"Richter isn't very friendly to your boss," I said.

"Karl is a Grade A louse," she said. "He is also a Grade A director. This business is full of talented louses—or is it lice?"

I gave the waiter the order for two very dry martinis on the rocks.

"Richter keeps trying to point us toward your boss and his friends," I said.

She looked at me, frowning. "It's absurd, you know. We all have alibis for both times—the time Frank was killed and this afternoon when Norman was attacked. You know that, Mark."

"Richter thinks we may not be asking about the right times," I said.

"What other times are there?" she asked. She didn't seem remotely disturbed. The waiter brought our martinis, and we clicked glasses and sipped.

"Mind if I ask you a question?" I said.

"Ask away," she said.

"When you all went down to dinner last night, Hansbury *was* in Saville's suite?"

"You want me to be very precise, don't you, Mark?"

"Yes, I do."

"I went downstairs ahead of Bob and the others—to make sure about the table reservation in the Grill Room. Frank was there when I left, arguing with Bob and George and Paul Drott."

"How much later did they come down to the Grill Room?"

"Oh, fifteen minutes," she said without hesitation. Then her clear gray eyes contracted. "Are you suggesting that something happened to Frank during that time?"

"Richter suggests it."

"That worm," she said.

"He calls your outfit the Mafia."

"I know." She sipped her drink. "You halfway buy it, don't you."

"When you're trying to put a puzzle together, and there's no glimmer of light—" I shrugged.

"From what I've seen of you, Mark, I write you down as a very nice guy," she said. "The way you've stood by Norman."

"Thank you, ma'am."

"And you're not simpleminded, Mark. You couldn't be and hold your job with Chambrun, who's certainly not simple-minded. You know something about the importance of public relations and publicity. That's your job. Nobody who isn't in the business can quite understand what the wrong kind of publicity can do to a man in Bob Saville's position. Or how important good publicity is to him and everybody connected with him."

"He's the golden egg layer for a lot of people," I said.

"He is that," she said.

"He plays it pretty dangerously," I said, "carting Miss Sheri Southworth around the country with him."

Her lips compressed. "Richter *has* been talking to you," she said.

"Well, she is a little risky, isn't she?"

Sally sat very still, turning her cocktail glass round and round in her fingers.

"I understand the kind of special love affair that girls have with the boss," I said, "even though it isn't for real. But let's face it. Saville's practicing a kind of brinksmanship, wouldn't you say? When something serious, like Frank Hansbury's murder, comes on the scene he's got to think of covering up so much else."

"I suppose you could say that I love Bob Saville," she said. "I've been with him for nine years—first as a script girl and then as his personal secretary. I know all the good things about him, and all the bad things. I know all his weaknesses and strengths, all his fears, all his dreams. They total up to something, Mark. If he wasn't always in Technicolor, always in the public spotlight, he'd be just another ordinary guy with ordinary weaknesses and fears. And dreams. That's how I see him, working with him every day. Would it surprise you if I told you I'd cut off my right arm for him if he asked it?"

"Knowing you, even as slightly as I do, it would," I said.

"What did Richter tell you about Sheri?"

"I don't think you're old enough to have it repeated," I said, grinning at her.

"Whatever he told you, it isn't true," she said.

"Since you don't know what he told me, how can you be sure?"

"I know Karl," she said. "Louse is too kind a word." She glanced at her small jeweled wristwatch. "Oh, brother, I was supposed to report back on Richter's availability. Would you excuse me a moment?"

She went off to the phones in the foyer again.

I signaled the waiter and asked him to bring a phone to the table. I'd written down Gillian's number when I got her address out of the phone book. When the waiter brought the phone and plugged it in, I dialed Gillian. She answered at once.

"Mark Haskell here," I said. "I have to ask you something in a hurry, Gillian. Are you *sure* it was Frank who called you last night asking for Norman?"

"Of course I'm sure."

"It's been suggested that it might have been someone imitating Frank's voice." She was silent for so long that I said, "Are you there, Gillian?"

"Yes, I'm here. I was trying to remember what he said. He asked if Norman had got here yet. I said no. He said to tell Norman he wanted to talk to him. And then, in that snide way of his, he said, 'And have fun, baby.' Yes, it was Frank."

"Well, thanks anyway," I said. "I'll explain it to you when I see you."

I saw Sally coming toward me from the foyer. So much for a faked phone call. But the question of times was still complicated. Maybe, after that, Frank had had his fatal argument with someone who had not yet gone to dinner. It could have happened that way. Sheri's testimony that she'd been alone with him could be part of the conspiracy.

"It's a good thing I called," Sally said as she rejoined me. "Lieutenant Hardy wants you up there in Bob's suite. Shall we go?"

I was playing cops and robbers, and I was in love with it. But I was an amateur. I was full of important suggestions for Hardy. It didn't cross my mind that if Hardy wanted me he would have found me direct, through Chambrun, who knew where I was.

It didn't cross my mind until five minutes later when I walked into Saville's suite with Sally and saw that Hardy wasn't there.

"I'm sorry, Mark," Sally said quietly. "I had to get you up here."

Saville faced me, looking pale and tense. As the door closed, I was aware that the muscular George Brimsek was standing behind me. Paul Drott, the vice-president, was standing over by the windows, looking down at the East River lights. It was now dark outside.

Sally walked over to the center table and got herself a cigarette. Saville held his lighter for her.

"Thanks, Sally," he said, his voice low and unsteady.

"Call me Mata Hari," she said, and turned away from him. "You've managed to make me hate myself, Bob."

"I'm sorry," he said. He turned to me. "I'm sorry, too, that I got you here under false pretenses, Haskell."

"No harm done," I said, trying to sound like the leading man in a soap opera. "I'll just take off."

"Not so fast, buster," Brimsek said. He was leaning casually against the door. He pasted on his white smile. "The so-called Mafia is now running the show."

Richter's nickname for them suddenly didn't sound so funny.

"Sally called up from downstairs to say that Karl Richter had been filling you full of it," Saville said. He was really trying the line of apologetic charm. Brimsek's muscular bulk against the door rather negated it. I like to be free to accept or reject apologies. "We're in a very tight spot, Haskell. We can't allow you and your friend Chambrun to get your hotel off the hook by throwing mud at us."

"I wasn't aware—"

"Hotels don't thrive on the news that guests are murdered and stuffed into closets and that attempts are made to throw other guests out of windows," Saville said. "But if you can dump it all in our laps, nobody will remember where it happened—just that it was us. There's too much at stake to let you play games with us."

"So I go out the window?" I asked, returning to my jaunty soap-opera role.

"Don't be absurd," Saville said. "We are going to convince you, once and for all, of the truth."

"Under the circumstances I might be easily convinced," I said.

The doorbell rang. Brimsek moved away and unlocked the door. Karl Richter stood outside looking pink and well-scrubbed. The steamroom and shower had done wonders for him.

"Ah, the delight of being wanted!" he said, sauntering into the room. Brimsek closed the door, and its lock snapped shut. Richter smiled at me. "Have you now also become a story expert, Haskell?"

It happened so fast I had no time to make even a joking answer. Brimsek swung Richter around and hit him flush on the mouth with a pile-driving right. Blood spurted like juice out of a grapefruit. Richter landed on a small straight-backed chair that crumpled under him like matchwood. He sat on the floor, his eyes blurred, fumbling at his shattered mouth.

"You jerk," Brimsek said, massaging his right fist gently. He had forgotten to take off his smile. There was now something obscene about it.

"You can begin, Karl," Saville said, "by telling Haskell the truth about Sheri."

Richter muttered something unintelligible. Brimsek reached down, caught him by the coat lapels, and dragged him up onto his knees. Then he hit him again, flush on the bleeding mouth. Richter screamed.

I moved in. "All right, tough guy," I said. "That's enough."

I didn't get as far as Brimsek. Saville moved deftly. My right arm was suddenly bent behind me in an anguishing twist lock. "You are here just to listen, Haskell," Saville said. "Go on, Karl. Tell him about Sheri."

Both murderous hatred and fear were reflected in Richter's pale eyes.

"One more, Karl, just for openers?" Brimsek asked, reaching for him.

"No!" Richter's voice was thick.

"Then tell the man about Sheri," Brimsek said.

Richter moved his bloody mouth. "Sheri is Saville's sister," Richter said. "The only way he can keep her out of trouble—"

"And out of the newspapers," Brimsek interpolated.

"—is to keep her under his thumb every minute." Richter touched his mouth. "What I told you is a rumor I've never bothered to correct—up to now."

Brimsek yanked him up to his feet again.

"No!" I heard Sally say.

"Now about a conspiracy to pin a murder on Norman," Brimsek said. He hit Richter again, a vicious uppercut that seemed to come almost from the floor. Richter literally went up and through the air and fell in a crumpled heap against the wall.

"You'll kill him, George!" Sally said.

"Too good for him," Brimsek said. He started across the room toward Richter.

The doorbell rang.

"Ignore it," Brimsek said.

He reached Richter, dragged him up to his feet, began to cross slap him—back of his hand to one side of the face, front of his hand to the other—whack, whack, whack, whack.

The door opened. My heart did a great big thud against my ribs.

Jerry Dodd was the first one into the room, a passkey in his hand. Chambrun, Hardy, and Norman were behind him. Jerry got to Brimsek and managed to spin him around. Richter sank to the floor. Brimsek and Jerry faced each other, Jerry about half the muscleman's size. I can't tell you exactly what happened, but suddenly Brimsek went through the air in a complete somersault and landed against the wall. Jerry stood over him.

"Don't move, big boy," Jerry said, "or I'll kick in your teeth."

Brimsek's smile was still there. "That was real good," he said. "How did you do it?"

"You, I suspect, are only a Brown Belt," Jerry said. "I'm a Black Belt. Take the lessons, and you'll find out. Now what the hell's going on here?"

It poured out of me. Richter had given me a lead. There was a way to make the time schedule fit the killing of Frank Hansbury. I dished it out, chapter and verse.

"It's an interesting theory," Chambrun said. "I thought about it without Mr. Richter's assistance. But other facts—" He turned, and for the first time I noticed that Hardy had Norman's arm in a firm grip. "You see, Norman forgot to cancel his milk delivery."

"Milk delivery!" I figured the Great Man had lost his grip on things.

"The time Norman had to account for was between six and a little after eight last night," Chambrun said. "He said he went to his apartment for his mail and clean clothes. I thought I'd have Jerry check it out. Norman needed that alibi. Well, there were four bottles of milk outside Norman's door and four days' collection of mail slipped under it. Norman certainly wasn't there last night."

I looked at Norman. He was staring at the rug pattern.

"We brought Norman here to have him confront your sister, Mr. Saville," Chambrun said.

"My sister!" Saville said.

"I've always known Miss Southworth was your sister," Chambrun said. "We have our own way of discovering facts about our guests. The information is on your file card. What happened last night is something like this. When you all went down to dinner and left Hansbury here, he did try to reach Norman on the phone. He called his ex-wife, because he knew Norman was headed there. But Norman hadn't arrived. He took a chance and called Norman's room. I've checked that out with the call slips at the switchboard.

"He found Norman still there and asked him to come down the hall to this suite. Norman protested, but he came. Sheri was in her room and couldn't hear. Hansbury and Norman got into an argument. Hansbury wanted Norman to stay here till you came back. Norman was to tell you he wouldn't write another word and was withdrawing his material—the original idea of 'The Masked Crusader.' Norman refused. Hansbury was his agent, so Hansbury should handle it. Besides, he was already late for a date with Mrs. Hansbury." Chambrun turned to Norman. He was almost gentle. "Then what happened, Norman?"

"He—he laughed at me," Norman said. "He said he'd been with Gillian a couple of nights ago. He said she wouldn't be eager for me to get there—not after the master had been with her. I—I hit him. Without thinking, I clipped him on the back of the neck. He fell down on the floor. He was dead—just like that!"

"No plan, no murderous intent. It just happened," Chambrun said. "Then Norman panicked. He could have called Jerry, told his story, and at the worst got off with a manslaughter charge. But he panicked. He has a quick mind, Norman. He knew if Hansbury were found here, all the others were alibied. They were in the Grill Room. The trail might quickly lead to him. If he could get the body out of here—somewhere else—

"Then he remembered Saville's wheelchair and his makeup equipment—the wig, glasses. He found them in the next room. He decked Hansbury out in the disguise and wheeled him out into the hall. I think he probably meant to dump Hansbury in the linen room or a cleaning closet. Right, Norman?"

Norman nodded. "But that damned woman was out there—Mrs. Kniffin—drooling at what she thought was Saville. So I had no choice. I unlocked my door and wheeled Frank in there. Then I had my bright idea." His laugh was mirthless. "If they found Frank there, it could be made to look as if somebody was trying to frame me. So I put him in the closet. I brought the chair and the makeup stuff back here. Then I hightailed it for Gillian's and stayed there.

"This morning I hunted up Mark with my story about needing a place to work. I didn't want to be the one who found Frank's body. So I asked for things to be brought from my room, including my slippers. I knew that whoever went for the slippers in the closet would find Frank's body."

"Hold everything," I said. "Maybe all this happened. But you're not going to say that Norman tried to throw himself out my window? Who was the man in the stocking mask?"

Chambrun's smile was wry. "The Masked Crusader," he said. "I suggested it once, not believing it. There was no one. A product of Norman's fiction writer's mind. Norman set the stage—overturned the furniture, opened the window. He cracked himself in the mouth. He clawed his own chest. Hardy's man has just taken some stuff from under Norman's fingernails to the lab. The result will almost certainly show bits of Norman's skin."

"I did it," Norman said. "I—I wanted to make absolutely sure you were convinced there was someone else."

"When the stage was set, Norman took the telephone off the hook and yelled for help," Chambrun said. He turned to Saville. "We came here in the hope that your sister just might have seen Norman coming in or going out or returning. It isn't too important, but Hardy likes to have his cases nice and tidy."

"If you could leave her out of it—" Saville said huskily.

"What about this mess?" Jerry asked, nodding toward the battered Richter. "Assault with something damn near like a deadly weapon."

Brimsek was on his feet. "Ask him," he said, always smiling. "Ask him if he'd like to bring charges. When I get through telling what I know about him in open court—"

"Forget it," Richter said in a voice that sounded as though it came from the bottom of a well.

Norman turned to me. "Would you try to explain to Gillian, Mark? I know she loved Frank. I didn't mean to kill him. But I couldn't bear it when he made those cheap cracks about her."

"I'll explain to her, Norman."

Saville moved forward. "Before you take Geller away, Lieutenant, could we talk to him a few minutes about the property—'The Masked Crusader'? I think we still want to use it."

Hardy looked at him, his eyes puzzled. "Don't you ever think about anything else, Saville?"

Saville's dark eyebrows rose. "Why should I, Lieutenant? It's my business."

# Pierre Chambrun and the War for Peace

I don't know whether Dr. Conrad Walbruck consciously modeled himself after the great Dr. Albert Schweitzer or not. Certainly their careers ran a curiously parallel course. They were both great physicians, great philosophers. They both shunned the opportunities for glory and wealth in the great sophisticated centers of the world. They both toiled twenty hours a day in jungle hospitals, struggling to save lives, fighting to get the funds for medical supplies and equipment. They both shone like bright stars in a desert sky. They were both the focal points for pilgrimages by the famous, the rich, and the humble.

These two great healers actually worked near each other in terms of today's world, the jet world, yet, so far as I know, they never actually met. Dr. Walbruck had not left his jungle hospital for more than thirty years until the occasion that brought him to the Beaumont, the world's top luxury hotel, in New York City. He came to address the United Nations. In Biafra, not far from his hospital, 16,000 children were dying each day—a child every five and one-half seconds, day and night, from the ravages of starvation and disease.

Dr. Walbruck, we knew from his wife, had decided he

could no longer stand by, helpless, and watch this happen. He would make his appeal in person to the highest tribunal in the world, the UN. If they could not stop the war in Biafra, they could at least put an end to the hunger and sickness. As a result of this public appeal, spotlighted around the globe, Dr. Walbruck also hoped to raise several million dollars from private sources to restock and reequip his own hospital for his war against the horsemen of famine and pestilence.

The Walbrucks—Dr. Conrad and his wife Gretchen—arrived at the Beaumont at two o'clock on a Wednesday morning. Their journey had been carried out in relative secrecy, so there were no reporters. They were taken, without fanfare, to their suite on the tenth floor, and, I assume, they slept the sleep of the just. It must have been an exhausting journey for the doctor because he was approaching his eightieth birthday.

At twenty-two minutes after nine the following morning, I was where I always was at precisely nine-twenty-two—standing beside Pierre Chambrun's flat-topped Florentine carved desk in his luxurious office on the second floor of the Beaumont. Chambrun is a dark stocky man with black eyes, which, hidden in deep pouches, can twinkle with humor or turn as cold as newly minted dimes. The Beaumont, under the managing directorship of Chambrun, is a world in itself, a way of life. I am one of the cogs in a machine that operates with Swiss-watch efficiency under Chambrun's watchful eye. I have a nice brass plate on the door of my second-floor office that says that I am MARK HASKELL, PUBLIC RELATIONS.

Chambrun eats only two meals a day: a hearty breakfast consisting of steak or chops or brook trout or perhaps a Dover sole, and quantities of gluten toast with sweet butter and English marmalade, and coffee—three cups of American coffee followed throughout the rest of the day by Turkish coffee, prepared on a sideboard by his remarkable secretary, Miss Ruysdale; and a gourmet dinner at seven P.M., also served in the office, for which Chambrun dresses, whether he has a guest or not.

Chambrun, born in France, came to this country as a boy and has been in the hotel business all his life, starting as a shoeshine boy in an East Side hotel operated by an uncle. He has reached the top of the heap at the Beaumont, having made an art of the business of hotel management. He speaks seven languages fluently, can assume a Continental manner that would please a duchess or a queen, and can be frighteningly tough with anyone, employee or guest, who upsets the routines of the hotel.

It is a world of exact routines—which is why it works so well. At nine in the morning a waiter brings the breakfast to the office, accompanied by Monsieur Fresney, the hotel's head chef, who waits for a nod of approval. At nine-ten Miss Ruysdale comes in with the registration cards of guests who have arrived since the night before. At nine-twenty-two I enter Chambrun's office. Chambrun is then on his second cup of coffee and his first Egyptian cigarette of the day. He instructs me about the new arrivals—whether they are news, whether they need special attention or special watching.

On this particular morning he passed me a card, and I saw that Dr. and Mrs. Conrad Walbruck had arrived. I had known they were coming and that Chambrun had considered the famous doctor sufficiently important for the manager himself to be on hand to act as official greeter.

"The old man made the trip in satisfactory shape?" I asked.

"Amazing person," Chambrun said. "He looks like an Old Testament prophet. Long white beard, eyes almost hidden by bushy white eyebrows. Somehow like one's childhood concept of Moses on the Mountain."

"I don't think I've ever seen a photograph of him."

"One of his foibles," Chambrun said. "No cameras. This, by the way, becomes part of your job, Mark. The good doctor is to be protected from any and every kind of intrusion. No cameramen, no interviewers, no autograph hunters. No one is to be permitted to go to his suite without prearrangement and only then accompanied by Jerry Dodd or one of his boys to make sure no one else gets in."

Jerry Dodd is our house officer, the Beaumont's security chief.

"He's afraid of something?" I asked.

Chambrun's smile was thin. "He's afraid of wasted time," he said. "He's got so little left at eighty that he insists on being protected from anything trivial, anything purely social. He will make his speech before the UN General Assembly this afternoon, and he will fly back to his hospital tonight. He will have taken thirty-six hours out of his life to help fight the war for peace and to raise some much needed money. It took considerable persuading to get him to come here at all, according to his wife. Someone else should have been able to do the sales job. But he was finally convinced there would be a special magic to his being here in person. The UN is to be his only public exposure. When the time comes for him to leave for the UN, we take him down on a service elevator to the kitchens. There will be a limousine waiting for him at the rear door. He'll come back the same way and take off for the airport later the same way. No chance of any approach from anyone anywhere. You are not to give out the word that he is here to anyone until after he is gone. Understood?"

"Understood."

The office door opened, and Jerry Dodd, the house officer, came in. Jerry, a dark wiry man with the sharpest eyes you've ever seen, is one of Chambrun's most trusted people. A pleasant professional smile doesn't hide the fact that Jerry is reading the maker's label on the inside of your shirt collar. He is tough and efficient, created in Chambrun's mold. He is one of three employees who would dare walk into Chambrun's private office unannounced; Miss Ruysdale and I are the only others granted that privilege.

"Sorry to interrupt," Jerry said. "We've had a high dive. From somewhere well up on the Fifth Avenue side."

Jerry was reporting a suicide.

"Bounced off the steel awning at the front door and onto the sidewalk," Jerry said. "Young girl, so far unidentified. No handbag."

Sudden, even violent death is not rare at the Beaumont. The hotel is like a small city, with its own shops and restaurants, its own small hospital and medical staff, its own police force, its city manager in the person of Chambrun, its own nightclubs and bars, its own brokerage office with ticker tapes and a miniature Big Board. Whatever can happen in a small city can happen at the Beaumont. People die of heart attacks; people fall and injure themselves critically; people take overdoses of sleeping pills or hang themselves from a coat hook in a closet or jump from a high floor. What is part of life in any community is part of life at the Beaumont.

Suicides outrage Chambrun but not for any moral or philosophical reason. They turn the unpleasant spotlight of publicity on the hotel, and what damages the hotel damages Chambrun.

"Why here?" he said that morning, his eyes bright with anger. "Why do it on *my* rug?"

Mystery is bad for the hotel. UNKNOWN GIRL LEAPS TO DEATH is designed to keep people focusing on the story, wondering who and especially why. Quick identification and burial of the story was what Chambrun would hope for.

I didn't have to look at the remains of the girl, thank God. However, we turned out to be lucky. When they undressed the body at the morgue, they found a little gold locket on a fine gold chain around the girl's neck. It gave her name—Karen Mosely. She was in the phone book. A horrified roommate told the police that she was a translator for one of the African delegations at the UN. She had spent two years in the Peace Corps—in, of all places, Biafra. That was coincidence Number One.

Coincidence Number Two was that Miss Mosely had told her roommate after breakfast that morning that she was headed for the Beaumont in the hope of seeing Dr. and Mrs. Walbruck, whom she had known—and loved—in Biafra.

A myth circulates among the employees of the Beaumont that Chambrun has a personal, built-in radar mechanism, or eyes in the back of his head, or secret peepholes into every room. The truth is that he knows the details of everyone's job down to the most inconsequential minutiae, so he knows who should be where and when and why. When he has a question, he knows whom to ask and why they should have an answer.

When the information came in on Miss Karen Mosely, I was with Chambrun in his office. We were about an hour away from the time when Dr. Conrad Walbruck would be whisked down a service elevator and taken to a waiting limousine for his trip to the UN.

Security had been set up around the Walbrucks, and Chambrun now checked it out. First there was Mrs. Veach, the chief operator on the hotel switchboard. There had been special orders about the Walbrucks. No incoming calls, house or outside. If anyone phoned, the caller would be asked his or her name and for a return number. Mrs. Veach would then relay the name and number to Mrs. Walbruck, and she could call back or not as she chose.

"Was there a call this morning for the Walbrucks from a Karen Mosely?" Chambrun asked.

Mrs. Veach checked her lists. There had not been such a call. There had been only three: one from the office of the secretary-general of the UN, one from the managing editor of the *Times*, and one from an airline official simply to report that the return journey was all arranged. Mrs. Walbruck had called back the secretary-general; she had ignored the other two calls.

Karen Mosely, whatever her intentions, had not announced herself to the Walbrucks.

"How would she know they were staying here?" I asked.

Chambrun shrugged. "United Nations," he said. "The girl is a linguist, a translator. She could have heard someone talking."

"But she didn't come after all."

"But she did," Chambrun said, "and jumped—or was pushed—from high up."

There is the right place to ask the right question. Chambrun found it on the tenth floor in the person of Mrs. Kniffin, the housekeeper. Mrs. Kniffin had had a special assignment that morning—to watch the door of 10G, the Walbrucks' suite. If anyone seemed to be loitering around who had no business there, Jerry Dodd was to be notified at once.

"Did a young girl—mid-twenties—try to gain admittance to the suite, Mrs. Kniffin?" Chambrun asked.

"No, sir," Mrs. Kniffin said. "That is, not exactly."

"So what did happen, exactly, Mrs. Kniffin?" Chambrun asked quietly.

"A young girl went in with Mrs. Walbruck."

"Went in with Mrs. Walbruck? Mrs. Walbruck had gone out somewhere?"

"Oh, yes, sir. Shortly after room service had brought them breakfast. She came out, looking a little vague, I thought. I—I asked her if I could help. I—I thought that was the right thing to do, Mr. Chambrun."

"Of course, Mrs. Kniffin. And were you able to help her?"

"She wanted some things from the drugstore. I directed her to the one in the lobby, sir. I asked her if someone could do her errand for her. She said no, she'd rather enjoy going out. 'No one will bother me,' she said. So she went down in the elevator and came back maybe twenty minutes or so later. There was this young girl with her. She seemed excited like—laughing and gay. I heard her say she couldn't wait to see Dr. Walbruck. I took it they'd met in the drugstore or the lobby."

"Quite probable," Chambrun said. "And did you see the young girl leave 10G?"

"Well, not exactly, Mr. Chambrun."

Chambrun's patience was monumental. "What exactly did you see, Mrs. Kniffin?"

"There was a phone call from the main office, sir. They'd sent me the wrong towels. I had the towels for 14, and 14 had the towels for 10. I talked for perhaps a minute or two. When I got back to the door of my cubbyhole here, the girl and this man were just passing my door."

"What man?"

"Just a—a man, sir. They were walking close together. I remember noticing that the girl wasn't laughing or happy anymore. I thought she looked frightened, Mr. Chambrun."

"What did the man look like?"

"Nothing special, sir. Tall, grayish hair. I—I didn't notice too clearly."

"Clean shaven?"

"Oh, yes, sir. I mean, he might have had a little mustache. I didn't really notice. Clean shaven, I'd say."

"You'd never seen him before?"

"No, sir."

"And they came out of 10G together?"

"I couldn't say that for sure, sir," Mrs. Kniffin said. "Of course the girl must have come out of 10G because I saw her go in. But I didn't see where the man came from. He could have come from 10G, or he could have come from down the hall. You see, I was on the phone, sir."

"It would seem she didn't go out the window in 10G," I said.

Chambrun looked at me as if I were an idiot. "Of course she didn't!" he said. "The windows in 10G open on the side street, not on the Fifth Avenue front. I think we'd better talk to Mrs. Walbruck."

Gretchen Walbruck answered Chambrun's ring at the door of 10G. She was a surprise to me until I remembered that she was Dr. Walbruck's second wife, a nurse who had been working in his hospital at Biafra not long after he'd become a widower. She could not have been more than fifty, I thought, with a strong face, a tight, grim mouth, and hostile gray eyes. She seemed to relax when she recognized Chambrun.

"You are early, Mr. Chambrun," she said. "We're not supposed to leave for another half hour. Conrad isn't ready yet."

"I'm afraid it's something else I've come about, Mrs. Walbruck," Chambrun said. "This is my associate, Mr. Haskell."

She looked at me without warmth. Then she stood aside and we went into the living room of the suite.

"You know a young girl named Karen Mosely?" Chambrun asked when we were inside.

"Of course," Mrs. Walbruck said. "Conrad and I knew her in Biafra. A charming girl. As a matter of fact, she's only just left here a little while ago."

"She came to call?"

"Yes and no," Mrs. Walbruck said. "She came to the hotel for that purpose, but before she could get in touch with us on the telephone I happened to run into her in the lobby. I'd been getting some things at the pharmacy. I brought Karen back up with me to see Conrad. They visited for a few minutes, and then she left."

"Accompanied by—?"

"She left by herself."

"There was no one here except you and Dr. Walbruck?"

"Of course not. See here, Mr. Chambrun, what is this all about?"

"I'm afraid you must be prepared for a shock, Mrs. Walbruck. Karen Mosely jumped, or was thrown, from an upper-story window of the hotel very shortly after she left you. She is dead."

"Oh, my God!" Mrs. Walbruck said.

"We identified her and traced her to you through her roommate. What was her state of mind when she was here?"

"Gay and laughing, as always," Mrs. Walbruck said, her voice low. "She was to have been the translator for one of the delegations when Conrad makes his speech at the United Nations. I didn't let her stay long. Conrad is very tired and very much concentrated on what he's facing. He must sway the diplomats and the private philanthropists, or we are lost, Mr. Chambrun."

There was the sound of a door opening, and Mrs. Walbruck reached out and closed a strong hand on Chambrun's arm. "Please, do not tell Conrad what has happened—not till after he's made his speech. It will upset him dreadfully."

We all turned and watched Dr. Conrad Walbruck come

slowly into the room. He was truly an extraordinary figure, tall, rugged, slightly stooped, with a mass of thick white hair, bushy white eyebrows, and a white beard that rested on his chest as he came vaguely toward us, head lowered.

"Is it time to go, Gretchen?" he asked in a voice that had distant thunders in it.

"Soon, Conrad."

The doctor had met Chambrun the night before, but he looked at him as though he were a stranger. He didn't look at me at all. He walked toward the windows, a man with the whole world carried on his bent shoulders.

"Conrad was so fond of Karen," Mrs. Walbruck whispered.

It was then that Chambrun gave me an unexpected order. "You will drive to the United Nations with Dr. and Mrs. Walbruck, Mark," he said. "Stay for the speech and come back with them. I don't want them out of your sight."

"There is danger?" Mrs. Walbruck whispered, glancing fearfully at her husband.

Chambrun's eyes had a hard, opaque look. "The world is sick with fanaticism, Mrs. Walbruck," he said. "I will feel easier if Mark is with you."

Let me say I was puzzled. To be perfectly frank, I am not someone Chambrun would normally pick for a bodyguard. I am a pleasant, not unattractive youngish man of thirty-five. I have a seven handicap at golf; I am a better than average bridge player; I have good manners; and twice a year I determine to do something about physical fitness—a resolution I give up twice a year after very short periods of time. Jerry Dodd and his men were the bodyguard types. It was obvious I was simply to provide the customary Beaumont courtesy.

The trip to the UN was uneventful. The Walbrucks were taken downstairs in a service elevator to the kitchen and out a side door where a limousine was waiting. I rode in front with the chauffeur. At the UN building we were greeted by a distinguished multination committee that conducted the doctor to the great hall where the General Assembly meets. Dr.

Walbruck was introduced to an attentive audience by the president of the Assembly and took his place at the speaker's rostrum. The delegates waited, many of them wearing earphones, so that they could follow the translators' words.

Dr. Walbruck put a sheaf of papers on the rostrum. Before this august body one does not ordinarily speak extemporaneously. One's words are history. But I don't think Dr. Walbruck referred to his written speech more than twice in the next half hour. I won't attempt to quote from the speech—it is a matter of public record, if you are interested. I can only say that this tired old man had a magic with words that I've never heard matched—except by Winston Churchill in his prime. He made a stirring plea for human life, for peace, for the great powers to direct their energies not against each other but against poverty, famine, and disease. He made an impassioned plea for help from governments and from private individuals. When he had finished, he was given a long, enthusiastic standing ovation.

In the outer hallways people crowded around Walbruck to shake his hand, to touch his sleeve. I heard a distinguished gentleman I knew to be the head of one of the great foundations tell the doctor that one million dollars would be placed to his account in his personal bank the very next day.

At last we reached the waiting limousine and pulled away from the UN. The old man sat with his head back against the rear seat, his eyes closed. He was exhausted.

"You were magnificent, sir," I said.

He didn't speak or move.

As we approached the side door to the Beaumont, I saw that something was wrong. The sidewalk was crowded with press photographers and reporters, many of whom I knew. Somehow the word had gotten out.

"I cannot subject him to that!" Mrs. Walbruck said in a shrill voice.

I ordered the chauffeur to drive straight past and around to the front entrance on Fifth Avenue. Things seemed quiet there.

"Let me have a look in the lobby first," I said.

I went across the sidewalk to the revolving door and then into the lobby. I was surprised to find Chambrun standing just inside the entrance and behind him another army of photographers and reporters, including a red-eyed television camera.

"Not interested in facing the cameras?" Chambrun asked, in a strange, hard voice.

"They were promised no cameras," I said. I didn't understand Chambrun's odd question.

"Perhaps I can persuade them," Chambrun said.

We went out and across the sidewalk to the limousine. Chambrun opened the door and got into the rear with the Walbrucks.

"I regret to say there seems to have been a leak," he said. "All the communications media are here."

"Conrad was promised!" Mrs. Walbruck said.

"Perhaps we can get him past them without their knowing who he is," Chambrun said.

"What nonsense!" Mrs. Walbruck exclaimed. "They all know him by sight."

"But not without his beard, wouldn't you say, Mrs. Walbruck?"

Chambrun didn't wait for an answer. I couldn't believe what I saw. He reached out, grabbed the white beard in his hand, and gave it a strong yank.

It came off!

"Now, madam, perhaps you wouldn't mind answering a question," Chambrun said, in his hanging-judge's voice. "Where *is* Dr. Walbruck?"

Chambrun sat behind the flat-topped desk in his office, sipping a cup of Turkish coffee, a Cheshire-cat smile on his lips. The rooftop fiddler in the original Chagall painting on the opposite wall seemed to be chuckling with delight. I was there, along with Jerry Dodd and Miss Ruysdale. The police had already taken Mrs. Walbruck and her unexpectedly beardless companion into custody.

"Ours is a business of detail," Chambrun said, lighting one of his flat Egyptian cigarettes. "When something goes wrong, it's a matter of routine with me to check every small detail, hoping for answers. I sent you with them to the UN, Mark, just to be sure the doctor didn't vanish into thin air while I checked."

He leaned forward and pushed a slip of paper to within my reach. I looked at it, with Jerry and Miss Ruysdale peering over my shoulder. It was a penciled list:

Toothpaste
Aspirin
Spirit Gum
Sleeping pill prescription
Kleenex
Medium toothbrush
Shaving cream

"That," Chambrun said, "is the list of things Mrs. Walbruck bought at the drugstore this morning. Interesting? Who has to use the shaving cream? The bearded Dr. Walbruck? It occurred to me, Ruysdale, that women do sometimes use razors—to shave their legs. It was possible the shaving cream was for the lady. Just possible."

"But the spirit gum!" Jerry Dodd said.

"Precisely," Chambrun said. "Spirit gum is a substance that actors use to fasten on false hair—beards, mustaches, sideburns. A small detail—but revealing. And so—and so—" Chambrun sighed and sipped his coffee.

"The Mosely girl inadvertently saw the man without his beard," Jerry said.

"I think not," Chambrun said. "Mrs. Walbruck met the girl in the lobby. She couldn't turn her away. If she did, it might arouse suspicion. The man posing as Dr. Walbruck—who, incidentally, turns out to be Mrs. Walbruck's brother—would not come out of the bedroom if there was anyone with Mrs. Walbruck. But something went wrong. The rooms, as you know, are soundproofed. Mrs. Walbruck let herself and the Mosely girl in with a key. No sound of the doorbell. So the imposter wasn't aware there was anyone with his sister. He appeared—not with his beard, Jerry, but as he told us a few minutes ago, with half of it on!"

"Sweet Sue," Jerry said. "He sure couldn't talk his way out of that!"

"So he took off that half of the beard, then escorted Miss Mosely down the hall with a gun in her ribs—you remember Mrs. Kniffin said they were walking close together, and the girl wasn't laughing anymore? She wasn't laughing because she was on her way to an open window and her death."

"But the speech!" I said. "I heard it. No stand-in could have made that speech."

"A stand-in could *make* the speech if the real Dr. Walbruck had written it," Chambrun said. He smiled. "I would like to continue to dazzle you by saying I knew the answer. I didn't. The police got it from Gretchen Walbruck. The good doctor died the day before they were to take off for this country. His speech was already written. He was prepared to make the great effort—the spirit was willing but the flesh was weak. He, quite simply, had died in his sleep."

"But why the fraud?" Miss Ruysdale asked. "They wanted the work to go on? Was that it?"

"My dear Ruysdale, you are the supreme sentimentalist," Chambrun said. "Dr. Walbruck was a saint. He was one of the few men in the world to whom hardheaded businessmen would give millions of dollars without comptrollers and accountants and committees to supervise its spending. Just over the rainbow there were millions of dollars to be had by Mrs. Walbruck and her brother, if they could carry out the fake for a very few days." Chambun put out his cigarette in the silver ashtray on his desk. "Well, my friends," he said briskly, "we have a hotel to run."

# Pierre Chambrun and the Last Fling

Walston Conyers had an old-world elegance. He looked as if he might be going to a formal function of some sort, even though it was early in the morning on an ordinary Saturday at the Hotel Beaumont. A great many United Nations diplomats make the Beaumont their home away from home. Many of them, particularly from new and underdeveloped nations, lean toward formal attire. Most of them look awkward and uncomfortable in black coat, striped trousers, and ascot tie. Except for a tiny black pearl tiepin in his ascot, Walston Conyers's clothes looked seedy and too long used; but he moved in them like—well, I find myself wanting to say, like a great gentleman.

There had to be a kind of magic about him. I am the public relations director for the Beaumont. The first item on my daily agenda is to go to the second-floor office of my boss, Pierre Chambrun, the Beaumont's resident manager. I report to the outer office at exactly nine-twenty and say good morning to the extraordinary Mr. Chambrun's extraordinary secretary, Miss Ruysdale. At exactly nine-twenty-two, as though it were the time mechanism of a bank vault, I am ushered into the Presence. At that precise moment Chambrun will be pouring his second cup of American coffee after a hearty breakfast of steak or chops or Dover sole or broiled lamb kidneys. He will be lighting his first Egyptian cigarette of the day, and on the sideboard the Turkish coffee machine will be making muttering noises. Chambrun will drink Turkish the rest of the day.

My first look at Chambrun each morning gives me an inkling of what the day will be like. There can be a cheerful "Good morning, Haskell," which means there is nothing out of the ordinary afoot. There can be a "Good morning, Mark," which means God is in his Heaven and all that. There can be no greeting at all, and the bright black eyes in their deep pouches can have the baleful look of a hanging judge—which means something has gone wrong with the Beaumont's Swiss-watch efficiency and there is going to be hell to pay.

"Good morning, Mark," Chambrun said. "Try the Dover sole for your lunch today, my boy. Fresney has outdone himself this morning." He nodded toward his breakfast tray. I would somehow get word to Monsieur Fresney, the Beaumont's master chef, that the Great Man was pleased. It would make the chef's day.

The business was routine. We went over the list of newly registered guests. There was a Hollywood actress who needed red-carpet treatment and a few press releases. There was a member of the staff of Britain's new Prime Minister who should get special attention. Then there was to be a wedding reception in the main ballroom that afternoon for the daughter of an outrageously wealthy deodorant manufacturer.

The routine was broken by the unexpected appearance of Miss Ruysdale. She never interrupted this moment except in an emergency.

"Yes, Ruysdale?" Chambrun's voice sounded sharp, but it was surprise, not irritation. Miss Ruysdale is hard to describe. Chambrun has many requirements in a personal secretary. She must never dream of regular working hours. She must be chic but not disturbingly so. Chambrun doesn't want the male members of his staff mooning over some "doll" in his outer office. She must eternally anticipate his needs.

Miss Ruysdale manages to meet all these requirements.

Her manner with the staff is friendly, but she draws a line over which no one dares to step. She is clearly all woman, but if she belongs to any man it is the best kept secret of the year. God forbid I should pass on the gossip that her man may be Pierre Chambrun himself. He neuters her by calling her "Ruysdale"—never Miss Ruysdale or Betsy. But Chambrun, among other things, is a talented actor.

The most unusual thing about Miss Ruysdale's entrance this morning was that she looked sheepish—as if she were a little girl who had been caught with her hand in the cookie jar.

"Well, Ruysdale?"

"There is a Mr. Walston Conyers in the outer office to see you," Ruysdale said.

"Conyers? Conyers?" Chambrun's fingers shuffled the registration cards on his desk. He stopped halfway through the pile. "'Conyers, Walston. Rittenhouse Square, Philadelphia.' His first visit to the Beaumont. You know very well, Ruysdale, that I don't see anyone—"

"—until you have finished the morning routines. I know that very well. Mr. Conyers started to tell me his story, and I thought you had better—"

Chambrun smiled. "Tall, dark, and handsome?"

"Old, tired, and somehow very winning," Miss Ruysdale said.

This was a "Hello, Mark" morning. "It is my pleasure to humor you, Ruysdale," Chambrun said. "Show Mr. Conyers in." He watched Miss Ruysdale leave. "Well, I'll be damned," he said. "She looked positively guilty."

"Maybe Mr. Conyers sold her the Brooklyn Bridge," I said.

As I have said, there had to be a kind of magic about him. To have persuaded Miss Ruysdale to get him into the Presence, I mean. She had kept kings and presidents cooling their heels while Chambrun finished his morning routines.

I had to guess that Conyers was in his early seventies, but he moved with all the grace of a trained actor. His little bow to Chambrun, not much more than a gentle inclination of his head, was somehow the very essence of good manners. His hair was white, but not that dead white that sometimes goes with age. It was almost electrically bright. He must have been an extraordinarily handsome young man; high cheekbones, a straight nose, a wide generous mouth, and blue, blue eyes. The eyes instantly won you. The little crow's-feet at their corners had been etched there by a lifetime of good humor and gentle amusement.

"I very much appreciate your seeing me, Mr. Chambrun," he said.

"My pleasure," Chambrun said. "This is Mr. Haskell, my public relations man."

The blue eyes made me feel that meeting me was a genuine pleasure.

"What can I do for you, Mr. Conyers?" Chambrun asked.

Conyers took an envelope from the pocket of his black morning coat. He put it down on the edge of Chambrun's carved Florentine desk. "In this envelope, Mr. Chambrun, is a certified check for five thousand dollars. I have endorsed it over to the hotel."

"You want me to keep it for you?" Chambrun sounded vaguely puzzled. It wasn't enough to explain Miss Ruysdale's extraordinary behavior.

"After a fashion, Mr. Chambrun," Conyers said. "I want you to keep it for me until the money is gone."

"I don't follow you."

Conyers's smile was gentle, patient. "I have come to a kind of crossroads in my life, Mr. Chambrun. A crossroads in time too. Aside from that five thousand dollars I have only a few dollars left in the world. I have decided, while I can still enjoy it, I would like to spend some time living fully, luxuriously. I do not want to know what I am paying for my room. I do not want to know what my meals and my mild alcoholic intakes are costing me. I want to simply sign for everything and to tip extravagantly. I do not want to know in advance how long the road will be, or what is around the next corner. One morning I will find a note from you in my box to the effect that I have, as you might say, run out of gas."

"And then?" Chambrun asked.

"I shall thank you for your courtesy and take my leave," Conyers said softly.

"I see."

"You find me childish and imprudent?" the old man asked, his eyes dancing. "There has to be sometime in a man's life when he throws his hat over the moon."

"And why have you chosen the Beaumont?" Chambrun asked.

"Because it is said to represent the quintessence of good living," Conyers said.

"I hope we can live up to your expectations, Mr. Conyers."

"Then you will do this?"

"Of course." Chambrun held a lighter to one of his Egyptian cigarettes. "Mr. Haskell will see to it that you have everything you want."

"I am deeply grateful to you both," Conyers said. He gave each of us his enchanting little bow and departed.

Chambrun watched him go, his bright black eyes narrowed against the smoke from his cigarette.

"I don't like it, Mark," he said.

"I rather admire him," I said. "He's giving himself a big birthday party instead of squeezing out what he has left, drop by drop."

"And after the party?" Chambrun didn't wait for an answer. "I don't like suicides in my hotel. Let all his tabs and his daily account come to me. I'll decide how long his road will be."

You may think that five thousand dollars would give Walston Conyers quite an extended birthday party. How well do you know the economics of a luxury hotel like the Beaumont? Just to start with, his small room and bath would set him back sixty dollars a day. Meals, tips, and a few drinks or some wine would set him back another sixty dollars. If he patronized any of the hotel's special offerings, like the Blue Lagoon Room, which is a very stylish nightclub, that would add considerably to his expenses. If he found friends and paid for part of their entertainment, that would take another big bite out of his capital. Would you guess one month? Three weeks? Even less?

During my rounds that day I passed the word about Conyers to Mr. Del Greco, who presides over the Trapeze Bar, and to Mr. Cardoza, the maître d' in the Blue Lagoon Room. They were to look out for Mr. Conyers and extend themselves a little extra for him. He might as well have a ball while he was at it.

I didn't actually see Conyers until late in the afternoon, at the crowded cocktail time in the Trapeze Bar. I spotted him at a corner table, sipping a vermouth on the rocks. His face seemed to be set in that bland half-amused smile that I had found so engaging when I first met him.

"He insisted on a table facing the door," Mr. Del Greco told me. "I thought he must be waiting for someone he knows."

"He didn't mention any friends," I said. "I wish there was someone I could steer his way—just so he'd have someone to talk to."

I went over to the table, and he gave me his graceful little nod. "Good evening, Haskell," he said.

"Good evening, sir. Everything all right?"

"Perfection," he said. "This is a really joyful room, isn't it? I suspect most of the high and the mighty pass this way at one time or another."

"You're looking for someone you know, sir?"

"Oh, I don't know anyone in New York. It would be a real coincidence if I should see anyone I know." His blue eyes twinkled. "This kind of plush place is not my usual habitat."

"Let me know if there is anything I can do for you."

"I will, Haskell. I will indeed."

I didn't come across him again until after midnight. He was in the Blue Lagoon Room then, sitting in lonely splendor at another corner table. His dinner jacket looked a little old and worn, but he wore it with a special elegance.

"He knows something about wines," Mr. Cardoza told me. "The best champagne—an obscure but very good year. He seemed to enjoy Zita very much. Much applause and a little gesture of pleasure."

Zita was the star on the bill that week. She is advertised as a "chanteuse." She is a dark Spanish-looking girl from Brooklyn. She sings a mixture of modern rock-message music and old-fashioned ballads, particularly Irish. She is very high-priced, and her records have made her a large amount of money. She has a boy friend named George Ortell who hangs around backstage, who clearly feels he owns her, and who looks as though he might be a highly paid gun for the Syndicate.

Conyers made a little gesture indicating that he wanted me to join him, and I went across the room to his table.

"Can I buy you a drink, Haskell?"

"I'd like to join you, but you needn't buy me a drink," I said. "Mine come on the house." I signaled to Cardoza for my regular Scotch on the rocks.

Conyers poured a little champagne into his glass from the bottle in the ice bucket beside his chair.

"I wonder if—if it would be inappropriate for me to send a bottle of champagne to—to Miss Zita in her dressing room?" he asked.

I gave him a wry smile. "It depends on what you think the result might be, Mr. Conyers," I said. "Zita has a boy friend who seems to own her, body and soul."

"My dear fellow, you overestimate my capacities. I simply wanted to express my pleasure and appreciation. She sang 'Molly Malone,' a song my mother used to sing to me when I was a small boy. I was strangely moved to hear it after all these years."

"I may be able to do a little better than that for you," I said. "I think I could persuade Zita to join you at your table for a few minutes before the next show."

"How very delightful that would be," Conyers said, beaming.

I was glad the old boy couldn't hear my conversation with

Zita. Her stage personality is that of a frail helpless child in need of love and help. In reality she is a very tough cookie, whose conversation is larded with earthy words. If she needs help, I imagine the glowering George Ortell supplies it. He is the muscle; she is the breadwinner.

"Why don't you get your friend one of the fancy call girls who hang out in the Trapeze Bar?" Zita suggested. She was alone in her dressing room.

"You've got him wrong," I said. "He's a nice old guy having a sort of final spree. You touched him with your rendition of cockles and mussels. His mother used to sing it to him."

"Hearts and flowers!" Zita said. "Look, really, Mark—"

"You owe me, friend," I said. I had gotten her out of a jam with the musicians' union some time back. "Give him ten minutes."

"After that, brother, you will owe *me*," Zita said.

I have left out her four-letter embellishments.

She put on a little mink jacket, and I led her out to the old man's table. He smiled with delight when he saw us coming. He stood, bowed low over her hand when I introduced them, held her chair for her.

Zita gave me a dirty look when I left them alone after the first pleasantries. In the lobby entrance I ran into Jerry Dodd. He is known as the "security officer"—we don't say "house detective" at the Beaumont. Jerry is a wiry, bright-eyed little man who is tops at his job.

"Your project seems to be having himself a whale of a time," he said. "How did you persuade Zita?"

"Slight arm-twist," I said.

"Odd thing about your old gentleman," Jerry said.

"Odd?"

"He's carrying a gun," Jerry said.

"You're out of your mind!" I said.

"I kid you not. Shoulder holster. It's my business to spot that kind of thing, Mark."

"Well, I'll be damned—"

"Maybe the suicide the boss is afraid of is closer than you think," Jerry said. "I suggest you pass the word on to Chambrun."

Chambrun rarely leaves the hotel, but that evening he had gone to a dinner given by the French Ambassador to the United Nations. Long ago Chambrun had been a figure of some importance in the French Resistance movement.

After the second show in the Blue Lagoon I saw, to my surprise, that Zita had rejoined Mr. Conyers, this time bringing her boy friend, George Ortell, with her. There was a fresh supply of champagne in the ice bucket. The old boy was positively glowing. How hungry he was for companionship, I thought. Maybe he would forget his dark thoughts of self-destruction for a while.

I didn't bother Chambrun that night with Jerry Dodd's observation about Conyers's gun. I thought of it as simply confirming Chambrun's fear that, when the old man "ran out of gas," he probably planned to do away with himself. There was still plenty of gas left in his tank after only one day, and he had seemed to be having too good a time to be despondent.

Sunday morning at nine-twenty-two I went into Chambrun's office and found myself confronting "the hanging judge." Chambrun is short, square, with wide, splayed fingers that can play an extraordinary piano. He has a small mustache, and when his lips are compressed it makes a straight black line above his mouth. His eyes were deep in their pouches that morning, glittering. I braced myself.

"You were right about the Brooklyn Bridge," he said.

I was lost for a moment.

"He not only sold it to Ruysdale, he sold it to you and me too. Our Mr. Conyers is a phony."

"Phony?"

"I was concerned about him," Chambrun said. "I thought if he had family or friends they should know that he was embarked on a last spree, which would probably be followed by his suicide. I am so clever! I am such a Good Samaritan!"

"So?" I said.

"The address on Rittenhouse Square is a phony. There is no Walston Conyers listed in any Philadelphia directory. I got a banker friend of mine out of bed who tells me that Conyers, or whatever his name is, came into the bank, handed over five thousand dollars in cash, and asked for a certified check. He was not a client. No one at the bank had ever seen him before."

"He's carrying a gun," I said.

Chambrun sat up very straight in his desk chair. I told him about the previous evening and what Jerry Dodd had noticed.

"We've been had," Chambrun said, slamming the palm of his hand hard on his desk. "He's here for quite another purpose than he led us to believe."

He reached for the telephone on his desk and asked for room service. "Henri? Mr. Chambrun here. Have you had a breakfast order from 1412? A Mr. Conyers. . . . Has the waiter brought the tray down yet? . . . Good. Now listen carefully. Was there fruit juice on the order? . . . Fine. Tell the waiter not to touch the juice glass, no matter what. You understand? I'll have Mr. Dodd waiting for it when it comes down. I want to get fingerprints from it. . . . Fingerprints, you idiot! You know what fingerprints are, don't you?"

Chambrun put down the phone. "There's just a chance we may find out who this old charlatan really is. I want him covered, Mark. I'll talk to Dodd. But I want you to see to it that all phone calls in and out of his room are covered—also, any orders he gives, any communications with anyone."

I had some answers fairly quickly, none of them helpful. Conyers had made no phone calls from his room except to room service to order his breakfast and to the newsstand in the lobby to ask for a Sunday *Times.* I looked over the restaurant slips from the Blue Lagoon of last night. Conyers had splurged. He had bought two more bottles of champagne and enough Kentucky sour mash for Otell to float a destroyer. There had been two cold-lobster suppers and a deluxe hamburger with onion, the last item presumably for the sour-mash drinker. Conyers had made friends.

The day wore on into the afternoon. I ran into Jerry Dodd a couple of times. He had placed one of his men on the fourteenth floor. Conyers had not left his room all day. He had asked for the maid to make up his room, but she'd had to work around him. She'd found him a charming old "gent," and he had signed a tip for her of five dollars. He was spending.

Just before five o'clock, when I was about to take off for cocktails with my girl who lives a couple of blocks from the hotel and who is my secretary on weekdays, I got a flash to report to the boss's office pronto. I found Jerry Dodd already there.

"We got lucky," Chambrun told me. "The fingerprints paid off. Our Mr. Conyers's real name is Dr. Morton Wallace—a doctor of philosophy. He's a professor at an upstate college—or was. He had a son who was murdered here in New York about a year ago. The son was found shot to death in an alley behind a Greenwich Village nightclub. Police never came up with an answer."

"How did our Mr. Conyers happen to have his fingerprints on record?" I asked.

"War work—long ago."

Jerry Dodd gave me an odd look. "Would you like to make a guess as to who the entertainer was at that nightclub in the Village?"

His face told me. I didn't have to guess. "Zita?"

"Bull's-eye," Jerry said. "Looks like the old man was planning to play the role of avenging angel. I've been trying to reach Zita but she doesn't answer at home."

"Well, there's no show on Sunday night, so she's safe enough for the moment," I said. "Conyers—Wallace—still hasn't left his room?"

"It takes a long time to read the whole Sunday *Times*," Jerry said wryly. "But the old boy was almost certainly setting her up last night—along with Georgie Ortell."

"Wouldn't she know who he is?" I asked.

Jerry shrugged. "Not necessarily. She was never implicated in the murder. Claimed she had never seen young Wallace in her life. There was no court hearing. Certainly she wouldn't have gone to the funeral where the old man could be seen."

Chambrun's phone rang. He picked it up. "Chambrun here. Yes, Charles." There was a long silence as Chambrun listened, and his face turned rock-hard. He put down the phone and stood up.

"That was Charles. He takes over from Henri in room service at three o'clock on Sundays. Henri left him written instructions, but he only just found them. It seems that our Mr. Conyers ordered a high tea for three people to be served in his room. He asked Charles if he could suggest anything that Miss Zita might particularly like. Very thin caviar sandwiches was Charles's recommendation. The high tea was taken up to 1412 twenty minutes ago.

"Let's go!" Jerry Dodd said.

We raced out to the elevators and got up to the fourteenth floor as quickly as we could. At the door of 1412 we rang the bell. There was no answer. I pounded on the door. You can't hear anything that's going on inside a Beaumont room because they're all soundproofed. Jerry pushed me aside and produced his special passkey.

Jerry was in first, his gun drawn.

The tableau inside the room sent the small hairs rising on the back of my neck. The elaborate high tea had not been touched. The three people in the room were standing. Zita was half crouching behind George Ortell. Ortell, poised on the balls of his feet, like an animal ready to spring, was facing Conyers, who was pointing a gun steadily at Ortell's heart.

As we barged into the room, the old man's voice rose in a kind of despairing wail.

"You damned interfering idiots!" he cried out. "Oh, damn you!"

And then he turned and tossed the gun onto the bed. In that instant Ortell sprang at him, but somehow Jerry Dodd managed to trip Ortell, and he crashed into the table of food.

The old man had turned away, and he seemed to crumple. His shoulders shook. He was sobbing.

"The damned old goat was going to kill us!" Zita said. Her face was the color of ashes.

Ortell had got himself straightened up, and he looked at Jerry, wondering whether he should go to work on him. I've seen Jerry handle guys three times his size, and I almost wished Ortell would try it.

While Ortell was wondering, Jerry moved in. He whipped open Ortell's jacket and came away with a gun.

"You got a license to carry this, buster?" he asked.

"What the hell is it to you?" Ortell asked.

"If you haven't, I'm charging you with violation of the Sullivan Law—carrying concealed weapons."

"Let's get out of here," Ortell said to Zita.

"Don't you want to bring charges against Mr. Conyers?—against Dr. Wallace?" Chambrun said.

"To hell with that," Ortell said. "Just see that he gets locked away in a padded cell where he belongs." He and Zita almost ran out of the room.

The old man turned very slowly to face us. His voice sounded broken. "How did you get to know my real name?" he asked.

"Did a little checking," Chambrun said. "I meant to help you, Dr. Wallace. Perhaps I have. Murder would have cut short your last fling."

"Oh, yes, it would," the old man said, his voice bitter. "There was to have been a murder, and it would have cut short my adventure in high living."

"Let me guess," Chambrun said gently. "Ortell was about to spring at you. Then you would have managed to let him get the gun, and he would have killed *you*."

"And he would have paid for it!" the old man cried out. "The waiter saw him here. Room service knew they were coming.

He couldn't have escaped the murder charge when my body was found."

"You think he killed your son?"

"She killed him. That woman killed him. Oh, she didn't pull the trigger, but she played with him, ruined him, and then had him destroyed."

"Evidence?"

"None. The police had nothing. But I knew—from fragments I had from my Johnny—that she was a sickness that was destroying him. I have nothing to live for, Mr. Chambrun—nothing but revenge. But I thought, by dying, I could square accounts for Johnny."

"How did you get them to come here for tea?"

"I played the foolish innocent last night. I let them believe they could hook me for a few thousand dollars. They were eager to come today. Oh, God, there is no chance for me to reach him again."

"We can send him up for a spell on a gun-carrying charge," Jerry said.

Chambrun put his hand on the old man's shoulder. "Perhaps we can find a way to reopen the case—Mr. Conyers. Meanwhile, please consider yourself my guest. The Beaumont will be proud to serve you." Then he turned to me, all business. "Get busy, Mark. We need someone to replace Zita in the Blue Lagoon."

# Pierre Chambrun Defends Himself

New York has changed since I first came to work here only a few years ago. Luxury landmarks, great hotels, and famous restaurants like the Stork Club, El Morocco, Toots Shor's, the Colony, and the Cafe Renaissance—all have disappeared from the scene. People are afraid to go out at night; they hear you can be mugged, robbed, cut up just for kicks. But there is one place where luxury is still the theme song and where you can feel safe—the Hotel Beaumont, where I work as public relations genius.

The Hotel Beaumont is still unmatched anywhere in the world. Its trappings are lavish, its culinary reputation is excellent, its wine cellar unsurpassed. Each room and suite in this great hotel is constructed to shut out the harsh sounds of a raucous world. It is like a small city in itself, run by an extraordinary executive named Pierre Chambrun, a legend in his time.

The security system is supervised by a wiry, sharp little man named Jerry Dodd. The Hotel Beaumont is *safe.* I've often come in late at night off the city streets and realized that I was letting out my breath in a long sigh of relief. Once through the revolving doors, the automatic anxieties I'd felt as I'd circulated in the outside world evaporated. I was home—home safe.

And yet on a spring night of this year a violent and shocking murder took place inside that safety zone. A man was "cut up" for what appeared to be more than kicks. He was stabbed a dozen times by a missing knife—a butcher knife, the police believed. He was mutilated in a way that seemed to suggest that his death was meant to serve as a warning to someone or to some other persons. The killer had obliterated an eye with the knife and cut a diagonal line across the victim's face, obliterated the other eye, and then cut a crossing diagonal line. The result was a bloody X. Someone suggested a gang killing, perhaps a Mafia vengeance.

The dead man was a West German diplomat, in residence at the Beaumont while he attended the current session of the United Nations. A gang killing didn't seem probable to me. Early evidence indicated that Erich Garber had been entertaining a lady who was someone else's wife. An outraged husband seemed much more likely to me than a gangster contract.

The Beaumont's staff was thrown a little off balance when the murder was discovered. It so happened that on that particular spring night Pierre Chambrun had made one of his rare excursions outside the hotel. We were, for a short time, a ship without a captain.

Pierre Chambrun, a short dark little man with the brightest black eyes you have ever seen, lives in the penthouse atop the Beaumont. He sunbathes there in decent weather. He exercises in the hotel's gymnasium. He rarely goes out. If people want to see him, they come to him, usually in his second-floor office, where a Picasso of the "blue period," a personal gift from the artist, is only one item of luxury in a large unofficelike room.

But on this night Chambrun had gone to a dinner. In what Chambrun referred to as the "black days," the early forties, he had fought in the French Resistance movement. The dinner had been a gathering of old friends and comrades-in-arms from that distant time.

Chambrun returned from the dinner accompanied by a friend, a French painter named Jacques Furneaux. He had insisted on Furneaux's stopping for a nightcap, a very special brandy reserved for very special occasions. He walked into a kind of organized bedlam. He found me in his office along with Lieutenant Hardy of Homicide, a friend from one or two other violences within the sacred gates.

I had been going over the dead man's card file with Hardy. We know more about most of our guests than they would care to have us know—their habits, their credit ratings, their past history as guests, how they handle their alcohol, and even their private lives as they are lived inside the hotel.

Erich Garber was from West Berlin, an army officer in Hitler's battalions in World War Two; a retread democrat, apparently. He was the vice-president of a large automobile manufacturing company, and his credit was impeccable. He had one of the most expensive suites in the hotel, and that means expensive. He gave small but costly parties. He was polite to employees, a generous tipper, and held his liquor like a gentleman. The one blemish on his record was a predilection for high-priced call girls. As far as the hotel was concerned, he handled this with discretion, too.

Chambrun, wearing a scarlet-lined cape over his dinner jacket, walked into his office with his friend Furneaux, took one look at Hardy, and his eyes became those of a hanging judge. I should say here that anything that upsets the Swiss-watch efficiency of the hotel's operations is taken by Chambrun as a personal affront.

"Who?" was all he said.

"Erich Garber, a West German diplomat," I said.

"14B," Chambrun said.

"Yes, sir."

He threw his cape over the back of a chair, took one of his Egyptian cigarettes from a silver case, and lit it. He muttered introductions to Furneaux. "Mark Haskell, my public relations man, and Lieutenant Hardy, Homicide Division of the

New York City police." Hardy, who looks like an ex-Notre Dame fullback, blond, a little battered, grunted something. I nodded.

"How?" Chambrun asked.

"Knife," Hardy said. "Dozen or more stab wounds—nearly every one of them would have done the job. A big ugly X carved on his face—eye to chin, eye to chin."

Chambrun looked as if he had turned to stone.

"Sweet Mother!" Furneaux said under his breath.

I thought they were overreacting a little. "Most of what we know comes from a room service waiter named Marcel," I said. "It seems he—"

"Marcel Durant," Chambrun said. He knew every employee's name and history. "Where is Marcel?"

"In the lobby office," I said.

"It would simplify things if I could hear the story from him instead of listening to it twice, first from you," Chambrun said. He walked over and sat down behind his carved Florentine desk. I called downstairs for Marcel, then walked over to the buffet in the corner and brought Chambrun a cup of the Turkish coffee he drinks from morning to night.

Chambrun waved to the buffet. "Make yourself a drink, Jacques," he said to his friend. He watched Furneaux go to the buffet and pour himself a stiff brandy. "When you mentioned the X cut on the man's face, Jacques and I were startled," he said. "We have just come from a dinner of former French Resistance fighters. Back in those days there was a Gestapo butcher who used to carve Xs on the faces of our men whenever he caught them, blinding them in the process."

"Same thing here," Hardy said. "You know Garber from those days?"

"Not by sight or by name," Chambrun said. He glanced at his friend Furneaux.

"Not by name," Furneaux said. "Of course I haven't seen him here."

Marcel Durant, as you will have guessed, was French. He

had been with the hotel for many years, a top waiter in his time. His gradual crippling had removed him from the dining room and Grill Room staffs—he no longer could move quickly enough. He had been reassigned to room service, where the functioning was more leisurely. He had a craggy, deeply lined face, and his eyes looked red and tired as he came into Chambrun's office.

"Monsieur Chambrun," he said in a husky voice, ignoring the rest of us.

"You've had a distressing evening, Marcel."

"It was horrible, monsieur," he said.

"Take your time, Marcel, and tell it to me from the very beginning."

"I'll do my best, Monsieur." Marcel took a deep breath. "An order came to room service—dinner for two in 14B. Vichyssoisse, roast veal, baby peas with onions, potatoes au gratin, a *vin ordinaire.* The dessert was to be ordered later. Dinner was to be served at eight o' clock."

"And you were prompt?"

"To the minute, monsieur."

"Good. Proceed, Marcel."

"I rang the doorbell, and Herr Garber opened the door for me, and I wheeled in the wagon."

"You had served Garber before?"

"Oh, yes, monsieur. Herr Garber often dines in his suite. Very polite, generous tipper. Never tries to hurry me, for which I am grateful. He generally asks for me."

"So you wheeled in the wagon?"

"Yes, monsieur. Herr Garber was not alone. There was a very beautiful young lady with him. She was sitting on the piano bench, watching me as I came in. You will remember there is a small spinet in 14B."

"Yes. Had you ever seen this young lady before?"

"No, monsieur. She was very beautiful, as I've said, twenty or twenty-five years younger than Herr Garber."

Chambrun glanced at Hardy. "You've found this young woman?"

"Not yet," Hardy said.

"She was gone when I found the body, monsieur," Marcel said.

"You found the body?"

"Yes, monsieur. When Mrs. Kniffin let me into the room—"

"Please, Marcel," Chambrun interrupted. "Tell me the story in sequence."

"Yes, monsieur. Herr Garber told me where to set the table. While I was doing so, the telephone rang, and Herr Garber answered. He spoke in what I suppose was German. I do not understand German. He seemed very agitated. When he put down the receiver, he turned to the young lady and spoke to her in French, which of course I did understand. 'It is a man I must see,' he said. 'It is urgent. Will you mind waiting in the bedroom, cherie? Unfortunately, this man knows both you and your husband, at least by sight.' And so the young lady—"

"'You and your husband,' he said?" Chambrun interrupted again.

"Yes, monsieur. His exact words. So the young lady hurried into the bedroom, and Herr Garber turned to me. 'I'm afraid the dinner must be delayed, Marcel,' he said. 'Will you be good enough to take it away and call me in half an hour? If the dinner cannot be kept warm and palatable, you will replace it with a fresh order. I will, of course, pay twice.' So I wheeled out the wagon, monsieur, and took it back down to the kitchen."

"So?"

"About twenty minutes later a call came to room service asking for me. It was Herr Garber. He said that his friend did not care for the wine he had in the room and would I bring him a bottle of Saint Cristobel, '57. Of course I said I would."

Chambrun's eyes widened. "Saint Cristobel, '57? That's what he asked for?"

"Yes, monsieur. So I took up the wine and Herr Garber answered the door and took it from me."

"You didn't see into the suite—who was with him?"

"No, monsieur. He said I shouldn't call for another half hour, that the dinner must now be replaced. When I called he would tell me exactly when to serve."

"Go on, Marcel."

"In a half hour I called 14B. There was no answer. I neglected to tell you, monsieur, that he had given me a ten-dollar tip when I first arrived with the wagon. My time was up, but I wanted to earn the tip, so I stayed on. In about ten minutes, I called again. No answer. And so, monsieur, I went up to the fourteenth floor and to the door of 14B. There was obviously a gay party going on inside, monsieur. Someone was playing the spinet, and they were playing an old French song and singing. The lady was singing, too. You remember the song, monsieur, 'Alouette, gentil' Alouette, Alouette, je te plumerai.'"

Chambrun had that frozen look. "I remember," he said.

"I rang the doorbell, monsieur, but nobody answered. So, not wanting to interrupt till I was wanted, I went back down to the kitchen. I kept calling at intervals, monsieur, without getting an answer. From my first visit to the room with the wagon until I became genuinely distressed must have been almost an hour and a half. I went back upstairs and listened outside 14B. There were no sounds now. I went to look for Mrs. Kniffin, the housekeeper. I was concerned—the dinner would be spoiled—the second dinner!

"If they had left, forgetting the dinner, I would remove the soiled glasses and the empty wine bottle. Mrs. Kniffin was unwilling at first. She had received a call from Herr Garber asking her not to send the maid to turn down the bed—the maid goes to turn down the beds at nine, as you know, monsieur. But in the end I persuaded her to let me into the suite. We could always apologize. So Mrs. Kniffin let me in with her key—and there he was, dead, bloody, that great X cut on his face."

"And no young lady?"

"Nor anyone else, monsieur."

Chambrun put out his cigarette and sat silent.

"The elevators are self-service at that time," Hardy said, "so no one saw a young lady leave that floor. Jerry Dodd is checking, but so far no report on her or on the visitor who phoned at eight."

"The visitor who phoned at eight is clearly the murderer," I said. "He'd have been as inconspicuous as possible. Garber's card indicates he had a penchant for call girls. If the girl Marcel saw was such a girl, she'd take off in a hurry. Being found there would be bad for her business."

Chambrun's eyes turned my way, and I thought he must hate me the way they glittered. "'Unfortunately this man knows both you and your husband, at least by sight.'"

He turned to the waiter. "Marcel, you would know this young lady if you saw her again."

"Oh, yes, monsieur. Dark, svelte, very young, very attractive."

"You heard Herr Garber talk in German on the phone to his unexpected guest but you did not, of course, hear the guest's voice at that time. When you brought the Saint Cristobel, '57?"

"No, monsieur."

"Later, when you heard them singing 'Alouette'?"

"I cannot be sure, monsieur. The girl was singing and one of the men. It was very loud, very gay. I couldn't say if it was the guest or Herr Garber. It was—how shall I say?—like a comic act?"

"Is there anything else of consequence that comes to your mind, Marcel?"

"No, monsieur."

"Thank you, Marcel. Will you wait downstairs again, please," Chambrun watched the old man go, and Chambrun's eyes narrowed to slits.

"Fingerprint men are going over the suite," Hardy said. "There are wine glasses and an empty bottle of wine—this Saint Cristobel, '57. In the bedroom were several cigarette butts stained with lipstick. The girl must have touched something. The girl puzzles me." When Hardy is puzzled, he looks like a baffled St. Bernard. "She was in the bedroom when Garber's unexpected guest arrived—hidden there because the guest would know her by sight and might tell her husband. She hides there, but later she joins the party, singing that French song. After that someone cut Garber to pieces with what could have been a carving or butcher knife. Had the girl left before that? If she was still there when it happened, why did the killer let her live? Unless she was, all along, the killer's accomplice."

"That occurred to me," Chambrun said. "To make sure that Garber would be where they wanted him to be, she had agreed to a date with him. According to his card he liked young women, though usually they were professionals and not other men's wives." Chambrun lit a fresh Egyptian cigarette and leaned back in his chair, his eyes almost shut. "What do we know about the killer?" he asked softly.

"Nothing," Hardy said.

"Oh, come, Hardy, we know a great deal. At least four things. First, he speaks German. Garber wouldn't have spoken to him in German on the phone unless the killer was also speaking German. Garber spoke to the girl in French, which presupposes she was French—or that she was more familiar with French than English. Second, the killer was a man of rather special tastes. He asked for Saint Cristobel, 1957. There are not two places in New York where Saint Cristobel is stocked. It comes from a vineyard in southern France. I discovered it some years ago, was entranced by its bouquet and flavor, and arranged to have a case delivered to me here each year. It is not ordinarily sold commercially. The vineyard owner keeps it for his friends. He produces only a small quantity each year. You are a connoisseur of wines, Jacques. Have you ever heard of Saint Cristobel?"

Furneaux smiled. "Yes. I have had it here with you, Pierre. But nowhere else."

"So our killer had knowledge of an almost nonexistent

wine," Chambrun said. "Third, he knows something about hotel routines. I have to assume it was he who called Mrs. Kniffin and asked her not to send the maid to turn down the bed. And fourth, it is possible he plays the piano. And doesn't it strike you as odd that these two German-speaking gentlemen should be enjoying themselves with an old French folksong?

"So we know this about our killer; he is a German-speaking wine connoisseur who knows the hotel routines and plays the piano, particularly the old French classic 'Alouette.' Suggest anyone to you, Mark?"

"No," I said. "Should it?"

Chambrun's smile was a tight little quirk at the corners of his mouth. "I speak German, along with several other languages. I am not only a wine connoisseur, I have special knowledge of an obscure wine—Saint Cristobel. I know the hotel routines better than anyone else in the world. I play the piano, as you very well know." He turned to Furneaux. "In the black days, when we could afford to be noisy, Jacques, do you remember that I played the piano?"

"Yes."

"And do you remember what song we sang most often when there was a group of us together?"

Furneaux seemed to have trouble swallowing. "'Alouette,'" he said.

"To add to the case against me," Chambrun said, "I obviously have access to a hundred carving knives and a hundred butcher knives." His smile became a real smile as he looked at the scowling Hardy. "Open-and-shut case, friend? A wild set of coincidences? Well, my blood is not running cold with anxiety. You see, I know something you don't know, Hardy. I know I *didn't* kill Erich Garber. Fortunately, I have an ironclad alibi. I was with Jacques, here, and our friends from the Resistance days from seven o'clock until I walked into this office a little while ago. You will swear to that, won't you, Jacques?"

"Of course. And so will a dozen others," Furneaux said.

"Is that good enough for you, Hardy?"

"Don't be a damned fool," Hardy said. "Sure it's good enough."

"It shouldn't be," Chambrun said, his voice harsh. "One thing we haven't discussed is the possible motive. I told you that the X carved on Garber's face was a shock to Jacques and me because that was what a Gestapo butcher did to our friends back in the days of the Resistance. If Garber turns out to be, and I daresay he will, an ex-Gestapo man—if he was one of those X-makers in the old days—I would have a motive, and my alibi would be worthless. Jacques and my other friends would lie their heads off for me if I told them I was bent on following the Biblical precept of 'an eye for an eye, a tooth for a tooth.' So my alibi is no good."

"What the hell do you want me to say to that?" Hardy asked.

"I want you to say that obviously it was meant to look like me," Chambrun said. "I want you to say that you realize as you head toward the truth someone will remind you of these incriminating facts about me. But let me cheer you up, my friend. I can provide an alibi that *will* stand up. Jacques and my friends might lie for me, but not the manager and the waiters in the restaurant where we dined tonight."

"So stop playing games with me," Hardy said, nevertheless sounding relieved.

"I can tell you one thing more about the killer. He is someone who knows a great deal about me—about my habits, my tastes, my talents. Someone who has known about me for thirty years—back to the black days of the Resistance." Chambrun's smile remained, a sort of Cheshire-cat smile. "Just one thing went wrong with the killer's plan to implicate me."

"Your alibi," Hardy said.

"In a way." Chambrun turned to me. "How many evenings do I spend away from the hotel, Mark?"

"Three or four a year," I said.

"Quite so. The killer had every reason to suppose I would

be here in the hotel, moving about as I do every night. He set it up and unluckily for him he chose one of the rare occasions when I was away from my bailiwick. So now we proceed, Hardy. You always say that detective work involves checking, checking, and rechecking until the truth becomes obvious."

Lieutenant Hardy is a dogged cop. He takes hold of a case by the hind leg, and he holds on for dear life, checking, checking, rechecking. Jerry Dodd, chief of security at the Beaumont, is by comparison mercurially dogged. He grabs hold, lets go, attacks from another point, lets go, until someone cracks under the pressure.

Jerry is a mad chain-smoker, and he paced up and down Chambrun's office listening to the Great Man's summing up of the case. Hardy had gone off to his dogged work of checking fingerprints, checking on Mrs. Kniffin, the housekeeper who'd gotten the call from 14B, checking the restaurant where Chambrun had dined—the last at Chambrun's insistence.

"So you make sense, or you're just building something up to irritate us," Jerry said to Chambrun. He is one of the few people on the staff who can speak his mind to the boss without bothering to be polite or careful. "Let's start at the top. Who is there in the hotel that fits the bill of speaking German, knowing your blasted special wine, knowing the routines—oh, to hell with listing it all. Who knows the hotel, you, and your habits of thirty years ago?"

"No one I know of."

"Because anyone could speak German without your knowing about it. Did you know I speak Japanese? Well, I do—never mind at the moment how it happens. Half a dozen maître d's, room service waiters, and chefs know that you drool at the mention of Saint Cristobel. No secret that. Anybody could play the piano. Ever hear me on 'The Darktown Strutters Ball'? There are a thousand employees in the hotel who know that the maids turn down the beds at nine o'clock unless otherwise instructed. Anyone living in the hotel, any employee has access to carving knives. It would take a year to check out all the possibilities."

"Please don't drop your ashes on my Turkish rug, Jerry," Chambrun grumbled.

"They're good for the rug," Jerry said impatiently. "There's just one phase of this we can narrow down. Who knows you used to play and sing 'Alouette' for your Resistance pals in 1943? That touch is just a little too elaborate, and it may hang somebody."

"I wish I had an answer to that," Chambrun said.

"Maybe it's not so hard as it looks," Jerry said. "This hotel is teeming with French chefs and French waiters and French chambermaids. You're a sucker for your native people. And you're a kind of hero they grew up on, most of them."

"You make me sound like the world's grandfather," Chambrun said. "I was twenty years old in 1943."

"And except for confusing things you're not a hell of a lot of help right now. That girl Garber was out to make could solve this for us, but unless Hardy comes up with fingerprints, or unless she's stupid enough to show herself to Marcel again, we can—we will have to—forget about her."

"So it would seem." Chambrun looked sleepy.

"So let's begin with Erich Garber. Was he a Gestapo man in the days they were carving Xs on dead Frenchmen's faces?" Jerry said. He started for the door and stopped. "How many of your old Resistance friends attended that dinner tonight?"

"There were eighteen of us," Chambrun said. He nodded his head like a schoolteacher who is pleased with a precocious pupil.

"They can alibi you—but can all of them be alibied?" Jerry looked from Chambrun to Jacques Furneaux, who had been silent in the corner all this time.

"Some of us arrived late," Furneaux said. "I was one of them."

"What kept you?"

"I work for the French delegation to the United Nations," Furneaux said. "I was held up decoding messages from the Foreign Office."

"What time did you get to the dinner?"

"About ten o'clock. That's why I came back here with Pierre. We'd had almost no time to talk of the old days."

"Garber was presumably dead by ten o'clock," Jerry said. "You can prove you were at the UN?"

"I didn't say I was at the UN," Furneaux answered quietly. "I was working in my own apartment—alone."

"No alibi?"

"No alibi," Furneaux said. "And to save you time, I fit most of Pierre's points. I speak German, I know about Pierre's fondness for Saint Cristobel, I can play the piano. I don't know the hotel routines, but I have stayed here. I could have remembered that a maid turns down the beds every night."

"Go home, Jacques," Chambrun said, smiling. "If they decide to arrest you, I'll let you know."

"So you want to make a joke of it!" Jerry Dodd said and stormed out of the office.

The time was creeping on toward morning. Chambrun had taken a few minutes to change out of his evening clothes and into a loose-fitting tweed suit. He must have drunk a gallon of his poisonous Turkish coffee and smoked a box and a half of his Egyptian cigarettes. He sat behind his desk, his eyes hooded. I could almost hear his mental machinery revolving, but I had no idea what it was producing.

About four in the morning Hardy turned up again—slow and solid Hardy.

"We've picked up a lot of fingerprints in the suite," he said. "The girl's must be among them, along with Garber's and Marcel's. If the girl's prints match something that we or the FBI have on file, fine. If not—not."

"Not, I imagine," Chambrun said.

"Marcel's story checks and double-checks," Hardy said.

"Garber—or at least someone in 14B—ordered the dinner. The veal was special—with a special wine sauce. The girl who took the order remembers that Garber was most painstaking about it, including a wish for some flowers for the table. 'I am entertaining a lady,' he told the order girl. He then asked, politely, if he could have Marcel to serve him. 'He knows my ways,' he told the girl.

"Promptly at eight Marcel delivered the dinner. Ten minutes later he reappeared in the kitchen with the word that Garber wanted the dinner held—kept warm, if possible—for half an hour. Later Marcel did call 14B, just as he said. The girl was at his elbow when he made the call. No answer. Just as he said, Garber had called in the interim and asked for a bottle of Saint Cristobel, 1957."

Chambrun's eyes opened. "Garber called?"

Hardy checked his notebook. "14B called—a man. Who else?"

"The killer who was trying to frame me," Chambrun said. "That's who else."

"At any rate, the girl located Marcel, who was puttering around the kitchen worrying about the dinner, and had him take up the wine. He came back in a sweat. Another half hour at least. The chef would have to prepare whole new servings. No answer when he called in half an hour. Something, he thought, might be wrong with the phone, so he went upstairs. That's when he heard the singing and piano playing. He came back down and told the room service girl about it.

"It was now getting late. Marcel was unhappy; he'd collected his tip, so he felt he had to wait. Eventually he went back upstairs. That's when he went to Mrs. Kniffin and explained his problem. In the end he persuaded her to open the door—and they found Garber dead and the girl gone."

I thought for a moment that Chambrun had gone to sleep while Hardy was talking, but he lifted his heavy lids to look at the lieutenant. "Is Marcel still here?"

"I asked him to stick around," Hardy said. "I've got an artist on the way from headquarters to see if Marcel can help him sketch a likeness of the girl. That girl is about our best bet."

"If she's a regular hooker, the people in the Trapeze Bar and the Blue Lagoon Room will recognize her," I said.

"Could be," Chambrun said. "I'd like to watch the picture process. Can it be done up here?"

Hardy shrugged. "Why not?" He hauled himself to his feet. "I have to check in at headquarters. Victim a diplomat. We'll be up to our necks in State Department characters."

I don't know if you've ever seen one of these Police Department experts work up a portrait likeness of someone simply from the description of an eyewitness. This one talked to Marcel, fooling away at a sketching pad as he asked the old man questions. Small eyes? Wide eyes? Set close together or far apart? Eyebrows thin or thick? Hair worn long, short, loose, or close to the head? Mouth wide and generous or tight and thin? Ears flat or protruding, small or large?

Marcel, obviously near exhaustion and suffering some pain from his arthritis, was nevertheless eager to help. The police artist sat in a chair near the office door, with Marcel watching over his shoulder. I was circulating, taking a look every minute or two at what the artist was coming up with: a dark girl with hair worn short and shaped to her head, wide come-hither eyes, a smiling mouth. Marcel appeared satisfied with the growing likeness.

"It is truly astonishing how you do this, monsieur," he told the artist.

The girl on the drawing pad would certainly have been attractive enough to interest a man like Erich Garber.

What happened then was so sudden, so unexpected, so terrifying that I find it impossible to describe it adequately, except to say that in the crisis I froze. I was still wandering and was at the opposite end of the office from the door. Marcel, near the door, was bending over the chair where the police artist worked. Chambrun, his eyes closed, was slumped in his desk chair.

The office door opened. When I say it opened, I'm not being precise. It burst open. An unbelievable figure stood there. He had some kind of stocking mask pulled over his face, and he was holding a gun in his right hand. He aimed it directly at Chambrun—and fired.

I saw Chambrun topple out of his chair. This monster took another step into the room to fire again.

As I've said, I froze. I couldn't move. But Marcel moved. He let out a great shout and stumbled toward the masked man, clawing at him with his crippled hands. They wrestled for an instant, and then the gun went off again.

Marcel seemed to bounce, but he clung to the masked man. Now the police artist was struggling out of his chair, and I saw Chambrun, on his hands and knees, opening a desk drawer where I knew he kept a gun.

Then the masked man wrenched himself free of Marcel, turned, and ran out of the office. Marcel dropped to his knees, then toppled over onto his side. The police artist was off after the would-be assassin, and Chambrun and I reached Marcel at the same moment. The old man was clutching at his stomach and blood trickled through his fingers.

I didn't have to be told to call Dr. Partridge, our house physician. Chambrun knelt beside the old man, talking gently to him in French. I came back from the phone. Dr. Partridge was on his way.

"I thought he got you," I said to Chambrun.

"You have to be damned good or damned lucky to hit someone with a handgun at thirty feet," Chambrun said. "Except on television."

"But who in God's name—"

Chambrun turned his head, his face grim. "Someone who believes I killed Erich Garber," he said. "As good a guess as any. Get Jerry on the job, and call Hardy and have him check Garber's staff at the UN." His eyes darkened. "This old boy is pretty badly hurt."

"He saved your life," I said.

"I owe him," Chambrun said. "Check his employment card. If he has family I'm afraid they should be notified."

The masked man had made good his escape. He'd raced down from the second floor by the stairway and out onto the street before the police artist could get close enough to stop him. Dr. Partridge, looking grave, had moved Marcel to the hotel's small hospital. I had checked Marcel's employment card and found a home number for him. A sleepy and quickly frightened woman answered the phone. She turned out to be Marcel's granddaughter, and she said she would leave at once. I told her to come directly to Chambrun's office.

Marie Durant was an attractive young girl, small, slim, with long, beautiful, quite natural red hair. She was deeply concerned for her grandfather. Dr. Partridge already had the old man on the operating table, so he couldn't be seen.

"I have to warn you, Miss Durant," Chambrun said, "that the signs are not hopeful." He told her how it had happened and how deeply in debt he felt to Marcel. "It took great courage," he said. "More than that, it was the instinctive reaction of a brave man."

Marie lowered her head and wept quietly. Chambrun walked over to the sideboard and poured some brandy into a glass. He carried it back, balanced in the palm of his hand.

"It will do you good, Miss Durant, to drink this," he said.

She took it from him, gratefully. She drank it and put the glass down on the table beside her. Then Chambrun did a peculiar thing. He took the handkerchief out of his breast pocket and used it to pick up the glass and carry it back to his desk.

"I am sorry to play such a trick on you, Miss Durant," he said in a flat voice. "Your fingerprints are on that brandy glass. You and I know they will match the fingerprints the police have found in Erich Garber's apartment. Shall we talk together, without the police, before we decide what is to be done?"

I thought he was off his rocker. This girl looked no more like the portrait the police artist had drawn than I did.

"Your father was Marcel's son, was he not?" Chambrun asked, quite gently.

She nodded.

"Your father was killed by Garber?" Chambrun asked.

Now I knew he was off his rocker. The days of the Resistance were thirty years ago. This girl couldn't be a day over twenty-one or twenty-two.

The girl had turned a deathly white. "Erich Garber was with the Gestapo in Paris in the days of the occupation," she said. "My father, I am told, was with the Resistance. Some of his friends were killed and—and marked with the X. And then—then the girl with whom my father was in love was abducted, turned over to the Gestapo swine for their pleasure, and eventually killed. My father swore he would track down the man responsible if it took his whole life.

"Five years after the war he had not succeeded. He met and married my mother. He had given up his plan for revenge, they tell me. I was born in 1952. My father had a job as a salesman for a pharmaceutical firm. He had to take a trip to Rome, and on that trip, on the train, he came face to face with Erich Garber.

"We never knew exactly what happened. My father fell—or was thrown—from the train. When they found him he was at death's door, and he muttered the name 'Garber' to the people who found him. It meant nothing to them or to the authorities, but my mother knew what it meant—and my grandfather.

"I was one year old, so it meant nothing to me. My mother died that same year. Marcel decided to come to America, and he brought me with him. I have been raised here, Mr. Chambrun, had my schooling here. I was like any other American girl, except for one thing. Every day of my life my grandfather reminded me of my father and how he had died, reminded me that someday we would find Erich Garber, someday we would even the score. And I—well, it was like a religion, Mr. Chambrun. I came to believe in it."

She drew a long shuddering breath. "Then, about a month ago, he came home in a state of great excitement. Erich Garber had a suite here at the Beaumont, the very place where he, my grandfather, worked."

"Then the planning began," Chambrun murmured.

"Yes. You see, my grandfather isn't a maniac, Mr. Chambrun. He wanted to square accounts for my father, but he also wanted to go on living. He was going to commit a crime, but he meant to get away with it. Circumstances helped him. Garber entertained a good deal in his suite, and my grandfather ingratiated himself with this villain as a room service waiter. He learned a great deal about him, among other things that Garber was attracted to young girls." She shuddered. "Grandfather developed his plan. One thing was essential. He had to be sure that Garber would be in his suite when the plan was put into action."

"And that's where you came in?"

She nodded. "I spent a couple of evenings in the Trapeze Bar and just as my grandfather knew it would happen, Garber picked me up. He invited me to have dinner with him last night in his suite and so—and so there it was."

"And the plan was to frame me for the crime," Chambrun said. His eyes had a cold light in them.

"Yes and no. Don't you know, Mr. Chambrun, that you are a great hero to my grandfather? From the old days of the Resistance? To him you are a knight in shining armor."

"But he was prepared to pin a murder on me!"

The girl's eyes widened. "Who on earth would really believe you had done it, Mr. Chambrun? It would merely blur the trail, but no one would believe you guilty. If, finally, you were thought guilty, I assure you my grandfather would have stepped forward."

The red button on Chambrun's phone blinked, and he answered, listened, then put the phone down. "Your grandfather is conscious, Miss Durant. It may be for only a very short time. Unfortunately, he's not going to make it." He glanced at me. "Take Miss Durant down to the hospital, Mark."

The girl stood up. "Am I under arrest, Mr. Chambrun?"

"I am not the police," he said.

I rejoined Chambrun after I'd left Marie Durant sitting by Marcel's bedside, clinging to one of his gnarled hands. The old man seemed curiously peaceful.

Chambrun was sipping coffee. He looked very tired.

"How on earth did you guess she was the girl in Garber's suite?" I asked.

"Guess? Hardly a guess. You see, I had come to the conclusion some hours ago that Marcel was our man," he said. "The girl, whoever she was, was his accomplice. Therefore the police artist's portrait, which came out of Marcel's description, was obviously worthless. There is no such girl as the girl in the portrait."

"But why had you fixed the guilt on Marcel? His story checked at every point."

"My dear fellow, it checked at so few points," Chambrun said. "Follow along with me. Garber did order dinner, and he did ask for Marcel to serve it. That came through the order girl at room service. Check. But from there on, Mark, almost nothing checks. Marcel said he delivered the dinner. While he was setting up the table, he said, Garber had a phone call from someone he spoke to in German. It could be—but it can't be checked. We don't keep a record of incoming calls at the switchboard, as you know. There may or may not have been a call. Marcel took the dinner back to the kitchen. That checks."

"Just a minute," I said. "Marcel said that after the phone call from the German-speaking person, Garber asked the girl to go into the bedroom. And she did go. We know that—fingerprints."

"Yes, she did. She went because Marcel did not want her to witness the savage and bloody killing. If I am right, and I'm sure I am, among the things on that serving table with the dinner was the murder weapon—a carving knife. Marcel could have taken it from the kitchen without being observed. I think he killed the unsuspecting Garber in the first two or three minutes he was in the room—murdered him, marked him with the gruesome X. Then he sent his granddaughter home. Think. After that he called the room and got no answer. Naturally—there was no one there to answer."

"But there was a call *from* the room—for the special wine."

"Do you remember what the room service answering girl said, Mark? There was a call from 14B asking for a bottle of Saint Cristobel, '57. She had some trouble finding Marcel, she said, who was 'puttering around' in the kitchen. I suggest to you that it was Marcel himself who made the call from one of the innumerable phones on the kitchen level. His use of the phone would have drawn no attention. He had been calling 14B periodically to inquire about serving the dinner.

"The Saint Cristobel was part of this plan to point to me. So he took the wine up, let himself into the suite, and left it there with the dead man. He says Garber took it from him at the door, but that can't be checked. No one saw it happen. Again, he called asking that the maid be kept away. Mrs. Kniffin says the call came from 14B. How could she know, except that someone said, 'This is 14B. Please don't send the maid.' The call could have come from anywhere in the hotel. Again, no way to check. All very clever, Mark. His story cannot be proved, neither can it be disproved."

"Then what made you think—?"

"One mistake. Marcel made one mistake. One thing that could *not* have happened the way Marcel said it did."

"What, for God's sake?"

Chambrun smiled. He sang softly.

"Alouette, gentil' Alouette,
Alouette, je te plumerai."

"He heard them singing. A macabre business, but he said he heard them," I said.

"The song was one of my favorites in the old days," Chambrun said. "It helped to point to me. But—how long have you worked in the Beaumont, Mark?"

"Six years."

"Then you know that part of Marcel's story must be a lie."

I started to say I knew no such thing, then my jaw sagged. "The rooms are soundproofed!"

"Head of the class," Chambrun said. "From the hallways, you can't hear anything that goes on inside the rooms. And one lie in Marcel's story made everything else suspect."

"What are you going to do?"

"He is going to die—having saved me from an assassin. I shall have to tell my story to Hardy in spite of that."

"And the girl? She is an accomplice."

He gave me an odd look. "Which girl, the granddaughter or the girl in the portrait?"

He was thinking, I knew, that Marcel Durant would never kill again; that he owed Marcel something. However, he didn't have to make that decision. Marie came forward to make a full confession of her involvement and Marcel's to Lieutenant Hardy.

Chambrun's would-be assassin, the man in the stocking mask, did not escape entirely. The police did manage to track him to the West German secretariat where he hid, for a time, behind the shield of diplomatic immunity. It seemed the word of Garber's death had reached his staff, and a young man with a hero impulse, interpreting the first evidence to mean that Chambrun had killed Garber in retaliation for old horrors, had decided to take the law into his own hands. But for Marcel he might have succeeded. There would be a long wrangle between governments over what was to become of him, but from our point of view the case was closed.

"And now we have a hotel to run," Chambrun said.

# Chambrun and the Electronic Ear

Mrs. Veach, the motherly-looking chief operator on the switchboard at the Hotel Beaumont, was the first one to detect something irregular about the telephone in Room 912. The noise she heard was a faint continuous buzzing the moment the line was open. Mrs. Veach promptly called Jerry Dodd, the Beaumont's security officer.

Dodd listened, gave Mrs. Veach an approving pat on her wide shoulders, and headed for the second floor.

The second floor is where the heart of the Beaumont beats—in the private office of Pierre Chambrun, the legendary resident manager of America's top luxury hotel. Chambrun is a short square man with bright black eyes buried in deep pouches—eyes that can twinkle with humor and compassion or turn frighteningly cold and hard when the efficiency of the Beaumont is threatened.

The Beaumont is the private world over which Chambrun presides—a small city within one building with its own shops, restaurants, nightclubs, cooperatively owned apartments, hospital, safety-deposit vaults, beauty parlors, ballrooms, bars, even its own police force. Chambrun is the "boss," the king with the uncanny ability to know exactly what is going on in his domain everywhere and at all times.

Some people think Chambrun has a kind of built-in radar system of his own, but those of us who work for him know his secret: it is simply that nothing even remotely out of the ordinary is ever kept from him by any of his staff. Jerry Dodd, the wiry little security officer, was perfectly competent to handle the suggestion from Mrs. Veach that the telephone in Room 912 might be bugged, but it wouldn't have occurred to Jerry not to go to Chambrun first.

I happened to be with Chambrun when Jerry reported. I am Mark Haskell, the public relations man for the hotel and as close to Chambrun as anyone on his staff. My office is just down the corridor from his.

Chambrun listened to what Jerry had to say, then pressed a buzzer on his desk. Miss Ruysdale, his fabulous secretary, appeared in the door to the outer office.

"Card on Room 912, please," Chambrun said. He took a sip of the Turkish coffee from the cup at his elbow and lit one of his flat Egyptian cigarettes. His eyes narrowed against the smoke.

"You know anything about the occupant in 912?" Chambrun asked Jerry.

"Name—Warren Wilson," Jerry said. "Checked in yesterday. I haven't had a chance to look at his card."

Guests of the Hotel Beaumont might have been a little disturbed to know how complete the record was on them. On their cards were symbols that indicated their credit standing, their marital status, whether or not they were cheating on a spouse, how they handled their liquor. On the card there could be a notation that Chambrun had something special about them in his private file that he didn't want to become general knowledge.

Warren Wilson's card showed that he had not been a guest of the hotel before. We had nothing yet on his habits or his private life. But there was one interesting thing about him.

His room had been reserved for him and his credit vouched for by a deputy director of the Central Intelligence Agency in Washington.

"Cloak and dagger," Chambrun muttered. His eyes glittered. "The whole damned country is playing spy games these days, a million phones bugged. Half the world takes it as some sort of amusing parlor game. Who's listening to whom? Not, by God, in this hotel!" He took a deep drag on his cigarette, then ground it out in the ashtray on his desk. "Call Mr. Wilson, Mark, and tell him we'd like to come up to see him."

Mr. Wilson didn't answer his phone. Chambrun decided we would make an examination of Wilson's room whether he was there or not.

There was very little of interest in the room. Wilson had one extra suit, half a dozen shirts, some fresh underwear and handkerchiefs, two rather plain neckties, and shaving things in the bathroom. There were no letters, papers, or briefcases, only a slightly aged canvas airplane bag. It was rather less than you'd expect to find in a seventy-dollar-per-day room.

I checked all this out while Jerry searched the room for a bugging device. He found what he was looking for in the telephone instrument itself. He had unscrewed the mouthpiece and sat looking at it, scowling.

"This is it," he said to Chambrun. "Sophisticated little doojigger. Sends the sound to a listener somewhere or to a tape recorder somewhere. Like a tiny radio."

"Be careful how you handle it," Chambrun said. "It's so small, it couldn't have been installed by a man wearing gloves. There might be a fingerprint on it."

At that moment there was the sound of a key in the door, and a man came in. Warren Wilson was, I guessed, in his early thirties. He had sandy hair, cut short, and what was normally a pleasant, boyish face. He was angry now.

"Who the hell are you, and what are you doing here?" he demanded.

"I'm Pierre Chambrun, the hotel manager," Chambrun

said. "This is Mr. Dodd, our security officer, and Mr. Haskell, our public relations man."

"You're not entitled to be in my room!" Wilson said. He was staring at the phone, which Jerry still held, taken apart, in his hands.

"We had reason to think your phone was bugged, Mr. Wilson," Chambrun said. "I didn't choose to wait for you to get back. Show him, Jerry."

Jerry held out the instrument. "Tiny radio device," he said. "Anything you said on the phone went out somewhere. I haven't had a chance to check it, but it may have reported anything that went on in here whether the phone was in use or not."

"That's crazy!" Wilson said. "Who had the room before me? It could have been for them—no chance to remove it."

"Your room was reserved for you by the CIA, Mr. Wilson. I assume you work for them," Chambrun said.

Wilson drew a deep breath and fumbled for a cigarette. "I guess there's no point in trying to pretend," he said. "Yes, I work for the CIA."

"You care to tell us why you're here at the Beaumont?"

"I can give you a surface explanation," Wilson said. "I'm what you might call a courier. I am carrying documents to be delivered to someone else registered here at the hotel."

"Who?"

Wilson studied the end of his cigarette. "I don't think I can tell you that, Mr. Chambrun. I will say that my contact is supposed to register here at the hotel. He hasn't done so yet."

"So you are waiting for him to show up?"

"Yes."

Chambrun glanced at the card in his hand. "You checked in yesterday noon."

"Yes."

"Did you ask for the man you're supposed to meet?"

"Yes."

"Whom did you ask?"

"The man at the desk who registered me."

"Atterbury," Jerry Dodd said. He knew exactly who was on duty every hour of the day.

"Whom did you ask for?" Chambrun asked.

"Sorry. I can't tell you that."

Chambrun turned to me. "Find out, Mark," he said. "Call Atterbury on the housekeeper's phone. We can't use this one." He looked at Wilson. "Atterbury will remember," he said.

Wilson shrugged. "I don't suppose the name matters," he said. "It isn't his real name. I asked for Curt Helwig. The man at the desk told me he had a reservation but that he hadn't checked in."

"And he still hasn't checked in?"

"According to the front desk."

"Have you any idea who might have wanted to overhear your conversations, Mr. Wilson?"

Wilson shook his head slowly. "No idea," he said.

"If you'd had any sensitive telephone calls to make, would you have made them on this phone that goes through a switchboard?" Chambrun asked.

"Of course not."

Chambrun was, I saw, controlling his anger. "I don't like this kind of mumbo jumbo going on in my hotel," he said. "The whole damn country seems to be in the hands of idiot children playing spy games. Privacy seems to be a dead privilege. Well, by God, it isn't going to happen in the Beaumont! If somebody will bug your phone, Wilson, they may also try to steal the documents you're carrying. I suggest you put them in the hotel vault."

Wilson grinned. "I put them there right after I registered yesterday," he said. "I intend to leave them there till Helwig shows up."

"Good. Meanwhile we'll remove this device from your phone. When they realize they're not hearing what's going on here, that may scare them off. Handle it carefully, Jerry. Remember, we may find a helpful print on it."

We left Jerry Dodd with Wilson and went down to the

lobby where Atterbury was on duty again. Atterbury wasn't some kind of memory genius, but he did have total recall about Warren Wilson.

"He asked me for a Curt Helwig," Atterbury told Chambrun. "Helwig wasn't registered. Wilson seemed distressed and asked me to check on whether Helwig had a reservation."

"And did he?" Chambrun asked.

Atterbury nodded. "He did—and not quite usual, Mr. Chambrun. The reservation was made by a Washington source we honor without question. Same people who reserved Wilson's room. The thing that was unusual about Helwig's reservation was that they weren't quite sure when he would arrive—yesterday, today, tomorrow, even the day after that. We were to make sure, however, that there was a room for him when he did appear."

"Damn!" Chambrun said.

I knew what irritated him. The Beaumont is not far from the United Nations building, and many foreign diplomats and attachés make the hotel their home-away-from-home. Quite often we are asked by the State Department or the CIA or top White House personnel to provide special accommodations. It isn't always convenient because the Beaumont rarely has any long-range vacancies.

So, more often than not, to accommodate the government, we'd have to turn away a regular guest. We had what we called "house seats," three or four rooms we kept open, day to day, for emergencies; but these were almost always quickly filled. To hold a room for an indefinite arrival tended to upset our smooth routine.

"Let me know when this Helwig checks in," Chambrun said. "Wilson will pass over his documents—which he tells me are in the vault."

"I put them there—a briefcase—myself," Atterbury said.

"Then let's get rid of these two cloak-and-dagger Johns as fast as we can," Chambrun said.

Mr. Wilson and his bugged phone went out of my mind

during the rest of that day. I knew Jerry Dodd had removed the electronic gadget from the telephone in 912 and that he was trying to check out its source—that is, the manufacturer. It wasn't, Jerry assured us, a homemade device. There was a fashion show that afternoon that I had to cover, and in the evening there was to be a coming-out party in the Grand Ballroom for some debutante chick. These are routines in which a PR man has to involve himself.

It was nearly three in the morning before I finally got to bed in my apartment on the second floor of the hotel. I was bushed, and I went to sleep the moment my head hit the pillow. Actually, I hadn't been asleep more than twenty minutes when my phone rang.

I dredged myself up out of some dark void and managed to answer it. It was Mike Maggio, the bell captain.

"Trouble," Mike said. "You're wanted in the lobby office on the double, Mark."

I mumbled something.

"Robbery," Mike said. "Somebody held up Carl Nevers, the night manager, forced him to open the vault, and took off with God knows what."

There had been robberies at the Pierre, the Plaza, the Waldorf-Astoria in the past. We had been waiting for our turn, although we thought our security setup was foolproof.

Behind the front desk in the lobby is a private office for use by the day and night managers. And behind that office is the vault. Only the manager on duty can open it. There's no time lock, because guests come in at all times of the day or night with possessions they want to keep safe. Those possessions are mostly jewelry. There have been so many gem robberies around town in plush hotels that we urge guests to keep their gewgaws in the vault. We make it easy for them by having someone who can give them access round the clock. Every room and suite in the hotel has a notice in it urging this precaution.

It seemed that, at a few minutes after three, the party in

the ballroom being over, a Mrs. Horace Paradine, one of the guests, came to the desk and asked Carl Nevers to place her jewels in the vault. They started through the back office to the vault when someone came up behind them and stuck a gun against Mrs. Paradine's head. Nevers and Mrs. Paradine both described him as medium tall, medium thin; he was wearing a raincoat and had a tan-colored stocking mask over his head and face. Nevers would turn off the alarm system and open the vault, or Mrs. Paradine would have her brains blown out onto the office rug.

Nevers is a cool character. He wasn't going to risk Mrs. Paradine's brains, if any, and he wasn't going to risk his own hide. He also knew exactly what would happen when he turned off the alarm system. There were two ways to turn it off which, Nevers felt certain, the gunman couldn't know. One way was the ordinary turnoff, used when a guest came to get something or deposit something. The second way turned off the alarm but set off another. The instant that second way was used, a silent-alarm system went into operation. The security office and Chambrun's penthouse apartment were warned, every maintenance office showed a blinking red light, and every doorman was alerted.

At the vault there was no sign of anything except the absence of an alarm. Within two minutes of that second turnoff, there was almost no way a thief could get out of the hotel undetected. The system was Jerry Dodd's pride and joy and Carl Nevers's comfort in a tense moment.

He used the second turnoff and opened the vault. Stocking Mask forced him and Mrs. Paradine into the vault, the woman sobbing hysterically.

It was a strange business. Mrs. Paradine, by her account, was wearing $100,000 worth of diamonds and other precious stones. The robber had only to snatch them off her, but he didn't.

Instead, the thief opened a couple of small lockboxes and took a handful of jewels without really looking at them.

"He didn't seem to have anything special in mind," Nevers told us. "He didn't examine what he took. Then he went to the box for Room 912, took out a small zippered briefcase, told us to go to the end of vault, went out, and shut us in."

Three minutes later Jerry Dodd opened the vault and let them out. He hadn't met anyone on his way in.

Dr. Partridge, the house physician, was called to deal with the weeping Mrs. Paradine who had lost nothing. Jerry went to cover all his checkpoints. When I arrived, Chambrun, that hanging-judge look on his face, was in the vault room, waiting with Nevers for Jerry's report.

"It seems quite clear," Chambrun said, "that he wanted it to look like a haphazard robbery, which is why he took a few pieces of jewelry. What he really wanted was Warren Wilson's briefcase. We'd better tell Wilson what's happened."

I called Wilson on the phone. He sounded sleepy. I told him what had happened, and he was suddenly wide awake.

"Be with you as soon as I can throw on some clothes," he said.

Chambrun fidgeted with one of his flat Egyptian cigarettes, walking around the vault room and actually into the vault itself, which was still open. His forehead was drawn together in a concentrated scowl.

"Carl, describe to me again just how he behaved here in the vault," he said, turning to Nevers.

"He forced Mrs. Paradine and me in ahead of him," Nevers said. "He was still holding his gun to her head. Once we were inside the vault, he shoved her away and ordered us to the rear of the vault. He was still covering us with the gun, though."

"How did he get the lockboxes open?" Chambrun asked.

"Master key," Nevers said. "He told me to throw him the master key. I did. I wasn't resisting, you understand, Mr. Chambrun. I figured there'd be help any minute."

"You did just the right thing," Chambrun said. "Go on."

"He opened two boxes that were closest to him. He

reached in them with his free hand and dug out some pieces of jewelry from each box. He didn't even look at what he had, just stuffed the things in his raincoat pocket. Then he walked directly to the box for 912 and opened it."

"He seemed to know exactly what he was doing?"

"Yes, sir. He opened the box, took out the small briefcase, tucked it under his arm, then backed out of the vault and shut us in."

Chambrun took a deep drag on his cigarette. "There's a raincoat hanging on the hat rack in the outer office. I noticed it when I came in. Is that yours, Carl?"

"No, sir. It was a beautiful night when I came on duty. I didn't wear any kind of coat. I wouldn't leave a coat in the outer office anyway. There's a coat closet for employees, as you know."

"Get that raincoat, Mark," Chambrun said.

The so-called "outer office" is not a space occupied by anyone in particular. It is a place where a guest can talk to the manager on duty, or to the credit manager, or to anyone else he wants to talk to in private. There is a table in the center of the room, several comfortable Windsor armchairs, a telephone on the table, and an old-fashioned hat rack in the corner near the door.

Chambrun rarely misses anything, and he hadn't missed the raincoat hanging on the rack. There shouldn't have been a coat there without someone to go with it. It's the kind of detail that is endlessly registering in his mind as he moves around the hotel—something out of place, no matter how inconsequential.

There was nothing special about the raincoat. I carried it back to the vault room and handed it to Chambrun. He felt in one of the pockets, and I saw a bright, hard look in his eyes. He brought his hand out, and in it was a tan stocking mask. He reached in the other pocket and produced a handful of jewelry, which he put on the table.

"The briefcase was all he wanted," Chambrun said. "Smart operator. He left you and Mrs. Paradine in the vault, took off his mask and coat, left them on the hat rack, and walked out of here with the briefcase under his arm, all casual and innocent-looking."

"Not so casual and innocent-looking," Jerry Dodd said from the doorway. We turned to look at him, and his face was pale and tense with anger. "Butch Schooley, whose job it was to cover the northwest fire stairs when that number-two alarm went off, is dead. Neck broken. Looks like a karate expert did him in."

Schooley was one of the night security staff. He had evidently responded to the number-two alarm and taken up his position in the northwest fire stairs. There are four inside fire stairs at the Beaumont, one at each corner of the building. They lead from the penthouse level down to the subbasement, where the elevator machinery, the heating and air-conditioning units, and the chief engineer's shops are located. From that lower level there are exits to the street.

Schooley's body had been found at the third-floor level by Jerry. Someone had killed him on the way up or down. There was no escape possible from the hotel from the upper levels, so I guessed the murderer had been on the way down to his only way out. I said so.

"No, he didn't get out through the basement," Jerry said. "All the exits were covered down there as soon as the alarm went into effect. The killer is still somewhere in the hotel."

At that moment Warren Wilson joined us. He seemed to have hurried into his clothes, not bothering with a necktie. He looked frightened, I thought.

"Did they really get my briefcase?" he asked.

"I'm afraid so," Chambrun said. "But Dodd thinks he's still somewhere in the hotel."

"I—I'd better get in touch with my chief in Washington," Wilson said. "If those documents are lost—even long enough to be photographed—I'm a dead duck, along with quite a few other people."

"There's a phone in the outer office," Chambrun said.

"Thanks," Wilson said and went to it.

There was nothing secret about the phone call. Wilson asked the night supervisor on the switchboard to charge it to his room. He gave her a number, and I could see that Chambrun made a mental note of it. Presently there was a connection.

"Mr. Tabor?" Wilson asked. "I'm sorry to call you at this time, sir. . . . There's been a robbery at the hotel, and the stuff I was carrying is gone. . . . Yes, I know that, sir. . . . No, Helwig hasn't checked in yet. . . . I don't know who knew, except the clerk who put it in the vault for me. . . . Yes, the manager is here." Wilson turned to Chambrun. "It's my boss, Mr. Clarence Tabor of the CIA," he said. "Would you please talk to him, Mr. Chambrun?"

Chambrun took the phone. I couldn't hear the other half of the conversation, but Tabor seemed to know Chambrun, and Chambrun appeared to know him. "Wilson hasn't told you the whole story," Chambrun said. "Earlier today we discovered that the phone in his room had been bugged. What happened tonight was an armed holdup by a masked man who seemed to know exactly what he was looking for in the vault. . . . No, but we don't think he can have gotten out of the hotel, and he won't get out carrying that briefcase. He can't hide it on himself. . . . No, but we are about to bring in the police because one of my people has been killed. . . . I don't give a damn about your top-level secrecy, Tabor! One of my staff has been murdered, and I don't intend to hold back for God himself!" He put the phone down hard.

Wilson was mopping sweat off his face, although the room was air-conditioned. "A lot of people in high places are going to be in big trouble if we don't get that stuff back fast," he said.

"I'm sick of people in high places who are so concerned with their own power that they have to operate forever undercover," Chambrun said. "I don't care who gets into big trouble."

"Since we have no idea who it is, what's to stop him from just checking out of the hotel with my documents in his luggage?" Wilson asked. "Will you subject everybody to a search before they leave the hotel?"

Chambrun's cold eyes seemed to be buried in their deep pouches. "I don't think that will be necessary," he said. He turned to Nevers. "However, Carl, let me know if anyone tries to check out before the normal time this morning. If anyone tries, stall until I get to them."

"Yes, sir."

Chambrun gave Wilson a thoughtful look. "You're a professional, Mr. Wilson, at this sort of thing."

"I don't follow you," Wilson said.

"Spy and counterspy, all perfectly legal, of course. Suppose you knew an enemy agent had important documents in our vault, how would you go about getting them?"

Wilson shrugged. "This fellow knew his job pretty well," he said. "I don't know that I could improve on it."

"Probably not," Chambrun said. "There's just one thing this man didn't know when he was planning."

"Oh?" Wilson said.

"That when the alarm was turned off in the vault a certain way, it set off another alarm, a silent one, that warned us the vault was being robbed. He couldn't have anticipated that. He thought he had plenty of time, with Nevers and Mrs. Paradine locked inside the vault. He'd planned his escape by way of the northwest fire stairs and unexpectedly he ran into Schooley. So he had to kill."

"In my experience," Wilson said, "there's always something unexpected happening. You have to be trained to act without hesitation in any emergency."

"But this man must have had an escape plan as well as his plan to get into the vault, wouldn't you say?"

Wilson nodded. "They'd be equally important," he said.

"So this man planned to make his escape by way of the northwest fire stairs," Chambrun said. "He only had to walk a few yards across the lobby to the stairway door, carrying the briefcase, of course. He assumed there had been no alarm, so he didn't have to move so fast that he'd attract attention."

"Sounds logical," Wilson said.

"He must have checked out the ground pretty thoroughly, wouldn't you say?" Chambrun sounded almost casual.

"As I've said, he was obviously a professional."

Chambrun put out his cigarette in an ashtray on the telephone table. He actually smiled at Wilson. "Since he knew the hotel so well," he said, "why do you suppose our man headed *up* the northwest stairway instead of *down*? There's no escape from the upper levels. He must have known that."

"That's pretty obvious, isn't it?" Wilson said. "He started down, found the way blocked by someone alerted by the alarm he didn't know about, and had no choice but to head up in the hope of escaping somewhere into the upper levels of the hotel."

"And ran into Schooley?"

"Must have," Wilson said.

Chambrun seemed to consider this for a moment. "There could be another explanation," he said. "He always *meant* to go up—to his room."

"Could be," Wilson said, "if he had a room."

"I'm inclined to think he does have a room," Chambrun said. He smiled again. "You know, I've had some experience with crime, Mr. Wilson. I always try to put myself in the criminal's mind and think as he might have thought. I assume these documents he stole would be worth a great deal of money to the thief—perhaps blackmail money?"

"You can say that again," Wilson said.

"Being a professional, this man must have recognized the danger of being caught with the documents in his possession. He'd want to get them off his person just as fast as he could, in case anything went wrong."

"You mean, hide them?" Wilson asked.

"Something like that," Chambrun said. "Of course, if he

was caught, he'd have some difficulty getting back to the hiding place."

"A confederate?" Wilson suggested.

"Would you share a big financial bonanza with someone else, Mr. Wilson?"

Wilson shrugged. "There might not be any other choice. Not in advance, I wouldn't. If I was caught I might get help from my lawyer, for example. But I wouldn't cut anyone in ahead of time."

"And he would know we'd search the hotel from top to bottom," Chambrun said, "so he'd have prepared a safe hiding place."

"Yes, he would."

I could see Jerry Dodd champing at the bit. Chambrun's theorizing wasn't getting us anywhere, and Schooley's killer was still at large somewhere in the hotel.

"And that hiding place would have to be somewhere not far from this vault room if he was to dispose of the briefcase quickly." Chambrun turned to Jerry Dodd. "Let's walk over what must have been his escape route, Jerry. He'd walk from here through the outer office. He stopped there to take off his mask and then his raincoat—"

We walked into the outer office, Chambrun pausing by the old-fashioned hat rack. He looked around the office.

"No place to hide a briefcase here," he said.

We went out into the lobby. It was buzzing with people, mostly staff, who knew what had happened. Ordinarily there would only have been the cleaning crew there at four-thirty in the morning. Chambrun headed toward the northwest fire-door exit, Wilson, Jerry, and I following him. He stopped at the door. Just to the left of it was a large mailbox, with slots for letters and larger packages. Chambrun looked at Jerry.

"Can you open that mailbox, Jerry?" he asked.

"At the risk of spending the rest of my natural life in jail," Jerry said. "That's a federal offense."

"Let's risk it," Chambrun said.

"What's the idea?" Jerry asked. He didn't like it.

"I'm trying to think like our man," Chambrun said. "I'd have come prepared to get rid of that briefcase quickly. It would not be easy to hide. But if I had a large envelope prepared that would hold it, all I'd have to do would be to drop it in a mailbox, addressed to some prearranged post office box, and let Uncle Sam protect it for me.

"He'd been over the ground. He knew this mailbox was here, only a few yards from the vault room. He probably put the briefcase in his prepared, stamped envelope when he discarded his coat and mask in the outer office. He walks, innocent as you please, across the lobby to this box and mails his package, quite openly. Open it up, Jerry."

Jerry produced some kind of kit from his pocket and went to work on the mailbox lock. It evidently wasn't very complicated, because he got it open almost at once. The big box was half full, and Chambrun fumbled around with the contents. Like a magician pulling a rabbit out of his hat, he produced a large manila envelope. He read us the address.

P.O. Box 1724
Grand Central Post Office
New York, N. Y. 10017

Chambrun handed the package to Wilson. "I don't think we should compound our federal offenses by opening it, Mr. Wilson, but would you guess from the feel of it that we might have your briefcase here?"

Wilson took the envelope and felt it carefully. "By God, I think you've found it, Mr. Chambrun," he said.

Chambrun almost snatched the package away from Wilson, and he wasn't smiling anymore. "Check this for the fingerprints Mr. Wilson just made, Jerry," he said. "I think you'll find that the prints on this package match the one you took off the electronic device on Mr. Wilson's phone."

Jerry opened his mouth to speak, then closed it. Chambrun turned to Wilson.

"You were headed upstairs for your room when you ran into Schooley, weren't you, Wilson? Your fingerprints on that package have blown the ballgame. You bugged your own phone, to make us think someone else was involved. You had to stage the robbery so that the people in Washington would never think of you as the thief. The subsequent blackmailing of higher-ups would appear to be the work of the man who robbed you."

Wilson was sweating again. He looked around like someone trapped, then made a quick move away from us.

"Hold it right there, Wilson!" Jerry Dodd shouted. He'd produced a gun. "Your body will look like a hunk of Swiss cheese if you take one more step."

A couple of Jerry's security boys took charge of Wilson. We stood, watching him being taken away. He would be charged with homicide and robbery.

"Those CIA boys are taught all kinds of things, including karate," Chambrun said, then sighed. "It was mighty bad luck for Schooley."

"I damn near blew it," Jerry said. "You know there was no fingerprint on that telephone gadget. It was too small to take a clear print."

Chambrun's smile was grim. "But Wilson didn't know that," he said. "I wanted him to make a move, just to be certain."

# Chambrun and the Melting Swan

He was a terribly nice kid, just out of Cornell, with a degree in hotel management. Pierre Chambrun took him on at the Beaumont. It was Chambrun's custom to give an opportunity to a recommended graduate from Cornell each year. They always came in, bright, shiny, and eager, and in the early days of my working for Chambrun I had the feeling these kids were after my job, which is public relations for the Beaumont. I discovered, after a couple of years of bracing my feet, that they weren't after my job. They were gunning for Chambrun himself. Only the very top spot would satisfy their egos. They came, and they worked very hard and finally they left, aware that Chambrun *was* the Beaumont and permanent as the Rock of Gibraltar.

Ted Springer was different from most of them. He really wanted to learn. He was endlessly curious, his questions were always to the point. If he had ambitions toward any particular job at the Beaumont, he kept them politely hidden. He was, Chambrun mentioned to me after a few weeks, that rare commodity, a born hotel man. Young Mr. Springer looked as if he might stay with us for a long, long time. I think he would have, if he had lived.

The security staff at the Beaumont consists of about twenty-five men and five girls under the efficient command of Jerry Dodd, a former FBI agent, a wiry, energetic, and very tough little cop. Chambrun assigned Ted Springer to Jerry Dodd's force. It was the ideal post from which to see and learn everything that went on in the hotel, from the penthouses to the cellars. The Beaumont is like an isolated city within a city, with its own restaurants and bars, its shops, hospital, communications systems, police force, and mayor or city manager. We have all the problems of a city including the problem of crime.

About the time Ted Springer came to work for us, we were in the throes of being victimized by a highly skillful hotel thief. There had been a rash of robberies in some of the best hotels in the city. The M.O. was simple: a knock on the door, a couple of thugs barged in, slugged the unhappy guest or guests, stole whatever wasn't nailed down, and took off.

Nothing like that had happened to us. Jerry Dodd had some kind of personal, built-in radar system that could smell out the wrong kind of person on the premises. Our man was a much slicker operator. He never burglarized a room when anyone was in it. He had a way with locks. He seemed to know exactly when a guest was out and exactly which guests were worth robbing. This meant a very close and constant surveillance. It suggested that our man was a guest himself, probably smiling at us cheerfully as he passed us in the lobby.

Jerry Dodd had gone over the list of some twelve hundred guests and boiled down his list to six—five men and a woman. After three weeks of watching those six and having four more robberies pulled off right under his nose, Jerry had pointed the finger at one man. His name was Wilson McVey. He was an attractive man in his middle thirties, blond, rather stylish in his style of dress, and said to be an art expert for a West Coast museum. I say "said to be," but it checked out. He was just that, with a first-class reputation on the Coast. Jerry had nothing positive on him, but he was convinced.

"There are two things we can do," Jerry told Chambrun. We were in Chambrun's second-floor office.

"We can tell him his room is needed and kick him out," Chambrun said, "or we can wait to catch him red-handed and send him up for a long time."

"And risk another robbery," Jerry said.

"I want him. I want him badly," Chambrun said.

So Mr. McVey was in for it, I thought. Chambrun and Jerry would get him sooner or later.

Jerry had gone a good deal farther than trying to identify the thief. He had drawn up a list of the most likely victims for McVey, trying to think like McVey himself. On that list was a Mrs. Framingham on the fourteenth floor—1407. She was a middle-aged, not unattractive woman, alone, and clearly on the make. She wore valuable jewelry in public and, as far as Jerry knew, kept none of it in the hotel safe. Mrs. Framingham, out on the town, undoubtedly left most of her jewelry in 1407. There were others, but they are not important to this story. Men were assigned to cover each of the possibilities, and Ted Springer, unluckily for him, drew Mrs. Framingham.

About six-thirty on the evening when it happened, Ted Springer checked in with Jerry. Mrs. Framingham had just left her room, dolled up for the evening.

"Stay under cover," Jerry ordered Springer. "If McVey—or anyone else—lets himself into the room, don't try to nab him. Call me. I want to take him myself."

Springer was a management student, not a cop. Caught, McVey might turn out to be dangerous, and Jerry didn't want a green kid confronting him.

I was aware of the stake-out, and I knew, as the evening wore on, that none of the men watching had reported any action on the part of Wilson McVey.

As public relations director of the hotel, I had other things to do beside stalking our hotel thief. On that particular night there had been a private banquet in one of the special dining rooms for the French ambassador to the United Nations. It broke up a little before eleven, and I made a point of putting myself in the ambassador's path to inquire if everything had been satisfactory.

"I'm Mark Haskell, sir," I told him. "Mr. Chambrun will be anxious to know how the dinner was."

It had been perfect, the ambassador told me. The Beaumont's wine cellar is unsurpassed, particularly in imported French wines.

"There was one small disappointment, however," the ambassador said. "My old friend Jacques Dubois had promised one of his fabulous ice sculptures as a table decoration. He never brought it. I know he's a temperamental devil, so I can only assume I must have offended him in some fashion."

I told the ambassador I didn't think that was likely. Only that afternoon Jacques had told me, with pride, that he was preparing something very special for the ambassador. I would try to find out what had gone wrong.

Jacques Dubois, in his late fifties, is the pastry chef at the Beaumont. He is a flamboyant and volatile Frenchman. More than that, he is a personal friend of Chambrun's. Back in the 1940s they had fought, side by side, in the French Resistance. It was hard for me to imagine Jacques Dubois, whom I'd never seen except in his white clothes and chef's hat, strangling Nazis in a Paris alley, but Chambrun remembered him as a man of courage and was fond of him.

As a sideline to his chef's duties, Jacques Dubois had become an expert in the almost forgotten art of ice carving. From a 300-pound block of ice he could carve a battleship, a bird, a rabbit, a deer, or any kind of special figure required by the customer. What a sculptor could do with stone, Jacques could do with ice, and he was enormously proud of his product. I suspected that the ambassador might also have been one of the old Resistance group, and I wondered why Jacques had let him down.

I had nothing else pressing to do, so I went down to the kitchens to see if Jacques was still there. No one had seen him since about seven o'clock, when he had gone to deliver an ice sculpture for the ambassador's dinner.

Puzzled, I decided to go down to the basement where Jacques did his carving. The area consists of a small outer room backed by a large walk-in freezer like a butcher shop's. The first thing I saw, resting on what looked like a butcher's carving block, was a slightly drooping swan carved out of ice. It must have stood where it was in the outer warmish room for some time, because there was a pool of water under the block and on the surrounding floor.

On the block beside the melting swan was some of Jacques's equipment—a carpenter's wooden yardstick, a piece of graph paper with the design of the swan drawn on its squares, a six-pronged ice shaver, and a V-shaped chisel. Jacques is usually as careful with his tools as a diamond cutter. It was out of character for him to leave them lying around, even if he had taken off in a temperamental pique.

I felt suddenly that something was wrong. I turned to the freezer, anticipating the chill, and walked in. The first room inside is kept at just below thirty-two degrees. That is where Jacques, wearing a sheepskin-lined coat, does his carving. In the back room Jacques keeps his 300-pound blocks of ice, and the temperature there is kept at five degrees Fahrenheit.

That's where I found Jacques, frozen rock-solid.

I took him by the heels and dragged him out, through the first room and out onto the floor beside the melting swan. I think I knew he was dead, but I found myself running around looking for something to cover him. Finally I made sense and called Dr. Partridge, the house physician, Chambrun in his penthouse, and Jerry Dodd. Then I knelt beside the frozen man, rubbing a hand that was a block of ice, hoping inanely that it might do some good.

Chambrun, Jerry, and the old doctor arrived almost simultaneously, the doctor grumbling over having been dragged away from a backgammon game in the Spartan Bar. Chambrun, his eyes glittering slits in their pouches, Jerry, and I watched the doctor make his preliminary examination. Finally the old man stood up, muttering about his arthritic knees.

"No use," he said. "He's long gone, Pierre."

Chambrun seemed almost not to be listening. He had picked up the carpenter's yardstick and was idly measuring the swan's delicately curved neck.

"Terrible thing for a man to get locked in his own freezer," Doc Partridge said.

"Nonsense!" It was like an explosion from Chambrun. "There are no locks, just to make certain such a thing is impossible. There's no way to get locked in. Could he have had a heart attack and frozen after he died?"

"It's slippery in there," Jerry said. "He could have fallen, hit his head, and frozen before he came to."

"I want the answers, Doctor," Chambrun said. "Was it his heart? Was he knocked unconscious by a fall—or by someone?"

"Have to thaw him out first," Doc said.

The doctor had called for a stretcher on his way down. It should have arrived by now. We heard someone pounding on the door of the service elevator.

"This thing is stuck about a foot from floor level," someone shouted to us. "Can't open the door. We'll have to go up a flight and bring the stretcher down the stairs."

"So move it!" Jerry shouted back.

A friend could die, a mistress could be clamoring for him, but if something didn't work properly in his beloved hotel, Chambrun stayed with it till he had an answer. He sent for the chief engineer. While Jacques's body was carried upstairs by the stretcher bearers, the engineer worked on the elevator.

A few minutes later we knew the grim reason why the elevator couldn't get down to the floor level. The horribly mangled body of young Ted Springer lay at the bottom of the shaft.

* * *

Lieutenant Hardy of Manhattan's Homicide Division was an old friend. As in any city, there had been murders before this in the city called Beaumont. Hardy was a big, fair-haired man who looked more like a bewildered Notre Dame fullback than a sharp criminal investigator. Hardy's chief attribute is a kind of dogged stick-to-itiveness. He digs and digs and digs until he finally comes up with something that makes sense. He was on the scene at midnight, an hour after I'd found Jacques's body in the freezer and we'd found what was left of Ted Springer.

Hardy began at the bottom of the service elevator shaft. Chambrun and I had stayed there from the moment Ted's body was found. Jerry Dodd, a white-hot rage shaking him, had gone in search of Mr. Wilson McVey. Jerry had no doubts about what had happened.

Ted had confronted McVey outside Mrs. Framingham's room on the fourteenth floor—or in it—had been overpowered by McVey and dropped down the elevator shaft. The service elevator door on the fourteenth floor had been tampered with, Jerry found. McVey, if it was McVey, was an expert with locks and catches. He had sent the elevator up above fourteen, gimmicked the door catch on fourteen, and dropped Ted—alive or dead—down the shaft.

Hardy, examining Ted's body without moving it, was able to set a time for us. Ted's wristwatch had been smashed at exactly seven minutes after nine.

Jerry Dodd, cruising about the hotel, came on Mr. Wilson McVey having a drink in the Trapeze Bar, which is located on the mezzanine just over the Beaumont's lobby. That was at half past midnight. McVey was entertaining an attractive lady. He regarded Jerry with a pleasantly insolent smile. Jerry said afterward he could have sworn McVey knew exactly what was coming and was particularly pleased because he knew he had the right answer.

Jerry got McVey away from his table and the lady and talked to him over by the bar. He identified himself and asked McVey where he had been that evening from eight o'clock on.

McVey could have refused to answer—Jerry had no legal right to interrogate him.

"I don't know why you're asking me, Mr. Dodd, or by what right you ask me," McVey said, smiling, "but I have no objection to telling you. I work for an art museum on the West Coast. Tonight I attended an auction of paintings at the McIntyre Gallery on West Fifty-seventh Street. I was there from eight o'clock until about eleven-thirty. The young lady at my table was with me all that time. If her word won't do, the gallery can verify it. I bought several paintings for my museum in the course of the evening."

It checked out. Like it or not, Wilson McVey had been nowhere near the fourteenth floor at seven minutes after nine. There was too much evidence to prove that the fourteenth floor was the starting point of Ted's fall. Not only had the catch on the elevator door been tampered with, but Hardy found signs that Ted's body had been dragged along the corridor from close by Mrs. Framingham's room to the back-hall area where the service elevator ran. McVey was a blind alley, a dead end.

"Whoever our man is, Ted moved too fast and showed himself. This kind of operator doesn't turn to violence as a rule." Jerry Dodd was expounding to us in Chambrun's office in short bursts of anger. He had been certain he had cornered a thief and a murderer, and now he was at the beginning of the line again. Chambrun sat at his desk, his eyes almost closed, sipping his Turkish coffee. I'd made myself a double Jack Daniel's on the rocks. I needed it. We were all under the surveillance of the three-cornered face in the blue Picasso original opposite Chambrun's desk.

"Ted showed himself too soon," Jerry went on. "He shouldn't have shown himself at all. He should have called me. Our thief knew the game was up. Ted could identify him, name him. So he turned to violence, knocked Ted out, and dropped him down the shaft. We'll never know what he hit Ted with or in what other way he overpowered him. Too much damage in the fall."

Chambrun opened his eyes. "Don't let McVey slip away from you, Jerry. I'm not satisfied."

"He couldn't have done it," Jerry said.

"Done what?" Chambrun asked in a strangely vague voice.

"Whatever was done. He wasn't here."

"He wasn't here at seven minutes past nine," Chambrun said.

"Which is when it happened."

"I wonder," Chambrun said.

Hardy had come into the room during this conversation. "No doubt about the time," he said. "The watch."

"You have the watch?" Chambrun asked.

"Of course."

"Fingerprints—if they aren't all yours?"

Hardy's face looked stern. "I don't think we've checked yet. You think—?"

"That's what I think," Chambrun said.

"I wish I knew what the hell you were talking about," I said.

Nobody answered me because old Doc Partridge joined us at that point. "I've got a rather surprising answer for you, Pierre," he said.

"It wasn't his heart," Chambrun said. He was suddenly talking about Jacques Dubois.

"He was heavily dosed with chloroform," Dr. Partridge said. "Probably held over his face on a cloth or handkerchief. It was enough to have made him unconscious for a long time, and it possibly killed him. The medical examiner isn't certain. The chloroform could have killed him in about thirty minutes. In that five-degree temperature, he couldn't have lasted more than three hours. In any event, the chloroform is why he didn't get out of the freezer."

"Is the chloroform easily detectable?" Chambrun asked.

"Simple."

Chambrun turned to Hardy. "Have your people check with what's left of young Springer, Lieutenant. It's just possible the same M.O. was used."

Hardy took off. Chambrun turned to Jerry Dodd. "I think you'd better bring Mr. Wilson McVey up there. I don't want him out of my sight."

"Suppose he won't come?"

"Then I'll go to him," Chambrun said.

Jerry left to find McVey. Chambrun lit one of his flat Egyptian cigarettes and squinted at me through the smoke.

"If a strange man came up to you in a bar and asked you for an alibi, would you give it to him, Mark?"

"I'd tell him to drop dead," I said.

"Unless you very much wanted to provide an alibi for yourself for a certain time," Chambrun said. "You asked me a little while ago what I was talking about. It's not very complicated. Ted Springer's watch was set to seven minutes past nine after he was dead. Because that *wasn't* the time he died."

"It could have been set before he was thrown down the shaft," I said.

"No," Chambrun said. "If it had been, the ambassador would have had his frozen swan to decorate the banquet table. Have you forgotten that my poor friend Jacques was also murdered? I will make you a bet, Mark. I will bet you a new suit of your choice, price no object, that Ted Springer was murdered a few minutes *before* seven o'clock, and that Jacques was murdered at almost *exactly* seven o'clock."

"You got a witness or something?" I asked. I thought I was being funny.

"I have a witness or something," Chambrun said, quite seriously.

After that he seemed to go into some kind of trance. I've seen him that way before when he's trying to think something through. I paced around the office, after pouring myself another drink, waiting for some word from Hardy and Jerry on the subject of Mr. Wilson McVey. You could have feathered me down when the office door opened and Jerry appeared with a smiling McVey.

"I ought to be outraged by whatever is going on here, Mr.

Chambrun," McVey said. "I am asked for an alibi. I am ordered to come up here to your office. I should have refused both requests, but curiosity has got the better of me. What is it all about?"

He was as relaxed as a man in church.

"There have been two murders committed in the hotel tonight, Mr. McVey," Chambrun said.

"Shocking. But what has that to do with me? I wasn't in your hotel when the crimes were committed."

"How do you know that?" Chambrun asked.

McVey's smile was completely disarming. "Because your Mr. Dodd asked me where I was from eight o'clock on. Obviously your murders happened then, or I would have been asked to account for some other time."

"So I ask you now to account for the time between a quarter to seven and a quarter after seven," Chambrun said.

I thought for just a flashing second McVey's smile seemed to fade. But he stayed with it.

"I was dressing to go out for the evening," he said.

"In your room?"

"Yes."

"You can prove it?"

"How? I was alone. I don't dress in public, Mr. Chambrun." McVey reached in his pocket for a cigarette and lit it with a lighter held in a perfectly steady hand.

The little red button on Chambrun's desk phone blinked. He answered. Of course we only heard his end of it. "Chambrun here. . . . Ah, yes, Lieutenant. . . . Interesting coincidence, what? . . . Ah, well, life is full of little disappointments. I think you'd better get back here. I've got your man."

Chambrun put down the phone, and his glittering black eyes fixed on McVey. "The two dead men were friends of mine, McVey—trusted friends. It is going to give me pleasure to nail you to the barn door."

"Fascinating, if improbable," McVey said, still smiling.

"You're a clever operator, McVey, but tonight the heat got a little too much for you." Chambrun's mouth moved in a tight smile of his own. "The heat got too hot for you, but I should add it was the cold that did you in."

"What kind of double-talk is that?" McVey asked.

"It will save time if I lay it out for you," Chambrun said. "You are a skillful hotel thief, McVey. You've been driving us crazy here for weeks. But tonight we were close to you. We'd begun to think your way, and we guessed you might be planning to rob a certain Mrs. Framingham. A young man on our security force named Springer was waiting for you on the fourteenth floor. We found him at about eleven o'clock at the bottom of the service elevator shaft. His watch had been broken in the fall at seven minutes past nine."

"Which would seem to let me out," McVey said, still at ease.

"Lieutenant Hardy has just told me on the phone that Springer had been chloroformed before he fell. I suggest you carry chloroform with you on your little adventures, McVey. You're not a violent man, until you are driven to it. You carry the chloroform in case someone walks in on you, unexpected. You were masked or disguised, I suppose. A whiff of chloroform, and there would be time for you to get away."

"And have other people been chloroformed in your robberies, Mr. Chambrun?"

"No, because you had no need to use it until young Springer walked in on you tonight. He recognized you, called you by name, didn't he? You knew he had you, and so you chloroformed him, dragged him to the service elevator, unlocked the door with your special skills, and dropped him down the shaft. That was a few minutes *before* seven."

"Prove that it was me. Prove that it was at the time you say." McVey moistened his lips. Strain was beginning to show. "You said Springer's watch was set at seven minutes past nine."

"Exactly the right way to put it," Chambrun said. "'Was set' at seven minutes past nine. Proof of the time and proof that it was you who did it are coming up, McVey. You must have come as close to panic as you have ever been. You had to be as sure as you could be that Springer had died in the fall. So down you go in the service elevator to the floor above the bottom. You walk the last flight, use your skills to open the basement door to the elevator shaft, and there was Springer—as dead as you could hope. Then you saw the chance to put the icing on the cake. You took Springer's watch off his wrist, set it at seven minutes past nine, then smashed it and strapped it back on his wrist."

McVey actually laughed. "And you have proof of all this?"

"Let me go on, McVey," Chambrun said. "Just as you had the watch back on Springer's wrist you heard a sound behind you. You turned and saw Jacques Dubois standing beside his beautiful ice carving of a swan. He had wheeled it out of the freezer while you were concentrating on Springer. You had no choice. You pretended to be explaining while you walked up to him—then a second dose of chloroform. You dragged Jacques into the freezer and left him there to die.

"As I have said, this was at about seven o'clock. How do I know the time? Because I know about everything that goes on in my hotel, McVey. I know many facts about ice carving from my friend Dubois. For example, I know that when a carving melts, its relative shape is retained because all parts melt in proportion. Ice actually melts at a rate of about half an inch an hour at room temperature." Chambrun turned to me. "Do you remember, Mark, when we first found Jacques I was measuring the swan's neck with that carpenter's yardstick?"

I remembered.

"The design on the graph paper showed me that the swan's neck had originally been four inches thick. My measuring showed me, at eleven o'clock, that it was then only two inches thick. So I knew that the swan had been out of the freezer for approximately four hours—half an inch to an hour. That's when poor Jacques was taken back into the freezer by you, McVey—at seven o'clock."

"So I need an alibi for then."

"Not really," Chambrun said. "Your fingerprints on the watch—"

McVey seemed, slowly, to shrivel before our eyes. Like the melting swan, I thought. "Never improvise," he said in a shaken voice. "I always planned everything down to the smallest detail, every eventuality. But as you said, Mr. Chambrun, it all happened too fast—the heat was too hot—one thing on top of the other. I had never killed anyone in my life, and there in the space of twenty minutes—"

Jerry took McVey away, and Chambrun went over to the sideboard to pour himself a brandy. He looked tired.

"It's amazing that you could tell time by that swan," I said. "If you hadn't measured it when we first found it—"

"But I did."

"Anyway, the fingerprints would have nailed him."

Chambrun sniffed the aroma of his brandy. "What fingerprints?" he asked.

"On the watch."

"The only fingerprints on the watch are Hardy's," Chambrun said. "He told me that on the phone, and I said, 'Ah, well, life is full of little disappointments.'"

"You let McVey think—"

"He killed two friends of mine in cold blood," Chambrun said. "Are there Marquis of Queensberry rules for dealing with such a man?"

# Chambrun and the Double Event

It is one of the legends surrounding the Hotel Beaumont, that Pierre Chambrun, its manager (himself a legend in his own lifetime), has a private radar system, probably internally installed. Chambrun is apparently able to foretell anything that may interfere with the Swiss-watch operation of his hotel. The truth is, there is nothing magical about it. No one who works for Chambrun, from Miss Ruysdale, his fabulous secretary, down to the lowest busboy in the room service, would dream of noticing anything remotely out of the ordinary in a day's business without passing the information on to the Great Man. He has an extraordinary capacity for putting two and two together and coming up with the right answer, which may just happen to be five.

I am Mark Haskell, the public relations man for the Beaumont. I probably know more about things that have happened in the hotel and have never been made public than anyone except Chambrun himself and possibly Betsy Ruysdale. Some of those things are funny, some are tragic. As in every hotel we have to deal with alcoholics, with elegant call girls, with old men who die in the wrong beds, with cheating husbands and cheating wives, with foreign diplomats claiming diplomatic immunity, and on and on. But there have been suicides and murders that cannot be kept hidden.

Take the case of a sixteen-year-old girl who now lies in a coma in a luxurious suite on one of our upper floors, all her medical expenses paid for by Chambrun himself. He visits her every day, praying, I suspect, to whatever deity he believes in, for her recovery, which the doctors tell him is possible if not probable. He visits her because she represents to him a personal failure. He should have guessed, he has told me over and over, what was likely to happen to her, or someone like her.

"The facts were all there, and I overlooked one of them," he says.

The facts may have been all there for him, but none of the rest of us saw them or even thought of trying to put them together until it was all over.

I had two major headaches on that particular day. There was the coming-out ball for Judy Horween, the steel heiress. Judy, whom I have never met to this day, may be the greatest girl ever, but her grandmother, Mathilda Horween, who was engineering the ball, makes the Wicked Witch of the West look like Florence Nightingale. She is, if I may say so, a domineering and impossible old bag. Decked out in jewels like a Christmas tree, she descended on us the last day with demands for changing dozens of details that were to drive the catering department, the security people, and the telephone switchboard crew out of their minds. The Dowager Duchess of Bilgewater, someone called her.

She stormed into Chambrun's office, almost literally brushing Miss Ruysdale aside—an off-tackle run—and made her demands to an astonished Chambrun, who sat behind his desk smoking a cigarette and sipping his inevitable demitasse of Turkish coffee.

"And I'm leaving Mr. Lucas behind me to see to it that my instructions are carried out to the letter!" Mathilda Horween said, and made an exit that would have put Bette Davis to shame.

Mr. Reginald Lucas, freed from his leash, gave Chambrun a

helpless shrug. Reggie Lucas is an aging queen. He dresses in outlandish clothes, adorns himself in a necklace and rings, and struggles to look twenty-two when he is nearer forty-two. But he has an engaging kind of acid humor.

"Her Majesty has spoken," he said to Chambrun, with a wry smile. "I suspect, my dear Chambrun, that you will carry on exactly in your own fashion. You will not, I trust, resent it if I tell her I *tried* to get you to do things her way. Your world will not come to an end if you don't follow her instructions, but mine certainly will if I haven't tried to persuade you."

"We aim to please here at the Beaumont," Chambrun said. "But only so far, Mr. Lucas."

Chambrun can look like a compassionate father confessor or a hanging judge, depending on his mood. He was midway between those two extremes at that moment, outraged by Mathilda Horween but with some sympathy for Reggie Lucas. "The late Mr. Horween, I take it, was beaten to death," he said mildly.

"He didn't wait for that eventuality," Reggie said. "An astute mixture of sleeping pills and bonded bourbon whiskey did the job. His last words to me, the night before he indulged in that fatal combination, were to the effect that I might be able to endure her since I wouldn't be expected to make love to her. Imagine what the poor devil must have suffered."

"It is beyond imagining," Chambrun said.

"All fangs and razor blades," Reggie said.

I have indicated that I had two hot potatoes to handle that day. The second one was Robert Gaynor, the movie star and sex symbol. He had no connection whatsoever with the Horween ball. I suspect Madame Horween belonged to a generation when actors and golf professionals were considered second-class citizens instead of national heroes. Gaynor's presence in the hotel's most luxurious accommodations might have convinced her the Beaumont was going to seed. His existence was of no consequence to her, and she didn't read the gossip columns because the gossipers of today cover very little of what Mrs. Horween considered the social aristocracy. That evening, when she saw the crowds in the lobby, she would assume the "bourgeoisie" had come to see the socially elite, when in fact they would be there to catch a glimpse of the glamorous Robert Gaynor.

They were not due to catch a glimpse of Gaynor that night because he had made plans for something very private. It is necessary to describe his accommodations at the Beaumont. There are three penthouses on the roof of the hotel. Two of them are cooperatively owned—one by Chambrun, and one by a very old lady who lives there with her memories and a particularly obnoxious Japanese spaniel. The third penthouse is reserved by the hotel for very special guests. Robert Gaynor fell into that category.

Gaynor had stayed at the hotel several times before, but on those occasions he had been eager for public attention. He had been gracious to autograph hunters, endured being swamped in the lobby by screaming females, all part of the promotion of his sensational career. This time it was something else again. His presence in the hotel was to be kept a secret.

Room service waiters and maids must keep their lips sealed. The famous star would not circulate in the hotel. He would register under a phony name—what we call "a John Smith" in the Beaumont. In case, by some misadventure, his presence became known, he must be put up where no one could get at him. Penthouse Number Three was the answer.

He arrived the morning of the Horween Ball, was registered in advance, and hurried, unnoticed, up to the roof. I was delegated to make sure everything was to his liking.

Gaynor wasn't quite real, I thought. You don't ordinarily use the word "beautiful" to describe a man. He had golden blond hair and a profile that could have come off an old Greek coin. He was slim, muscular, and for all the delicate beauty, his face was strong. He was a very, very male man. He was the kind of heroic figure romantic lady authors of another time must have dreamed of at night and written about immediately after breakfast.

He was relaxed and rather charmingly sardonic when I met him.

"You may wonder why all the secrecy, Mark," he said, jumping to first names as many people in show business do. Maybe it was a way of indicating he was a "regular fellow."

"Having seen you swarmed under in the past I can understand it," I said.

"There's a special reason," he said, "and I'm going to tell you what it is to make certain there's nothing slipshod about my protection."

"Knowing the reason won't make us any more attentive to your wishes," I said.

He turned away from me and looked out the windows across the roof. "It's a woman," he said.

"Am I supposed to be surprised?" I asked him.

He turned back to me, brooding. "You may wonder why I have chosen such a very public place for such a very private meeting," he said. "Private places are almost impossible for me to find. One glance at my face, and the whole damn city will be hammering on my door. You can save me from that. Another important fact is that the lady is a guest here in the hotel. She can slip up here without attracting attention."

"Simply arranged," I said.

"It has to be tonight, Mark, because tonight her husband will be out of town."

"Oh, brother," I said. We don't like cheating wives or cheating husbands in the Beaumont. They often lead to explosions.

He must have seen something in the look I gave him. "This isn't a tawdry affair," he said. "She is the only woman I have ever really loved in all my life."

"So good luck," I said, wondering what Chambrun would think when I told him. I would tell him, of course, because that was routine.

"I'll be ordering dinner," he said. "When the room service waiter brings it, we'll be out of sight. He is just to leave the dinner and go."

"No problem," I said.

"I could run the risk of your waiter recognizing me, but not recognizing the lady," Gaynor said.

That was all there was to that conversation with Robert Gaynor. I certainly didn't think of it at the moment as a prelude to violence. Angry or jealous husbands don't react predictably to being cuckolded, but carefully planned murder is not a usual option.

When I got back to my office, which is down the hall from Chambrun's on the second floor, I found a message summoning me into the Presence. Chambrun was surrounded by hotel personnel. Betsy Ruysdale stood at his elbow, dictation pad ready. Mr. Amato, the banquet manager, was there. So was Jerry Dodd, our chief security officer with his sharp fox-face, and Douglas Muir, our Scots maintenance engineer, chewing on the stem of an unlighted pipe. Mr. Atterbury, the desk clerk, was there, and Claude Lavalle, the head man in the hotel's Grand Ballroom, where Judy Horween was to burst on society as a debutante that night. There was Miss Veach, the chief switchboard operator, and hovering on the fringes of this group was Reggie Lucas, representing the Dowager Duchess of Bilgewater.

"Mrs. Horween has made more last minute demands on us," Chambrun said. "On some of them we will deliver, others we will not."

"Oh, my!" Reggie Lucas muttered.

"To start with, she insists that four elevators in the main bank in the lobby be reserved exclusively for her guests. They will, she insists, run only from the lobby to the ballroom on the nineteenth floor."

"That will make it very inconvenient for—" Mr. Atterbury began.

"That will be impossible," Chambrun said. "Too many of

our regular guests will have to find different routes to reach their rooms."

"Oh, dear!" Reggie Lucas said.

"We will, however, make the elevators in the west wing exclusively available to guests at the ball. The doormen will be instructed to pass this along to people arriving by car or taxi. Jerry," Chambrun went on to Jerry Dodd, "you will have men stationed to guide people, to keep the lobby uncluttered as usual."

"Mrs. Horween will be very distressed," Reggie Lucas said. "Perhaps I can make it clearer by saying she will blow her stack."

"Make a note," Chambrun said to Miss Ruysdale, "that Mr. Lucas tried."

"Thank you, love," Reggie said, smiling at Miss Ruysdale.

"Speaking of elevators," Douglas Muir, the engineer said, "the number two car going to the roof is out of order." There are only two elevators that go to the penthouses on the roof.

"What's wrong with it?" Chambrun asked.

"If I didn't know better, I'd say it was sabotaged," Muir said. He is a big, gray-haired, unsmiling man with a walrus mustache and is enormously efficient.

Chambrun's eyes narrowed. "But you do know better, Douglas?"

"No way for anyone to get at it unnoticed," Muir said. "A Stilson wrench fell into the clutch mechanism and ripped it to pieces. Take two days to get new parts shipped in from Detroit. But there are only three people on the roof, sir. You, old Mrs. Haven and her dog, and the movie star. One elevator should handle your needs without too much discomfort."

"No strangers in the engine room?" Chambrun asked.

"Only a safety inspector who checked the whole place out yesterday," Muir said.

"Man you know?"

Muir shook his head. "New man, who seemed to know his stuff, however."

Chambrun nodded and turned to Mr. Lavalle, the ballroom

manager. "In the reception room outside the ballroom, Lavalle, there are two bars, one to the right and one to the left as people enter."

"Correct," Lavalle said.

"Beyond that the official reception line is to be set up—Mrs. Horween, the girl, a couple of male relatives. Mrs. Horween wants the order reversed. Reception line first, then the two bars."

"No problem," Lavalle said. "The bars are movable."

"You are overlooking one stage in the procedure, Mr. Chambrun," Reggie Lucas said. "I come first, checking out the guests at the door—examining their teeth for flaws, their bodies for birthmarks. Just to make sure no one who isn't invited gets in. Actually, I will have a checklist. The reason for the bars beyond the reception line is that Mrs. Horween would like to be sure people are not smashed before they meet the debutante."

"Not unreasonable," Chambrun said.

"Supper will be served at precisely one o'clock," Chambrun said. "It was originally scheduled for twelve-thirty. Mrs. Horween wants it moved forward half an hour."

"Which brings me to an unrelated question, Mr. Chambrun," Amato, the banquet manager, said. "Robert Gaynor, in Penthouse Three, has ordered a dinner for two. He wants fresh salmon with sauce Beaumont. It seems he had it here sometime. Unfortunately there is no fresh salmon on the market except half a ton that Mrs. Horween had flown in from the state of Washington. I doubt if she would miss two servings."

"Naughty, naughty!" Reggie Lucas giggled. "You will have to be supersweet to me, Chambrun, or I might tell?"

"On another problem presented by our movie star," Amato said. "He demands a certain brand of Spanish sherry. I can't produce it for him."

Chambrun raised a disapproving eyebrow. "It is my understanding that there is no wine worth serving that we don't have in our cellar."

"That's the difficulty. The sherry Gaynor asks for isn't worth serving," Amato said. "It's a cheap cooking sherry no one I can find would consider stocking. But the gentleman insists. This is some kind of anniversary. He and the lady drank this cheap sherry on the occasion they are celebrating. I'm damned if I can find a bottle of it anywhere. I understand they stopped exporting it from Spain about five years ago. No market for it here."

"Do your best," Chambrun said. He sat frowning for a moment, then he went on with a dozen small demands made by Mrs. Horween. He and the others settled them. As far as I could tell, Mrs. Horween had scored on all her major points except the elevators. I do remember that Reggie Lucas was to have a telephone at his elbow as the guests arrived. Any phone calls from anyone, for anyone at the ball, were to be delivered to him.

Miss Veach, the night superintendent on the switchboard, had arranged for Reggie's phone. "Robert Gaynor seems to keep coming up," she said. "He has instructed us to put no calls through to him after seven o'clock tonight. He must be planning quite a celebration with his lady."

The meeting was over, but Chambrun stopped Mr. Atterbury at the door. "Be good enough to send up our folder on Robert Gaynor," he said.

Finally Chambrun, Miss Ruysdale, and I were alone. Reggie Lucas had dashed off to report an almost-victory to Mrs. Horween. Everyone else had gone back to work.

"Speaking of Gaynor," I said. "The lady he's celebrating with tonight is the wife of someone who is a guest in the hotel."

"How do you know?" Chambrun asked.

"He told me. Wanted me to understand why there's so much secrecy and hush-hush around his being here."

"Who is she?" Chambrun asked.

"No idea. That's something he didn't tell me."

"I don't like the feel of the whole thing," Chambrun said slowly.

"She is maybe the five thousandth cheating wife in my time," Ruysdale said. "I know you don't approve, but what's so different about it?"

Chambrun crushed out his flat Egyptian cigarette in the ashtray on his desk. "I don't know. I wish I did," he said.

I make it sound as though Chambrun were playing some kind of hunch, having some kind of psychic premonition. If you knew him as I do, you'd know he played no such games with himself. It was hours later before I knew what was bothering him. I found myself too busy to deal with the fragments he never overlooked.

My problem was that in the late afternoon someone on radio tipped Robert Gaynor's presence. The word got out that he was in town, staying at the Beaumont. Excited young girls seemed to appear out of the woodwork and were obviously prepared to camp out in the lobby, waiting for Gaynor to show.

The front desk did their best to persuade these sensation seekers that the story was false, Robert Gaynor wasn't registered at the Beaumont. That was the technical truth. He was "a John Smith," registered under a phony name. Extra precautions were taken by Jerry Dodd and his security people to keep these young people from infiltrating to the upper floors to search for their idol. With only one elevator operating to the roof, it was easy enough to keep that car blocked off. I took it upon myself around six o'clock to call Gaynor and tell him that the secret was out and that an army of admirers was flooding the place.

"Can you keep them off the roof?" he asked.

"Of course," I said.

"Then it doesn't matter—I'm not leaving this penthouse," he said.

"I called you now because I know you're not taking calls after seven o'clock," I said.

"What are you talking about?" he said sharply.

"Your orders to the switchboard," I said.

"I gave no such orders," he said.

Some kind of confusion by one of the switchboard operators, I thought. "I can have the order canceled," I said.

He laughed. "Never mind," he said. "It's not a bad idea."

It didn't occur to him or to me to wonder who could have given the order to the switchboard. We both assumed it was some kind of misunderstanding. Of course, I should have known better. Chambrun's staff doesn't make that kind of mistake.

It was white tie and tails for me and for Chambrun for the night of the ball. I took time to dress after my conversation with Gaynor and was pleased with the results. I went down the hall to Chambrun's office. The first thing I noticed was that he was wearing a black tie with his full-dress suit.

"You put on the wrong tie," I said.

He seemed far away. He glanced at himself in the wall mirror. "So I did," he said.

"Shall I get you a white tie? I have a spare," I said.

He reached into his trouser pocket and pulled out a white tie. "I'll be ready when the right time comes," he said. "Who wears a black tie with a dress suit, Mark?"

"A maître d', a waiter," I said.

"I am about to become a room service waiter," he said.

I was not a witness to what happened after that, but when it was all over we got the details from Chambrun. He had put together some of the fragments I've mentioned, and he'd anticipated violence. And he almost prevented it, but not quite.

No one ever questions anything Chambrun does in the hotel, and when he appeared in the kitchen and took over from the room sevice waiter who was about to take dinner up to Penthouse Three, no one asked a question. Whatever he chose to do in the Beaumont was law.

I need to explain that there are three ways to reach the roof other than the fire stairs. There are the two elevators in the lobby, one of which was out of order, and there is a service elevator at the back that is used by room service and by maids and other personnel at the proper times. The three penthouses are separated at the front by garden space, but they are connected at the rear by a service hallway into which the service elevator opens along with the fire stairs.

Chambrun, a napkin draped over his arm, went up in the service elevator with the wagon that carried Robert Gaynor's dinner—which included some of Mrs. Horween's State of Washington salmon. At the roof level he ran into a horror that sickened him. Stretched out in the hallway was the body of a girl, brutally beaten around the head—pistol-whipped, he thought. On the room service's hall phone he called for Jerry Dodd and the house physician, Dr. Partridge. The girl, a total stranger to Chambrun, was still breathing faintly.

He waited for help, cursing himself for not having foreseen this possibility. When the girl was in the doctor's care, he gave instructions to Jerry Dodd.

"You're going in there?" Jerry asked, pointing to the back door of Penthouse Three. Chambrun, his face grim, nodded.

"I'm going with you," Jerry said.

"Just handle your orders, Jerry," Chambrun said. "Let us hope I'm not too late."

With a service key, he opened the rear door of Penthouse Three and wheeled in the dinner wagon. He waited in the kitchen area, straining to hear something. He was aware of the scent of an exotic perfume. Then he heard a woman laugh.

"Thank heaven," he said, under his breath.

He wheeled the wagon into the living room. Gaynor had said that, when the waiter brought the dinner, he was just to leave it and go away. He was not to see who Gaynor's guest was. Chambrun walked to the door that led to the penthouse's bedrooms.

"Gaynor, it's necessary that I talk to you," he called out.

There was no sound from the rooms beyond.

"You will force me to come looking for you," Chambrun said.

Gaynor appeared, his face flushed with anger. "I gave strict instructions—" he began. "Mr. Chambrun!"

"There isn't much time to talk," Chambrun said in a cold voice. This was the hanging judge.

"Talk about what?" Gaynor asked.

"What you do with your life, or other people's lives, is your affair," Chambrun said. "But *where* you do it is mine."

"Are you taking a moral tone with me, Mr. Chambrun?"

"I don't give a damn about your morals," Chambrun said. "Already you may be responsible for a death. One of your fans, a child almost, has just been found outside the service door here, severely beaten. The person responsible for that is waiting for the proper moment to attack you and your lady."

"Why—for God's sake?"

"Because he has been hired by the lady's husband to eliminate you both. The husband is not one to forgive treachery."

"You're not making sense!" Gaynor said.

"I know a good deal about you, Gaynor. It is my business to know everything there is to know about famous guests. Five years ago you had your first big success, an Italian-made Western movie shot in Spain."

*"The Silver Spurs,"* Gaynor murmured.

"The leading lady in that film was a ravishingly beautiful Irish girl named Kathleen O'Connor. That was her maiden name. She was actually married to a wealthy Spanish businessman named Manuel Santana. He was one of the backers of the film, which is how Kathleen got the job. There were rumors about you and Kathleen at the time, but there are always rumors about romantic leading men and their leading ladies. Today you told Mark Haskell, my public relations man, that your dinner companion was a married woman who is staying here with her husband."

"I wanted him to understand why all the secrecy was necessary," Gaynor said.

"You discreetly didn't mention the lady's name, but there was something you did do, Gaynor. You ordered a cheap Spanish sherry to go with a gourmet dinner."

"Sentimental reasons," Gaynor said.

"I understand. It was a wine you drank when you had your first romance. A very bad wine, I may say, but it revealed the lady's identity to me. Married, with a Spanish background. The only lady married to a Spaniard in the Beaumont was Madame Santana, or the former Kathleen O'Connor, your former leading lady. How you got together again, how you arranged this meeting, I do not know. But it was slipshod, because Señor Santana became aware of it and set a trap for you."

A beautiful woman appeared behind Gaynor in the doorway. "That is impossible, Mr. Chambrun," Kathleen Santana said. "My husband is in Washington on diplomatic business."

"A perfect alibi for him," Chambrun said, "but it will not interfere with the operation of a hired killer who is, I tell you, just waiting for me to leave before doing his job."

"I can't believe my husband would—" Kathleen said.

"Believe," Chambrun said. "The trap is set, rather elaborately. Yesterday, posing as a safety inspector, this hired killer put one of the two front elevators that come to the roof out of commission. That left only one elevator to watch, to make certain you were in the trap, Mrs. Santana. It also meant that, if you changed your plans and decided to dine out somewhere, he had only one elevator to cover. He gave instructions to the switchboard that you would accept no phone calls here after seven o'clock. No chance that way that anyone would become concerned by your failure to answer the phone. No one would be sent to check on you at a critical moment."

"But if what you say is true—"

"It is true, and there is no time to waste. Something has already gone wrong—that unfortunate girl in the service hall. He may not wait for me to leave. He can't use the service elevator—the way he came—because the place is swarming with security people. He will have to come here, finish his job, and leave by the one working elevator at the front. You will stop for nothing. You will slip out through the kitchen to the service area. My man Dodd will get you out of the hotel, take you anywhere you choose to go."

"But where?" Gaynor asked.

"Your problem, not mine, Gaynor," Chambrun said. "Now move. There is no time!"

The frightened couple took off for the kitchen and their one way of escape. Chambrun went back into the living room. He hesitated a moment, then opened the curtains at the French windows that looked onto the roof. He was clearly visible to anyone out there. Like a perfect waiter he began resetting things on the dinner wagon.

He heard the front door to the penthouse open, but he paid no attention. He kept his back turned. The waiter's napkin was draped over his right hand.

"Where are they?" a harsh voice asked.

Chambrun turned and found himself faced by a grotesque figure wearing a black ski mask. A deadly looking handgun was aimed straight at "the waiter." Chambrun give his shoulders a Gallic shrug and nodded toward the bedroom area.

The man in the ski mask evidently thought a waiter could be handled later. He moved quickly across the room toward the bedroom door, stepped inside for a moment, then returned.

"Where have they gone, buster?" he demanded. The hand holding the gun stretched out toward Chambrun, who took a step backward and raised his right hand, covered with the napkin, in a defensive gesture. A gunshot blasted the quiet of the room. The man in the ski mask screamed, dropped his gun, and clutched at a shattered elbow.

"Breaking and entering," Chambrun said in a quiet voice. He dropped the napkin, revealing his own gun. "Assault with a deadly weapon on that poor girl, intent to commit several murders. Señor Santana cannot claim diplomatic immunity for you."

The man, clutching his arm, his body twisted in agony, cried out, "Who are you?"

Chambrun's lips moved in a tight smile. "Under this roof, in this hotel, I am supreme ruler," he said.

There was a call to the security office. And then the supreme ruler removed the black tie he was wearing and replaced it with the white one he had in his trouser pocket. The Horween ball was the next thing on his agenda.

# Chambrun and the Obvious Clue

I got a right to sing the blues,
I got a right to feel lowdown—

I don't know if those are the true words of the song. They are the ones Freddie Lukes sang each night in his whiskey-tainted voice as a prelude to Marilyn Stark's entrance. Then came his special magic on the keyboard as he played the rest of it, without any vocal. Freddie manages a distillation of the joys and the sentiments of Fats Waller and Duke Ellington. Liquor may be the reason he never made it as big as those jazz giants, because there are moments when he could sweep you away with the sheer brilliance of his improvisations.

"I got a right to sing the blues" was the nightly notification to the audience in the Blue Lagoon that Marilyn was about to make her appearance. The spotlight on the black man at the piano would shift to the entrance, center stage, and Marilyn, with her golden hair, her elegant figure, her expressive face, would pick up the lyric and come downstage to a thunder of applause.

For the next hour she held the people spellbound. Twice a night she did her thing, at eight-thirty for the people who were not going to the theater, and at twelve-thirty for those who had been and were looking for more. And there were those who stayed for both shows, determined to see and hear all there was to see and hear that night.

I am the public relations man at the Hotel Beaumont. For a month now I had managed to make my rounds so that I could catch each of Marilyn Stark's nightly performances. I would appear behind the red-velvet rope at the entrance, and Mr. Cardoza, the maître d', would greet me.

"Good evening, Mr. Haskell," he would say.

"Good evening, Mr. Cardoza," I would say.

I've had reason every night of my life for the last ten years to contact this elegant gentleman who looks like a Spanish nobleman. He has never called me by my first name, Mark, and I have never called him Luis. He has a gift for making the formality seem closer than the casual use of first names.

On this particular morning—at twelve-thirty—I arrived just as Freddie Lukes was beginning "I got a right to sing the blues," and Cardoza gave me his enigmatic smile.

"Prompt as usual, I see," he said.

The stage darkened. The spotlight moved slowly away from Freddie Lukes and his flying fingers to the center entrance. You could hear a little whisper of expectancy run through the rich-looking audience. But Marilyn didn't appear.

The Hotel Beaumont is run with a kind of Swiss-watch precision. No fixed routines ever vary by a hair, not even the entrance on cue of its star chanteuse in its elegant nightclub. I remember Cardoza and I glanced at each other. Marilyn was three bars of music late—unheard of. Freddie Lukes at the piano began to repeat the theme music, this time a louder, stomped-out version, as if he thought that for some reason Marilyn hadn't heard the cue. It could be a number of things, of course: a heel caught in the hem of her skirt at the last moment with Lucy, her dresser, making frantic repairs; a coughing fit because of something swallowed the wrong way.

I remember wondering if Pierre Chambrun was aware, wherever he might be in the hotel at the moment, of this momentary break in an established routine. We who work with Chambrun are convinced he has some kind of built-in personal radar system that warns him of any deviation in procedure, from the penthouse rooftop to the subbasement. The truth is, of course, that the moment anything goes even slightly wrong there is someone to notify him. I was actually turning toward Cardoza's reservation phone when the spotlight at Marilyn's entrance point went out, and the dimmed houselights came up. There was to be no show, at least not for the moment.

Cardoza hurried between tables toward the stage. Freddie Lukes ended his theme music on a jangling chord and took off for the backstage area. Then someone backstage let out a blood-curdling scream. It was an announcement of violence that none of us is ever likely to forget.

Somewhere else I have written that every six months of my life I fall in love. I am, I guess, what you might call a one-woman-at-a-time man. I remember almost all my gals with affection, one or two with both affection and regret, one with love and enormous gratitude. That one is Marilyn Stark.

It happened eight years ago. I was young, full of enthusiasm for my job at the Beaumont, encountering famous people every day of my life, imagining that I was an incomparably sophisticated man of the world. I told myself that no woman who had an affair with Mark Haskell would ever forget him. I was, I thought, really something. Women were easy to come by in that glamorous setting, so easy that I was actually a little shocked by that fact from time to time. I put it down to my own irresistible charm.

Then there was Marilyn. Today, onstage, she looks in her late twenties. She is actually in her late forties. She came to fill a six-week engagement at the Blue Lagoon, and I was hopelessly lost to her in the first week. She was the first "older woman" in my life. She taught me tenderness and how to laugh and the skills of lovemaking. I promised her everything; she promised me nothing but the moment at hand. It was six weeks never matched in my life, before or since. It was she who said goodbye, not me. For me, it was forever. She was moving on to an engagement in Las Vegas.

"You've made me feel very young again, Mark," she said that last time. "I love you for it."

A year later she came back for another run at the Blue Lagoon. I rushed in to pick up the old relationship. It wasn't to be.

"Let's leave it as it is, Mark," she said. "I'd rather remember what we had—just as it was."

There had, of course, been other women in my life during that year, and there were new men in hers. She was right, I guess, though at the time I didn't think so. It could never be quite the same again.

And so, each year when she came back to play the Blue Lagoon, I would send flowers to her dressing room and a bottle of champagne, and we would chat, like old friends, about nothing in particular. Never about love, or what had been.

I didn't go to watch each of her shows because I was grieving for her or lost without her. She had known, among other things, how to write "The End" to our story without drawing blood. I went to watch and listen because this woman belonged among the greats of all time. I am too young to have ever heard Nora Bayes or Helen Morgan or Ruth Etting, but I have heard Ella Fitzgerald and Sarah Vaughan and Lena Horne. Marilyn belonged in their class. Those gals begin where the average singer leaves off.

So that night, like every night, I was there to hear the best there is. I was aware of at least three men in the audience, one of whom might be the man in her life at the moment. They were Richard Loring, a handsome young man-about-town, a wealthy sportsman, bubbling with animal energy; George Canaday, multimillionaire industrialist, much older, but able to buy Marilyn half of the world if she asked for it; and Peter Sebastian, the bearded artist, sought after, admired, obviously mad about Marilyn.

These three came to hear her almost every night, and they

were there the night that ghastly screaming started backstage. They—and the thousands of other people who adored Marilyn as a performer—were never to hear her sing again.

Death, I imagine, never comes as less than a shock, except perhaps in very old people—I mean, to those still living. Sudden death, without the preface of illness, death as the result of an accident or an act of God, is always shocking. But death that comes as a result of purposeful violence by another human being goes beyond shock.

Marilyn—lovely, vivacious, tender, joyful Marilyn—lay on the floor of her room, dressed in an evening gown in which she would never perform again. Her head had been beaten unmercifully, and her golden hair was matted with dark blood. She had also been struck time after time across the face, and her beauty had been completely obliterated. For one wild moment I told myself it couldn't be Marilyn. It had to be someone else wearing Marilyn's gown. And then I turned away, fighting a terrible nausea.

For a moment the faces that circled Marilyn were all familiar. There were Cardoza, his elegant composure shattered; Freddie Lukes, who had come running off the stage, his black face streaming sweat; Danny Haines, the stage manager who handled the backstage at the Blue Lagoon. And there was Lucy Morris, who had screamed us all to attention. Lucy is perhaps sixty years old, ugly, gnarled by arthritis, Marilyn's dresser for the past twenty years. Lucy would have put her arm in an electric meat grinder for Marilyn, if Marilyn had asked it.

Lucy's mouth was open for another scream when she saw me, someone Marilyn had cared for, a friend, and she catapulted herself into my arms, shaking and sobbing.

Then others were crowding into the room and at the door, including the three men who dreamed of Marilyn—the sportsman, the tycoon, the artist. It was George Canaday, the tycoon, looking old and gray, who said, "Someone call the police!"

I thought that must be in character. Get someone else to do what must be done.

Something better than the police arrived at that moment, a dark, wiry, intense little man named Jerry Dodd, who is the Beaumont's security chief.

"Out!" he shouted at Canaday, Loring, Sebastian, and the others crowded around them. "Out!" He slammed the dressing room door in their faces and fastened the inside bolt.

Jerry Dodd knelt and took a close look at Marilyn. I heard him swear under his breath. "Anyone thought to call Doc Partridge?" he asked. "Not that there's anything he can do for her." Doc Partridge is the house physician. Then Jerry looked at me. "You notified Chambrun?"

"For God's sake, Jerry, I just got here!"

It was Cardoza who went to the dressing room phone and tried to locate The Man. Old Lucy Morris and I clung to each other, as though to lose one another was to be lost forever.

People have seen Pierre Chambrun in many kinds of crises over the years at the Beaumont. They would say, I think, that no circumstance, however serious or bizarre, ever changes his outward aspect. He is always well-tailored, wearing exactly the right clothes for the moment. Like a good actor, he seems never to be caught in an awkward gesture or movement. Short, he walks with such a firm stride that he seems taller than he is. A Hollywood producer was once interested in doing a movie about the Beaumont with Chambrun as the central figure. He asked me which actor I would choose to play the role. Unfortunately, the perfect actor is no longer available—the late Claude Rains.

Those of us who knew Chambrun well could always find a clue to his feelings in his heavy-lidded eyes. Those eyes could be as compassionate as the Good Samaritan's, as curious as a mischievous child's. When he walked into Marilyn's dressing room that night, the hanging judge was in command. You couldn't look at her without feeling an intense and fierce rage at the person who had done this. I remember feeling reassured as he stood there, looking down at what was left of Marilyn. He would nail the person responsible for this if anyone could.

I look at what I have written, and I have to say that a dinner jacket was not exactly the right dress for a murder. He was dressed for all the various events taking place that evening in the hotel, the events he would cover on his nightly rounds. He was always just a little more elegant than his most elegant customer or guest.

He looked at Jerry Dodd, his eyes cold enough to freeze one's blood. "Weapon?" he asked.

"Not so far," Jerry said. "Looks like it was carried away."

Those frightening eyes circled the ring of faces. "Well?" he said.

It was Lucy Morris, still clinging to me, who broke the silence. "I—I found her," Lucy said. "She—she had sent me to the drugstore for—for something, and when I came back I found her—like that!" Her body was still shaking.

"What were you sent to get, and when did you go to get it?" Chambrun asked in a voice that was cold and flat.

"Poor Marilyn!" Lucy said. "She suffered from migraine headaches. She felt an attack coming on and discovered she was out of the medicine she takes for it. It's a prescription, and she sent me to the drugstore in the lobby to get it refilled."

"What time was that?" Chambrun asked.

"It was exactly twelve fifteen," Lucy said.

"Exactly?"

"I know because Danny gave her the fifteen-minute call just as I was going out the door." She looked at Danny Haines, the stage manager, for confirmation.

"I don't know where Lucy was at twelve-fifteen," Danny said. "But Marilyn was here. There's an intercom system between my control booth, where I handle the lights and other cues, and this room. For the second show, at twelve o'clock,

Freddie takes the stage with his piano, and I give Marilyn the half-hour call. 'Half hour, Marilyn,' I say. And she always says, 'Thank you, Danny.' At twelve-fifteen I call again and tell her fifteen minutes. And she answers."

"And she answered tonight, at twelve-fifteen?"

"Yes. Perfectly normal, perfectly ordinary. Lucy could have been at the door, like she says, but I wouldn't know, of course. All I know is that Marilyn was alive and in no trouble then. But ten minutes later—"

"What happened ten minutes later?"

"I gave her a five-minute call," Danny said. "Sometimes she answers, sometimes she doesn't. Tonight she didn't. But, like I say, that wasn't unusual. She often goes out into the wings and waits for the music cue from Freddie."

Chambrun looked down at the tragedy on the floor. "But she wasn't in the wings tonight," he said. He turned to Lucy. "You left for the drugstore at twelve-fifteen, you say. It takes two or three minutes to walk down the back corridor and into the lobby. The pharmacist had to fill your prescription."

"It's just tablets, Mr. Chambrun," Lucy said. "He had to type a label, that was all."

"And you came back here with the pills," Chambrun said. "In time to hear Danny give that five-minute call?"

"Oh, my God, I don't know, Mr. Chambrun!" Lucy moaned. "I saw her. I don't know what I heard or didn't hear. It—it could have been after the five-minute call, because I knew she only had a minute or two to take a pill, get into her costume, and get on stage."

"She's in her costume!" Chambrun said.

Lucy twisted her head from side to side. "I know. That's another odd thing," she said.

"Odd?"

"She never dresses without me," Lucy said.

"But the time was short, if she was to make her cue."

Lucy pointed to something I hadn't noticed before. It was a metal frame, standing on four legs, made of tubing. "I hang the gown on that frame," Lucy said, "and raise the frame. She stands under it and I lower the dress over her head. It's for quick changes, and to keep from messing up her hairdo. When I left for the medicine, the gown was on that dressing frame."

"Because you weren't there, she did it herself," Chambrun said.

"No," Lucy said.

"She must have."

"She never did before. No, she wouldn't have. It only takes ten seconds for her to stand under the dress. I lower it and zip her up from behind. She'd have waited for me."

"But she didn't," Chambrun said.

Lucy looked puzzled.

"How was she dressed before you left for the drugstore?"

"Pantyhose, evening slippers, brassiere," Lucy said. "She'd done her makeup and her hair before I went to the drugstore."

"So someone knocked on her door, and she got into her gown," Chambrun said.

"Not anyone who had any business being here," Lucy said. "Not me or Freddie or Danny. We'd all seen her hundreds of times almost naked that way. It's show business. If—if it was one of the gentlemen, she might have slipped into a dressing gown." She pointed to a kind of negligee hanging over a chair next to the dressing table and its mirror.

"What gentlemen?" Chambrun asked.

"There are three men who have been in constant attendance," Cardoza said. "They're outside in the hall now."

"But she wouldn't have got into the gown for them," Lucy said stubbornly. "She'd have waited for me. The dressing gown, maybe, but not the costume."

"Somebody came here and killed her," Chambrun said. "No one saw anyone who didn't belong here?"

"I was at the drugstore," Lucy said.

"I was on stage, at the piano," Freddie Lukes said.

"I was in my booth," Danny Haines said. "I can only see the stage and the audience from there. It's a one-woman show, Mr. Chambrun. There are no stagehands, no other regular people backstage."

"So there was no problem for the killer to come and go, unseen," Chambrun said.

"Carrying a weapon," Jerry Dodd said. "Why didn't she scream for help?"

"This room is soundproofed," Chambrun reminded him. "It was done so singers could vocalize without being heard. She could have screamed her head off, and only the killer would have heard it."

The Beaumont is like a small city, with its own security force, its own shops, restaurants, bars, its own hospital, even its own bank. The nightlife time when Marilyn had been killed was one of the busiest in the hotel's schedule, which is why the drugstore stayed open so late.

Like any small city, the Beaumont has suffered its share of crimes, including murders. Lieutenant Walter Hardy of Homicide was not a stranger to us. We were grateful to have the Marilyn Stark case assigned to him and not to some detective unknown to us. Chambrun and Hardy have worked together before, and they have a mutual respect for each other, even though their approaches to a problem are totally different.

Hardy, a big slow-moving blond, travels the painstaking, detailed route, covering every possible angle, collecting every scrap of evidence, sifting every point for and against every possible theory. He must build an unshakable case for the district attorney, must have every doubt answered in advance before he makes an arrest.

On the other hand, Chambrun is intuitive, a hunch player; he has done his rejecting and accepting almost before Hardy has picked up the first stone to look under it. Chambrun's approach might seem almost frivolous to a stranger—he looks like a man in a hurry to get his hotel running normally again. Those of us who know him well are aware of how invariably right his intuition and his hunches are. Hardy had learned over the years to listen to and follow the leads Chambrun gives him.

The inquiry had shifted to Chambrun's office on the second floor, while the crew from the medical examiner's office, the fingerprint men, and the police photographers had taken over the grim scene in Marilyn's dressing room.

I was there with Cardoza and Jerry Dodd as Chambrun laid out his preliminary findings to Hardy.

"The timing is the most unusual factor in the case," Chambrun said. He was smoking one of his flat Egyptian cigarettes and sipping at a demitasse of Turkish coffee, which was always kept brewed in a samovar on the sideboard. "We are dealing with something like twelve minutes. She was alive and untroubled at midnight and at twelve-fifteen, when Danny Haines gave her the first two warning calls. Lucy Morris was with her when she got both those calls. Everything normal, Lucy comes back in about twelve minutes and finds Marilyn dead. That's the crucial period—those twelve minutes."

"Probably even less," Hardy said. "The killer had to wait for her to be alone—and had to be gone before Lucy came back from the drugstore. Ten minutes at most, I'd say."

Chambrun nodded. "Okay—ten minutes in which the following takes place. The killer arrives—knowing the schedule backstage, by the way, knowing that when Freddie Lukes started his warmup that the backstage area would be clear."

"How could he know Lucy Morris would be sent to the drugstore?" Hardy asked.

"Perhaps Lucy just got lucky," Chambrun said. "Perhaps the killer had counted on having to deal with Lucy, too. So—the killer arrives, carrying with him a weapon of some sort—an iron wrecking bar, a fireplace poker, something of that sort. Marilyn wasn't killed with a toothpick! An awkward weapon to carry in—and out. It's summer. Overcoats are not in order."

"A raincoat," Hardy suggested.

"Possible," Chambrun said. "Absolutely no threat of rain, but possible. So he comes in, carrying his weapon, slips backstage, and knocks on Marilyn's dressing room door. Eight minutes left? And what does Marilyn do?"

"Lets him in," Hardy said.

"No, no, no," Chambrun said. "She asks him to wait a moment. She knows him, of course. She goes and stands under the dressing frame, lowers the dress over her head—an awkward procedure, according to Lucy. She zips up her gown. The zipper is at her back—another awkward procedure. She manages, however, taking at the shortest a minute. She goes to the door, fully dressed in her handsome gown, and lets the caller in."

"Seven minutes left," Hardy said, making a note in his little book.

"At most," Chambrun said. His face had become a cold hard mask. "The killer had come prepared to kill, not to converse. Right? This was a crime motivated by an almost unbelievable rage, certainly. No talk. The door is closed, all sound from the rest of the world shut out. The onslaught begins before Marilyn can speak a word. A dozen blows with that wrecking bar or poker—to the head, across the face. Nothing in the room is touched, which is why you won't find any fingerprints."

"The doorknob?" Hardy asked.

"Perhaps gloves, perhaps his hand protected by the raincoat or his suit jacket when he had to let himself out," Chambrun said. "The whole horror could have taken as little as a couple of minutes. He came to kill—Marilyn is dead—he still has two or three minutes left in which to walk away before Lucy came back with the medicine from the drugstore."

"Rage, I buy," Hardy said. "But what could drive a man to such uncontrolled fury?"

Chambrun shrugged. "A rejected lover," he said.

"So we have three gents outside who might fit that bill," Hardy said. "It's time we talked to them, isn't it?"

Cardoza broke in. "If you're talking about Richard Loring the sportsman, George Canaday the tycoon, and Peter Sebastian the artist, I would have to swear under oath that not one of them could have been backstage after midnight when Freddie Lukes started his warm-up. Each one of them was at his table in the Blue Lagoon the whole time."

"You're sure of that?" Hardy asked.

"Positive. It's the kind of thing I notice, it's part of my job," Cardoza said.

"Well, one of them or all of them may know something about other lovers, other rejected suitors," Hardy said. "Let's have the first one in."

The first one was handsome Richard Loring, the playboy sportsman. I had a feeling his shock and grief were genuine. He listened to the rejected-lover theory, frowning.

"Were you Marilyn's lover, Mr. Loring?" Hardy asked. The subtle approach was not in his arsenal.

"I'm not a kiss-and-tell boy, Lieutenant," he said. "Let us say that at one time Marilyn and I were close—but that was some time ago."

"And yet you came nearly every night to hear her sing?"

"I was fond of her, and she was a great artist," Loring said.

"You weren't prepared to prevent anyone else from having her?"

"You have to be joking, Lieutenant," Loring said.

Chambrun lifted his heavy eyelids. "Are you married, Mr. Loring?"

"Lord, no," Loring said. "There are too many lovely women in the world to anchor oneself to one."

"How about Sebastian and Canaday? Are they married?"

"Sebastian, no," Loring said. "And a thirty-year marriage has just ended in divorce for the Canadays. I think George dreamed that he could buy Marilyn for himself. But George didn't kill her—if she'd turned him down. I was sitting at the table next to him the entire critical time. I can alibi him, he can alibi me—and Sebastian, too, for that matter. I wish I could help. I would do anything in my power to catch the maniac who did this dreadful thing."

"Thank you, Mr. Loring," Chambrun said.

When Loring had gone, Hardy said, "Let's have the next one."

"Let's wait a moment, Walter," Chambrun said. His eyes were narrowed, almost closed. "I think I have been an idiot."

We all waited for him to go on.

"There is a famous play of Frederick Lonsdale's," he said, "in which a sophisticated man-about-town says something like: 'I've been dealing with women all my life and do you know what I've found out about them? Nothing!' From the very beginning I've been refusing to look at the obvious clue in this case."

"Nothing's obvious to me," Hardy muttered.

"Why did Marilyn go through the awkward business of getting into her costume gown before admitting her visitor—the killer? Professional glamor was her business, but sexual glamor was, I daresay, her life. Think for a minute, gentlemen. A lover or an ex-lover calls. She has on only pantyhose and a bra. If it were someone she had been intimate with, she could receive him that way—not unheard of in the theater. She could slip on her dressing gown, and a man would find that intriguing. But for her actual performance she would have waited for Lucy to dress her.

"But, gentlemen—and I don't pretend to know more than Lonsdale's character about women—I suggest that if a *woman* was calling on her, a woman who was her enemy, Marilyn would have chosen to receive her only with all the exterior glamor she could provide—in full stage costume. Semi-nudity or the dressing gown covering it would not have impressed another woman. In full costume Marilyn would have been showing a jealous woman how unbeatable, how truly glamorous she was."

"Are you saying it was a woman who could have delivered that beating?" Hardy said.

"A desperate, enraged woman, yes. A woman who came prepared to do it, yes. A woman from whom Marilyn expected nothing but tears, or pleadings—yes." Chambrun punched out his cigarette in the ashtray on his desk. "From the beginning I have overlooked the obvious. It had to be a woman. It explains why Marilyn chose to appear at her very best for her caller. Her best for a man and her best for a woman were two different things. If I were you, Walter, I would take off for the Canaday house on Fifth Avenue and ask Mrs. Canaday to provide you with an alibi for the critical time. And I would look around in the Canaday house for a weapon that might still reveal traces of blood at the police laboratory. Smashing a thirty-year marriage could drive a woman into a homicidal frenzy."

Those of you who followed the Marilyn Stark case in the media will know that Clarissa Canaday confessed to killing her husband's mistress backstage at the Blue Lagoon. It appeared that Marilyn, approaching fifty, had decided that Canaday's great wealth could give her the security she suddenly felt she needed. Perhaps I am running Canaday down. Perhaps he had charms I couldn't recognize. At the trial he tried to aid his wife by claiming his cruel affair with Marilyn had driven her to insanity. The jury agreed, and Clarissa Canaday is living out her life in a mental hospital.

And Chambrun? Well, as he has said so often, there was a hotel to run, and we got back to it.

# Pierre Chambrun's Dilemma

After ten years as public relations director for the Beaumont, I tell myself that I have come to know Pierre Chambrun better than anyone else on the staff. There is, of course, Betsy Ruysdale, his fabulous secretary, who appears able to read his mind in advance, but there are some of us who think she may be much closer to him than just a member of his efficient crew. That is another story, a secret that only Chambrun and Betsy could reveal.

Chambrun is king of his world. The Beaumont is like a city within a city, with its own security force, hospital, shops, restaurants, bars, and living quarters for a thousand people. Chambrun knows everything there is to know about its operation—exactly what is happening in every nook and cranny of his elegant establishment almost moment to moment. The difference between the Beaumont and an ordinary town is that, except for a few people who own cooperative apartments on the upper floors, the residents are transient, coming and going from all over the world. It is a home-away-from-home of many diplomats involved in work of the United Nations. Movie stars, social luminaries from London, Paris, or Monaco pass in and out.

In addition, Chambrun knows all there is to know about every guest—their credit ratings, their love lives, their political affiliation, their habits, good and bad. It might have embarrassed some of them to know how much intimate information we had about them. The information wasn't difficult to collect with an efficient front office, with a security service and housekeeping staff, with maître d's, bartenders, and sharp and observant bellmen.

It might have surprised the staff even more to know how much Chambrun knew about those who worked for him, their home lives, their children, their special problems. This was in no way a method of checking up on employees for security reasons. It was his way of being a friend. It equipped him to offer help before anyone had to ask him for it. These people, hundreds of them, were his family. It was his concern for one of his "family" that projected Chambrun, one summer day, into a terrorist plot to commit a murder that threatened to shake the power centers of the world.

General Achmed Hassan, the Middle Eastern diplomat, had come to New York for negotiations at the United Nations. He came from an area dominated by terror and confusion. His goal was some kind of peaceful solution of the problems of oil and the Western economy. His enemies—fanatics for the most part—were as numerous as his friends and supporters. Every moment of his life was threatened by terrorists who would gladly assassinate him given an inch in which to maneuver.

I can't tell you much about the outside forces set up to protect General Hassan. I suppose the FBI, the CIA, and certainly the New York police, covered every move he made in the city and at the UN. They had in the past protected Sadat, a friend, and Castro, an enemy, with calm efficiency. Protecting the general in the Beaumont without turning the place into an armed fortress that would frighten its regular guests was Chambrun's job, and Jerry Dodd's, our security chief, and mine, and every other employee of the hotel.

The general had four personal bodyguards who shared his suite on the twenty-first floor. Jerry Dodd's men patrolled the hallways. I, Mark Haskell, kept the press away. When times came for the general to leave the building, an elevator was reserved for his private use, which took him to the basement garage where a car, surrounded by police, waited to take him to the UN.

The general had all his meals in 21A. The food was prepared by the general's own special chef, watched over by an FBI man. The meals were served by a waiter, chosen by Chambrun, who had been with the Beaumont for more than twenty years. "I would trust my own life to Luigi Cantora," I heard Chambrun say when he selected the waiter to serve the general. "And I care quite a bit more for myself than I do for our guest."

On the summer day in question, Luigi Cantora did not report for work. It was the first time in twenty years he didn't report for work. He didn't call in sick. He just didn't show. Chambrun replaced him, but that wasn't good enough for him. There was something wrong with a member of his "family." He could have sent me, or one of Dodd's men, or Betsy Ruysdale, to check. He went himself. Luigi was his friend.

Not long ago a movie company was considering making a film out of one of the stories I've written about Pierre Chambrun. I was asked if I could suggest an actor who would be right for the role. Unfortunately the actor who would have been perfect was not available, the late Claude Rains. Short and stocky, like Chambrun, but moving with the grace of a dancer. Pouches under eyes that could be bright with humor, dark with anger, or cold as a hanging judge's. A touch of vanity shows in his expensive and impeccable taste in clothes. When he goes out on the streets of the city, he carries a blackthorn walking stick. Walking sticks have gone out of style until recently, when men have started to think again about self-protection in a violent city. Chambrun is, I suppose, in his late fifties, but I wouldn't recommend tangling with him, not when he is armed with his blackthorn. In what he calls "the black days," the time of the occupation of Paris by the Nazis, he had, in his late teens, learned all the arts of head-on confrontation.

That summer day Chambrun walked east toward a small building near the river where Luigi Cantora lived. Occasionally people would turn to look at him, his hat worn at a rakish angle, and swinging his stick. He was actually headed for a friend in trouble.

Chambrun knew things that morning about Luigi Cantora that I didn't know. Luigi was a dark Italian in his early sixties, with a deeply lined face; he was stooped a little with the years. His wife, Serafina, was twenty years his junior. Their only son had been killed in Vietnam. They were close, Luigi and Serafina, dependent on each other to survive their grief. If Luigi was too ill to go to work, Serafina would have called Chambrun, knowing that Luigi had a special job serving General Hassan. The only explanation Chambrun could think of for Luigi's not calling was that something had happened to Serafina—an accident, a sudden severe illness. Luigi would not act responsibly if something had happened to his beloved wife.

Chambrun knocked on the door of the Cantora apartment. There was no answer.

He rapped sharply with the knob of his blackthorn stick. Still no answer. Then he called out.

"Luigi! It's Pierre Chambrun!"

After a moment there was a sound from inside, the turning of the lock, and Luigi opened the door. He looked ravaged.

"Oh, my God, Mr. Chambrun," he said.

He stood aside, and Chambrun walked into the neat little living room, so perfectly cared for by Serafina.

"What has happened to Serafina, Luigi?" Chambrun asked. "I know something has happened to her, or you would have called in."

"Oh, my God, Mr. Chambrun!"

"Tell me, Luigi. I'm your friend. I want to help you if I can."

The old Italian turned away, and his body convulsed with sobs. "You cannot help! There is no way to help me."

*"Tell me what has happened, Luigi!"*

"The terrorists have her!"

"What terrorists? What are you talking about?"

"The enemies of General Hassan," Luigi said. "They have taken her to be a hostage."

"Stop blubbering, and tell me! How can I help you if I don't know what has happened?"

Luigi turned back. "I must help them commit a murder, or they will kill Serafina."

"How on earth are you supposed to help them commit a murder?"

Luigi was silent.

"You must tell me," Chambrun said. "I am your friend. I am Serafina's friend. You know that."

"I have been warned not to go to the police, not to go to the FBI, not to go to you."

"You haven't come to me, I have come to you," Chambrun said.

"They will know you are here, Mr. Chambrun. They are watching. They will think I've sent for you to help me. They may already have—have dealt with Serafina. You couldn't know, but your coming here may have cost her her life!"

I can imagine how that jolted Chambrun, but I doubt he showed it in any way.

"If you had to commit a murder to save her, why are you sitting here doing nothing?" he asked Luigi.

"I couldn't! I couldn't move! I was unable, like a man who has suffered a stroke. But it must be tomorrow morning or—or else. They have been in touch with me again. I—I have a last chance."

"To kill General Hassan?"

"To make certain he dies."

"How?"

"If I tell you, and you prevent it—"

"I promise you, Luigi, I will do nothing to risk Serafina's life. How are you supposed to make certain the general dies?"

Luigi turned away, his face working. "They cannot get to the general directly," he said. "There are his bodyguards, there are Jerry Dodd's men, there are FBI agents in the hotel. He is thoroughly protected from all ordinary violence. But I—I take him his food and drink."

"Poison?" Chambrun asked.

Luigi nodded.

"Impossible," Chambrun said. "He has his own trusted chef. The chef is watched, in all stages of his preparations, by an FBI agent."

"They know that," Luigi said. "There is one weak link in all of the protection they've set up, Mr. Chambrun. I take the food wagon up from the kitchens, on the service elevator, to the rear door of the general's suite. I am not watched because you selected me, I am to be trusted. Tomorrow morning, when I take up the breakfast wagon on the service elevator, I will be intercepted somewhere between the kitchens and the twenty-first floor. Someone will poison the food, and I will go on with it—and serve it."

"And if you sound an alarm?"

"For God's sake, Mr. Chambrun, they have Serafina! If a dozen generals have to die, I would save her first. Before you came, I made up my mind. I will go through with it. Now you will try to stop me!"

I can visualize Chambrun taking a flat Egyptian cigarette from his silver case, his eyes narrowed against the smoke as he lit it.

"I will not try to stop you, Luigi," he said. "You will do exactly what the assassins have ordered you to do. What I do—well, that is something else again."

* * *

"It is a very neat dilemma," Chambrun said. He was sitting behind the carved Florentine desk in his plush office on the Beaumont's second floor. Jerry Dodd and Betsy Ruysdale and I were with him, the three people I think he trusts implicitly. "We prevent Luigi from delivering a poisoned breakfast to the general, and Serafina dies. We don't prevent him, and the general dies."

"You haven't any choice," Jerry Dodd said. He is a dark, wiry little man, intense, expert at his security job. "You have to protect the general."

"I have to protect Serafina," Chambrun said. "She is my friend's wife. I've promised him not to endanger her."

"You have to make a choice, Pierre," Miss Ruysdale said.

Chambrun smiled at Miss Ruysdale, a sly, almost mischievous smile. "I know, and I have made a choice," he said. "I plan to save them both."

"You have no idea where Serafina Cantora is being held," Jerry Dodd objected. "You have no way to find her."

"So I will have to find a way, won't I?" Chambrun replied.

"Do I notify my people and the FBI that we are expecting trouble?"

Chambrun's smile vanished. "You don't mention any of this to a single living soul," he said.

"You're playing some kind of fancy game with human lives," Jerry said. He always has the guts to stand up to Chambrun.

"Only a fancy game can save them both," Chambrun said. "What I want from you, Jerry, is to tighten your protection of the general, don't let anyone become complacent. But I don't want you to change the routine by a hair—no sudden surveillance of the service elevator, no watchful eye on Luigi. What I have told you is as sacred and secret as if you were priests in the confessional."

"Just don't blame me if we mess up on the general in some way," Jerry said. "Is that all, boss?"

"That's all," Chambrun said. "The zero hour isn't until tomorrow's breakfast."

Jerry took off, obviously not convinced that Chambrun was making sense. There was, however, no doubt he would carry out his orders to the letter. When the day comes that we can't follow The Man blindly, our world will have collapsed.

"You have appointments," Betsy Ruysdale reminded Chambrun when Jerry was gone.

"I'll keep them," Chambrun said. "Remember, Ruysdale"—he never calls her by her first name, just "Ruysdale"—"nothing is to change. All routines as usual—until tomorrow's breakfast."

Ruysdale nodded and took off for her private office.

"What can I do to be useful?" I asked Chambrun.

He sat very still for a moment, staring down at a blank pad on his desk top. Then he looked up at me. "If I muff this, Mark, there won't be much flavor to living."

I didn't say anything.

"The general's breakfast is served at eight-thirty," he said. "I want you here with me at eight o'clock."

"Right."

"I may need you very urgently then, Mark. Meanwhile, today, don't let the press and media people develop any kind of special or sudden interest in the general. Invent something, if necessary, to keep them looking somewhere else. The Queen of England may be coming to stay with us; Greta Garbo is planning a party to announce her return to the screen. Anything to keep them looking away from the general."

"Count on it."

"You think I'm out of my mind, Mark?"

"No, but I don't know what's going on in it—in your mind."

"It's quite simple," he said. "I hope to save two lives."

If it had been anyone but Chambrun, I might have protested, loud and long. No individual has the right to play games with life and death. The general, forewarned, could be kept perfectly safe. He was surrounded by an army of trained people. Serafina Cantora was an unfortunate victim of fanatical evil. All hostages are such victims. Someone playing games with the situation was running intolerable risks.

But not Chambrun. If any man could assess the odds for success and against failure, that man was Chambrun. He had lived and succeeded all his life by taking calculated risks.

I have to tell you that I went through the next hours—the rest of that morning, the afternoon, and a long evening—under a kind of tension I wouldn't have believed. The Beaumont seemed to operate with its usual Swiss-watch efficiency, but for me violence seemed to be waiting around every corner. We all live with violence, but for me, that day, it was pinpointed, focused on the Beaumont.

The big trouble was expected tomorrow morning, but somehow I expected it might erupt long before that. I had an ear to the ground. I knew when the general left for the UN about ten in the morning. I knew when he returned about six in the afternoon. I knew when the changing of the guard took place, when a new group of FBI agents took over, when Jerry Dodd's crew changed.

The general lived through the day without incident. The newspaper and other media people had shown no interest in him. I was exhausted when I went to my apartment on the second floor and fell into bed, alerting the switchboard to call me at six-thirty in the morning. I wouldn't have believed it possible, but I slept as though I'd been slugged.

I must have jumped three feet clear of the bed when the phone rang. It was only the operator telling me it was time to get moving. The sun was streaming through my windows. This was the day when one of two people was scheduled to die, and both of them might.

Chambrun was already in his office when I got there at a quarter to eight, fifteen minutes ahead of the time I'd been ordered to report. He was wearing a light gray tropical worsted suit with a little white flower in the buttonhole. He looked as if he'd slept like a baby; he was refreshed, ready for anything. I knew from my shaving mirror that I looked as if I'd been on an all-night binge.

"We are sharing the breakfast hour with the general," Chambrun informed me.

With murder scheduled for eight-thirty, I told myself.

We went to the twenty-first floor, and Chambrun rang the bell to the general's suite. The door was promptly opened by one of the dark-faced bodyguards.

We were led into the luxurious living room where General Hassan was already at work at his desk. He got up from his chair to greet us, a handsome man with the brilliant smile of a professional public figure, a neatly trimmed beard and mustache, and dark eyes, bright with pleasure.

"It is a delight to see you, Mr. Chambrun," he said.

The general wasn't alone. The guard who had admitted us stood by the door to the vestibule. Another was at the opening of the corridor that led to the bedrooms. A third, I guessed, was at the rear of the suite waiting for Luigi Cantora to arrive with the breakfast wagon.

"It's rather early in the day, general, but there seemed to be no other time to fit myself into your busy schedule," Chambrun said. "Have you met Mark Haskell, our public relations director?"

The general's handshake was firm and friendly. "Like everything else in this establishment, Mr. Chambrun, the machinery turns soundlessly. Mr. Haskell has kept me well protected from the press. Please sit down. You will share coffee with me when it comes. It should be here any moment. And now, what can I do for you, Mr. Chambrun?"

"I just wanted to make certain everything is as you wish it to be," Chambrun said. "That you are satisfied with the routines, that the service is satisfactory."

"My own people in my own palace could not be more perfect," the general said. "Ah, here is Luigi with the breakfast."

Luigi Cantora looked like a man about to face a firing squad as he wheeled in the breakfast wagon, followed by a guard. When Luigi saw Chambrun, his eyes bulged like marbles.

"We missed you yesterday, Luigi," the general said.

"My—my wife was ill, sir," Luigi muttered.

"I trust she is feeling much better today," the general said.

"Thank you, sir."

Luigi wheeled the breakfast wagon into place in front of the general. Luigi's hands were obviously shaking as he shifted some of the silver-covered plates and moved the silver coffee pot into position. I felt the inside of my mouth go painfully dry. Almost certainly, from Luigi's panicked appearance, death was lurking there for the general.

The general was evidently in high good humor.

"I think you will find extra coffee cups in the pantry, Luigi," he said. "Please fetch two for Mr. Chambrun and Mr. Haskell."

Luigi seemed frozen where he stood.

"Luigi—" Chambrun said, very quietly.

The coffee! It had to be the coffee! The old waiter made a despairing sound, turned, and stumbled out of the room. The general filled the one coffee cup on the wagon with a flourish, picked up the cup, and held it out toward Chambrun.

"For you, my friend," he said.

Chambrun's face looked carved out of stone. He didn't move in his chair. One of the guards took a quick step forward, apparently to pass the cup. He stumbled as he reached the breakfast wagon, reached out to prevent himself from falling, sent the coffee cup flying, spilling most of the contents on the front of Chambrun's immaculate summer suit. The guard's other hand overturned the coffee pot on the wagon.

Both Chambrun and the general were suddenly standing.

"How could you be so clumsy, Abdul?" the general said sharply.

The guard muttered something apologetic in a language I didn't understand. He was blotting at Chambrun's stained suit with a napkin. Then he turned to the breakfast wagon to work on the coffee spill there. I glanced past him and saw Luigi in the entrance to the pantry, clinging to the door jamb like a man whose legs had turned to gelatin. Chambrun spoke quietly to the old waiter.

"Help clean up the mess, Luigi, and bring General Hassan a fresh cloth and napkins—and a fresh pot of coffee," Chambrun said.

Luigi nodded and began puttering, almost aimlessly.

"I'm deeply sorry for Abdul's awkwardness, Mr. Chambrun," the general said. "I trust you will wait for fresh coffee."

"I'm afraid not, General," Chambrun said. "I have a rather busy schedule this morning, and I'll have to change into a more presentable suit of clothes."

"Another time," the general suggested.

"It will be a pleasure, General."

Out in the hall I grabbed Chambrun's arm. "That was no accident," I said. "You'd forewarned them!"

He gave me an odd, cold look. "I agree with you, Mark. It was not an accident. But I assure you, I've talked to no one about this but Luigi, you, Jerry Dodd, and Ruysdale."

"Then why—"

"If I had taken a swallow of that coffee and dropped dead on the spot," Chambrun said, "it would have closed off the only avenue they have for getting at the general. As it is, tomorrow is another day."

"And you won't be there for breakfast tomorrow."

"If I have to be," Chambrun said, "it's 'Goodbye, Serafina.'"

It was pretty hard to concentrate on the routines of the day. Chambrun, I knew, would never tell me anything but the truth. He hadn't warned the general or his guards about a planned assassination by poison. That meant there was treachery within the ranks of the general's close and personal protectors—specifically, the man called Abdul. One rotten apple in the barrel. If the plan to use Luigi, forced to cooperate out of fear for his wife, was to be tried again it would have to be delayed until tomorrow's breakfast.

The general would have his lunch at the UN, and who could know where he might dine. Our unexpected presence this morning had aborted the plan, but Abdul—he must have thought very cleverly—had saved them a second chance. Serafina Cantora was still a hostage, and the terrified Luigi would continue to cooperate. Abdul and his co-conspirators must have felt certain of that. We, on our side, had a day and a night, but what could we do with that time?

A little after ten o'clock that morning I was in my office, down the hall from Chambrun's, when I got a call from The Man.

"I need your help, Mark," he said.

"Anything you say."

"Meet me at the elevator. We're going places."

Two or three minutes later we met. He was wearing his rakish hat and carrying his blackthorn walking stick. Apparently we were going somewhere outside the hotel.

Chambrun pressed the down button, and we descended to the garage in the basement of the hotel. He didn't explain anything until we reached his own private Mercedes, which was waiting for us with Jerry Dodd at the wheel. Chambrun got in up front with Jerry. He turned to me in the back seat as the car started up the ramp.

"I figured Abdul would have to report to his pals," he said. "So I alerted Jerry. Abdul wouldn't, I thought, make an outside call through the hotel switchboard. The general's guards change when he leaves the hotel for the UN."

"The boss was right," Jerry said, as he maneuvered the car out into the city traffic. "The first place Abdul went when he was relieved was to a pay phone in the lobby. I was on his heels. I could see him dial a number. He spoke, excited, in a language I couldn't understand. But I checked with a chum at the phone company and got an address for the number he'd called. About ten blocks away on the Upper East Side."

"That's where we're going," Chambrun said.

"To do what?" I asked.

"Not to whistle 'Dixie'!" Jerry said.

Our target turned out to be a dilapidated brownstone not far from the river. Jerry parked the Mercedes about a block from the house he indicated.

"Let me case the joint," he said, and took off.

We waited for what seemed an interminable length of time. Then Chambrun sat up straight. On the front steps of the house down the block we saw Jerry. He'd removed his suit coat, and he was, of all things, industriously sweeping the front steps of the house.

We left the car and walked briskly down the block to the house. The front door stood open behind the sweeping Jerry.

"The janitor was a sucker for a ten spot," he said. "Foreigners have rented the rear apartment on the first floor." He grinned at Chambrun. "I have the passkey."

We went into the dark hallway and down the corridor to the rear. Jerry signaled us for silence. He slipped a key noiselessly into the lock, again indicating we should stay behind him. He turned the key and was instantly three steps into the room beyond.

"A leak in the bathroom," we heard him say. "I thought you guys were out."

Chambrun pushed forward, I right behind him. Two dark-skinned men faced us, startled by our sudden appearance.

"Chambrun!" one of them said. They knew The Man by sight. They had probably scouted the Beaumont thoroughly before they'd put their murder scheme into action.

"I assume Mrs. Cantora is in the back bedroom," Chambrun said, coldly. "Will you be good enough to bring her out here, Mark?"

I must have looked like a sleepwalker as I started for the far door. One of the terrorists recovered and took a quick step to block the way. There was a gun pointed straight at my chest.

Chambrun's heavy blackthorn stick moved in a short arc.

There was a sound like splintering kindling, the gun went hurtling across the room, and the terrorist screamed and went down to his knees, cradling his shattered arm. The second man was down, with Jerry Dodd sitting on his chest, a gun pressed against the terrorist's forehead.

As if he were taking a stroll in the park, Chambrun stepped over the man he'd struck and went into the back room. A moment later I heard a woman's voice, frightened but relieved. She had been tied to a chair, a gag in her mouth, Chambrun told us later.

He reappeared, his arm around Luigi Cantora's beloved Serafina. "It's all right, Serafina," Chambrun said gently. "It's all over. I'll take you to Luigi. He'll be overjoyed to see you." He turned to me. "You can call the police to take care of these scum, Mark," he said. And then to Jerry, "Get in touch with General Hassan at the United Nations. He may want to disinfect his private army." He gave Serafina a little hug. "We must be going, my dear. I have a hotel to run."

# Chambrun Gets the Message

There is an old story about two wealthy gentlemen having dinner together in one of their homes. After dinner they retire to the library where the butler serves brandy and coffee and passes the cigars. The host stands with his back to the fireplace where, over the mantel, is a stuffed moose head. "Did I ever tell you about my moose hunt?" the host asks. "No, but don't," says his friend. "Because I know how it came out."

This story would be a kind of a "moose head" to anyone who is a regular patron of the Beaumont. If you were to go into the Trapeze Bar for a cocktail any evening after work, you would see Victoria Haven at her usual corner table, accompanied by her Japanese friend and holding court as usual. There is no way to create suspense over whether or not she survived the attempt to murder her, because there she is, "alive and well and living in Paris" as the song goes. This cannot be called a "whodunit," because it wasn't "dun," but the story of how Victoria Haven kept herself from being murdered in cold blood is, I think, worth the telling.

In a time when everyone calls everyone else by his or her first name, Victoria Haven calls me Haskell, never once using my first name, Mark. It reminds me of when I was a kid in prep school, and I was Haskell, M., when they called the roll in study hall. I have a crush on the lady, which may produce a snicker here and there. Mrs. Victoria Haven admits, without a blush, to having been born in 1900. I am thirty-five, the public relations director of the Hotel Beaumont. Mrs. Haven lives in a penthouse on the roof, and I see her almost every day of my life and look forward to it. She is something!

The Beaumont is famous for a number of things, primarily for its legendary manager, Pierre Chambrun. He is the king, the mayor, the boss of a small city within a city. He presides over his own police force, a shopping center, restaurants and bars, a bank, a health club, hospital facilities, and the living quarters for a thousand guests. Some of us who work for him think he has a magical radar system located behind his bright black eyes. He seems able to sense a malfunction in the Swiss-watch operations of the world he rules even before it happens.

Unfortunately Chambrun can't change human nature. He can't eliminate greed, or jealousy, or a passion for revenge, or the impulse toward treachery and betrayal in the individual man or woman. And so, as in every other place on earth, these ugly psychoses erupt in Chambrun's world too and hamper man's efforts to lead peaceful and orderly lives.

It was one of these dark and twisted impulses that threatened the life of Victoria Haven in the spring of this year.

Chambrun, too, has a very special place in his heart for Victoria Haven. It is whispered backstage that long ago there was a young man-older woman relationship between the two of them. She obviously has some kind of special drag with Chambrun, because she is allowed to break so many house rules.

Chambrun became the managing genius of the Beaumont in the early fifties, and, at the same time, Victoria Haven bought one of the three penthouses on the roof, a cooperative arrangement at that time. She was obviously a woman of means, because even in those days it was an expensive piece of real estate. There are two other penthouses flanking the lady's residence. Chambrun lives in one of them, and the other is held in reserve for visiting foreign diplomats, in New York on United Nations business.

At present, only one elevator goes to that top level, and the man who operates it won't take you there without word from the front desk that Chambrun, or Mrs. Haven, or the guest in Penthouse Number Three has approved, in effect has given the green light. You are as safe up there from unwanted intrusion as if you were detached from the rest of the world. Or so it seemed.

I have mentioned Mrs. Haven's Japanese friend who sits with her in the Trapeze Bar at the cocktail hour. He is one of the house rules that Mrs. Haven is allowed to break. He is a small, snub-nosed Japanese spaniel, snarling, unfriendly, contemptuous. He sits on his own chair, on his own red satin cushion, and indicates clearly that he is bored with the sophisticated social world of the Beaumont. His name is Toto.

Actually, in my time at the hotel, there have been two Totos, and I understand that there was still another before that. Pets are not allowed in the hotel, but Toto is the exception. Mrs. Haven and "my Japanese gentleman friend" are, you might say, landmarks. If for some reason they miss the cocktail hour in the Trapeze, or are late appearing, Mr. Del Greco, the maître d', is swamped with anxious inquiries from the regulars who fear something may have happened to the lady and her companion.

She is not inconspicuous.

At eighty-one Victoria Haven is tall, ramrod-straight. She walks briskly, like a woman of thirty. Her hair, quantities of it, is piled on top of her head, a henna red that God never dreamed of. She wears plain, black silk dresses, sedate and proper, but she has on enough dazzling rings, bracelets, pendants, and earrings to send the manager of Tiffany's racing back to his store to check on the inventory.

"I have been a kept woman all my life, Haskell," she told

me one day, "but not one of these baubles came to me for any other reason than love—good, sensuous, passionate love."

She had started out toward the end of World War One as a dancer in a cabaret, Chambrun told me. "She had legs that put the Betty Grables of her time to shame."

At eighty-one she is an outrageous and altogether charming flirt. I've never seen her with a woman friend, but men of all ages flock to her table in the Trapeze, ignoring Toto's growling hostility. She is still all woman, and fifty years ago she must have been the living end.

She was dangerously close to another kind of end that spring day. Afterward she told me she had wondered. "I felt a little like William Saroyan," she said, "who said to the press just before the end that he'd been told that all of us have to face death, but he'd supposed an exception would be made in his case. I've always thought that, Haskell, but yesterday I wasn't so sure. Not sure at all."

The complex problems of maintenance in an establishment like the Beaumont are beyond imagination. I'm not talking about maid service, cleaning crews, waiters and maître d's, chefs, kitchen staffs, bellboys, telephone switchboard operators—services supplied by people. I was thinking of the maintenance of machinery. I'm talking about a forty-story building that has to be heated in winter, air-conditioned in summer, about two banks of elevators that have to be kept in service around the clock, about ice machines, refrigerator rooms, hundreds of different electrical gadgets that supply special luxuries to the guests—portable broiler-ovens, toasters, drink mixers, and on and on. There are three chief engineers, each working an eight-hour shift, plus a crew of men who know exactly how everything works and where everything is located.

That staff of experts is prepared to deal with any sort of emergency that might develop in the hotel's equipment and to maintain regular maintenance checks. Occasionally, however, outside specialists become involved. Twice a year the two banks of elevators are checked out by experts from the manufacturer. If any parts or cables or controls need replacing, these outsiders deal with the problem. It is a part of some kind of warranty.

Their presence is never particularly noticed, because they put only one car at a time out of commission. In the case of the roof and its three penthouses, however, this makes for a brief dislocation for the top-level residents—Chambrun, Mrs. Haven, and whoever may be in Penthouse Number Three. Since only one elevator goes to the roof, when that is being checked out, it means the boss, Mrs. Haven, and the guest in Number Three will have to use the fire stairs from the fortieth floor to the thirty-ninth, to come and go for perhaps two or three hours.

Chambrun, of course, knows when it is going to happen and arranges accordingly. Mrs. Haven and the guest in Number Three are notified a couple of days in advance, reminded, and re-reminded. The period of non-service is always from ten in the morning till about two in the afternoon.

One of the extraordinary things about Chambrun is his knowledge of the personal lives of all the hundreds of people who work for him. He knows family histories, how many children there are, the schools they go to, medical problems, and so on. People will give an arm for him because he is aware of their problems before he is told. He does not have this kind of special knowledge, however, of the people who come in from the outside, like the elevator experts. That lack of knowledge came close to costing Victoria Haven her life.

The hotel's security force, commanded by Jerry Dodd, a wiry, bright-eyed, very tough former FBI agent, is a marvel of efficiency. You go into the hotel and wander down some corridor where you are not supposed to go or open the door of some anteroom, and someone is almost instantly at your elbow, asking you what cooks. But when special service people come in no one checks on them. They have free run of the place to do their jobs, whatever they may be. So what happened to Victoria Haven could not be blamed on Chambrun or Jerry Dodd. Neither one of them is psychic, although I sometimes wonder about Chambrun.

One more note before the curtain rises on a beautiful spring day with Death threatening to play the leading role. When I first came to know Mrs. Haven, she had a routine that has since been abandoned. Three times a day and once in the latish evening she charged through the lobby with Toto under her arm. The little spaniel had to "do his duty." On a summer day, when a topcoat wasn't necessary, she was quite a sight, her jewelry glittering and flashing. I remember remarking to Chambrun that she was asking for trouble with all the junkies and muggers populating the streets. Every day we heard of someone snatching a gold chain or some other piece of jewelry off a lady's neck, or wrist, or hand. Victoria Haven was too inviting a target, I thought.

Chambrun gave me a wry smile and said nothing. But I learned, doing my own snooping, that every time she went out one of Jerry Dodd's men strolled after her. If anyone had even so much as taken a step toward the lady, he would have been instantly confronted by an armed and tough security man. No one, I learned, had ever told the lady she was being protected, but I think she was too clever, too observant, not to have noticed it. I tell this only to show how closely Chambrun watched over her. When the city passed a law that pet owners had to follow their dogs equipped with scoopers, Mrs. Haven abandoned her outdoor forays.

"I would not be caught dead following Toto around with a shovel," she announced to the world at large.

A special place in her roof garden was set aside for Toto's problem, which explains why, on the day the elevator to the roof was out of service, Mrs. Haven had no reason to leave her penthouse.

On that day, a few minutes after noon, Victoria Haven came face to face with Death. He didn't look like Death or anyone dangerous. He was a small, dark young man sitting just outside her garden hedge, eating his lunch from a brown paper bag. Mrs. Haven was made aware of his presence by Toto, who, spotting a stranger, made bloodcurdling noises of protest through his upturned nose. Looking over her garden hedge, Mrs. Haven saw the man, and that he was wearing grease-stained coveralls.

"Toto!" she called. "My dog isn't partial to strangers. You are working on the elevator?"

The man—almost a boy, she thought—gave her a bright smile. "Lunch break," he said.

"What is your name?" she asked.

"Carl," he said.

"I'm not partial to first names," Mrs. Haven told him. "What is your last name?"

"Stratton," he said. "I am Carl Stratton. And you, ma'am?"

"I am Mrs. Victoria Haven," she said.

His smile became even brighter. "Victoria is a nice name—Victoria."

There was a kind of impertinent flirtatiousness about him that pleased the lady. "It's pretty hot out here in the sun," she said.

"After working in the dark shaft all morning, it is pleasant," Stratton said. "But if I'm in the way—"

"Would you like some iced tea to go with your sandwich?" she asked. "I have some already made in the refrigerator."

"That would be most pleasant," he said. He was not looking her in the eyes any longer. His attention seemed to be directed toward her conspicuous display of rings, bracelets, and pendants.

"Come on inside, and I'll pour you some," Mrs. Haven said.

Toto expressed his outrage with a snarl and disappeared into the garden. Mrs. Haven preceded the expectant Stratton through the front door into her penthouse.

I imagine Stratton was as astonished by what confronted him inside this obviously rich lady's living quarters as I was the first time I saw it. You expected elegance and grandeur, but that wasn't what you saw. The first impression one had was of total disorder, a crowded storage space for junk. There was twice as much old Victorian furniture as the place could comfortably contain. Heavy red velvet drapes shut out the world, day and night. Bookcases overflowed into stacks of books on the floor and stacks of newspapers from God knows how far back.

When you first recover from this apartment's incredible collection of rubble, you make a discovery. There isn't a speck of dust anywhere. The entire apartment is spotless. What appears to be total disorder is obviously perfect order to Mrs. Haven. "Ask for an article from the op-ed page of *The New York Times* from ten years back," Chambrun once told me, "and she will reach out, probably not moving from her chair, and produce it for you. She knows exactly where anything she cherishes is located."

Mrs. Haven left Stratton in this antique dealer's paradise and went to the kitchen to get him the promised iced tea. He looked around him, intently curious, not daring to move anything from a chair in order to sit down. Mrs. Haven reappeared with the tea in a frosted glass.

"Just throw that stuff off that chair, there, Stratton, and sit," the lady said.

He picked up some papers from a Windsor chair as if he might find a black widow spider hiding beneath them. He accepted the tea, his eyes focused on the diamond-studded pin that decorated the front of her dress.

"You have jewels for a queen," he said.

She smiled at him. "I have more fun acquiring them than most queens do," she said.

"The way things are today, you must have a good safe to keep them in," Stratton remarked.

"Jewels are no fun if you keep them locked away," she said. "Will the elevator be running when they promised—at two o'clock?"

"Before that if all goes well," he said.

"Splendid. I have an appointment at five—as usual."

"You're not afraid of thieves?" he asked.

"I am as well guarded in this hotel as if it were Fort Knox," she said.

Casual talk over, the time came for Carl Stratton to get back on the job. He thanked the lady politely, carried his empty glass back into the kitchen, thanked the lady again, and departed.

A nothing moment, if you had asked Mrs. Haven just then. She had done a kindness for a maintenance man who was, indirectly, making certain a service she counted on was in working order. She would have given a cold drink to almost anyone on a hot day. An unmemorable moment in an unmemorable day—so far.

At five o'clock that afternoon Mrs. Haven and Toto went down for their customary cocktail hour in the Trapeze Bar. It was an early evening when many friends stopped by her table to chat. A British diplomat whom she'd met years ago in Cairo was delighted to encounter her again and invited her to dine with him.

"Lord Ormsby," she told us later. "Willie Belton when I met him just after World War One. Damned near as old as I am. Horrible shape, though. Walks with a stick."

They dined in the Blue Lagoon, our nightclub. Toto is not allowed in the main dining room. The two old people apparently had a lovely time reliving half a century or more. It was nearly eleven when Mrs. Haven and Toto returned to her penthouse.

"Willie offered to escort me up to the roof," Mrs. Haven told us later, "but I told him chivalry didn't have to go that far. Good thing he accepted the idea. The dear old boy might have gotten himself killed!"

So it was that she returned to the roof alone, except, of course, for Toto. The little dog was left in the garden. He had a special "dog door" in and out of the kitchen, which he could manage by himself. Mrs. Haven let herself in at the front door, switched on the lights, and found herself facing Carl Stratton standing in the doorway to the kitchen.

"How did you get in here?" Mrs. Haven asked sharply.

"Fixed the lock on the kitchen door when I was here earlier," Stratton said. "Where do you keep them?"

"Keep what?"

"Your jewels, Victoria. Where do you keep them? I've turned the place upside down—no safe, no strongbox. Where are they?"

Maybe she made some kind of instinctive gesture, because he stepped forward and snatched away her suitcaselike handbag, and backed away, opening it.

"My God!" he said.

"Safest place to keep them is with me," Mrs. Haven said.

"My God!" Stratton said again. "In here—and on you—there must be a million bucks' worth!"

"I should have estimated it a little higher than that," Mrs. Haven said. She dropped down in the big armchair that Chambrun called her throne. "So you've got them, Stratton. Would you mind very much leaving me the privacy to go to bed?"

He moistened his lips. "How old are you, Victoria?" he asked.

"Eighty-one—if it matters," she said.

"It matters," Stratton said, his eyes very bright. "Eighty-one years is quite a lot of living. It makes what I have to do a little less difficult."

"What do you have to do?"

"Well, I can't go off with your million dollars and leave you to tell the police who was responsible." He shifted her bag under one arm, and from inside his coat he produced a switchblade knife. "I'm going to have to silence you rather permanently, Victoria. I'll try to make it as painless as possible."

He took a step toward her and out of the kitchen came Toto, snarling fiercely.

"I'll cut your stinking little head off, buster, if you don't stay away from me!" Stratton shouted.

"Toto!" The old woman's voice was clear and controlled. "Go somewhere and tend to your own business!"

The little dog gave Stratton a parting snarl and headed back for the kitchen. Mrs. Haven leaned back in her chair.

"I suppose you have no choice, Stratton," she said. "Perhaps you would let me have one cigarette before you cut my throat."

Without waiting for Stratton to answer, she began fumbling in the stack of newspapers next to her chair. When she turned to face him again, she was holding a giant handgun, a small cannon, aimed straight at his heart.

"Now, my young idiot," she said, "you will bring me that telephone, and we'll put an end to this. It has a nice long cord on it."

He stared at her, like a bird fascinated by a cobra. "The phone won't work, Victoria. I cut the wires when I first let myself in."

"Then we'll just have to wait, won't we?" Mrs. Haven said.

"Wait for what?"

"Why, for someone to come."

"When will that be?"

"Who knows? I rather doubt there will be anyone before the maid who comes about nine in the morning."

The heavy gun was steady as a rock in Mrs. Haven's hand, her elbow resting on the arm of her chair. Stratton must have been thinking the old woman couldn't keep it steady for too long. He moistened his lips, and there were little beads of sweat on his forehead. The light glittered on the blade of his knife.

"Do you really know how to use that thing, Victoria?" he asked.

"Oh, my, do I know how!" Mrs. Haven said, smiling at him. "One of the first men in my life was a very rich oil man from Texas. He saw me at a nightclub where I was dancing."

"You were a dancer?" The young man was playing for time, trying to judge the distance between himself and the "throne."

"A very good one," Mrs. Haven said. "But my Texas friend was traveling around the world in those days. He wanted me with him, and I wanted to be with him. He was afraid someone might try to get at him through me, so he taught me how to handle a gun. Would you believe I can still hit a fifty-cent piece at fifty paces?"

"Not really," Stratton said.

"You had better believe." Mrs. Haven smiled grimly. "My Texas friend gave me this diamond clasp I'm wearing." She touched the pin on the front of her dress with her free hand. "That was over fifty years ago. I suggest you sit down, young man. It will be a long time until the maid comes."

He sat down, facing her, wondering how long it would be before the gun hand wavered. It couldn't be too long now.

"My friend from Texas taught me to shoot with both hands," Mrs. Haven said, almost casually. "I am as good left-handed as I am right-handed." With which she shifted the gun from one hand to the other. That way, Stratton realized, she could hold out for a long, long time.

Could she really handle the gun, he wondered? If he made a quick lunge at her, would she react in time? Something in her cold blue eyes warned him to wait. In time fatigue would overtake this aged crone.

"If you'd care for a little music while we wait," Mrs. Haven said, "you can turn on the hi-fi set over there in the corner."

"You're as crazy as a bedbug, Victoria," Stratton said. "I can last longer than you can last."

"I know what you're hoping for, Stratton," she said. "Don't count on it."

An hour went by, with two people staring at each other, with Death waiting for one of them in the wings. Then Toto reappeared, snarling and whimpering.

"Toto! I told you to go somewhere and tend to your own

business!" Mrs. Haven said, a sharp edge to her voice.

The little dog gave her a sullen look and padded back into the kitchen.

A little after midnight I went up to Chambrun's penthouse with him. There was some kind of convention being held in the Beaumont the next day, and Chambrun had a list of names he wanted me to have that he hadn't brought down to his second-floor office. We sat there, having a drink and going over the next day's details, when I heard an unusual sound.

"You got rats in the woodwork?" I asked Chambrun.

"I think not," he said. He walked over to the garden door and opened it. There, looking up at us sullenly, was Toto, Mrs. Haven's Japanese friend.

"I didn't know you and Toto were friends," I said.

"We're not," Chambrun said. "He hates my guts." Even as he spoke, he was picking up the phone. "Get me Jerry Dodd," he said. A moment later he had our head security man on the line. "There's something wrong in Mrs. Haven's penthouse," Chambrun told him. "Get the passkeys, and get up here on the double."

I couldn't believe it. "She's sick, you think? Let's get over there, boss."

"We'll wait for Jerry," he said.

It seemed like forever—I suppose it was less than ten minutes—before Jerry Dodd arrived. We could tell there were lights on in Mrs. Haven's penthouse, but we couldn't see in.

"Damned drapes are always drawn," Chambrun said. "Give me the front door passkey, Jerry. You take the back." He glanced at his watch. "Twelve seventeen. We'll all go in at precisely twenty past."

And we did.

Mrs. Haven sat there, holding her gun on Stratton. When he saw Chambrun, he decided to make a run for it. As he passed the kitchen door, Jerry Dodd knocked him cold with the butt of his gun.

Mrs. Haven's pale blue eyelids lowered for a moment as she put her cannon down on the stack of newspapers beside her chair. Then she gave us a report on what had happened.

"Would you have shot him, Victoria?" Chambrun asked.

"I haven't fired a gun for more than fifty-five years," Mrs. Haven said. "And anyway, I took the bullets out of this thing years ago. I was afraid someone would stumble on it and hurt themselves."

"An empty gun!" I heard Jerry Dodd mutter. He was handcuffing the unconscious Stratton's hands behind his back.

"I always said, Dodd, that I could have been a very good actress," Mrs. Haven said. "That misguided young man seems to have bought my performance. I had to be good, you know. He was going to kill me."

Toto was sniffling on the floor beside her chair.

"Extraordinary that he had the instinct to go for help," I said.

Chambrun gave Mrs. Haven a wry smile. "We'd better show Mark how it works, Victoria," he said, "or we'll have a whole new folklore about animals."

"Go somewhere, Toto, and tend to your own business," she said.

Toto gave her a bored look and went out to the kitchen. I could hear his little dog door open and close. Mrs. Haven went to one of the windows and opened the drape. She beckoned to me, and I could see Toto trotting across the roof to Chambrun's penthouse. We watched him reach the garden door and scratch on it.

"I have trained him to follow that command—'go tend to your own business,'" Mrs. Haven said. "Pierre has always been concerned about my having so much of value here. If Toto ever scratched on his door, he'd know I had more trouble than a stomachache. Tonight I had to send him twice before you came upstairs, Pierre."

So that was how Chambrun got the message.